Readers love t.
series by K.C. WELLS & PARKER WILLIAMS

Endings and Beginnings

"If a series has to end, then KC and Parker have just shown us how to do it properly."

—Prism Book Alliance

"Overall, this is an amazing, emotional ending to a brilliant series. The Collars and Cuffs Series will always be one of my all-time favorites."

—Rainbow Gold Book Reviews

Dom of Ages

"This book was amazing, taking me on a journey from tears—my heart shattered for Jarod—to carefully optimistic, to heartwarming joy."

—The Novel Approach

"…this is a wonderfully written tale of two realistic men who show us that most things in life are not dependent on age."

—Long and Short Reviews

Damian's Discipline

"Thank you, K.C. and Parker—a wonderful addition that I loved!"

—Rainbow Book Reviews

"…a book that is so full of tender emotions, courage and strength, the will to overcome and survive with characters that not only captured your heart but took you with them on the path to healing…"

—Crystal's Many Reviewers

By K.C. WELLS

With Parker Williams: Before You Break
Debt
First
Love Lessons Learned
Step by Step
Waiting For You

COLLARS & CUFFS
An Unlocked Heart
Trusting Thomas
With Parker Williams: Someone to Keep Me
A Dance with Domination
With Parker Williams: Damian's Discipline
Make Me Soar
With Parker Williams: Dom of Ages
With Parker Williams: Endings and Beginnings

DREAMSPUN DESIRES
#15 – The Senator's Secret

LEARNING TO LOVE
Michael & Sean
Evan & Daniel
Josh & Chris
Final Exam

SENSUAL BONDS
A Bond of Three
A Bond of Truth

Published by DREAMSPINNER PRESS
www.dreamspinnerpress.com

By PARKER WILLIAMS

With K.C. Wells: Before You Break

COLLARS & CUFFS
By K.C. Wells: An Unlocked Heart
By K.C. Wells: Trusting Thomas
With K.C. Wells: Someone to Keep Me
By K.C. Wells: A Dance with Domination
With K.C. Wells: Damian's Discipline
By K.C. Wells: Make Me Soar
With K.C. Wells: Dom of Ages
With K.C. Wells: Endings and Beginnings

Published by DREAMSPINNER PRESS
www.dreamspinnerpress.com

BEFORE YOU BREAK

K.C. WELLS
PARKER WILLIAMS

Published by

DREAMSPINNER PRESS

5032 Capital Circle SW, Suite 2, PMB# 279, Tallahassee, FL 32305-7886 USA
www.dreamspinnerpress.com

Before You Break
© 2017 K.C. Wells & Parker Williams.

Cover Art
© 2017 Reese Dante.
http://www.reesedante.com
Cover content is for illustrative purposes only and any person depicted on the cover is a model.

ISBN: 978-1-63533-697-9
Digital ISBN: 978-1-63533-698-6
Library of Congress Control Number: 2017903376
Published May 2017
v. 1.0

Printed in the United States of America
∞
This paper meets the requirements of
ANSI/NISO Z39.48-1992 (Permanence of Paper).

To all those readers who loved the *Collars & Cuffs* series
and have followed Eli and Jarod on their new journey.
Welcome aboard.

Acknowledgments

As always, a thank-you to our wonderful betas.

A very special thank-you to Sharon D. Simpson for her invaluable help with regards to Ellis's situation.

And we would like to extend our gratitude to LM Somerton and Pride Publishing, as well as Elizabeth North, for allowing Joe and Olly from the fantastic series *The Edge* to visit on the opening night of Secrets.

PROLOGUE

July 2016

WAYNE DWYER sat in the back seat of the ARV, Ellis Mann beside him as usual, and Shaun Temple at the wheel. Wayne's loaded carbine lay across his knees, a pistol strapped to his thigh. The early morning was wet and quiet as the convoy of seven police cars, two police vans, and an ambulance crawled its way across South London, the drizzle misting the windscreen.

Wayne was calm, his thoughts focused on the briefing that had taken place an hour previous. They were on their way to arrest a suspect the police had reason to believe was in possession of a weapon. Intelligence came from the officers who'd spent the last few hours reconnoitering the address.

"If anything goes wrong," Shaun commented in his quiet voice, "this could be a long night."

Beside Wayne, Ellis twitched, clenching and unclenching his hand on his thigh.

Wayne chuckled, more to ease the tension in Ellis than for any other reason. "And he could already be tucked up fast asleep in his bed by the time we get there." The surveillance team had reported their suspect was home. As they neared the target's building, an ARV and another police car, this time with local officers on board, veered off to cover the back of the building.

"Then let's hope he doesn't wake up and decide to seize a hostage," Shaun muttered. He pulled the car over to the curb, and the other vehicles did the same. "Okay, rendezvous point."

Wayne knew they were out of sight and sound of the flats. He'd studied the Google Earth images and the large-scale maps of the property and neighboring area.

"I'm with you," Ellis murmured. "I hope he's off in the Land of Nod. Makes things a damn sight easier." They already knew what had occurred earlier that evening; the suspect and another man, both with records of violence, had threatened someone, demanding money they claimed was owed to them. The report said both men were armed.

The three men got out of the car and were joined by four more officers, all of them armed and fully kitted out with helmets, goggles, and body armor. Lewis was in command.

"Okay, check mobiles are off and radios turned down," he instructed in a low voice. "Cassidy and Phelps have a carbine and pistol trained on the fourth floor in case our man gets desperate and decides to try and escape through the window."

In a close-linked single file, they moved stealthily to the ten-story block of flats, part of the depressing seventies concrete jungle of gray with its raised footbridges and stone stairwells. Lewis was the first at the downstairs glass door, which he opened with a key as quietly as possible. Shaun slipped inside first, a bulletproof shield held up to protect himself, his Glock in his hand. Behind him the six officers made their way up the flights of concrete stairs, and Wayne's nose twitched at the faint yet unmistakable aroma of stale urine. Peters carried the battering ram.

The building was silent when they lined up outside the flat's door. Lewis signaled for Peters and Derwent, and the quiet was shattered as they rushed forward, breaking down the red front door. All of them rushed in, weapons ready, and Lewis called out, "Armed police! Armed police! Come on out. And let's see those hands!"

Wayne trained his carbine at the bedroom door as it opened and a young man emerged from it, unsteady on his feet, dressed in a pair of boxers. He blinked at them, mouth falling open.

"Okay, okay," he said, waving his hands in the air. "Not armed, all right?" His chest heaved.

"Find something to cover him with before you take him outside," Lewis directed. Shaun cuffed him, all the while reading him his rights. Wayne ducked into his bedroom and grabbed the black bedspread from the bed. He returned to the scene, threw it over the suspect's shoulders, and watched as Shaun led him from the flat.

Ellis jerked toward the second bedroom door and froze when a small girl appeared, rubbing eyes that went wide when she saw the officers. She began to wail, and another child and a woman spilled out of the room.

"What the fuck are you doing in my home?" the woman screeched, automatically indicating for the girls to stand behind her before pulling her robe around her.

Lewis ignored her indignant shrieks. "Peters, escort these people downstairs to the third floor." Peters did as instructed, and Ellis guided them through the door. Once they were safely out of the way, Lewis got on his radio. "Okay, bring in Troy."

Wayne remained still while they waited for Troy, the police dog, and his handler. He gave Ellis a glance as his buddy came back into the flat. This was the nerve-racking part of such an operation—the meticulous search of the property to ensure there wasn't a second hidden armed man. With the suspect and his family taken care of, the seven officers and dog searched all corners of the flat for the next twenty minutes. Once they were assured it was empty, it was time to go. The local officers would be in next to search for weapons.

They filed out of the flat and downstairs to the vehicles. "Debrief back at operations," Lewis announced. Wayne knew it would be quick; everything had gone smoothly. Only two hours left until his shift ended at 7:00 a.m.

"Well, that was textbook," Ellis commented as he climbed into the back of the ARV.

"Yeah, it's nice when that happens." After six years as a Specialist Firearms police officer, Wayne was accustomed to the pattern, the sudden changes in pace. One minute they could be out on a quiet patrol, the next thrown into action. *From one extreme to the other.*

Shaun's radio burst into life. "Nine-nine-nine call made from an address that's on your route," the tinny voice stated. "A neighbor has heard a woman in the upstairs flat screaming. She has reason to believe there's a weapon involved. We haven't got enough to corroborate this, but given the address, you might want to check it out. Local officers have been called to this address before. Can you assist? You're three minutes from the scene, and your commander has been advised."

Ellis's face fell, and Wayne knew what was going through his mind. Strictly speaking, it should have been passed on to uniform or possibly the armed officers unit. They were still on duty, however, and he knew Ellis wouldn't suggest leaving the call to the locals, not if they were closer. Wayne leaned forward. "Take it, Shaun. If we're closer than uniform, it makes sense. Besides, Lewis has okayed it."

Shaun nodded and spoke into his radio mic. "Affirmative." After receiving the details, he spoke again. "We are en route. Please ensure there will be backup."

"Affirmative. Over and out."

Shaun pulled away from the curb. He drove quickly through the empty streets. It seemed like no time before they were arriving at the address, a two-story house. Wayne and Ellis got out and hurried to the front door. A middle-aged woman in a blue dressing gown met them. Her eyes widened when she saw them.

"Oh my God, what have they sent me, the Flying Squad?"

"Not quite. Nearest available officers, ma'am," Wayne said politely.

With a trembling finger, she pointed to the staircase. "They're upstairs. You be careful now. He's a bad'un. Everyone around here knows about—"

"It's okay, ma'am," Ellis interjected in a whisper. When a low cry reached them, he signaled for her to go back into her ground-floor flat before he led them toward the stairs. They inched their way up the narrow steps, Ellis's gun drawn. When they reached the first floor, the door to the flat stood ajar. Ellis put his finger to his lips and crept inside, Wayne right behind him.

The first room was empty, but Wayne caught sight of the first signs of a struggle. A chair lay overturned, a man's shoe beside it. Wayne quickly assessed the situation. There wasn't enough evidence to indicate what was going on, but a loud noise from along the hallway had both of them stiffening.

"Help!" A woman's voice, clearly frightened, pierced the quiet house. "Anybody, please!"

Before Wayne could react, Ellis shouted out, "Armed police! We're coming in!" He darted out of the room and along the dimly lit hallway, his gun held high.

What the fuck? Wayne hurried after him, adrenaline pumping through him. *What is he playing at?*

When he reached the room at the end, Ellis flung open the door and Wayne followed him inside. In the middle of the room was a double bed, where a man lay on top of a woman. She was struggling beneath him, but he was clearly stronger. With one hand he pinned her wrists to the pillow above her head while the other wasn't in sight. Her satin slip was torn at the shoulder. A large knife lay on the bed beside them, and before Wayne could react, the man clambered off her and picked it up. He brandished it at Ellis.

"Back off." His eyes were huge, darting his gaze from Ellis to Wayne.

Ellis pointed his gun at the man. "Put the knife down," he ordered. "Now!"

The man paled and dropped it onto the floor, where it clattered against the varnished floorboards. Wayne gave an inward sigh of relief and Ellis's tension diminished visibly.

When the woman made a lunge for the bedside cabinet, Ellis froze. Wayne watched in disbelief as a second later she pulled out a revolver and pointed it at her assailant. *Aw fuck.* What dismayed him more was Ellis's reaction.

His partner hesitated, his weapon at his side.

Wayne took control, his heart pounding. "Put that gun down now!" he shouted. He aimed his Glock, making sure she saw it.

Her face crumpled and she collapsed onto the bed, sobbing, and dropped the revolver onto the duvet.

Wayne shuddered with relief. "Cuff him," he barked at Ellis before approaching the bed. He holstered his pistol and helped the woman to her feet. He spoke into his radio. "Shaun, has backup arrived yet? I need transport for two people as fast as you can."

"Got it."

Wayne guided her out of the room, leaving the revolver where it had fallen. He'd deal with that once she and the assailant were safely in police custody. Wayne followed Ellis and the man down the stairs and out of the house. By the time they reached the car, two more came around the corner and pulled up in front of it. Two local officers got out of each and separated the couple, helping each into the back seat of their cars, both of them cuffed. After a brief conversation with Wayne, the officers got into the cars and left.

"Just got to pick up the knife and revolver," he told Shaun. He signaled to Ellis to follow him back into the house and up the stairs. Once inside the flat, Wayne couldn't hold in his emotions any longer.

"What the fuck is wrong with you?" he growled.

Ellis frowned. "What are you talking about?"

"I'm talking about you apparently leaving your brains in the car." Wayne took a deep breath. "First off, since when do you shout out before you've even seen what's going on? You had no fucking idea what was going on in that bedroom. All you did by yelling too soon was announce our presence to that guy. You put us in danger."

"What?" Ellis gaped at him.

"You gave him time to prepare for us entering the room. We could have walked in there to find a loaded gun pointed at our chests." He clenched his gloved fists. "But what worries me more is your lack of reaction. Why didn't you aim at her?"

Ellis froze, his face ashen. "Instinct. I judged her to be the victim. I mean, she *was* the one screaming, right? And I... I didn't think she'd shoot."

"Why—because she's a woman? Damn it, Ellis, you know better. You've come up against armed women before, same as I have, but this time you held back."

"She... she collapsed."

"But you couldn't have known she'd give up so easily."

"She wasn't a threat," Ellis insisted.

"Not to *you*—but that guy was in immediate danger. You should have issued her a warning and then fired to protect him, damn it!" Wayne pushed down hard on his anger and bewilderment. "Okay, so there were a couple of options open to you, and yeah, there's never a right or wrong answer to the question 'should I shoot?' But in my opinion? I'd have gone for it." He stared at Ellis, unblinking. "What concerns me is that you didn't."

Ellis swallowed. "You think I fucked up." His chest heaved, his eyes full of dismay.

His obvious distress put a damper on Wayne's emotions. "Let's bag the weapons and get out of here, all right? We still have a debrief to take care of back at operations."

"Are... are you going to mention what happened here?" Ellis locked gazes with him.

Shit.

Wayne assessed his buddy and came to a rapid decision. "No," he said at last. "Though I should." In his heart he knew it was the latest in a series of incidents that worried the hell out of him. *Jesus, what the fuck is going on here, Ellis?*

This was getting out of hand.

"Let's move before Shaun gets it into his head that we're taking too bloody long." He reached out and patted Ellis's shoulder. "We can talk about this another time."

Ellis nodded, albeit with obvious reluctance.

Wayne bagged the knife and the revolver and followed Ellis from the flat. He stared at his retreating colleague's back as they descended the stairs.

And we are *going to talk about this.*

It was time to act before Ellis did something stupid and jeopardized not only his own life, but those of his fellow officers. And Wayne knew exactly what was needed.

Time to take you in hand, boy.

CHAPTER ONE

JAROD PEARCE followed his Dom, Eli Jameson, as they stepped off the jet that had brought them from Manchester to London. They'd landed at the far end of the runway, where other private planes sat. The day had turned decidedly grim, with heavy clouds that seemed eager to let loose a torrential downpour. As far as Jarod was concerned, it matched his mood, which had dimmed considerably after they'd had to leave behind their friends—their family—to start a new life. Even the ache in his arse, the result of Eli initiating them both into the Mile High Club, hadn't been enough to lift his spirits.

"We don't have to do this," Eli reminded him once again.

"We do," Jarod insisted. He'd wanted this for his Master. A chance to try something new, to create a business that would be all theirs, which they would run together. It certainly wasn't Eli's fault Jarod had trouble letting go.

"It's not the other side of the world, pet," Eli murmured as he reached out a hand and stroked the back of Jarod's neck. "Manchester is a couple of hours away by train. We can go back to visit any time you like."

Jarod appreciated the sentiment, but he knew they weren't likely to be visiting in the near future. They'd spent months taking courses, studying bookkeeping, and getting advice from Leo Hart and Thomas Williams, the owners of Collars & Cuffs. Everything had been leading them to this moment when they would be opening the doors to Secrets, the newest BDSM club in London.

"Sirs?" came a voice from behind them.

Jarod turned to find a smartly dressed man holding a placard that said "Pearce and Jameson." He did his best to smile, but he knew it wouldn't seem genuine. Fortunately Eli stepped forward and shook the man's hand.

"I'm Eli Jameson. Can I help you?"

For a minute the man's expression conveyed his confusion. "I'm Maxwell. I have your limousine waiting," he said simply.

"You have our...?" Eli arched his brows and turned to Jarod. "This has *your* dainty fingerprints all over it, pet. Care to explain?"

Jarod couldn't help but grin. "We took a private jet. How did you think we were going to get to our new place?"

"They have these things called taxis. Ever heard of them?"

The driver's cheeks pinked as Eli continued to berate Jarod, lovingly, of course.

"You are in such hot water, pet, you have *no* idea. At the rate you're burning through it, you won't have any money left by the end of the year."

Jarod suppressed the urge to roll his eyes. "I'm certain we won't end up on the streets, Sir. Besides, once the club takes off, we won't need to touch that money again. We'll make enough to support us all."

The all included Jarod's mother, Maggie, who had come to London ahead of them. They'd had the top floor of their new building divided into two apartments, one for his mother and the other for Eli and Jarod. They'd also invested heavily in soundproofing because the last thing Jarod wanted was to see his mother's knowing grin after every time he and Eli had sex. One thing was certain: Eli had a very healthy sexual appetite, which thrilled Jarod to bits.

"We will be discussing this later, pet."

"I never doubted it for a minute," Jarod answered with a smirk.

Eli grinned and kissed him, which caused Maxwell's cheeks to flush. *Too bad. He'll be seeing a lot more displays of affection in the future.* Which would probably be something he needed to mention to Eli at some point. Eventually. Maybe he could do it after they got home.

A long time after—they had a new bed to break in. The thought sent a shiver of anticipation skating down Jarod's spine, but when his hole clenched, he winced. *Ah. Yes. The Mile High Club.*

Breaking in the bed might have to wait awhile. A couple of hours at least.

Maxwell strode quickly toward the waiting car, and Jarod realized if they'd had to carry anything, they'd never have kept up. *Thank God we don't have to worry about the move.* Jarod found himself grateful that they'd had a removal company pack up their belongings and send them on ahead. The driver spoke animatedly about the city, the places to be seen, restaurants that were not to be missed, and touched on more details than Jarod could remember, but he let Max carry on chattering, enjoying the man's energy.

"Sir?"

"Yes, pet?"

"I suppose it's really not a good time to say this—"

"You bought the car and hired Maxwell to be our chauffeur?"

"I—yes. How did you know?"

As he reached out to stroke Jarod's cheek, Eli grinned. "I didn't, but I do know you."

"In other words, you guessed."

"I did. I want to protest, but I know you have valid reasons. I don't think you'd ever do something without thinking it through."

It warmed Jarod to hear Eli talk about him like this. Always effusive in his praise, there were times when Eli's gaze would take on a dreamy quality, as if he couldn't believe how lucky he'd gotten.

"Mother may want to shop or go out into the city. I hired Maxwell to be our chauffeur, but also to be her companion during the times I won't be able to be with her. He's taken first-aid classes, understands her needs, and is familiar with the city."

"And he's cute enough to make Maggie happy."

Jarod gave an exaggerated gasp. "Sir, I'm shocked. Do you think my mother would…? Oh hell, who am I kidding? Yes, she'll like that too."

"I think it's a brilliant idea, pet."

They got into the car, and Jarod leaned back in the comfortable leather seat, Eli automatically curling his hand around Jarod's.

So here we are, the first day of our new adventure.

Jarod had never been so grateful to have Eli at his side.

ELI PAUSED at the wide main door. "Ready to see how it's all turned out, pet?"

Jarod nodded, his heart pounding. Months of preparation, consultation, and any number of phone calls were finally over, and the results of their endeavors lay beyond that door. "Ready as I'll ever be." He took a deep breath. Eli unlocked the door and ushered him inside. The interior lay in darkness, and with one hand, Eli plunged them into light.

"Oh my God." Jarod gasped.

The place was *gorgeous*.

A wide reception desk in dark wood sat to one side, and beyond it was the social area, with leather-topped stools placed neatly along the length of a gleaming bar. The rest of the area was filled with tables and chairs, and the hardwood varnished floor reflected the LED recessed lighting up above.

"And we haven't even seen the main floor yet," Eli reminded him excitedly. He led Jarod through the bar to another wide door, and once through, the atmosphere changed. The floor was covered in a black material that appeared eminently more suitable for a BDSM club, and the lighting was cooler. Mirrors interspersed with racks covered the walls, and various benches and chairs stood around. Equipment cabinets hinted at delightful implements and devices hidden within them. There were slings, three or four set up against one wall, and wide frames complete with rings set into them, ready for someone to be restrained. The stage was located midway along the left wall, commanding attention even without being set up for any demonstrations. They'd had all of the gear custom made, and the quality shone through.

At the far end of the floor was the former service elevator, which Jarod knew had been renovated to allow access to the floor above, where the private rooms, group room, lockers, and showers were located.

"Fuck," Eli whispered reverently. "It's even more amazing than I'd imagined."

Jarod agreed. The workers had done an amazing job and somehow managed to come in under budget. He stood in the middle of the main floor, gazing at the club. *Not long now and it won't be so quiet in here.* He could almost hear it: the soft *swish* of a flogger, a single-tail whip slicing through the air, the *thwack* of a paddle connecting with a bare arse, and below all that, the sound of men engaged in various activities, low cries of mingled pleasure and pain.

"Check this out, pet," Eli called from the bar.

Jarod joined him at the opposite end of the club, where the office was located and a lift provided access to their accommodation on the top floor. Eli pressed the call button, and the gleaming metal door slid open to reveal deep-burgundy carpeting with polished stainless steel on the lower half of the wall and mirrors on the upper half.

Eli grinned. "Okay, we are *definitely* going to be christening this." He cupped Jarod's buttcheek and squeezed. "I'm thinking you, arse tilted, facing the mirrors while I fuck you."

Jarod raised his eyebrows. "We christened the jet an hour ago, remember?" Not that he was about to object—Eli's words already got his dick filling. *I guess an hour is enough after all.* Inwardly he chuckled. *We're as bad as each other.*

Eli leered. "What can I say? I get turned on easily around you."

Jarod stifled a giggle and instead pressed his arse into Eli's hand. "Maybe if Max takes my mother somewhere." There was no way he was even contemplating sex if she was within earshot.

Eli cleared his throat. *Oh. Max. Damn.* Jarod groaned. He'd completely forgotten the man was behind them. "Sorry," Jarod said.

"I'm not," Eli said with a chuckle.

"I'll wait for you down here, sir," Max said respectfully as Eli got into the lift, pulling Jarod with him.

"Thanks, Max," Eli said with a brief nod. The door slid shut and Eli grinned. "Let's go see our new home."

STEPPING INTO their new place felt like walking into a showroom. Everything from the woodwork to the dining room chandelier gleamed. The deep-pile lounge carpet, a glorious shade of red, was offset by the black leather furniture. Never in his wildest dreams had Eli ever thought he'd live in a place like this. Then he looked over at Jarod and saw the same awe.

"Pet?"

"This… is remarkable. The designs we saw don't even do this place justice. They made this into a house. A home."

Eli swept Jarod into his arms, then whispered in his ear, "Our home."

They explored the loft, lingering in the bedroom with the king-size bed and wrought-iron scrollwork Eli could hardly wait to put to use. When he noticed the dark wooden steamer trunk at the foot of the bed, Eli smiled. He had an inkling what was in it.

"You have a good eye, Jarod. These things are beautiful."

The bathroom had a walk-in shower large enough for four men, with benches inside. The frosted windows would allow a glimpse of Eli's body as he stroked himself while Jarod stood outside and watched. He noted that for a future punishment.

The kitchen held state-of-the-art appliances, including a coffeemaker that promised a perfect cup every time. This would be Jarod's domain. Eli might be in charge, but when it came to the kitchen, Jarod always got his way.

"This place is four times the size of my house," Eli murmured as he ran his hand over the formal dining room table. He'd seen Jarod's house, the one he shared with Phillip. The place had had an austere feel to it, but *this* felt organic, alive. Plants stood in front of the large floor-to-ceiling windows, green and vibrant. The windows themselves overlooked the St. Katharine's docks, and Eli marveled at the ships and boats moored there.

"We should take a ride on one of the boats," he remarked.

"We could buy a boat—"

"No."

"But—"

"No," Eli repeated firmly. He faced Jarod, looking him in the eye. "We used your money to buy this business and to refurbish the building. I want to be an equal partner in this, do you understand? I like participating, but when you hand out money to buy things, I feel like I'm not really a part of it." *Is this always going to be a bone of contention between us?* Eli hoped not. *Maybe it will just take time to get accustomed to it.*

"It's your money too." Eli could hear the frustration in Jarod's voice.

"Yes, it's *our* money. But I don't want to be *given* everything. I want us to earn it *together*. Do you understand that?"

Jarod's brow crinkled. "I never thought of it like that," he answered, his voice soft.

Eli took Jarod's hands. "Please think about it. What would mean more? Us earning the money and going out together to buy a boat, or just having it because there is money in the bank?"

When Jarod closed his eyes, Eli hoped he would ponder what he'd said.

"I understood the money situation, and I know there is more than enough to last us several lifetimes, but I don't want that. I want to risk it all, to take a chance on each other. Succeed together or fail together. I don't want a safety net, pet. I need us both invested in our lives. Can you do that for me? For us?"

Jarod gave him a patient look. "Unless we give the rest of the money away, there is always going to be that safety net, but I do understand. I'll talk to the lawyers. I'll tell them that we won't be drawing any money from the fund for the foreseeable future."

Bless him. Eli leaned forward and kissed Jarod on the lips. "Thank you. And I don't want you to think it's completely off-limits. We have Max and a limo to take care of, after all."

Jarod laughed. "Only until we're operating in the black. Once that happens we'll live within our means. Budget if we have to, but I don't think we will. This place is going to be outstanding. Because it's going to be run with a firm hand and a warm heart."

Eli stroked his fingers over Jarod's cheek. "I think you're right. And speaking of which, are the invitations ready?"

"They are. I went through the membership lists, checked who was okay to be contacted, then wrote emails to those who chose that preference. I'm sending cards to those who left a mailing address."

Eli stepped behind Jarod and nuzzled his neck. "We're really doing this, aren't we?"

Jarod hummed and tilted his head to allow Eli easier access. "Two weeks from today. I sent cards to Masters Leo and Thomas and invited everyone else. I… um… may have offered to pay for those who couldn't afford the trip."

"That's a nice thing, Jarod. We'll dip into the petty cash and buy tickets."

"But I thought—" Jarod must have noticed the unhappy look on Eli's face because he dipped his chin and said softly, "Yes, Sir."

"Hey, none of that," Eli told him. "Let me ask you something. You never spent any money at all until you met me, right?"

"That's correct, Sir. The lawyers handled all the financial things. Paid the taxes and for the upkeep of the property. Until we decided to look into the club, I didn't even realize how much money Phillip had put away."

"So why now? I mean, I understand about the club. We never could have done this if you hadn't. But now you seem more than willing to spend money, whereas before you never touched it. I'm curious as to why. Is it because you missed the life you had with Phillip? Where you could do anything you wanted and not be concerned about money?"

His pet squirmed as Eli allowed his fingers to trail over Jarod's neck. He wanted to make sure Jarod answered without a lot of thought.

"No, Sir. That isn't it at all," Jarod protested. "It's the club."

"Can you explain that to me?"

Jarod heaved a sigh. "I'm not sure I can. I love taking care of you. I could be happy doing that for the rest of my life."

"Oh, don't worry about that," Eli assured him with a grin. "You will be."

Jarod leaned back against him, and Eli knew he needed the connection. He wrapped his arms around Jarod.

"After we gave money to the boys, and the house to Masters Thomas and Leo, I realized how good it felt to take care of others too. When we decided to open the club, it became clear to me that maybe we were meant for this. It gives you an opportunity to be in charge of more than me. You will be able to control your life. No boss to please. You would be responsible for everything. And me? I'd have the chance to take care not only of you, but my mother, and maybe the people who come to Secrets. I thought it would give us both an opportunity to be *more*."

The honesty in his voice told Eli everything. Jarod had such a capacity for giving, and he wanted to make everyone happy. Eli rarely felt humbled, but Jarod had done it.

"Thank you, pet. That means a lot to me. But what I said before? That's what I'm talking about. You don't need money to take care of me or anyone. You—*we*—built this club to do that. We wanted to give people a place to be who they are. But we need to agree that we'll stand by each other. The money could solve any problem that cropped up, but then what would be the point of us? I wouldn't be in charge, trying to solve an issue, because the money would be there to take care of it immediately. And you? You find someone who needs help, you just pay to make their problem go away. You wouldn't need to be involved at all."

Jarod tilted his head back. "Is that what I'm doing?"

"I think so. Scott and Ben can't afford to pay for a ticket, so let's just give it to them. No need to find a creative solution because money solved it for us. Do you see what I'm saying?"

Jarod paled, and Eli's stomach clenched.

"I'm sorry," Jarod whispered. "I never thought of it like that."

"No, don't be sorry!" Eli said stridently. "Your heart's in the right place. But maybe if you want to help people, do what Thomas and Leo did. Set up a foundation, help people who need it. Runaways, throwaways, kids who've been abused. Pay for people to help them. Volunteer your time. Hell, I'll help out too. And maybe Maggie would enjoy mentoring. That's every bit as important as the money. But the club? That's where the two of us need to pull together to make it work."

Jarod grinned. "I could have the lawyers set up something," he said. "That's a brilliant idea."

"Well, I have been known to have a few on occasion." Eli buffed his fingernails on his shirt, and Jarod chuckled.

"And you're right about the club too. We're going to make it work without the money. Together."

"That's the spirit, pet."

A tingle went through Eli. They were *really* going to do this.

He couldn't wait for the open-house night.

CHAPTER TWO

WAYNE WAS beginning to feel sorry for the new guy.

Roberts had finished his probationary period and joined them for their three days' training at Gravesend. With sixty men serving as Specialist Firearms Officers in the Met, it was understandable he hadn't met the majority of guys, but Wayne quickly realized Roberts hadn't come across any of the men involved in the training. He was still trying to size Roberts up when the day came to an end.

The locker room was the place for a lot of banter, some of it extremely witty and sometimes involving quite a bit of leg-pulling and teasing, albeit good-natured. Wayne was used to that. From day one he was upfront with all the guys he served with, not wishing for there to be any secrets or miscommunication between them. These were men who'd have his back in an operation, under tense, stressful conditions, and Wayne wanted to know he could rely on any of them. They didn't say anything at first, but Wayne knew they were leery about working with a gay man, the only one, as far as he could tell; if there were others, they were doing a damn good job of staying in the closet. Wayne did everything he could to earn their respect and trust, but in the beginning, he had to put up with a lot of teasing and the usual remarks about them having to watch their backs. Nothing he didn't anticipate, however, and in time, they all warmed to him. If anything, it helped them become a more tight-knit group.

Roberts was already off to a bad start.

During the morning briefing before they headed out into the fake town used for training exercises, Shaun commented on Roberts's physical appearance. It was obvious he worked out; his *muscles* had muscles. But his face…. There was no way to describe him other than *pretty*. Not remotely Wayne's type—if he had a type, that is—but he knew someone was bound to say something sooner or later. He silently counted to ten before the first salvo was fired, and of course it was Shaun, he of the sharp tongue and razor-like wit. Roberts bristled initially, but Wayne moved swiftly to ensure Shaun's victim knew there was nothing to it, only words. Shaun had grinned, affirming Wayne's attempt to smooth Roberts's ruffled feathers.

The training exercise went well. The aim was to prepare them for a terrorist attack during a foreign diplomatic visit, and the debrief was useful. Wayne always treated these activities like they were the real thing. That way any errors or misconceptions could be eradicated, and should the situation arise, they would be ready. Once training was over, it was a case of off with the jackets, helmets, and other paraphernalia, into the shower, and then the rest of the evening was free.

Of course a training day wasn't complete without some teasing.

Fourteen officers piled into the locker room, and soon steam puffed out of the showers, accompanied by loud voices telling jokes, sharing tales of football, pub crawls, sexual conquests, and holiday plans.

Wayne usually spent his locker time trying his best to avoid looking at Ellis, afraid all it would take was one glance that lingered too long on his friend's solid body to give the game away. Of course he'd been doing this for years. Wayne had worked it out: Ellis joined the unit six years ago. Wayne reckoned they became friends about a month later. However, he'd been thinking about that magnificent body for five years, eleven months, three weeks, a couple of days, and maybe a few hours.

Thinking was all he did; Ellis was out of bounds. There was no way Wayne was about to jeopardize their friendship by making a move on his best friend—his very *straight* best friend.

When Roberts emerged from the showers, a towel wrapped around his waist, revealing a chiseled torso that wouldn't have looked out of place in a magazine, Wayne knew it wouldn't be long.

"Oh, you wanna watch out, Roberts," Shaun called out, a wicked grin all over his face. "You'll have our resident gay guy drooling so much you'll need to take another shower." Snickers echoed around the locker room.

"Ugh, gay drool. That shit gets everywhere," Cassidy joked, and Phelps snorted.

Wayne said nothing, but watched the proceedings with a smile. His colleagues weren't about to out him—not that he cared. They were still assessing Roberts.

Roberts opened his eyes wide. "One of you is gay?" His tone provided no clue as to his feelings about that.

Shaun's grin widened. "Why? Is that gonna be a problem?" He flashed a glance at the others who stood around, drying off or getting dressed.

Uh-oh. Wayne knew that look.

Ellis caught Wayne's gaze, his lips twitching. Apparently so did he.

"Uh, no…." Roberts didn't sound too sure. "So who's the gay bloke?" His tone was nonchalant enough, but Wayne hadn't missed a bit of tension creeping in across his shoulders.

Shaun's eyes gleamed. "That's for us to know and you to find out." He walked over to where Roberts stood and trailed a single finger down his bare back. "I'm sure a big, strong man like *you* can work it out— sweetheart."

Wayne had to fight hard not to laugh out loud. Shaun was six feet two in his bare feet, with hands the size of dinner plates. To hear the endearment, uttered in his deep voice, was just… weird.

Roberts stared at him, unable to repress a shiver.

Here we go.

Phelps took the hint and sauntered over to Roberts, sashaying his hips in an exaggerated fashion. "It can't be *that* difficult, surely, sweetheart." He stroked Roberts's shoulder before walking off in the direction of the shower.

Wayne wanted to laugh so hard, watching at least six more of his colleagues approach Roberts, every last one of them making their movements effeminate. Their voices lilted as all of them made sure to touch or stroke poor Roberts, and of course every one of them called him sweetheart. Derwent placed both hands on Roberts's shoulders and bent down to whisper that he gave a *wonderful* massage, if Roberts was interested.

It took a minute before he saw the funny side and waved them off with a grin.

"You're having a laugh, aren't you?" Around him the guys burst into laughter, and he relaxed.

Shaun chuckled. "Yeah, we are. The important thing is so are you now." He patted Roberts on the back. "You'll do."

Wayne smiled to himself. It wasn't the first of such initiations he'd witnessed, and he doubted it would be the last. He knew none of it was meant to cause bad feelings—they wanted to know Roberts could take a joke, that he'd fit in with the rest of the men.

Shaun gave Wayne a wink before he addressed Roberts. "I gather it really isn't a problem."

Roberts shook his head. "Nah. Just never worked with a gay copper before."

"That you know of," Cassidy added with a sly smile. "Not all gay men are stereotypical, you know." He flashed a look in Wayne's direction and his expression sobered. "You just need to know we look out for each other around here."

"Fair enough." Roberts squared his jaw. "Just don't call me pretty, all right?"

Wayne groaned. "And you were doing *so* well too." When Roberts stared at him, Wayne shook his head. "Face it, you just handed them all the ammunition they needed."

Roberts's forehead creased into a frown.

Shaun rubbed his hands together with obvious glee. "Okay, fellas, we've got Roberts's nickname sorted. From now on he's Pretty Boy." Guffaws and snorts rebounded around the room.

The penny dropped and Roberts sighed heavily. "I guess I walked straight into that one, right?" He dropped his towel and began to get dressed.

"Afraid so," Wayne said with a smile. He patted Roberts's shoulder. "Don't worry, you'll get used to it—after the first couple of hundred times."

Roberts shook his head, laughing. "What's your nickname, then?"

Before Wayne could reply, Cassidy piped up, "Well, we *wanted* to call him Babe. You know the little pig who rounds up all the sheep? But that didn't go down so well, so we're still working on it."

Roberts guffawed. "Babe?"

Cassidy shrugged. "He makes sure we're focused, doing our jobs." He gave Wayne a warm look. "A good man to have around in a crisis."

The sentiment made Wayne feel good.

Derwent slung his jacket over his shoulder and headed for the door. He paused and turned back to regard Ellis. "By the way, thanks for helping me out."

"No problem," Ellis replied with a wave of his hand. Derwent smiled and exited the locker room.

Wayne gave Ellis a curious glance. "What was that about?"

"Oh, it was nothing important," Ellis said with a nonchalant air as he stepped into his jeans. Before Wayne could push him further, he called out to Phelps in the shower. "Do you *have* to sing while you're showering?"

"Fuck you, I'm practicing for *Britain's Got Talent*. I'm gonna be the next SuBo," Phelps yelled back.

Ellis cackled. "I wouldn't be handing in any letters of resignation, if I were you." Around him there were snorts and guffaws and murmured agreements.

One by one the officers disappeared, all with a wave or a smile, until only Wayne and Ellis remained.

Ellis closed his locker and sighed. "And we get to do it all over again tomorrow."

"Different day, different scenario," Wayne said briskly. "It's all good." He glanced into his bag, and a shiver ran through him when he caught sight of the stiff envelope poking out from under his towel. *Not long to go now.* As Saturday drew closer, his anticipation increased until he was buzzing from it.

"What's got you all riled up?"

Shit. Wayne hadn't realized he'd been that obvious. But then he thought about it. *This is the perfect opportunity.* If he was going to help Ellis, he'd have to say *something*, right? Six years they'd been friends, and although Ellis knew Wayne was gay, part of Wayne's private life—the important part—remained something he kept secret.

Maybe it's time to share it.

Wayne sat on the wide wooden bench that stood in the middle of the room. "I'm not going to be able to make it out with you guys on Saturday," he said. "Something's come up, and I've got other plans."

"Ooh, hot date?" Ellis teased.

No, definitely not a date. He hadn't had a real date in years. Not since he realized the depth of his feelings for Ellis. He'd done a few scenes at the club, but nothing even remotely sexual for quite some time. That would have felt like he was cheating—even though he wasn't—and that wasn't how he was built.

"No, a club I belong to is having a reopening. I got an invite, and I want to go."

Ellis cocked his head, and Wayne grinned to himself. His friend had always been the curious sort, and his reaction was exactly what Wayne counted on.

"I didn't know you belonged to a club," Ellis said, sitting down next to Wayne.

"Yeah, have for a few years. The owners were getting on, so they sold it to someone else. They've remodeled, and they're going to be showing it off to the members and their guests."

"Really? Sounds great. Who's all going to be there?"

"Hopefully a lot of the members will show up. We've lost a few people over the last year, so this is a good chance to bring the numbers back up to what they used to be."

"What kind of club?" Ellis asked.

"Oh, nothing you'd care about," Wayne answered with a dismissive wave.

"Oh. Okay."

It wasn't okay, however. Wayne could see Ellis's feelings were hurt. Wayne felt like a jerk, but he needed this to be Ellis's idea. He knew his words would push Ellis's buttons, because the man hated being in the dark about things. It took him all of two seconds to ask again.

Wayne sighed dramatically. "I'm not really comfortable talking about this because it's a part of my private life. I don't really share it with anyone."

Ellis jutted his plump lip out slightly and squeezed his big brown puppy-dog eyes into a squint. "Wow. I didn't know I was just *anyone*. Sorry I asked."

When he stood to go, Wayne reached out and grabbed his bicep. Instead of pulling away, Ellis stopped and waited.

"It's not that I don't want to tell you. You'd actually be the only person I would tell. But this isn't the kind of club that mixes well with what we do for a living. And you'd have to swear to keep it a secret."

Ellis turned back to face him, his cheeky grin making Wayne's heart stutter. He held up his hand as though he were swearing. "I won't tell. You have my word."

Wayne looked around, playing it up for Ellis's benefit. "Okay, I belong to a very exclusive BDSM club."

Ellis's eyes were as wide as saucers. "You? So I just call you Mr. Fifty Shades or something?"

"No," Wayne growled. He'd heard that one before, and it pissed him off to no end. "This is a real BDSM club. That other crap was… tripe. No self-respecting Dom would ever treat a sub like that."

Holding up his hands, Ellis took a step back. "Whoa, mate. I'm teasing. So what's it like?"

"I'm not sure I can answer that. I mean, it's different things to different people. No two relationships are alike."

"There are relationships like that?" Ellis asked, rubbing his chin, his eyebrows squished together.

"Yes, and before you ask, they're not just about sex. Some relationships are, of course. But others have a deep bond that brings the people together in a way that benefits them both. For instance two of the men who used to come to the club found a third that they really fell in love with. The three of them were together quite a while, but then their submissive—do you *know* what a Dom or a sub is?"

"To be honest I read some of that book. I didn't really care for it. But I know the basics, I guess."

"Okay. I'm a Dom."

Ellis snorted. "Yeah, no kidding. Like I didn't know *that* from the way you boss everyone around."

"Cheeky sod." Wayne laughed. "I make no excuses for how I am. I like control."

Ellis gestured impatiently. "Yes, I know. Carry on."

"Okay, their submissive decided he didn't want to be part of the relationship anymore, so he left them. Now they're lost without a third to love."

"But they still have each other, right?"

"They do, but they're both Doms, and that doesn't make for a sexually fulfilling relationship. They stayed together, though. I guess they're hoping that their third will come back, or maybe that they'll find someone else." Wayne shrugged. "They're just an example. There are so many types of BDSM relationships that it would probably boggle your mind."

Ellis huffed. "And you think finding out that you're into that stuff *doesn't* boggle it?"

"See? You don't know everything about me."

"So I'm just beginning to realize." Ellis looked away. "So what kind of things are you in to?"

"Why? Afraid I'll be too kinky for you?"

Ellis's gaze snapped back. "No, nothing like that!" He paused. "You're not, right?"

Wayne laughed. "No. In the BDSM world, I'm considered pretty vanilla. I like control. I enjoy taking charge in a relationship, where what I say goes."

Ellis nodded. "I can see that. It's how we all see you, anyway."

"And that's how I am at home too. I've never had a submissive there, though. I confine all my playing to the club."

Ellis regarded him closely. "Okay, this might be a stupid question, but why?"

How the hell do I answer that? "Well, see, the thing is, the idea of having sex with a sub sort of makes me feel like I'm cheating on you." Yeah, he could see that remark going down like a lead balloon. "I haven't met anyone who interested me," Wayne answered. Not technically a lie, but not the full truth either.

"And no one else knows you're in to… this?"

Wayne arched his eyebrows. "The people at the club. No one else."

Ellis gave him a cheeky grin. "Your mum and dad? What do you think they'd say if you brought a young man home all hog-tied?"

Wayne frowned at Ellis. "Okay. One, they know I'm gay. They're okay about it, but I think they still hold out hope that I'll meet a woman one day. And two, I'm not into hog-tying people." He grinned. "I'm trying *not* to picture attempting to get a hog-tied man through my parents' front door. Yeah, that isn't me. Though I do know a few men who are. One is a dentist, believe it or not."

Ellis shook his head, then must have realized Wayne was serious. "No kidding?"

"Not at all. Like I said, the people who are interested in BDSM come from all walks of life. I haven't been to the club in a while, so I'm looking forward to seeing them again."

Ellis chewed the cuticle on his thumb, a familiar nervous habit. Wayne had to bite back the desire to smack his hand away from his mouth and tell him to stop. He waited, knowing as soon as Ellis worked it out in his head, he'd say whatever was on his mind. Fortunately it didn't take long.

"Are you… um… going alone?"

Wayne wanted to shout. He knew getting Ellis's interest would be the only thing needed before the man asked about coming with him to the party. "Well, the invitation does say I can bring a guest, but I haven't asked anyone yet. Why? Know someone who might want to come along?"

"Well… maybe me?" Ellis asked with a grin.

"You?" Wayne did his best to act surprised.

"Sure. I mean, if you don't mind. You're my mate, so if it interests you, I should give it a fair shot, right?" Ellis blushed. "Will there… uh, be women there?"

"It's a gay BDSM club, so no, no women."

"Oh." Ellis brightened instantly. "I guess that's still okay. I mean, I like learning things."

And if Wayne had his way, Ellis was about to step onto the path to learning a whole new way of life. One where Wayne would hold the reins as he brought Ellis back to being the strong man he'd fallen in love with long ago.

CHAPTER THREE

ELLIS LOCKED his front door, shrugged off his jacket, and hung it on a hook by the hall mirror. The drive home from Gravesend had been… interesting, but not in a good way. He'd had to fight really hard to concentrate on the traffic, not that this was anything new. When he had a near collision with another car on a roundabout, he pulled off the road into a lay-by, his heartbeat racing, palms clammy. When his pulse returned to normal, Ellis pulled out onto the main road and continued his journey home.

It's all Wayne's fault.

He flopped into his comfy armchair, his mind not on what he was going to have for dinner but still turning Wayne's revelations over and over.

BDSM?

Okay, so it wasn't a huge surprise, knowing how Wayne was. But still… a BDSM club?

What really burned him was that Wayne hadn't felt sure he could trust him. After six years of friendship, yeah, that stung. From the sound of it, this was an important part of Wayne's life, and he hadn't shared it. Not that Ellis expected him to blab to all and sundry—that wasn't Wayne's style—but to not tell *him*? As far as Ellis was aware, theirs was one of the tightest friendships in the unit.

He did his best to push aside his hurt and focused on this new facet to Wayne. Deep down Ellis knew why he wasn't surprised. He'd come to depend on Wayne. He felt like Wayne was always there for him. Maybe that was Ellis responding subconsciously to that part of Wayne's nature. He knew it felt good knowing Wayne was looking out for him and the others.

Ellis didn't know a whole lot about BDSM barring what he'd read in fiction. *Maybe I need to rectify that. Especially if I'm going to this opening night.* The last thing he wanted to do was embarrass Wayne with an unguarded reaction. He still wasn't completely sure why he agreed to go in the first place.

He forgot about dinner and instead reached for his laptop, his curiosity getting the better of him. What he found was an overwhelming array of articles, blog posts, forums—yeah, and videos. He opened up one that seemed more intended to relay information and less designed to… shock. A couple of guys sat on chairs, calmly discussing how BDSM was part of their lives, what they got out of it, and how it brought them together. It was obvious who was the Dom in their relationship, and Ellis found himself watching him with particular interest. The guy wore a black leather harness fitted snugly across his chest, metal rings set into it. His long legs were encased in a pair of tight leather pants laced across his crotch.

Is that how Wayne looks? It didn't take much effort to picture him in that getup. Ellis imagined Wayne would look more in control than ever. But when the screen shifted to show them about to do… whatever, Ellis switched off. That wasn't him.

It could never be him. And as long as he kept telling himself that, he'd be fine.

He went back to his research and soon was lost in a rabbit warren, each site leading him down another path, and another, and another….

When the message appeared on his screen informing him he needed to switch to another power source, as his battery was currently at 6 percent, Ellis stared at the clock at the bottom of the screen. Four hours. He'd been online for *four hours*. His growling stomach complained, and Ellis quickly went into the kitchen and made a piece of toast. It was way too late to think about cooking, and it wasn't as if he was about to fade away, not with his build. It was only when he'd finished eating he realized how utterly exhausted he was. His feet heavy, Ellis trudged into his bedroom, shrugged off his clothes, and made a quick trip to the bathroom before collapsing onto his bed.

Except he couldn't sleep.

Not that this was an unusual situation. Insomnia was fast becoming part of his life, unfortunately. He couldn't switch off his thoughts. His head was full of a new vocabulary: *power exchange, domination, submission, contract, safeword, scene, flogger, tawse….* The list went on.

And then there were the images of Wayne that flitted through his brain.

A very different Wayne, a black leather harness tight across his furry chest. A Wayne who stood, booted feet apart, taut leather hugging his thighs, a leather snake of a whip coiled in his hand. A Wayne whose piercing blue eyes seemed to see right into Ellis's head.

I know what you need.

Fuck, those eyes. The voice that had Ellis's belly in knots. The lean body he'd seen so often in the locker room, only this time it sent something shuddering through him, *racing* through him, something hot, almost primal….

His phone rang, shattering the quiet and rousing him from the dreamy state into which he'd drifted without even realizing it. One look at the screen had him groaning out loud.

What the hell can she want at this hour?

Wiping his eyes, Ellis connected the call. "Hey, what's up?" Like he didn't know what was coming.

"Oh, thank goodness, you're still awake." His sister sounded relieved.

The words were right there on the tip of his tongue. *Well, I wasn't, but your call saw to that.* He bit back the terse reply and waited for the request he knew was imminent.

"Listen, can you come over and watch the kids? I need to get out of the house for a while."

Ellis stared at the alarm clock beside his bed. "Barb, it's eleven o'clock." She had to be kidding.

"I know," Barbara whined, "but they're already in bed asleep. I just need you to come over and sit until I get back. I won't be long, I promise. I just need a break. Please, El?"

He wanted to shout down the phone that *he had a fucking life too.* That she couldn't keep doing this. Only he knew he wouldn't. Anything to keep the peace and make her happy.

Hell, he was far too keen on making everyone else happy. *Why isn't there someone out there who wants me to be happy?*

"Fine, fine. Give me twenty minutes, all right?"

"Aw, thanks." There was that note of relief again, and it was that more than anything else that ensured Ellis would keep saying yes when he ought to say no.

He disconnected the call with a sigh and clambered off the bed. It was only then he realized Barb's call couldn't have come at a more welcome moment. It might have broken his sleep, but it also shattered his dream.

He didn't want to think about Wayne like that.

THE CROWD was larger than either Eli or Jarod was expecting. Nearly everyone on their mailing list had come, some with a guest. There were a few men who grumbled about not liking the new place, how it didn't have the character of the old club. Jarod had wanted to talk to them to see what could be done to make it more to their liking, but Eli dragged him off to the side.

"No, pet. If they're not happy, let them go."

"But Sir, I thought we could—"

"What? Change everything we did to make a few disgruntled people happy? I know it's part of your nature to take care of people, to make them smile, but you can't please everyone, Jarod. No matter how hard you try, there will always be a few people that are too mired in the past to try and see what's in their present."

His words made sense, of course. Still, Jarod thought maybe with time, he could have done.... He sighed. Probably nothing. Eli was right. If the men didn't like the place now, there would be little *they* could do to ensure they'd stay in the future. Maybe some of them would come around, but more likely they'd try to find a club that better suited their needs.

The numbers at the bar continued to increase. The new bartenders they'd hired were doing their best to keep up, but the demands for drinks kept coming. Jarod stepped behind the bar to wash glassware and wipe down the marble counter, hoping to free up the young men who were serving patrons, when a familiar voice shocked him to his core.

"So who does a guy have to fuck to get a drink around here?"

He shivered as he turned around, unsure if he had heard what he thought. When he saw a bright smile aimed at him, his heart soared.

"Hey, Jarod," Scott said sweetly, no longer faking a deeper tone.

"Scott! You made it." Jarod breathed a sigh of relief. Before they left Manchester, the members of Collars & Cuffs were a family to him. When Thomas, one of the owners of the club, approached Jarod with the idea of opening their own club, the first thing through Jarod's mind was how much he didn't want to leave the people who had come to mean so much to him.

The idea that Eli was wasting away, though, gave him the push he needed to make the decision to broach buying the club. When it was agreed they would, Jarod's heart sank because he knew how much this change in location would hurt.

When they said goodbye at the airport, Jarod truly worried it would be the last time he'd see everyone. But now? Seeing Scott there, a huge smile on his face, his suit coat and tie pressed, simply reminded Jarod how much he loved those people who'd pulled him into their lives and made him one of them.

Scott grinned. "Yeah, and I brought some friends."

He pointed in the direction of the door, where Ben, Leo, Alex, Thomas, Peter, Darren, and JJ were coming through. Jarod's heart thudded. The Manchester contingent hadn't RSVP'd, and when Jarod had called to check, he got no answer.

Scott threw his hands in the air and beamed. "Surprise!"

It was a surprise, but the most pleasant one he could think of. Seeing Leo and Thomas, the owners of Collars & Cuffs, along with their subs, Alex and Peter, soothed Jarod's frayed nerves. Having Darren and JJ show up was icing on the cake. He'd missed them all so much. But the boy in front of him? He missed Scott most of all.

"And just in time, from the look of it," Ben added as he joined Scott at the bar. Scott's Dom looked wonderful. His cheeks were flushed, probably from the nip in the air. Or maybe it was the impending fatherhood that had made these two seem to stand taller. Jarod couldn't wait to catch up, to hear about the baby that Ben's sister was carrying for them. God, he hadn't realized how much of their lives he'd missed in these few short months.

Jarod was severely torn between spending time with his friends and doing the dishes to help his staff. He laughed when Ben came around the end of the bar and took the glasses from his hands.

"I've got this. If you don't spend some time with him, I may have to tie him down, gag him, and plug him. He's been talking nonstop ever since we got on the train. Several people moved to a different carriage, probably because of his incessant chatter about seeing you."

Jarod frowned. "But you're a guest. You shouldn't be—"

"Please. For me. Between Annie's grousing about how big she's gotten and Scott's unending chorus of 'are we there yet,' I can use the peace and quiet. Besides, I think he may burst if you don't go now."

Jarod handed over the bar towel and hurried to where Scott, Alex, and Peter waited for him. They grabbed him in a hug, Peter and Alex saying how good he looked, and Scott launching into a litany of questions about the club. He kept it up until Alex put a hand over Scott's mouth.

"You know what? If you shut up, he might actually have a chance to answer you." He grimaced when Scott licked his palm. "Sometimes you can be such a gross little shit."

Scott ignored him. "Can we see upstairs where you guys live? It sounded awesome in your email."

"Of course." Jarod led the three subs to the lift. "Take it up to the top floor. Ours is the only door. I'll be up in a while." He caught Peter's gaze. "I'm putting you in charge of Scott." He grinned.

Peter laughed. "Fine, give *me* the hard task, why don't you?"

Jarod laughed too. He left them there and turned to walk back to the bar. Behind him he caught Scott's squeal. "Ooh, mirrors!"

Shaking his head, Jarod went in search of Eli, who he found in the kitchen, rushing around stacking plates in racks by the dishwasher.

"I'm dashing around like a blue-arsed fly. Isn't this why we hired help?" he grumbled.

"You're loving it," Jarod said, a smile on his face.

Eli stopped and cocked his head for a moment before a huge grin split his face. "I am. This is exciting, pet. I know it will all level off, but I never thought we'd have this many people here tonight."

"More than you thought. Masters Thomas, Leo, and Ben are out there. I've got the boys in our place because… well, Scott's here."

Eli laughed. "I'm glad they made it. Put them at a table and send one of the boys to take care of them. Tell him they're his only responsibility for the remainder of the night and that we'll make sure he receives a great tip. I'll get out there as soon as I can while you go entertain." Eli turned to one of the cooks. "Marco, do me a favor. Throw on eight cheeseburgers and crisps for some friends of ours, okay? One of the guys will come to collect them and deliver them shortly."

"No problem," said the unflappable young man manning the kitchen line with grace under pressure.

Eli stepped closer to Jarod, reached out, and cupped his chin. "Are you happy, pet?"

"Yes, very much."

"Is it because our friends are here?"

Jarod thought for a few moments. While seeing the boys definitely qualified as a highlight of the night, being here with Eli and starting this new club overwhelmed it all. They were doing this. Together. While he missed his friends, the ache had lessened significantly as he'd found his footing in London.

"No. Because *we* are. I love our life here."

"Good. Now get upstairs before the three Musketeers find the sex toys."

JAROD GOT a call from the kitchen that the food had been prepared, and Eli said he would be sending it up to their place so Jarod could visit. After the boys wolfed down the burgers, Jarod glanced at his watch. There were still hours to go, and it didn't sit well with him that Eli would be alone while he stayed out of the fray.

"You can go downstairs, you know," Alex murmured. "We don't need a sitter."

"But I don't want to leave you. You came all this way, and it would feel wrong."

"We're big boys, Jarod," Peter told him.

"Except for Scott," Alex tossed in.

"Wanker."

Alex cackled. "Ooh, been here for a couple years and he's finally turning into a proper Brit." Scott raised his middle finger, and Alex burst out laughing. "I guess you can take the boy out of America, but you'll never get America out of the boy."

Peter laughed before addressing Jarod. "Seriously, Jarod, if we can watch television, we're fine by ourselves."

Jarod bit his lip. "I could see if my mother wants to come and visit. She's probably sitting at home knitting." And "home" wasn't exactly all that far away.

Scott piped up. "Jarod, we could come with you. We'd love to see more of the club. And you wouldn't need to watch us. We'll sit with our men. Then after the club closes, we'll go out to an early breakfast."

Again Jarod was torn. Eli told him it would be okay to stay with their friends, and he really wanted that, but he also wanted to be downstairs helping. Meeting the members and seeing what they thought of Secrets. If the boys came downstairs, he'd feel the need to entertain them.

Scott stood and walked over to Jarod. "Go on. Help Eli. This is your night to shine. We'll talk to our guys and see if they'd mind if we sit at a table together so they can have their Dom talk. I'm sure it'll be okay."

Jarod locked gazes with Scott. He could sense his earnestness, and his stomach unclenched a little.

"Thank you," he whispered.

"Least I could do after everything you've done for us." Scott gave Jarod a quick hug. "Now shoo while I call Ben."

Jarod laughed. "Bossy." He left them and went for the lift, his heart feeling lighter.

ELI HAD to break away from the guys from Collars & Cuffs when more and more people began to walk through the door. He did his best to greet them, offering to show them around or answer any questions. He'd just finished telling someone about the improvements they'd made to the club when he was approached by a tall, handsome man, a younger man close behind him.

"Good evening, gentlemen. Welcome to Secrets."

"It's a pleasure to be here." The man was an obvious Dom. His submissive stood at his heel, eyes to the floor.

Eli held out his hand. "I'm Eli Jameson, one of the owners."

A warm hand engulfed his. "I'm Joe Dexter, and this is my boy, Oliver. Olly—or sometimes Royal Pain in the Arse—for short." He turned to the younger man. "It's okay to say hello."

The young man turned his blue eyes toward him, and for the first time, Eli could see his beauty. A mop of blond curls lay atop a stunning face. The two men were a portrait in contrasts, and Eli could see Joe was very protective of his submissive.

"It's a pleasure to meet you, sir," Olly said.

"The pleasure is mine, I assure you."

Eli saw Jarod leading the Musketeers to a table, then fretting over them. He couldn't help but stifle a laugh. Not for the first time, he wondered what Jarod would be like as a parent. If his interactions with the boys were any indication, he'd be incredible. Maybe when Scott and Ben had their baby, a visit to meet the little one could be arranged.

He pointed to Jarod. "That gent over there is my pet, Jarod. He's the other owner. Those young men he's with are from another club, Collars & Cuffs, in Manchester."

"Ooh, Sir, may I go meet them?" Olly pleaded.

Joe gave his submissive a keen glance. "Will you promise to behave yourself?" Olly pouted beautifully, which caused Joe to sigh. "No, of course not. I don't even know why I bothered to ask." He turned his attention to Eli. "Are you sure it's okay?"

"Definitely. They came down to see the opening, and I'm guessing Jarod is feeling guilty because he can't do everything at once. It'll be good if Olly could keep them occupied."

Joe tucked a knuckle under Olly's chin. "Remember, boy. You're here as a guest. What you do reflects on me. Behave yourself."

"Don't I always?" Olly asked, his eyes wide.

Joe snorted. "No, and that's the problem!" He swatted Olly's arse. "Go on, then."

Olly turned and rushed to the table, where the boys stood to welcome him. Jarod turned and looked at Eli, who gave him a wink. One of the waiters came over to deliver a round of soft drinks, and Alex pointed to Olly. The server, Lawrence, if Eli remembered correctly, hurried to the bar.

Joe sighed. "He's not going to remember the no-sugar rule."

On cue Lawrence returned with a tall glass of orange Fanta.

Joe scrubbed a hand over his face. "*Someone* is going to be spending time in the corner when we get home, gagged and plugged."

"He seems like a great young man."

"Oh, don't let looks fool you." He chuckled. "Olly is my life."

"I get that," Eli replied, glancing toward Jarod, who was back behind the bar, washing glassware.

"I see that you do."

Eli returned his attention to Joe. "You're wearing the visitors' bracelet. Are you thinking about becoming members?"

"We're members of a friend's club here in London, and my partner and I run a corporate training facility. But we didn't want to miss the chance to welcome you to the scene."

Eli was gobsmacked. He hadn't thought people would go out of their way to welcome a rival club, but he didn't doubt Joe's sincerity.

"Oh hell no," Joe growled.

"What?" Eli asked, confused as to the glare Joe shot at the table where Olly sat.

"He is *not* getting a second Fanta." He turned back to Eli. "It's a pleasure to meet you. I hope one day we can see you at The Edge." He rose to his feet and slipped a business card into Eli's hand. "For now I need to go rescue your club from my soon-to-be-in-chastity boy."

Joe stalked over to the table where Olly sat. When Olly looked up, he beamed Joe a smile. Joe pointed at the glass, and Olly shrugged, giving such an innocent smile that Eli had to laugh. Joe reached out and grabbed Olly's hand and dragged the protesting boy to the door. The last thing Eli heard from them as they walked out was Olly shouting, "Call me!"

Eli chuckled as the two men left Secrets, then turned his attention back to the table with the Collars & Cuffs contingent.

"Thank you for your patience," he said, sitting down and waving to the waiter to fetch another round of drinks.

"You've got a great place here," Thomas said.

"Thank you. We really love it."

"I noticed the man with the sub he had to practically drag out of here."

Eli chuckled. "That would be Joe Dexter."

Leo's eyes lit up. "I've heard of him. He and his partner run a very exclusive training center."

"The Edge, right?" Thomas asked.

"Yeah," Eli replied. "He gave me the card. Maybe we'll head over there one day to see what it's all about."

"You should," Thomas said with obvious excitement. "I've heard nothing but good things about the place. Plus then you'll be able to tell us if we need to check it out too when we're next here."

Ben laughed. "Count me in. Scott could use a few good classes. With the baby coming and him working on a new book, he's become a bit lax."

"What's he become lax in? Servicing your dick?" Eli asked with a smirk. He winked at the others. "Because I've lost count of the number of times when I'd phone you and you were otherwise engaged with his mouth."

"Oh no. He's doing that most nights. But since you and Jarod moved, he's thrown himself into his work and our upcoming bundle of joy. He needs to remember whose collar he's wearing, though. If he needs a distraction, I'll be happy to provide it."

The laughter warmed Eli. He was glad that their friends had come for the opening night. Having them there meant a lot to both him and Jarod. He was about to say as much when the doors opened again and a new wave of visitors made what Eli hoped would be the first of many visits to Secrets.

CHAPTER FOUR

WAYNE PARKED his black Jeep Cherokee in an empty parking space in front of the building that housed Ellis's flat. Wayne's palms were damp as he waited for him to come out. He raised his eyes to the bright sky. "I hope tonight isn't a disaster in the making," he muttered. He'd expected questions the last two days while they were training together, but there had been nothing.

Maybe he's changed his mind and he's embarrassed to tell me. Maybe that's what the silence meant.

None of this helped quell his nerves.

When Ellis stepped out of the building, Wayne couldn't help the shiver that ran through him. Though the air still had a slight chill to it, Ellis wore tight jeans and an even tighter black T-shirt that stretched across his broad chest. Wayne had seen Ellis in the locker room many times, but no matter what he wore, Ellis always looked like a gift Wayne wanted desperately to unwrap.

Ellis slid into the passenger seat, and Wayne glanced at him out of the corner of his eye. He'd never get tired of this man. The dark, wavy hair plastered to his head because it hadn't dried yet, the thick eyebrows that framed his mocha-brown eyes. The pouty lips that gave him an air of innocence, even if Wayne knew there wasn't much that was innocent about Ellis.

"Did we run out of time today?" Wayne asked, arching an eyebrow as he pulled out of the parking space.

"Sod off. I didn't get nearly enough sleep last night and I'm cranky, so zip it unless you want an earful."

Jealousy clutched Wayne in an iron grip. He knew he shouldn't be upset, but the thought of Ellis with anyone else pissed him off.

"What was her name?" he asked, trying to remain casual.

"Jack, and *he's* my neighbor. The bastard decided to join a band and they were practicing all bloody night. I couldn't get any sleep. I went over and told them I was a cop, for all the difference it made. Certainly there was no change in the volume. I've got to call my landlord. I can't be having this on a nightly basis."

It was on the tip of Wayne's tongue to let Ellis know he had room for him; he only had to ask. Wayne wanted the man near him all the time. But as far as he knew, Ellis was straight. At least it seemed that way when they went out to the pubs and the girls wrapped themselves around him.

"So… tonight should be… um… interesting," Ellis stuttered.

Wayne fired a glance in his direction. "Are you sure about this? Because it's okay if you've changed your mind." *And you haven't said a bloody word about it since I asked you.*

Silence.

Wayne sighed. "What's up, Ellis. Cold feet?"

"No, it's not that. It's just.… Look, it was a bit of a shock, finding out you were into this kind of thing."

"There's a lot about me you don't know," Wayne muttered. *Like how I wish it were you kneeling by my side in the club. Or stretched out on my bed.*

Fuck. He needed that image like he needed a hole in the head.

"And what I'm wearing is okay?" Wayne could hear the anxious edge to Ellis's voice.

Okay? The skin-tight black shirt and the pants hugging every curve of Ellis's arse drew Wayne in and held him there. God, he was sex on a stick, though Wayne wished it were more "sex on his dick." He shook his head to clear out the pornographic images he'd stored away for those nights spent alone.

"You're fine. You'll have to beat the men off with sticks." He chuckled at the panic in Ellis's eyes. "Don't worry," he soothed. "No one will bother you while you're with me. Club rules state that you're respectful until you have an agreement for whatever they're asking about."

"I'm not into this, you know," Ellis muttered.

And yet he'd asked to come. Having been a practicing Dom for the last twelve years, Wayne knew there was at least curiosity there. He wondered if Ellis had done any research, and if so, what he found. God, he wanted to see inside Ellis's head right then.

"I told you, Ellis, you don't need to come. I'll take you back home if you want."

"No," he replied quickly. "It's fine. I'd rather spend some time with you than listen to Jack strangle 'Stairway to Heaven' again."

Wayne chuckled. "And you're right; it *will* be an interesting evening."
He couldn't wait to see Ellis's reaction.

THE MORE Ellis saw of the interior of Secrets, the bigger the butterflies
in his stomach became. Hell, he thought maybe they were hippos in
tutus doing *Swan Lake*, the way everything flipped and bounced. From
the entryway it hadn't seemed any different than some of the posher
clubs they'd been to. Wayne had talked to the guy behind the desk before
turning back to Ellis.

"Are you sure you want to do this?" he asked.

"Honestly? I thought I did, but now that we're here, I'm fucking
nervous."

Wayne chuckled, then put a hand on Ellis's shoulder. "Don't be.
I promise you'll be okay." He handed Ellis a wristband. "Slip this on.
It shows that you're a visitor and a guest. No one will bother you, I
promise. There may be some people I need to speak with, but I'll always
stay where you can see me. If you get too uncomfortable or things get to
be too much, you let me know, and we'll go."

"Really? You won't mind?" Ellis's slow smile and shining eyes spoke
of his relief.

"No, of course I won't mind. You're doing this so you can see
who I am. And that is someone who is always respectful of a person's
limitations. I wouldn't think anything less of you if you couldn't handle
it. I wouldn't tease you about it. And I certainly won't rub it in after the
fact. I need you to trust me on this."

And Ellis did. He trusted Wayne like he'd never trusted anyone
else in his life. Wayne never asked for more than Ellis could give. He
never made him feel stupid like his family did at times. No, Wayne was
always there. Strong, dependable. In the direst situations, he kept Ellis
level-headed and safe. Ellis smiled at the thought of how much better the
world would be if more people were like his friend.

*Stop being such a wuss. If Wayne's bringing me here, how bad can
it really be?*

"Okay, I'm ready. Let's do this."

Ellis had taken two steps, then stopped when Wayne put a hand on
his shoulder. "I'm serious, Ellis. Don't do this just for me. I don't want
you uncomfortable. That wouldn't make me happy at all."

During the six years they'd worked together and all the time they'd been mates, Ellis had never seen that expression on Wayne's face. Serious but… searching. Like he needed to ensure Ellis was okay with this. His heart hammered when he stared into the depths of Wayne's eyes. Ellis could see why he would be a Dom because the look he was getting made him feel safe and reminded Ellis who he was.

"We're good," Ellis promised. He tried to reassure Wayne with a smile. "Let's go before we miss the party."

When Wayne opened the door, whatever Ellis thought lay behind it went straight out of his head. He'd worked it out in his mind that the place would be dark and dingy. He had envisioned something creepy, with men splayed out and being beaten by guys who were taking turns. But the reality was a stark contrast. Secrets was absolutely gorgeous. And the name really made sense because, from the outside, you would never expect what this place held.

"Shit," Ellis muttered.

Wayne was instantly by his side. "What's wrong?"

"Nothing. This place. It's… wow."

"Not what you were expecting?" Wayne asked, his amusement obvious.

"Not in the least. Where are the kinky things?" he asked, and then his face heated when Ellis realized what he'd asked.

The question brought a laugh from Wayne, but Ellis knew it wasn't directed at him. Wayne might tease him, but he had never in his life been cruel about it.

"There will be, as you say, 'kinky things,' but not until later. Right now this is just a meet and greet. In about thirty minutes, they'll do demonstrations for the new people who might become members. Fair warning: I don't know what they have planned, and some demos can be pretty intense. Remember, if you need us to leave, we will. No questions asked."

"I've been in some really shitty situations," Ellis reminded Wayne. "I'm pretty sure I can handle anything this place has to offer."

Wayne wrapped an arm around Ellis's shoulder. "Keep telling yourself that." Then the bastard laughed. "Okay, I see a few people I need to say hello to, but I'll be back with you before the demo starts. I'm going to take you to the bar so you can have a drink. No alcohol and no caffeine. You didn't sleep well, so you don't need that to get you all worked up. Sound good?"

Ellis saluted. "Yes, sir!"

An oddly serious expression flitted across Wayne's face and his nostrils flared. "Let's go," he growled.

He put his hand on Ellis's arm and led him to the bar, then went off to talk with a group of men in harnesses, one of whom had a young man kneeling by his side. Ellis couldn't take his gaze off them. The younger man rested his head against the man's—Dom's?—leg, smiling widely when the other man stroked blunt fingers through his hair.

"Welcome to Secrets," a voice from behind him said. He turned to find an older gentleman decked out in a suit but wearing an apron. "Forgive the attire. I was washing glassware." He held out a hand. "I'm Jarod, one of the owners here."

Ellis shook his hand. It was warm and a little damp.

"Ugh. Sorry." Jarod wiped his hand on his apron.

"No problem." Ellis waved a hand around the room. "This place is amazing."

He turned back to Jarod in time to see him blush. "Thank you. There has been a lot of work put into it. So this is your first time here?"

"It is. I'm a guest of a friend."

"Would that be the sexy man over there who hasn't taken his eyes off you?"

Ellis whipped his head around and caught Wayne staring. When Wayne noticed, he turned his attention back to the men, but Ellis could see he was looking out of the corner of his eye.

"He's worried about my reaction to the place," Ellis said. "This isn't really my scene. I'm just here to give him support."

"Well, great. Everyone needs a friend. Say, I need to get back to washing glassware. What can I get you?"

"How about a tonic and lime? Wayne doesn't want me having any alcohol or caffeine because he thinks it will keep me awake all night."

Jarod arched an eyebrow and gave Ellis an odd look, but he filled a glass, then placed it on the bar. "If you need anything else, let me know."

"Oh, but I haven't paid," Ellis reminded him.

"It's all free tonight. There is a buffet set up over on the side if you want something to eat." One of the guys behind the bar called to Jarod. "I've got to go. Thank you for coming!"

Ellis picked up his glass and took a long drink.

Okay, so far this is fine. I can cope with this.

THE OPEN-HOUSE turnout was the largest crowd Wayne had seen at the club. He'd been a member for four years and watched as membership dwindled a little. It held steady with a core group of people, but by and large, it needed an infusion of new blood. If even a third of the people who turned out for the evening became members, then Secrets would once again be one of the finest places for people in the lifestyle.

He glanced over at Ellis and grinned. His friend looked so lost, but at the same time, he seemed utterly fascinated by what transpired around him. Wayne had suspected this would be the case, and he was overjoyed Ellis asked to come. Though Ellis had proclaimed his heterosexuality on occasion, usually when they went to the pub to meet up with friends, Wayne had noticed a few things when Ellis thought no one else was watching. Like the fact he never picked up a woman but always was the one who got picked up. He'd wait until she approached him, then they'd go off together. Not like the rest of his group, who tried their damnedest to find a little company for the evening. Then there was the fact Ellis never bragged about it the day after. None of this proved anything, but it definitely made Wayne curious.

They'd been friends for six years, and Wayne thought he knew Ellis pretty well. Lately, he'd begun to notice what started out as subtle changes in Ellis's behavior. At first he distanced himself from colleagues, not going out after work or on their days off. He seemed more highly strung, more prone to anger. Things that used to make him laugh now had him clenching his fists. Recently he'd arrived late a couple of times, which was so out of character for the man who once blasted someone on the team for being two minutes late to a briefing. It went downhill from there. In the last six months, Ellis had begun to snap at everyone, and when asked if everything was all right, he'd say yes, but Wayne could hear the truth in his tone. All the signs pointed to Ellis falling apart. He needed someone to take him in hand.

He needed Wayne.

He couldn't be sure Ellis would accept, of course. If nothing else he'd become more headstrong since they met. But Ellis—the one person he could admit to truly caring about—wasn't the same man he met on a sweltering June day. The bright smile had increasingly become gritted teeth, hard glares, or outright hostility toward people. The only one who had never been on the receiving end was Wayne.

He'd always known he exuded a subtle influence over Ellis. If he found himself struggling, he'd come to ask Wayne's opinion. Unlike everyone else on the team who asked questions of Wayne, Ellis asked questions to help him sort out his own thought processes. But that too changed over the last year or so. Now unless Wayne sought him out, Ellis stayed away. That couldn't happen. Ellis was the one Wayne looked to for a smile, a laugh, or just to remind himself he still had feelings for his friend.

ELLIS JERKED his head up as the PA system crackled into life.

"Good evening, gentlemen! Welcome to the opening of Secrets. I'm Eli Jameson, and that sexy thing behind the bar is my pet, Jarod. We're very happy that so many of you came tonight. We hope you're enjoying yourselves, and if you need anything at all, don't hesitate to give us a shout. For now, though, we've got a special guest here. Direct from Collars & Cuffs in Manchester, one of the co-owners, Leo Hart, has agreed to do a spanking demonstration with his submissive and husband, Alex Hart."

Two tall men walked up on stage, both dressed in very sharp-looking suits.

A chuckle snapped Ellis's attention away from the stage. Wayne stood beside him, his gaze fixed on the two men. "Yeah, that's a little… different."

Ellis said nothing but looked back at them. Despite his claims he could handle anything, he was glad to find Wayne at his side. Whatever was about to happen on stage was definitely a step beyond his comfort zone. *Spanking? Really?* Somehow it felt better knowing Wayne was there for him.

The older man addressed the audience.

"Okay, I'm sure you know that when a sub gets spanked, it's usually for punishment or maintenance. My boy happens to find it an erotic prelude, or foreplay, if you prefer. So we're going to do a quick demo, then try out one of the private rooms." He waggled his eyebrows.

The audience laughed.

"I know we're not really dressed for the occasion, but sometimes you have to work with what you have available."

Leo pulled a chair onto the raised platform and sat. He glanced up at Alex. "Pants down to your knees," he instructed.

Ellis stared. *What the fuck?* He watched as Alex undid the waistband of his pants without hesitation. He pushed them down, giving his butt a little wiggle, and revealed a pair of white briefs.

Leo patted his knee, and Alex bent over, positioning himself. Leo locked his leg around his partner's. "Are you comfortable?"

"Yes, Sir." Alex's voice was calm.

Leo raised a hand and brought it down with a solid *thwack*. Alex cried out, but it wasn't one of pain. There was a note of... something in his voice Ellis couldn't identify. Leo repeated the motion, his hand never landing in the same place in succession. Now and again he paused, rubbing Alex's firm cheeks before bringing down another blow.

Ellis couldn't believe he was standing there watching a grown man get his arse spanked—a grown man who loved every second of it, judging by the occasional low moan of pleasure that burst from his lips.

Fuck. It really is *turning him on.*

Leo stopped and slowly pulled down Alex's briefs, to reveal his rosy cheeks, Alex lifting himself up to help him. He caressed them, squeezing them and digging his fingers into the blushing flesh. "Ready for more?"

"Yes, yes, Sir," Alex whispered.

Over and over Leo rained blows on the younger man's rear end with no particular rhythm, and with each one, Alex's eyes grew wilder. Not with pain or anger, but with unbridled lust; Ellis couldn't miss Alex's erect dick that hung down between Leo's knees. *Oh my God, the sight of them.* Ellis couldn't take his eyes off them; they were so in tune with one another.

"Five more, boy," Leo called out.

The last five were harsh, and the sound echoed in the near silence of the room. As soon as they'd been delivered, Leo spread his legs. Alex slid off his lap and dropped to his knees in front of him, grasping for his Dom's zipper. Ellis couldn't believe it when he reached inside and fished out a hard cock, then went down on him. Leo placed his hand on Alex's head, urging him to go deeper, and with every thrust of his hips, buried himself in Alex's mouth.

Ellis shifted uncomfortably.

That small reaction was all it took.

Without hesitation Wayne turned to him and said, "Okay, we're gone."

WAYNE LED him out to the parking lot, unlocked the doors, and held open the passenger door for a seemingly shell-shocked Ellis. Wayne hoped he wasn't too far gone, because Wayne had hoped tonight would be the right moment for the conversation he had been rehearsing for the past two months. The one where he told Ellis of his plan and could only hope his friend would see things as Wayne did.

After starting the engine, he turned to Ellis. "So what did you think?"

Ellis blinked a few times. "Well. It was… different, I have to say." His voice was subdued.

Wayne wasn't sure where to go from there, and silence fell between them for a few minutes.

"You're really into that stuff?" Ellis still sounded quiet.

"Okay, you're going to have to help me here. Clarify 'stuff.'"

Ellis cleared his throat. "The leather. Guys on their knees. Guys with leashes attached to collars. Spankings."

Something in Ellis's tone finally broke through, and Wayne had a sinking feeling there might be a problem. "Some of those things, yes."

"What do you get out of it?" Ellis demanded.

"I like helping to get a sub out of his head, to shoulder his burdens. I like the control, I guess would be the best way to put it."

"So what you're saying is how you are on the job extends to how you act outside of it?"

"Precisely."

"So did you ever have a… what did you call it?"

"A submissive? No. I've played with some at the club, but I've never considered taking on a full-time sub. With our job I wouldn't have much time to give them." Wayne took a deep breath. "But lately I've been giving it some thought."

"Really?"

"Let me ask you a question. Why did you want to come tonight?"

Ellis gave a one-shoulder shrug. "I dunno. I thought I knew everything about you, but this was a shock. I guess I really want to know who you are. You're my mate, and if it's interesting to you, then I should know about it."

His words lessened the anxiety in Wayne's chest. Maybe this *was* the time to plunge in to the deep end.

"I can appreciate that," he said before taking a deep breath. "You know I just said I'd been giving some thought to taking a submissive? Well, I have my eye on someone who seems to be in need of help, and I want to provide that." He paused. "No, scrap that. I *need* to help because this person is important to me."

"Do I know him?" Ellis asked.

Wayne's stomach turned over. He'd known this was going to happen, but he also knew there was no way to sugar-coat it. "Yes. It's you, Ellis."

He didn't have to see Ellis's face to gauge his reaction. His shout of "What the fuck?" made it extremely clear. At that moment he was glad they were moving so Ellis couldn't jump out. He plunged ahead.

"As I said, one of the things that calls to me is someone who I think needs to be taken in hand. I have to be honest, mate…. Right now no one needs it more than you do. Do you know how many times I've covered for you in the last two months? After we talked about the woman who you should have shot to protect the man, you've messed up no less than five times. That can't stand. You've always been good at your job. One of the best I've ever seen, if I'm honest. But the last year or so, you're not the same man."

He could hear Ellis's harsh breathing and decided to press on before he had a chance to respond.

"You've been charging in like a bull, huffing and puffing, riding roughshod over your team. The same men you haven't been out to the pub with for the last six months. You're snapping at them, dressing them down for no good reason or, worse, for something you yourself did. You've got bags under your eyes, and you're even drinking the swill coffee in the office like it's lifeblood. Now do you want to tell me what's going on?"

He waited a few moments, and then Ellis snarled, "Nothing. If I made a mistake, then you should be getting me fired. That's what this is about, isn't it?"

Wayne sighed. "No, that's not what this is about. It's about you needing help. Specifically my help."

"Stop the car," Ellis thundered.

Wayne pulled to the side of the road. Ellis threw the door open and got out. "You know, I thought we were mates. I didn't know you didn't see me as a real man."

"That's not what I said and you know it."

"Fuck you, Wayne. You're telling me you want me to be a submissive to you. I saw what went on up on that stage. No way in hell would I ever allow someone to do those things to me. It's sick and wrong."

It couldn't have hurt more if Ellis had shoved a knife in Wayne's chest and had given it a good twist. But he knew the anger Ellis was experiencing had to do more with internalized feelings than actual upset with him, and he had to focus on that.

"You know that isn't true," he replied as calmly as he could. "Everyone needs help now and again, Ellis. I want to provide that for you."

"No! You're saying that I'm incapable of doing my job, that I'm a risk to everyone on the squad. Instead I should be fucking kneeling at your feet like a dog. Listen to me good, mate, because this is the last thing I've got to say to you. Fuck you. Fuck your club. And just… go fuck yourself."

The truck rattled when Ellis kicked the door shut and stalked off down the street. Wayne desperately wanted to go after him, but in his anger, anything could happen. As it stood right now, Ellis needed time to digest what Wayne had said. He only hoped his friend would realize Wayne's intentions were only to help.

If not, Wayne had just messed up everything between them.

CHAPTER FIVE

ELLIS STORMED into his flat and slammed the door. Neighbors be damned. He'd just lost the best mate he'd ever had, and his heart hurt over the fact. *What the hell could Wayne have been thinking? No one knows me like he does.* He went to the refrigerator and yanked it open. Thank goodness there were still at least eight beers left, because the way he felt, he'd probably need them all. He grabbed three of the bottles, then went over to his chair, placed the bottles on the table, and flopped down to enjoy them.

His stomach rumbled, and he thought about ordering a pizza, but a glance over at the clock reminded him everywhere would be long closed. He should have had some of the food they were offering at the club. The smells that were coming from the kitchen had tantalized Ellis's taste buds all night.

Ellis chugged down the whole bottle, then opened another. *That damned club.* Why had he insisted on going with Wayne? He wasn't into that scene, and those men down there were the cause of the row between him and Wayne. He'd sat there and talked with that man... Jarod? He seemed like a nice enough guy, quiet and respectful, and nothing like Ellis, that was for sure. *He* was loud and boisterous. As far as his colleagues were concerned, his favorite leisure pursuits were drinking with his mates and picking up women to take home.

How could Wayne even think something like that? It boggled Ellis's mind completely. They'd trained together; hell, they'd even sparred. True, he'd never beaten Wayne in a match, but it was damn close. Wayne had to know Ellis was every bit a man like him. So why? Biting back his anger, Ellis stood and went to the mirror. He ran a hand through his hair, then leaned close to look at himself. His dark blond spikes and brown eyes probably wouldn't win any beauty contests, but they always attracted him attention. More than one woman said his eyes were magnetic and drew them in. Sure, it was nice to hear the compliment, even if it probably was bullshit.

The thoughts going round and round in his head were getting him nowhere. He went back and popped the top off another bottle of beer, sat down, and dropped his head back. This night had screwed up everything. Would he be able to look Wayne in the eye again? Hell, could he even work with him? The thing of it, though? He loved his job and the men he worked with. They were tight and always had each other's backs. The nature of the Specialist Armed Officers was they spent a hell of a lot of time waiting around for the next op, so that left time for training. A *lot* of training. He *knew* those men. He couldn't see himself in another job, nor did he want to be. But right now he couldn't see working with Wayne either.

Ellis would never deny logic wasn't really his strong suit. Wayne had told him he was more of a hands-on, visual-type learner. He could do anything that needed to be done, but when he had to work through a particularly difficult question, he always asked Wayne for help. That definitely wasn't going to happen tonight. Or maybe ever again. His stomach clenched at the thought he wouldn't have Wayne in his life anymore. He had never once let Ellis down. Whenever there was a problem and Ellis couldn't see a way out, Wayne talked him through it. And he gave good advice. He'd probably saved Ellis's job more than once.

"Fuck," he muttered as he stood up, grabbed the remaining bottle of beer to put back in the refrigerator, then went into his bedroom and stripped down to his underwear. He plugged his phone in before he crawled into bed. With as little sleep as he'd been getting, he should have been completely exhausted, but now all he could think about was Wayne and his stupid desire to take Ellis in hand or whatever the hell he'd said.

"Don't need nobody's help," Ellis growled. He reared up and punched his pillow a few times before he put his head back down. Surprisingly he drifted off to sleep.

AFTER ELLIS vanished from sight, Wayne let his head drop to the steering wheel. This whole thing had gone so wrong. He replayed the incident in his head, and he could see clearly where he'd made his mistakes. He should have been with Ellis the entire time, answering any questions he had. He'd thought it best not to hover, to let Ellis take things in at his own pace. But he knew Ellis was more action than reaction, more prone to see something and dive in rather than sit there and question it.

"Fuck. You're a stupid git," he chastised himself.

If he had been with Ellis, he could have seen the changes as they came up. Been close enough to judge his reactions and able to do something about them right away, rather than leaving him to his own devices. He'd hoped it would open a dialogue, give them a chance to talk, but instead he'd jumped in with both feet, essentially ambushing Ellis about his intentions, giving him absolutely no chance to ask questions or talk about what he'd witnessed.

"You know why too," he told himself. "You wanted Ellis from the start. You can tell yourself that your intentions are noble, and they probably are, but there's also that bit about your feelings. You want him, so you threw away all that training, all your best intentions, and just tossed him into the deep end without a by-your-leave."

And that was exactly what he'd done. Years of instincts he'd honed, making sure to read a sub, to know when he needed to step in, and he'd just gone in the opposite direction and let his heart override his mind.

"Damn," he muttered.

He could sit there for hours and mull over this, but it wasn't going to change the fact he'd messed up and scared the hell out of his friend. Ellis was his responsibility, and Wayne had failed him. What kind of ramifications would he have to deal with at work? Would Ellis complain? Get him sacked?

Wayne lay back against the seat. He'd have to deal with whatever was coming up.

ELLIS REARED up from the bed shouting Wayne's name. Sweat drenched him, the bed, and his pillow. He couldn't recall what the nightmare was about, only it had terrified him. He looked at his phone and reached out with a trembling hand to pick it up, but froze. He had the insane need to call Wayne, but had no clue what he would say to him. *I had a nightmare and had to talk to you.* Yeah, that would go down well.

Snatches of the dream zipped through Ellis's mind, but he couldn't latch on to any of the bits. He looked at the time: not even four. He'd only been asleep thirty minutes, and right then he was too keyed up to go back to sleep.

He crawled out of bed and went into the shower. He turned it on as hot as he could stand it and stood beneath the pounding cascade of water. Knotted muscles relaxed and the heat helped to drain away some of the residual tremors from the dream. Ellis soaped himself down with the caju-and-lime body wash, allowing it to tickle his nose for a bit before he scrubbed himself off. He stumbled as he got out of the shower, barely managing to catch himself on the towel rack. His motor skills were shot. Lack of sleep really messed him up.

His stomach rumbled again, and this time he couldn't deny the need to eat. He toweled off, trudged to the kitchen, and threw a few pieces of bread into the toaster while he scrambled up a couple of eggs. The dream had scared the shit out of him, and the only thing he could recall was the fact Wayne was in it. Ellis leaned on the counter and closed his eyes, his mind chasing the elusive fragments. He could almost see it. Something in the shadows had grabbed Ellis and was dragging him in. Wayne was there, and when Ellis cried out for Wayne's help, his friend grabbed his wrist, holding him tight and not letting the darkness take him. Then Ellis shouted something about not being like Wayne, and he jerked free. This time when the darkness consumed him, Wayne stood by and watched.

A shudder went through Ellis. *Wayne let me go.* It was something Ellis knew was impossible. Wayne would never—

The memory of the club came rushing back. Wayne hadn't let him go; Ellis had *shoved* him away after their talk and in his dream. It was all on Ellis. He still couldn't understand how Wayne couldn't see him as a man, but right then, it didn't really matter. He needed Wayne in his life. With his sister asking him to babysit most nights and the guys on the squad asking him to pick up extra shifts for them, Wayne was the only thing Ellis had to depend on. But he couldn't let go of his hurt and anger, and he had no one he could talk to about it.

The smell of scorched eggs drew his attention back to the stove, where smoke rose from his now Cajun-style eggs. *Fuck.* He scraped the mess from the pan into the dustbin. He nibbled on the toast, but his stomach had begun twisting itself up again, and he'd lost his appetite. Ellis flopped down into his armchair, his head buzzing. He really wanted to call Wayne, hash out whatever had gone wrong between them, but Ellis knew he wouldn't be able to face him without getting angry again.

The thought started up the whole cycle of mental conflict once more, and Ellis closed his eyes as if that would shut it all out.

When he opened them again, he was amazed to realize he'd drifted off to sleep. Not good sleep, that was true, but even a nap was better than nothing. He still had so many questions, but there was no way he was about to seek Wayne out.

Then it struck him. There was one person he might be able to ask. He glanced at his watch. Just past seven. The party must have gone on until late, and he doubted very much the man would be awake, but Ellis needed to talk, and there was only one person he could think of right now who might be able to help him.

He grabbed his jacket and hurried out the door. If he sought answers, there was only one place he could go—back to where the problems started. Back to Secrets.

THE MAIN door to Secrets was shut, and Ellis's heart sank. *What was I thinking? At this hour on a Sunday morning?* The street was silent, but in the distance was the faint hum of traffic.

This was a mistake. I should be in my bed, trying to get some more sleep. Heaven knew he needed it.

"It's Ellis, isn't it?"

Ellis turned around to see Jarod crossing the street, a paper bag clutched in his hand from which issued forth a wonderful aroma.

Ellis gave him a sheepish smile. "Hi. I didn't think you'd be awake, not with the party finishing so late." And yet he'd turned up, hoping....

Jarod's relaxed smile eased the knots in Ellis's belly. "Force of habit. I'm an early riser." He tilted his head to one side. "What brings you out here at this hour?"

Ellis's heartbeat raced. "I actually came hoping to talk to you. I... I have a few questions for you."

Jarod arched his eyebrows. "For me? Oh. Okay. I was about to have coffee and croissants with Eli. Do you want to join us?" He regarded Ellis closely. "Or would you rather keep it between you and me?"

Relief flooded through him. "I'd prefer that, to be honest." He didn't know Eli. He was sure the club owner was a nice guy, but there was already a connection with Jarod that made Ellis feel more comfortable.

"No problem." Jarod opened the door and led him inside. "Take a seat at the bar while I pour us some coffee. It's already brewed."

Ellis sat at the bar and glanced around. The place seemed so different in the light of day. There were no leather-clad men strutting around. The smell of pine cleaner had replaced the earthy male scents he'd noticed the previous night. And the smack of Leo's hand on Alex's arse had been replaced by a cleaning crew who chattered amongst themselves.

"I have to say, this is a pleasant surprise," Jarod called out, strolling across the room with two mugs of steaming coffee. He placed them on the bar top, the rich aroma making Ellis groan with need. Jarod chuckled and pushed a cup toward him, which Ellis gratefully accepted.

"I'm sorry to bother you," Ellis began, then stopped. How the hell could he tell this relative stranger why he'd come?

"It's fine, really. I enjoyed talking to you, so it's no hardship to do so again."

As he tried to gather his thoughts and make sense of the jumble of emotions in his head, Ellis noticed a door opening. The other man— Eli—came into the room, carrying a plate with a lid on it. He set it down and uncovered the plate, revealing some flaky golden croissants.

"You left these in the kitchen. You need to have something to eat with your pills, pet," Eli murmured, taking a quick kiss before addressing Ellis. "Good morning."

Jarod slid one of the croissants toward Ellis while he smiled at Eli. "Good morning, Sir. This is Ellis. He came last night with a friend to see what we were all about. He's got some questions for me and stopped in to talk."

Eli's affection for Jarod couldn't have been more obvious. He slid his fingers through Jarod's hair and smiled when Jarod pressed into his touch. "Very well. Unless you need me, I'm going to the gym. I'll be lifting weights in about an hour, and I need a spotter. I expect you to be there."

Jarod's cheeks pinked, and his voice grew husky when he replied, "Yes, Sir."

Eli's eyes gleamed. "And make the most of your croissant. Buttery pastry is not on your approved foods list, is it?" He gave Jarod a fond smile. "Enjoy your treat."

After Eli left, Jarod glanced at the clock. "I don't mean to be rude, but I only have an hour to talk. Will that be enough?"

Would it? Hell, Ellis didn't even know where to begin, let alone what to say. *What will he think if I just blurt everything out?* Ellis sighed. "Maybe we can do this another time. I don't want you to be late."

He made to stand, but Jarod placed a hand on his arm. "Hey, sit down. Eli will wait for me. What's wrong?"

Warmth flooded Ellis's cheeks. He took a deep breath to steady himself. "How did you know you were… you know?"

"Gay?" Jarod suggested, his face impassive.

"No. I mean… um…." He lowered his voice to where he barely heard himself. "Submissive."

Jarod smiled. "The day my mother told me that if I wanted to take care of someone, I needed to learn the skills."

"Your mother?" Ellis asked incredulously.

"You'll understand when you meet her," Jarod promised. "I take it this has something to do with the man you were here with last night?"

Ellis nodded. "His name is Wayne. He's my partner at work."

"Okay. He appears to be very protective of you."

Startled, Ellis replied, "What do you mean?"

"He didn't take his eyes off you while you were talking with me. He seemed… I don't know, edgy?" Jarod took a bite of his croissant and let out a soft moan of pleasure. "Damn, this tastes good."

"He's always keeping an eye open. We're usually both on the lookout for trouble. It sort of comes with the job."

"It felt like there was more to it than that," Jarod said quietly. "He wasn't watching the club, only you. Even during the demonstration, you seemed to be more the focus of his attention."

The words rattled Ellis. If Jarod noticed, would other people?

"Is there a problem? You are friends, right? He's not pressuring you, I hope?"

If only it could be that simple. "No, nothing like that. Last night after we left, Wayne drove around and we… talked."

Jarod's brow furrowed. "Okay. I'm still confused, so please bear with me. I take it the conversation made you nervous, which is why you came to see me, right?"

Ellis glanced away from the cool gaze that seemed to see right into him. "Wayne said he has been noticing things about me. He said I'm not eating right, I'm quick to anger, and I'm not sleeping well. He said if I couldn't or wouldn't take care of myself, then he would have to…."

"Take matters into his own hands?" Jarod guessed. When Ellis stared at him with wide eyes, Jarod shook his head. "God save me from Doms."

"What do you mean?"

Jarod let out a sigh. "Doms like to fix things. Take control of many aspects of life. If Wayne sees you struggling, it calls to him to make it better. It's part of who he is."

"But I'm not… gay." Ellis swallowed. "Not that there's anything wrong with being gay. It's just not me."

Jarod didn't seem fazed at all. "It doesn't matter. As his partner you are part of his world. He's going to do what he thinks is best to fix whatever the problems are. Like I said, it's who he is."

"And what if I don't want him to?" Ellis demanded. "I'm not a kid."

Jarod cocked his head again. "Have you ever read Shakespeare?"

"In school. Wasn't really my thing. What's that got to do with anything?"

Jarod gave him a speculative glance. "You trust Wayne, yes?"

"With my life," Ellis answered without hesitation.

Jarod nodded as if pleased by Ellis's reply. "In one of his sonnets, Shakespeare said, 'To give away yourself keeps yourself still.' Based on what you're telling me, it sounds like this is what Wayne does for you, at least while you're at work."

Ellis thought about it before nodding.

"So," Jarod continued, "if he brings you peace while you're in a tense situation on the job, maybe he thinks he can do the same thing outside of it? Being taken in hand isn't for everyone. Not many people are willing to let themselves submit, but for some people, it can calm their mind and body, knowing that someone else is there who won't let them fall."

Ellis tried to reply, but his tongue seemed thick. He'd always looked to Wayne for instructions. To guide him in tense situations. Wayne always had his back, and Ellis knew deep down he relied on that. Maybe Wayne could see something in Ellis that told him he needed help.

Still…. *Taken in hand.* "But what does that mean?"

Jarod's smile was warm. "I think it means you need to figure out how you feel and then talk with Wayne. If he's your friend and you are adamant about not accepting his help, he won't like it, but he will understand and back off."

The thought of Wayne's calming presence not being there wasn't something Ellis had ever considered. Sure, he'd been mad at his friend, but they'd been angry before and gotten over it. Even when he was upset, there was never a time Wayne hadn't been there. And even though he wasn't ready to say it out loud, he needed Wayne because, without his direction, Ellis knew he'd be lost.

"Eat your croissant," Jarod said, taking a sip of his coffee.

Dutifully Ellis ate, but he didn't taste anything. His mind whirled with Wayne's proclamation.

CHAPTER SIX

WHEN ELLIS wasn't there Monday morning, Wayne's stomach clenched. Okay, so it was only training—there were no planned operations for the foreseeable future, and barring calls with more information, it was likely to remain that way—but it wasn't like him. When the call had come in that he was sick, Wayne wondered at the truth of it. By the end of the day, when everyone was changed and ready to leave, he was still pondering it.

Is this down to me? He gave an internal snort. *Stupid question.* His gut was still in knots at the thought of what he'd done. It hadn't been Ellis's fault at all. Wayne had to go and open his big mouth, frighten the man off, and now the team would pay the price for his hubris.

"What happened to the little woman?" Shaun asked, displaying his permanent smirk as he entered the social lounge, where Wayne sat at one of the tables, his phone in front of him.

The temptation to mouth off at him was enormous, but Wayne pushed down hard on his irritation. "Not now, Shaun. Not in the mood."

Shaun held up his hands. "Just joking, mate. You know me." He glanced more closely at Wayne. "Everything okay?"

"Yeah, it's fine," Wayne answered absently. He glanced up at the clock. "What are you still doing here? Surely it's pub time by now." It was a habit they'd gotten into after training days—they'd head off to their homes, only to meet up at a pub as soon as possible.

"You don't have to tell me twice," Shaun said with a laugh. "Did you wanna come along?"

Wayne couldn't deny he was tempted, but right then, it was best if he kept a level head. He could only imagine himself on the phone at two in the morning, crying to Ellis to forgive his stupidity.

"No, not tonight. I need to get home—and stay there," he added with a half smile for Shaun's benefit.

Shaun dropped his voice. "Wayne, if you need to talk, you know you've got a friendly set of ears here. And I wouldn't ever repeat something you told me in confidence."

"Yeah, I know. And I do appreciate it, but there isn't anything to tell." A lie, but he wasn't about to share his mess with Shaun. "Look, you get off out of here and enjoy yourself. Just not *too* hard—the powers that be are coming here tomorrow to talk to us about becoming C-Men, so you'll need to be alert." Their bosses were recruiting for the Counter Terrorism Specialist Firearms Officers team, and Wayne knew they'd already spoken with other teams.

Shaun picked up his newspaper from where he'd left it that morning. "Okay, but if you want to talk, you always know where to find me." Shouts rang through the open door, and Shaun laughed. "All right, you load of inebriates. First round is on me!"

Cheers rose up as Shaun went through the door. Seconds later Wayne heard Shaun call out, "Thought you were sick, Mann? You missed out on training for an armed siege on a school today. We're heading to the pub if you want to come along."

"No, thank you. I need to talk to Wayne. You go ahead. Maybe I'll catch up when we're finished."

"Suit yourself. Just be gentle with Wayne. He's not had a good day."

The door creaked open and Ellis stepped inside. Wayne's stomach clenched again when Ellis met his gaze. With deep lines bracketing his eyes, Ellis looked completely knackered. He went over to the machine and poured himself a cup of the crap Shaun told them was coffee that would put hair on their chests. He'd seen Ellis in the locker room. Maybe Shaun was right because with the amount of body hair Ellis had, he could definitely be a bear.

"Feeling better?" Wayne asked, not sure what else he could say. For the first time, it occurred to him Ellis would be within his rights to file a complaint. If it came to that, Wayne would step down without being asked. He owed it to his team to not let them become embroiled in something he had started.

Ellis strode back from getting his cup of black coffee, turned the chair around, and sat. "No, not really."

Wayne took a deep breath, then leaned forward, chin resting on his hand. "Look, I understand that you're upset. I ambushed you, and that wasn't fair of me."

Ellis narrowed his eyes. "Gee, you think? You take me to a—" He lowered his voice. "—BDSM club, all with the purpose of telling me you think I should allow you to—what was the phrase you used?—take me in hand."

"You're right. I messed up. I'm still human, you know."

If Wayne had hoped for a grin, he found himself disappointed. Ellis's expression didn't change a bit. *That won't do.*

"Right. Okay. If you've come to file a complaint, let me know. I'll tender my resignation so neither you nor the team has to be sullied because of my stupidity."

That got a reaction. Wayne knew the signs. Ellis was *pissed off.*

"You're a stupid bastard, do you know that?"

Wayne snorted. "Believe me, I know."

Ellis took a long draw of his coffee, then plunked the mug back onto the table. "You think after all you've done for me, I'd come here to complain? You're a stupid one. What happened was between us, and I intend for it to stay that way."

Wayne breathed a sigh of relief. "So why did you come?"

Ellis stared into the depths of his mug. "I needed to take the time off to think. I've been doing a lot of that since Saturday. Yesterday I went back to… you know."

Snakes squirmed in Wayne's stomach. The thought of Ellis in the club without his protection didn't sit well at all.

"Stop growling," Ellis chastised. "I went in the morning to talk to the owner, Jarod."

Wayne stood up, pushing the chair back with a squeal as its legs scraped across the floor. He had to get control of himself, otherwise he would end up in the same position he was before—with Ellis pissed off, and no one wanted that. At least he came to talk. He could just as easily have come to punch Wayne or get him fired. Either of those options would have been preferable to losing his friend, even though he'd convinced himself it was worth the risk if it helped Ellis.

"So what happened?"

"We had coffee and a croissant. It was really nice. The croissant was buttery and flaky, and the coffee was way better than the shit we have here."

Wayne couldn't help the snort. Ellis's expression showed no reproach at all.

"Can you sit down, please? You're making this worse than I thought it would be."

"Look, can you tell me—"

"Sit down," Ellis grumbled. "We're not talking until you stop hovering. I'm nervous enough as it is, and I don't need you adding to it."

Though he wasn't used to following orders, Wayne sat.

"Thank you. See how much easier things can be when you work with me?"

Cheeky sod. "Are you going to tell me what happened now?"

Wayne could see Ellis tighten his grip around the mug. He'd watched him—all of his team—for years. He knew their habits and mannerisms, how they'd react in most situations, but right now he couldn't read Ellis at all. He was tense; that much couldn't be more obvious. But beyond that Wayne hadn't a clue.

"He asked me about Shakespeare."

Definitely *not* what Wayne expected. "Shakespeare?"

"Shakespeare said something that Jarod likened to—that stuff."

Wayne slumped down a bit in his seat, the hardwood slats digging into his back. "We're the only ones here, Ellis. You can say BDSM."

"Fine," Ellis said, exhaling sharply. "Jarod told me Shakespeare said something like, 'To give away yourself keeps yourself still.' He told me about this thing that guys like you need to do. To take control of a situation, or of people, to make things right in their world. He asked me to think if maybe that's what you were trying to do with me."

Though he hadn't had much of an opportunity to talk with Jarod, Wayne found himself liking the man already.

Apparently Ellis wasn't done. "But see, there are a few things I don't understand."

"Ask me anything you want. I'll do my best to answer for you."

"Going to need another cup if we're going to talk now." He turned to head over to the machine. There was probably about one cup's worth left in it.

"No," Wayne said sharply. "Have water."

Ellis stiffened and faced him, scowling. "Excuse me? What the hell?"

"One look at you and I can tell you've not been asleep, probably since Saturday morning. Adding more caffeine on top of that won't help and will probably make things worse. So no coffee for right now. In fact, why don't you give me a few minutes to finish up, then we can go somewhere and talk?"

"Not sure...."

Wayne knew he was treading on dangerous ground, but Ellis's health had to come first. Everything he could see certainly proved his point that Ellis needed help. If not from Wayne, then someone.

"Give me five minutes to finish up my notes on today's training, then we'll leave. Why don't you leave your car here and come home with me? I'll bring you in tomorrow."

"Er… okay." Ellis seemed less sure of himself.

"Good. That way we can talk. Or you can take a nap in the guest room, and *then* we'll talk when you wake up." Wayne wasn't sure appealing to his common sense would do the trick, so he decided to sweeten the deal with Ellis's favorite food. "I'll order us a pizza from Carlotti's."

There was a pause. "Thick crust?" God, Ellis was practically *drooling*.

"With extra cheese if you want. But if we have pizza, we're going to have to work out harder tomorrow to burn the extra calories."

"Got any beer?" Ellis asked, waggling his brows.

"I do, but it might be best to hold off on that too. When we talk, both of us should have a clear head."

Ellis scrunched his brows, obviously considering what Wayne had said. "Yeah, that might not be a bad idea."

"Okay, five minutes."

By the time Wayne glanced up from his notes a minute later, Ellis had already fallen asleep in one of the world's most uncomfortable chairs. His head had fallen back, mouth open, from which loud snores emanated. His arms, heavy with muscle, had dropped to his sides. The man was a picture of innocence. *Exhausted* innocence.

Deciding against making him wait anymore, Wayne stuffed the remainder of his work into his bag. He'd tackle it first thing in the morning. Right now Ellis had to be his main priority.

"Ellis, you need to wake up," he said softly in his ear. When he didn't stir, Wayne called a little louder. Still nothing. Wayne reached down and wrapped Ellis's arm around his neck, helping him stand. Ellis mumbled groggily but started moving. "Damn, you're *so* going to be doing extra reps tomorrow. You're getting a bit on the chunky side."

Ellis mumbled something Wayne couldn't make out. It didn't matter, though. Helping Ellis felt right. Like Wayne had finally found the piece of his life that was missing. He hoped to hell their conversation went as Wayne wanted because he refused to let Ellis break, no matter what.

WHEN ELLIS opened his eyes, he couldn't figure out where he was. He tried to remember if he'd gone home with someone, because the bed was a lot more comfortable than his. The mattress was soft, without that annoying dip in the middle his thin one had. The duvet was thick and warm, and the pillowcases smelled like the ones his mum used to hang out in the sun to dry. He didn't want to get up, but the call of nature wouldn't be denied.

He tossed back the covers and noticed the room wasn't frilly or anything. It seemed to be more masculine, with dark wood trim offsetting the light blue walls. And the old wooden desk that sat in the corner wasn't an antique, but simply ancient. Nothing about this room had a feminine touch, so he doubted he'd spent the night with a woman. It took him a few minutes to realize he was in Wayne's guest room.

Then he realized he was fully dressed; only his shoes had been removed. He could smell pizza in the air, and then everything rushed back with startling clarity. He'd gone to see Wayne, who had told him they'd talk at his place. He swallowed hard. What Jarod said made a lot of sense. He tried to see things from Wayne's viewpoint. He was one of the most senior members of the team, taking responsibility for all of them, but that didn't mean Ellis was about to let him get away with anything. He still had questions, and Wayne needed to provide the answers.

He hurried to the bathroom and took care of business, then washed his hands. He took a deep breath, steeling himself of the conversation to come. As he pulled open the door, the scent of the pizza made his stomach rumble. He hadn't eaten anything since his croissant with Jarod, and he was starved. The whole group had been to Wayne's house a few times for pizza and football. It wasn't a big place, but it was nice. They'd teased him about missing out on the gay decorating gene, though. Everything was muted colors. Dark woods, light trims, table lamps that looked like they'd come from a charity shop. But it was a decidedly masculine place, and it fit Wayne perfectly.

"Perfect timing," Wayne called. "I just got back with it."

"How long was I asleep?"

The answer could be read in Wayne's dark expression. "Not nearly long enough. Two hours tops. And that includes the car ride back here."

Ellis stared at him. "You carried me? Please. *You* can't lift me."

Wayne laughed. "No, you're right. You're freaking huge. You need to work out more."

"Fuck you." Ellis slapped his stomach. "I've got 3 percent body fat. Everything else is pure muscle."

Another chuckle. "No, I didn't carry you. You were groggy, but you still helped me get you into the car and to the bedroom." He waved a hand at the box on the table. "I can put this in the refrigerator for later if you want to sleep some more."

Sleep sounded so good right then, but Ellis knew he'd only toss and turn. That had been the pattern for months, anyway. "Nah, I'm good. Besides, I'm hungry."

"Okay, I'll grab some plates. Have a seat. Do you want some water?"

"Got a Coke?" Then he recalled what Wayne had said about caffeine. "Yeah, okay. Water is good."

After Wayne disappeared back into the kitchen, Ellis opened up the pizza box. God, Wayne knew him so well. A jumbo Carlotti's thick-crust pizza piled high with pepperoni, sausage, mushrooms, and onions, and a double layer of the cheese that held the whole thing together. He could eat this for every meal and be perfectly content.

"Don't stand on ceremony. Dig in," Wayne told him as he came out of the kitchen, two chilled bottles of water and a couple of plates in his hands.

This seemed nice. Normal even. After he'd blown up at Wayne, Ellis feared he'd ruined everything, and that his friend would be gone. *Hell, who knows? After we talk, that could still happen.* It was a sobering thought.

"Only a slob eats pizza without putting it on something," Ellis replied, reaching for a plate.

"You're right, of course. So what's your excuse?"

Ellis laughed, and it went a long way to draining the tension that had knotted his insides. They ate in a comfortable silence, Wayne seeming as lost in his own thoughts as Ellis. When they'd finished, Ellis put his plate on the table and patted his stomach. He couldn't recall the last time he'd had such a good meal.

Wayne cleared the dishes, then came back out of the kitchen. "Should we go into the lounge?" he asked.

"Sure." *May as well get this over with. See how it's going to go.* Ellis grabbed his bottle of water and went to sit on the sofa. Wayne took the chair opposite him and leaned forward, resting his elbows on his knees.

"Okay, so—" they both started.

Ellis laughed. "Go ahead. You bought dinner. Least I can do is hear you out first."

"Thanks. First off I want to apologize to you. I chose a bad time to spring my thoughts on you. You were already keyed up after the party, and I should have understood and respected that. The thing is, you're my mate, and I've been watching you fall apart. Every time I tried to talk to you about it, you shut me down. I don't know what else I can do."

"Right. What I need to know is why?"

"Excuse me? Why what?"

"Last year when Phillips's wife told him she wanted a divorce, did you offer to 'take him in hand'? He was a wreck, but I didn't see you rushing to help *him*."

"No, I didn't. But then again Phillips isn't my best mate, is he? He was sad too, but he didn't go around biting everyone's head off. He didn't avoid us for the last few months when we went out after work. He wasn't nearly passing out at his desk. And, most important, he talked to us when he needed to. He didn't go shutting us out. Not like you."

Ellis thought back. Phillips had talked to him more than once. He'd spoken with the whole team, and though he was sad, he'd separated it from work as much as he could.

"Would apologizing help?"

Wayne shook his head. "No. You've apologized too often. You've got something going on, and you either need to let us in or—"

"Or let you take over my life."

"I wouldn't put it that way," Wayne replied. "I'd help you to get back on track, but you'd have to do things my way."

"So you'd take over my life," Ellis repeated.

Wayne frowned. "When you put it like that, I can see what you're saying. If I'm honest? Yes, I would. You're important to me, Ellis. You're hurting, so the team is hurting. I'm hurting because there isn't anything I can do to help you. And I don't like that feeling."

"What do you get out of it?"

Wayne smiled. "I get my friend back."

CHAPTER SEVEN

"I SHOULD get home."

Wayne peered across the room to where Ellis was stretched out on his couch. "How? Your car's at the center, remember? And who says you have to? I've got a perfectly good guest bedroom—as you well know." He raised his eyebrows. "That *was* you asleep and snoring earlier on, right?"

"Bastard." Ellis sat up and yawned. "Thanks for that, though. I feel much better."

Wayne got a sinking feeling in the pit of his stomach. "I'm glad about that," he began slowly. "But we were talking about ways to help you, as I recall. Have you made a decision about that?"

Ellis's expression tightened. "Look, I appreciate the fact that you've been worrying about me, which I suppose is sort of... sweet, but I'm fine," he stressed. "Personally? I think you've blown this up out of all proportion."

Damn. Wayne should have known it wouldn't be *that* easy. Still, at least he'd planted the seed in that overtired brain.

"It's late," he said matter-of-factly. "Way too late to be going home. And look at you: you're still exhausted. How about I make us some popcorn and we watch a film on Netflix or something before going to bed? Your choice."

"Honestly I really am okay."

Wayne knew better. He could hear the strained edge to Ellis's voice.

"What harm can it do? Hmm?" He was not about to back down on this. It was too fucking important.

Ellis let out a weary sigh. "Fine. I'll stay." He glared at Wayne, but there was no heat to it. "What do you feel like watching? I'm guessing chick flicks or musicals. Maybe a combination."

Wayne rolled his eyes. "Why don't you take a look at the DVDs if you're not interested in searching for something on Netflix? I have a few new ones on the bottom shelf of the bookcase. You've seen virtually all my others."

Ellis grinned. "What about the top shelf?"

Wayne chuckled. "Gay porn. You're welcome to watch that too, if you want." Ellis raised his eyebrows. "You never know; you might enjoy it." Without waiting for a response, Wayne got up and went into the kitchen to make the popcorn. He chuckled to himself at the idea of Ellis perusing his porn collection—if he dared to look.

They were five minutes into watching the thriller Ellis had chosen when Wayne looked across at him. Ellis was out like a light. Wayne glanced at the DVD cover and smiled. Perfect choice—*Before I Go to Sleep*. He gave Ellis a nudge. Another nudge. Yet another. Yeah, this wasn't happening.

He went into the guest bedroom and grabbed the duvet from the bed. Wayne covered Ellis with it, noting how he shifted in his sleep, a frown creasing his brow.

Fine my arse.

He switched off the DVD player, picked up the bowl of popcorn, and retreated to his bedroom.

The first call came at eleven thirty. The shrill sound of Ellis's ringtone was loud enough to wake Wayne from the doze he'd slipped in to. The second call came at twelve forty. And the third just before two.

Who the hell is calling him at this hour? Wayne jotted the times down. *Yet something else we need to talk about.* He wondered briefly if these calls were a regular occurrence. He was still wondering about that when he fell asleep.

The next morning Wayne made them breakfast. Nothing fancy, just some eggs and toast. Ellis inhaled the food, claiming starvation.

Wayne watched him with amusement. "Wow. Come up for air, why don't you?" He took a bite of his toast. "And you missed a good film last night."

Ellis cocked his head to one side. "Did we watch one?"

That exchange added pieces to the puzzle Wayne was constructing. Ellis's late-night calls, his lack of sleep, and his angry outburst all seemed to be connected.

"We started to, but you fell asleep."

Ellis's brows scrunched. "Oh shit. You made popcorn. Ugh. I'm so sorry. I was really out of it."

"I noticed, believe me."

"Maybe we can watch it later?"

"Sure." He paused. "Want me to run you to your place to pick up a clean set of clothes?"

Ellis yawned and stretched. "Nah, I'm good. There are clean clothes in my locker." He gave a tired smile. "I wonder what delights today has in store for us."

Wayne gave a low groan. "If we're really unlucky, Lewis has a new training scenario all figured out, and by the end of the day, we'll all be knackered."

And then I'll be every bit as exhausted as you are—except I'll have a good reason to be. He regarded Ellis closely. *What is going on with you?*

Now more than ever, he was determined to get to the bottom of it.

THE NEXT two weeks crawled by. No calls came in for their team, so a lot of training was scheduled. At the end of each day, they dragged themselves out of the locker rooms and to their rides, utterly exhausted both physically and mentally. Each morning Ellis came in looking no different than he had when they'd left: bags under his eyes, dark lids, and a slack face that screamed he needed help. Each time Wayne mentioned it, Ellis blew him off. His neighbor kept him awake again, he claimed. Their music wasn't getting any better either. It was meant to be a joke, but Wayne wasn't laughing.

By the time Friday came, it felt like everyone on the team was looking forward to the weekend. They'd practiced how to handle so many different scenarios that they were beginning to blur into one another. Wayne started to wonder if maybe Lewis was a sadist; every time he thought up a new training scenario, there were groans from the team.

After picking up all the dirty mugs, Wayne went into the large kitchen that served the training center. *God, these guys can be real slobs.* While he was running hot water into the washing-up bowl, a shout echoed from the locker room. Wayne dropped the mug he was cleaning and ran into the room.

Roberts was pinned up against the lockers, Ellis's hand tight around his throat. Roberts's face was chalk white, his eyes focused on Ellis, who glared at him, snarling.

"You wanna repeat that?" Ellis growled.

"Ellis, get the fuck off him," Phelps shouted, trying to pull him off, but he and Cassidy were having little luck with that. Ellis's muscles were taut and his arm shook.

Wayne had never seen him in such a rage. He launched himself at Ellis, grabbing his beefy arm. "Ellis, let him go," Wayne ordered.

Almost as if someone flicked a switch, Ellis dropped Roberts, who slumped to the floor. Ellis backed up against the lockers, his chest heaving, his eyes wild. Wayne stepped back, ready to say something when Lewis strode into the room.

"What the hell is going on here?" he yelled. "Dwyer?"

Wayne stiffened. "Not sure. I was in the kitchen when I heard the shouts."

Lewis's gaze switched to Ellis. "Mann, what happened?"

Ellis turned, his expression almost feral. "That son of a bitch called Wayne a queer," he snapped.

The room went silent, and all eyes turned toward their comrade.

"Roberts?" Lewis regarded him with cool eyes.

"What?" Roberts stared back at him, his manner belligerent. "They told me someone on the team was queer, and I said I figured out who it was."

"We never said queer," Phillips shouted. "We said we had a gay man on the team. That's all *we* said."

"What's the difference? He *is* one, isn't he?" The distaste on his face was obvious. Wayne regarded him, a sour taste in his mouth. *And there you have it. Pretty Boy has an ugly side to him too.*

Shaun's face was contorted with disgust. "And here we were thinking you were okay with it. You had me fooled, that's for sure."

Roberts had his hand to his throat. "I was biding my time until I worked it out, that was all. I knew I'd get to the bottom of it eventually."

Cassidy tried injecting a little humor to diffuse the situation. He snorted. "He said 'bottom.' How apt."

"That's enough of that," Lewis declared instantly.

Ellis lunged forward, a murderous look on his face. Wayne got in front of him and held out his hands. "You need to calm down," he said, his voice pitched low.

Ellis's confusion was obvious. "But Wayne…. He can't…."

"Right," Lewis shouted. "You lot go on home. Roberts and Mann, you're with me."

Wayne's heart ached at the sadness in Ellis's posture. *Shit. There's nothing I can do to help him out of this one. I've failed him.*

ABOUT SIX that evening, there was a knock at the door. Relief filled Wayne when he opened it to find Ellis standing there, his shoulders hunched over.

"Come on in," Wayne said, stepping back to let him enter. He couldn't keep the words inside him. "Where the hell have you been?" Ellis left the center hours previously and hadn't answered a single call.

"Good to see you too," Ellis murmured. He walked into the living room and dropped onto the sofa.

Wayne regarded him from the doorway. "Want some water?"

"Got anything stronger?" Ellis asked.

"For you? No. You're already angry and hurting. You've seen enough to know how bad it gets when you add alcohol to the mix."

He expected an argument, but Ellis merely nodded. "Yeah, okay."

Wayne took a seat next to his friend. "Do you want to talk about it?"

Ellis stared at the dark TV screen. "I'm suspended for a week," he whispered. "I've never been suspended before."

And it would have been earlier if I hadn't covered for you. Not that Wayne was about to say that out loud. "What about Roberts?"

"He's going back to his last station. They want him to see the LGBT liaison officer. He's also going to have to take sensitivity courses. Lewis was fucking *livid* that Roberts mouthed off like that."

Wayne chuckled. "Which one of you do you think was angrier?"

"Definitely me," Ellis replied. "If they hadn't pulled me off him, I would have hurt him. I've never lost my temper that badly before."

But Wayne knew it had been building. Ellis was like a volcano, ready to erupt. Wayne had been able to calm him, but there was only so much influence he could exert over Ellis. In order to properly help him, Wayne needed to see him more frequently than just at work or in the bar. He needed Ellis in the house, with him—more importantly, agreeing to let Wayne help.

Wayne couldn't keep silent any longer. "Why did you do it?"

Ellis fluttered his hands. "He called you a queer. I couldn't let him do that."

Wayne arched his eyebrows. "I'm a big boy, you know. I've been called worse. I don't need you to stand up for me."

"But…." Ellis's eyes went wide. "You look out for me. I should do the same for you."

"No," Wayne corrected. "We look out for *each other*, but not to the point where we have to hurt someone. You should have gone straight to Lewis and told him what was said. You know violence doesn't solve anything."

Ellis winced, and Wayne regretted hurting him, but the time for coddling was over. He'd allowed it to go on too long, and now Ellis was paying the price.

"Did Lewis talk to *you* about seeing someone?"

Ellis shook his head. "He said I acted out, that I should have talked to him, but that under the circumstances, he could see why I'd been so angry."

"Right. But he doesn't know about the other stuff, does he?"

Ellis stiffened. "Other stuff?"

Wayne softened his voice. "I haven't mentioned to him about the problems you've had in the past. I kept those things out of the reports."

"Maybe you should have told him," Ellis said morosely. "Maybe I can't do this job anymore."

"Bollocks!" Wayne snapped. He put his hand on Ellis's arm. "You're one of the finest officers I know. You've hit a rough patch, but come on, we *all* do at some point." Ellis shrugged and Wayne drew in a deep breath. "You need to talk to someone. The department will suggest a therapist if you ask."

Ellis looked up, panic in his expression. "I can't do that! If they find out, they'll—"

"They who?"

His friend turned away. "The department. If they find out, they might decide to sack me."

"Then I don't know what to suggest. You're fraying at the seams, and you need help."

ELLIS STOOD up and sat in the other chair. Having Wayne so close made it hard for him to think. He'd almost told Wayne the truth about why he couldn't see the psychologist, and that just wouldn't do.

And if that option is a no-go, then I'm left with….

Ellis took a deep breath. "What if I agree to what you suggested?" he asked hopefully.

He expected Wayne to jump at the chance, but his friend surprised him. "I don't know that you really want that. And unless both of us are invested in helping you, it would be a wasted effort. As much as I want to help you, I won't bother if you're not genuinely interested."

Fuck. Ellis knew he had to do something. He hadn't gone after Roberts with the intention to hurt him. He'd wanted to kill him. To beat him until there was nothing left beyond a telltale smear on the floor. In his mind he could see Roberts's eyes pleading with him, and Ellis hadn't cared one bit. He'd spoken ill of Wayne, the only person Ellis really gave a damn about. Roberts deserved everything he'd gotten and so much more.

The truth of the matter was, Wayne was right. *I should have gone to Lewis. Should have filed a complaint.* He couldn't stop himself, and that made him dangerous to work with. He wouldn't want anyone getting hurt because of him. And if Wayne's idea helped….

"I'll do it," Ellis said softly.

"What?"

"You can do… what you said. I mean, if you still want to." The words were bitter on Ellis's tongue. He hated the idea he'd fallen so far that he now had to ask for help.

"Stand up," Wayne ordered.

Ellis stood, waiting to see what he would say.

"Okay, I'm going to be totally honest with you. If you say this is what you want, we'll try—"

"Okay!" Ellis thought he'd burst from sheer relief.

"No, don't say that yet. It's not going to be easy. You'll have to agree to what I say. There won't be any room for discussion. If I say it's going to be done a certain way, you'll do it. No arguments, no debate. We will discuss your limits before we begin, but once you've signed my contract, that's it. Unless you choose to break it and walk away, you'll do whatever I say for the next three months."

Three months. Ninety days. *Really, how bad can it be?* "Okay."

Apparently Wayne wasn't done. "I'm not having you make a spur-of-the-moment decision. You're going to go into the guest room and sleep. Tomorrow we'll talk. We have the weekend to suss this out, so for now, I just want you to think about it." When Ellis hesitated, Wayne regarded him, eyebrows arched. "Guest room. Now."

Shit. He really isn't joking about this, is he?

Ellis nodded. "Okay." Without another word he left Wayne and went to his room. It wasn't until he was sitting on the bed, staring at the walls, that the questions started coming.

Why did I agree to let Wayne take charge? Agree? Hell, he'd been eager for it. He knew the reason, though. It was because he *had* lost it. And Wayne would want to know more. How Ellis was never able to say no to people, always having to show them how much they could count on him. And it had been tearing him apart. Five nights a week babysitting for his sister, picking up extra shifts when asked, plus his regular duties had left him barely able to make it to the bedroom. More often than not, he'd get to the couch and collapse.

He listened carefully, familiarizing himself with the sounds of the house. He could hear Wayne in the kitchen, probably grabbing a snack. There were cars that passed by on occasion, filling the room with brightness from their lights. The people next door were in the backyard talking. He couldn't hear the words, only the low mumbles. They were soft, affectionate. A sliver of jealousy ran through Ellis.

A light rapping at his door, followed by it swinging open, had him sitting up. "I brought you some tea. I know sleeping in a new place can be disconcerting."

"Thanks," Ellis murmured.

Wayne placed the teacup on the bedside cabinet, then sat on the bed next to Ellis. "You know I'm only doing this because I care, right?"

"So I hear," Ellis replied tartly.

Wayne huffed a breath. "I know you don't understand it. Hell, I barely do myself. But I can't watch you self-destruct. It kills me to see you working so hard, running yourself into the ground. You're my friend. My partner. And honestly this was the only way I could think of to fix it."

Ellis turned to face Wayne. "Why do you need to fix anything?" he snapped, then immediately felt contrite. "I'm sorry."

"You're important to me," Wayne answered, reaching out and putting a hand on Ellis's shoulder. "You are the best friend I ever had. My reasons for wanting to do this are completely selfish. I need you. I can't stand the thought of losing what we have."

"Do you still think we'll be able to be mates after this?" Ellis couldn't see that far ahead, and it worried him. *I want to know where this is going.* It felt like driving at night with the car headlights turned off, a scary, scary prospect. *I just want to see daylight again.* Preferably with Wayne still around.

Wayne shrugged. "If making you healthy again means I lose your friendship, it's a risk I'll have to take."

The thought staggered Ellis. Wayne would be willing to lose him in order to make things better for him. No one had ever done that for him before. He'd never known it could be possible. "I'm not going to fall all over myself, you know. If I don't think what you're doing helps, I'm going to walk away."

Wayne nodded sharply. "I understand. Drink your tea and get to sleep. We've got to be up early tomorrow."

Before he left Wayne turned around and held out his hand. "Your phone, please."

Startled, Ellis asked, "What?"

"I want your phone. This will prove to me you're serious about wanting my help."

"But I need my phone in case—" He clammed up.

"In case what?"

"I just need my phone, that's all." There was no way Ellis was telling him why. He didn't need to know.

"Is there anyone you need to speak with tonight? And I mean, is it a dire emergency?"

Fuck. "No, not really."

Wayne gave him a patient look. "Then you'll have to do without it for tonight. Tomorrow when we talk, we can revisit phone privileges. But for now...."

The thought of not having his phone terrified Ellis. He'd never been parted from it. *What if I were to get a phone call in the middle of the night and Wayne answers it?* He shuddered at the possibility of Wayne finding out everything. Because then he'd give up on Ellis.

Still, if he wanted a chance at keeping his job, staying friends with the guys, and helping people, he needed to do as Wayne said.

That meant he had to trust him.

He glanced up at Wayne, who curled his fingers with a "give me" motion. Ellis sighed and fished the phone from his pocket, then put it in Wayne's hand. Inwardly he said a little prayer the phone would stay silent tonight. He held back a snort because how likely was *that*?

Without another word, Wayne walked out and closed the door behind him. Ellis had to admit it was nothing like he'd expected. When he thought he had a handle on something, Wayne would go in a different direction. He picked up the cup and sipped his tea. A little milk, just like he liked it. Who else knew him well enough to know how Ellis liked his tea? He drained the cup, then placed it back on the bedside cabinet. Afterward he switched off the light and pulled the blanket up to his shoulders. He lay back, loving the softness of the pillow beneath his head.

As he drifted toward sleep, the last thing he remembered thinking about was Wayne, the way he knew Ellis, the way he looked out for him, and the pleasant thoughts helped him find his way to a restful slumber. The first he'd had in months.

Chapter Eight

WAYNE SWITCHED the phone to silent before throwing it into the drawer of the bedside cabinet. He had a feeling it wouldn't be long before it started to ring, and there was no way in hell he was going to wake and answer it.

Wayne stripped down to his boxers and stretched out on the bed, his back supported by pillows. *Ellis is sleeping in the next room.* Just like that his cock started to fill and he gave it a thump, glaring at it. *Behave, you.* This wasn't about sex—this had to do with bringing Ellis back from the brink.

He grabbed his notepad from beside the bed and began to go through the list of things they were going to discuss in the morning. *Maybe I should put a rating next to each item, as to how much I think each one will piss Ellis off when he sees the new rules.* Wayne grinned at the thought of Ellis ranting about how unfair Wayne was being. *Bring it on, boy.*

The word—and the rightness of it—startled him. Ellis *was* his boy. He had been for a long time. Wayne had guided him, pushed him when the going got tough, and never once given up on him. Wayne expected perfection, and Ellis never disappointed him. Even if he struggled to do something, he always gave it his all and made Wayne proud.

"We're going to make it through this, Ellis. I promise." His throat tightened. *We have to.*

He put down his notepad for the night and opened the drawer, curious to see what had transpired in the thirty minutes since he'd put the phone out of sight. Two missed calls from Ellis's sister. Wayne felt a flash of guilt. *What if something is really wrong? Maybe they need Ellis. Do I have the right to keep him in the dark about his family?*

He didn't have to think too hard about that last point.

Yeah, he had no doubt it was the right choice. If Ellis had needed his phone, he would have said so. He clearly hadn't been happy about giving it up, but he did it because Wayne insisted on it. He had to wonder if Ellis was aware of his submissive tendencies. How he always deferred to Wayne in any circumstance. Even when he went after Roberts, he stopped as soon as Wayne ordered him to do so.

He got up and crept out of his room, walking as silently as possible to the spare bedroom, where he pushed the door open as quietly as he could and peeked inside. Ellis had stripped down to his underwear and was lying on his side, one curled leg rested on top of the duvet. He looked innocent—which wasn't something you'd say about a man who stood a shade over six feet tall and had weighed a tad over fifteen stone when they'd completed their last physical.

Wayne drank in the sight of him. *You've got it bad.* He knew it was true. Ellis was *perfect* for him. Wayne liked bigger men. He had no interest in twinks, no matter how beautiful. Ellis's muscles, the sounds he made when they were lifting weights together, the sheer, raw power he possessed—*that* was what Wayne wanted, to see all that strength on display as Ellis submitted. *God, what a glorious sight that would be.*

Wayne knew that every time they sparred, Ellis held back. He had no doubt if Ellis really let go and went for it, he could take Wayne down. It would definitely be a fight to remember, but Ellis would probably win. It reminded Wayne of Lawrence from the club, who was forever looking for a Dom who could take him down, get him to submit through strength. He wanted someone to earn his submission, but he hadn't found anyone he thought was worthy.

And that's *what I have to do with Ellis. Show him I'm worthy of it.*

Wayne closed the door silently and went back to his own room. He checked Ellis's phone once more: two more missed calls. His sister certainly was persistent. On impulse he checked Ellis's texts. There were several from her, all in the same vein, asking him to babysit so she could go out. *Yeah, we definitely need to talk about this.* Tomorrow. Wayne ached to get inside Ellis's head and plumb those secrets he knew his friend had been hiding.

Starting tomorrow, Ellis Mann, you're going to belong to me for three months.

If Wayne had anything to say about it, those three months would only be the beginning.

WAYNE COULD almost read the words in Ellis's eyes. *What. The. Fuck?*

"No coffee?" Ellis shouted. "How the hell do you expect me to get through the day without coffee?"

Wayne gave a quick shrug. "You can have decaf."

Ellis's eyes bulged. "You might as well be telling me to drink water!"

"Well, it would be better for you," Wayne teased. "After your body becomes accustomed to no caffeine, you'll find you won't need it."

"*You* drink coffee!" Ellis growled, his frustration obvious.

"On occasion I'll have one after dinner. I don't need it to get me through the day." His gaze met Ellis's. "Unlike you."

Ellis ignored Wayne as his eyes scanned the list Wayne had printed out. He stabbed one of the items with his finger before staring incredulously at Wayne. "So this no-alcohol thing, do I get to have one when we go out after work?"

"No." Wayne waited for the eruption.

"Oh my God. I can't believe you. And what's this? No phone? This is total *bullshit*. You can't expect me to not have a phone. I need it for work, for one thing."

Wayne forced himself to maintain a calm, steady voice. One of them being angry was already way too many.

"I didn't say you won't have one. I'm just stating that I'm going to be carrying it. If someone wants to talk to you, they'll have to talk to me first."

Ellis set his jaw, his eyes glinting. "Really. And what am I going to say to the guys? 'Oh, sorry, I can't talk to you right now,'" he simpered. "'Wayne won't let me.'"

Keeping his cool was definitely proving a struggle. "You don't need to explain anything to them unless you feel the need to do so. For now we'll simply tell them that your neighbor's music is keeping you awake, and you're using my guest room." He eyed Ellis closely. "Unless you'd rather not admit that you're staying in the house of a known gay man?"

Ellis glared at him, his frustration obvious. "You fucking *know* that's not it at all. When have I *ever* had a problem with you being gay?"

"Then what is it?" Wayne wanted this out in the open. *Come on, Ellis. Talk to me.*

Ellis dropped his gaze to the table. "I've been on my own for years. It's not easy to just say 'Oh, here, you tell me what to do.'"

Wayne sat at the table with Ellis. "It takes a strong man to take control," he said quietly. "It takes an even stronger man to give that up."

Ellis snorted. "Oh, that's bullshit."

"No, it really isn't. Let me ask you a question, and you have to be honest with me. When you think of a submissive—let's say Alex from the night of the party—what do you think of?"

ELLIS THOUGHT back. How Alex had willingly bent over and allowed another man to spank him. How he'd then dropped to his knees and blown Leo in front of everyone who was there.

"I think he was weak," Ellis admitted. "He should have said no. What Leo did to him was humiliating."

"Okay, that's your opinion. Now answer some questions for me, if you will. Did it seem as though Alex was humiliated? Was he crying? Begging for Leo to stop?"

Ellis remained quiet for a moment as the scene played through his head again. "No. Alex seemed... at peace."

Wayne nodded. "Because he was. He trusted Leo to give him what they both needed. That's what giving up control is—trusting that your partner or partners will always have you. Alex wasn't humiliated: it was obvious he loves what the two of them do together. And just so you know? If Alex *hadn't* wanted it, he could have said his safeword, and Leo would have stopped immediately. You might think the sub is weak, but they hold the power in any transaction. They only need to say *one word*, and all play stops."

Ellis shook his head. He knew Wayne wouldn't hurt anyone. But all of this seemed so... bizarre. He couldn't wrap his head around any of it.

Wayne pointed to the sheet Ellis clutched in his hand. "I need you to make sure you finish reading the contract. There are still a few points you've not yet gotten to."

Intrigued, Ellis looked farther down, and a cold hand trailed down his spine.

"Punishments? *Punishments*? And what the hell is maintenance?"

Wayne gave an easy shrug. "Punishment means exactly what it sounds like. You do something wrong, you get punished for it."

Ellis folded his arms across his broad chest. "And *you're* the one who will punish me?"

Wayne simply nodded.

"You can't be serious," Ellis scoffed.

Wayne tapped his fingers on the tabletop and pinned Ellis with an intense stare. "Tell me something. If there is no fear of recrimination, what's to stop you from simply ignoring our agreement?"

Fuck. He had a point.

"Well… you know I wouldn't," Ellis blustered.

"You may *think* you wouldn't," Wayne countered. "But you get to work, and that coffee pot is calling your name—not that you can call that sludge coffee. What happens when you can't resist it? If I'm out of the room, how do I know you'll keep your promise to me?"

"You can trust me." Then in a softer voice, he added, "Can't you?"

Wayne sighed. "Trust is earned, as you well know. You've never given me a reason to doubt you, but that was before we agreed to take this… relationship, for lack of another word, in a different direction. As for your question about maintenance, we will sit down once a week on Saturdays. I will ask you if you've been honest with me for the week. If you tell me no, and you're honest about it, you will receive ten swats. If you've lied to me and I find out, there will be additional punishments."

"How the hell is maintenance different from punishment?"

"Because it reinforces our roles. It shows you that I'm committed to your success."

Ellis gaped at him. "That makes absolutely no sense!"

"Remember I told you that trust is earned? *This* is how you begin to show you're deserving of it. If you're honest with me and take whatever you have coming to you, *then* we begin to build trust. If you lie to me and I find out—and by the way, I *will*—it shows me you can't be trusted. This means we'll have to work harder to attain our goals. And if we need to step up the punishment, then so be it."

Ellis's head swam. "This is ridiculous. I'm not a child."

"You're right, you aren't. But you *are* at the end of your rope, aren't you? Answer me honestly."

Ellis really didn't want to. This whole situation was so far outside of his comfort zone that he didn't know what to do. On the one hand, yes, he knew Wayne was right. He was ready to leap headlong into the abyss.

On the other hand, grown men didn't get spanked.

But Alex did. And you saw how much it calmed him. What's more, it obviously turned him on.

Ellis teetered on the edge of the abyss, his heart pounding. "I'm in trouble," he said quietly.

Wayne's smile lit up his face. "Good. Thank you for your honesty. Remember this is the time for negotiation. While I would prefer the contract to stay as is, you've certainly got the right to ask to discuss some terms."

"What if I refuse the punishments and maintenance parts?"

Wayne picked up a pen and nibbled on the end. "Well, if you refuse, I'm not sure we can actually move forward. I want to trust you, Ellis, but like I said, trust has to be earned." He put down the pen and gazed frankly at Ellis. "This is a huge change in your life. Right now you may think you're prepared for it, but it all comes down to this: either you let me control your life, or you keep hold of that control. The difference between those two options couldn't be any wider."

"Can I think about it?"

Wayne chuckled. "I'd be disappointed if you didn't. Take the contract to your room and go over every bit of it. Then when you're done, we can discuss it in depth. Any questions or concerns you have can be addressed then. Keep in mind this is all down to *your choice*. You can choose to see the psychologist, you could decide to try things my way, or you can do nothing at all."

"Really?"

Wayne smiled. "Of course. No one is *forcing* you to choose. BDSM isn't a replacement for therapy, but honestly? I could be wrong, but I don't know that you need that as much as you need someone to make sure you're taking care of yourself. But you've got to make sure you understand the ramifications of whichever decision you make."

Ellis rose to his feet. "Then I guess I'd better go and do some thinking."

The contract in his hand, he hurried to his room. Once the door closed behind him, he sat on the bed and went back to his reading. Everything he saw showed how much thought Wayne had put into this. Ellis couldn't see anything that wasn't clear and concise; from his responsibilities to Wayne's, nothing had been left open to interpretation or could easily be misunderstood.

Ellis chuckled. "This is how he does his paperwork too. Then he wonders why most of us just let him go with it." He went back to his reading.

The contract Wayne had given him consisted of eight pages. Ellis's part was laid out in specific terms: no alcohol, no late nights unless they were related to an assignment at work, no coffee, no telephone calls unless they were vetted by Wayne first, and on it went. Just reading it

Ellis felt as though he were a prisoner with no rights at all. He threw the papers, which fluttered onto the bed and then the floor. Ellis lay back and closed his eyes.

"No matter how I look at this, I'm fucked," he muttered. "I choose to see someone, and they're going to dissect my life. I go with Wayne, and I lose all my freedom. If I decide to do nothing, I'm going to end up out of a job."

And that was the crux of the issue. He knew, especially after his suspension, that the ice had gotten very thin. Now that they'd seen what was happening, they would be watching him a lot more closely. He had to tread a very fine line, and there could be no slipups.

Wayne says the choice is mine, but is there really a choice here?

Ellis's stomach clenched.

I need time to think.

Except he didn't need to think, did he? He already knew what a mess he was in, not that he'd shared that with Wayne. He'd known he was on a downhill slide for over a year. Every time he found himself floundering, he tried harder. And then he'd redouble his efforts, but they always led to the same conclusion.

You're a failure.

He'd constantly tried to prove to people he could do anything they asked. And he never turned someone down when they needed him.

Oh, you want me to cover your shift? Sure. I can do that. Nah, it's fine. I don't mind pulling a double.

You need me to babysit? Absolutely. No, don't worry about it. I only worked a double. You need your time away. Sure, I can be there in an hour.

Yet no matter what he did, they always wanted more. Even when Ellis tried to say no, the guilt would gnaw at him until he agreed. He'd tried his damnedest to be the good guy, and where had it gotten him? In an even deeper mess, his job in jeopardy. And all those people he'd tried to please? Would they be there for *him*?

Hey, I got fired. I'm probably going to lose my place. You think I could come and stay with you for a few weeks until I get my head back on straight?

He knew for a fact what he'd hear.

Oh, my wife wouldn't let me.

I would, but you know, the kids. With the hours you keep, they wouldn't get any sleep.

Of course, Ellis. As long as you need.

That last one would be Wayne. Ellis knew with absolute certainty if he needed a hand, Wayne would be there. Even if Ellis told him no to doing things his way, Wayne still wouldn't abandon him. While he might not be able to keep Ellis from being fired, he would help him in any way he could.

But to let Wayne take over his life? Had things really gotten that desperate?

Do you really need to ask that question?

He didn't. Hell, he was surprised he'd lasted this long. If Wayne had seen him at the club the last time he'd gone out with the guys, he would probably have arrested Ellis. The guy hadn't even done anything much beyond bumping into Ellis and making him spill his beer. Ellis had crowded the guy into the corner of the bar, out of the sight of everyone else, and threatened to punch him. He'd clenched his hands until the skin on his palms ached.

What made it worse? The fact Ellis was ready to beat him up, eager, in fact. He'd finally felt in control, having this man look at him with such fear.

Then what happened? Oh yes. The guy begged you not to hurt him. You were shocked that you had all that rage bubbling up from someplace inside you. You ran out of the bar and went home. You buried your head in your pillows and cried. All that over a drink? You're a mess.

God, how he wanted someone to talk to. Someone who wasn't Wayne, because Ellis knew he couldn't be in the same place as him and still think rationally. A large part of him wanted to simply say yes, to let Wayne take control, because when was the last time Ellis had had control? Not for a long time.

And he had no one to pick up the pieces.

Sure, Ellis. Take some time to think. This isn't a limited-time offer, you know that. I'll always be here for you.

White-hot anger coursed through Ellis, and he snarled, "Fuck you!"

Who are you screaming at? Wayne? The men you work with? Your family? Who are you really angry with?

"Myself," Ellis whispered with a sigh. "It's no one's fault but my own."

So what are you going to do about it? You're the only one who can make that decision. The only one who knows exactly what you're going through. Wayne doesn't know everything because you've hidden things from him. How do you think he'd react if he knew the truth? What do you think he'd say if he knew what you've done to your family?

"Shut up!" Ellis growled.

His internal voice chuckled. *You're only hurting yourself, you know. If you lost your job, who'd miss you? Not those guys. Sure, they'd miss your easy capitulation when they wanted something. Your sister? She'd be fucking* overjoyed. *You'd be available to babysit twenty-four hours, but she wouldn't help you. The kids, you know. Got to remember the kids.*

"I said shut up!"

Ellis pressed his hands to his ears, desperate to block out the voice that continued to mock him.

"Wayne," he whispered. "Please, I need you."

WAYNE SAT at the table, going over his own copy of the paperwork one more time. He'd done his best to make sure everything had been spelled out properly, but he had to be sure Ellis had a safety net. If he decided to allow Wayne to help, then Ellis's well-being would become Wayne's primary responsibility. And in that respect, failure was *not* an option.

When the door opened, Wayne looked up. Ellis shuffled into the room. His face was pale.

"I've decided," he muttered. He pulled out a chair and sat.

Wayne's heartbeat raced, but he did his best to push down hard on his growing excitement. "Before you tell me your decision, do you have any questions?"

Ellis nodded. "If I go with 'none of the above,' do you think I'll lose my job?"

Though he'd expected that to be a concern, Wayne was surprised that was the first thing Ellis went to.

"If I'm honest? Yes. Not right away, but with how you're behaving lately, I think it's a very real possibility. A year ago nothing Roberts said would have ruffled you at all. You might have been annoyed by it, but you would have told the guys what happened, and we would have taken care of it ourselves. There would have been no fight, no suspension. Right now you're going to be on their radar."

"That's what I thought," Ellis replied sadly. "I really fucked up."

Wayne's heart went out to him. "You did, but admitting there is a problem is the first step to fixing it."

"You make it sound like a twelve-step treatment plan," Ellis tried to joke.

Wayne tempered his irritation. "This isn't funny, you know."

"Believe me, I know." Sadness clung to him, and Wayne had to fight the urge to hug Ellis.

Then he reconsidered. *Fuck it.* Ellis might become his responsibility, and there was nothing wrong with a hug between mates. He stood and spread his arms.

"Come here," he said.

Ellis glanced up and appeared stricken.

"Ellis, get over here," Wayne said, his voice deep.

For a moment Wayne wasn't sure what Ellis would do, but then he got up and stepped into Wayne's embrace. He sighed deeply as he put his head against Wayne's shoulder.

"I decided I'm going to try things your way."

"Thank you for trusting me," Wayne answered, bursting with pride. *He chose me.*

They stood together for a few more moments before Ellis stepped back and dipped his head.

"How did it get so bad?" he asked.

"I don't know," Wayne responded. "But I promise we'll do whatever we can to make things better."

A wave of protectiveness washed over him. *Whatever it takes to make sure you're okay.*

CHAPTER NINE

ELLIS'S ALARM clock went off, the loud buzz rousing him from his second consecutive night of restful sleep.

I could get used to this. For the first time, he had to admit giving Wayne his phone might have been a good idea. He got off the bed, stretched, scratched his stomach, and started to think about what he had to do for the day. Then he remembered. It was Monday morning and he'd been suspended.

"Breakfast is ready in ten, Ellis," Wayne called.

The memory of what he'd done to bring about this change in his circumstances caused Ellis's stomach to knot up. "Not hungry," he replied.

When the door opened, Ellis cupped himself. "Hey, I could have been naked here!" he shouted.

Wayne snorted. "Right, like I haven't seen you in the lockers five days a week for the last six years," he replied. "Or do I need to remind you about those two little freckles you've got on your—"

"No! For fuck's sake!" Heat rushed through Ellis's body. "Go away, will you?"

"I said breakfast is ready."

"And I said I wasn't hungry," Ellis answered icily.

Wayne's expression was one of solid stone. "Funny, I don't recall asking if you were. I told you breakfast is ready. When I tell you a meal is done, I expect you to come to the table, ready to eat."

"Even if I'm not hungry? That's ridiculous," Ellis snapped.

Wayne's features softened. "I know what you're thinking. Yes, it's your first day under my guidance, and it's also the first day of your suspension. I'm going to let the rudeness slide this time, but if it happens again, it will count against you."

Crap. Bad enough to be suspended, but I'd completely forgotten our agreement.

"I'm sorry," Ellis said honestly. "I'll be out in a minute."

Wayne nodded sharply, then closed the door as he left. Ellis quickly grabbed the clothes he'd worn for the last two days. He gave a quick sniff of the shirt and winced.

"Okay, yeah. That won't do." He cracked the door open. "Wayne? Do you have some clothes I could use?"

"Sure. Give me a second."

He could hear the bastard chuckling. A few moments later, he appeared with a pair of gray sweatpants and a black T-shirt.

"You know these are going to be… snug, right?" Wayne asked, grinning like a loon.

"Yeah, I know. Why I chose someone so short for a best mate is beyond me. How are we supposed to share clothes?"

Wayne gave an exaggerated eye roll. "You've got five minutes to shower, then I'll expect to see you at the table." He left Ellis.

Not certain he should push Wayne at this point, Ellis grabbed what was possibly the fastest shower of his life and got dressed quickly. He sat down at the table just as Wayne brought out their breakfast.

Wayne placed the bowl in front of him. "Just a little muesli and fruit this morning."

"Thank you," Ellis muttered.

"Let me make something clear right now. When you speak, it needs to be audible and concise. I expect to be able to hear you from across the room."

"Okay, sorry."

"And another thing. While you're under my care, you'll address me as 'Sir.'"

What the hell? Ellis stared at him. "Oh, come on. Now you're just taking things too far."

Wayne arched an eyebrow. "You need to show me the proper respect. Right now I'm not just your friend. I'm the man who is going to sweep up all those little pieces that have broken off and do my best to put you back together. That alone deserves your compliance."

Ellis wasn't about to back down on this. "But what the hell will the guys at work say?"

Wayne nodded. "That's a fair point. When you come back to work, you'll address me by my name while we're there, but in this flat, you will refer to me as Sir."

"And what if I don't?" Ellis challenged. He knew he was pushing, but he had to see how far Wayne could be pushed.

Wayne's eyes glinted. "We talked about punishment. I've forgiven you once, but it won't happen again."

Fuck. He's serious. The realization sent a shiver through Ellis.

"I have to leave for work soon. While I'm gone I want you to tidy up. Do the dishes, vacuum, and the like."

Ellis gaped. "So what am I now? Your maid, your bitch?"

Wayne stood and pushed his chair back, almost knocking it over. He levelled a sharp gaze at Ellis, his eyes narrowed. "Okay, that's enough. I've tried to be patient. I know this is different for you, and I know you're lashing out because you're angry at the situation, but I will *not* allow you to take out your attitude on me."

Ellis swallowed hard and droplets of sweat trickled down his sides. He wasn't sure what scared him more: the thought that this Wayne was so very different from the friend he'd known for years, or that even though he could see the anger, it was controlled. *How much willpower does he possess?*

Dropping his gaze to the tabletop, Ellis said softly, "I'm sorry, Sir."

He hated the word. This was his *mate*, someone he'd known for years, and this new angle on their relationship freaked Ellis out completely.

"What are your tasks for today?" Wayne asked.

Ellis clamped down hard on the urge to say something sarcastic. "To clean your flat."

"Thank you. That includes making the beds, just so you know. Since it seems I have to spell everything out for you, I thought it best to mention that fact."

Anger simmered below the surface. Ellis had to bite the inside of his cheek to keep from spouting off again.

"Going on the assumption that there will be no problems at work today, I should be home by six. After you've cleaned, I want you to take a nap. Now while I'm gone, you have the use of your phone in case you need to contact me."

Thank God. "Okay."

Wayne crossed his arms and stared at Ellis.

Shit. "I mean, okay, Sir." He was *not* going to get the hang of that.

Wayne handed the phone back, and relief surged through Ellis.

"Thank you," he said, sliding the phone into the pocket of the sweats.

Wayne glanced at his phone. "Right. I need to go. You have your phone, so you can call me. By the way, you did receive several calls from your sister last night."

Goddammit. Barb was going to be really pissed off.

"If you want to call her back, you can. But unless the calls are important, I expect you to focus on your tasks for the day."

Ellis repressed the urge to sigh. *Yeah, like Barb's going to leave me alone after she thinks I've ignored her.*

Wayne put his bowl in the sink, then went to his room.

Ellis stared at his bowl of muesli, his appetite nonexistent. His stomach was in knots. The prospect of being alone with his thoughts was not a happy one.

Wayne emerged a few minutes later, dressed for work. He walked over and put a hand on Ellis's shoulder.

"I know this isn't easy for either of us. I'll try to keep in mind that you're nervous, but don't think I'm going to go easy on you. This is no different than a training session. You'll be scared, but you know I'm there with you, and that means it will all be okay."

Ellis had no snarky comeback because it was true. Wayne always had his back, and even though it might seem weird, maybe he really did know what was best.

"Thank you, Sir. Be careful at work."

Wayne held out his arms, and Ellis grinned. "What—another one?" Even so, he slid into the embrace like it was the most natural thing in the world.

"Hugs are powerful medicine," Wayne whispered in Ellis's ear. "I think maybe we ought to make this a habit."

It was sappy and sentimental and so very unlike Wayne, but Ellis didn't mind the hug. In fact, it warmed him. When Wayne broke the connection, Ellis felt the loss of contact and immediately missed it.

"See you tonight… boy."

Before Ellis could think up a reply, Wayne was gone out the door.

Ellis looked around the flat. *Maybe Wayne has the right idea.* At least carrying out his chores would keep Ellis occupied.

"Better get to it, then." He regarded the bowl on the table. "After breakfast."

HE'D JUST finished scrubbing the last of the dishes when his phone rang. He grinned. *I wondered how long it would be before he checked up on me.* A quick glance at the time had Ellis chuckling. Already two thirty. Ellis was impressed. Wayne had almost made it through a full shift without calling. He was ready to tease Wayne about separation anxiety until he saw the number on the caller ID. Then what had been a halfway-decent mood went to hell.

"Where have you been?" That was Barb all over—no greeting, no "how are you?"

"My phone died and I forgot to put it on the charger," he lied.

She sighed into the phone. "I needed you last night, and you weren't there. Why aren't you ever there for your family?"

She did not *just say that.* He wanted to snap at her, to remind her of the damned phone calls at midnight where she was complaining she needed a break, demanding he help her. *Every single fucking time* he'd got up in the middle of the night and rushed over there. But one night—one fucking night!—he didn't answer, and suddenly he was never there for them?

Ellis took a deep breath. "What do you want, Barb?"

"I need you to babysit. I had to cancel a date last night because you weren't available, so we rescheduled for this evening."

Her voice grated on Ellis's nerves. Fingernails on blackboard wouldn't have irritated him more.

"I don't know if I can. I've got something going on tonight." He hated how his voice sounded—defeated, lost, weak—and he knew she'd pick up on it and launch into her tirade any second.

"After everything we've done for you. The support you've got from us. I ask for one favor, something small and insignificant, and you're going to turn me down? Mom and Dad were right."

Ellis winced. "Fine. I'll be there. What time?"

Barb's voice brightened considerably. "If you could come now, that would be great. I want to go get my hair done before Martin comes to pick me up."

Yeah, you're all sweetness and light now you've got your own way.

A quick glance at the clock showed it was almost three. Wayne would be home soon. *How much trouble am I going to be in if I'm not here when he walks in the door?*

Ellis didn't want to think about that. Barb was still waiting on the phone.

"I'll be there as soon as I can."

Without even a thank-you, Barb hung up.

"Fuck my life," Ellis growled. He resisted the urge to fling his phone across the room.

WAYNE GOT out of his car, locked it, and headed for the main door to his building, his body aching all over. It had been a slow day, so he'd spent most of the afternoon in the center's gym. Of course some of the guys asked about Ellis, and Wayne kept his answers short. He knew he'd really pushed it with the weights, but it helped keep his mind off Ellis. At least Roberts was gone. Wayne wasn't sure he could have faced him without wanting to say something. When he finished for the day and went to grab a shower, there was no water pressure in the building, which did nothing to improve his mood. The dried sweat prickled his skin and annoyed him. All he'd wanted was to go home, check on Ellis, then have a hot shower to remove the caked-on grime.

He unlocked his front door and stepped into the quiet flat. "Ellis? I'm home."

The place was *too* quiet, and a surge of anxiety pulsed through him. *Has he given up already?* It didn't seem like the Ellis Wayne knew, but then again, he'd never been confronted with this type of situation before. He pulled out his phone to call, hoping Ellis would pick up, when he saw the note on the table.

Wayne,
Had to go out. I'll be back as soon as I can.
Ellis

He jammed his finger on Ellis's number, growling with every ring. "Hey."

"Don't you 'hey' me. Where the hell are you?"

"I left a note," Ellis protested.

"Not good enough, damn it. I gave you back your phone so you could contact me if you needed to. And I think leaving qualifies as a reason to call. I want you back here right now."

There was a pause before Ellis replied. "I can't. I'm not sure when I'll be able to get back."

Wayne counted to ten. He knew better than to lose his temper when talking to his sub, but right now Ellis was pushing every last one of his buttons.

"Where are you?" Wayne demanded.

Ellis didn't reply for a moment, then quietly he said, "I'm at my sister's house. She needed me to watch the kids."

Relief flooded Wayne's body. At least he knew Ellis hadn't simply gone. "You could have refused. Said you were busy."

"I… I couldn't do that. I… have responsibilities."

The hesitancy in Ellis's voice was setting off alarm bells. "Why are you responsible for your sister's children?"

Ellis didn't answer right away.

"Ellis, I asked you a question. Why are you responsible for your sister's children?"

"I… I can't really explain it right now. Please don't ask me to."

Wayne kept a lid on his anxiety. "When you get home, we are going to talk about this, all right? I am *not* going to let this go."

"Fine. Look, I've got to go." All went quiet as Ellis disconnected.

Wayne stared at the phone. *What the hell is going on?* The smell of stale sweat assaulted his nostrils. The shower took priority. Then he would wait for his sub to walk through the door.

Wayne had questions, and Ellis was going to damn well provide the answers.

ELLIS PULLED into an empty space in the car park in front of Wayne's block of flats. He switched off the engine, rested his head and arms on the steering wheel, and closed his eyes. The thought of walking into Wayne's flat—and what might be waiting for him there—sent a wave of panic through him.

I can't do this.

There was no way he could tell Wayne the truth, but he had a feeling Wayne wasn't going to accept "I can't tell you" as an answer. Ellis just *knew* he would push and push until either Ellis pushed back—or worse still, cracked under the pressure.

A sudden tap on his window made Ellis jump out of his skin. Wayne was staring at him. He beckoned Ellis with his finger.

Aw shit.

Ellis sighed and opened the car door. He didn't have to wait long.

"It's 2:00 a.m. Inside. Now." Wayne didn't sound pissed. He just sounded tired.

Ellis got out, locked the car, and followed him into the building. They climbed the stairs in silence until they reached Wayne's floor. Wayne opened the flat and pointed to the living room.

"In there. I want you on your knees, palms flat on your thighs."

Ellis was *right there* on the brink of telling Wayne where to get off, but Wayne's expression killed all such thoughts. Slowly he walked into the room and did as instructed, his heart pounding, his hands suddenly clammy.

Wayne stood in front of him, feet apart, arms folded across his chest. "You left this flat without having a key. Did that even cross your mind before you left?"

With a shock Ellis realized it hadn't. He'd been too busy thinking about Barb's call.

"I didn't think so." He speared Ellis with an intense gaze. "I know you were at your sister's. Now tell me why."

"She needed me." Except he knew Wayne wasn't going to let it lie.

Wayne cocked his head to one side. "Want to tell me why in the space of half an hour, she called you three times last night? And we're talking late, by the way."

Shit. Shit. Shit. He couldn't. Just... couldn't. Because talking about Barb would entail talking about his parents, and Ellis did *not* want to go there.

"Let's try another topic, then. When was the last time, before this weekend, that you got a full eight hours' sleep?"

"I told you, my neighbor is—"

"Right. Try again without the lies."

Even though Wayne was right, Ellis didn't like the accusatory tone. "Excuse me?"

"Do you honestly think I don't pay attention to the people in my unit? I do. No one plays music every night, and you're an officer. You could have had them shut down any time. So don't hand me a line about how you couldn't sleep because he was up playing with his band all night."

Fuck. Ellis should have known Wayne wouldn't be put off that easily. As much as he hated to admit it, though, the thought of Wayne worrying about him did help to soothe Ellis. It proved to him that at least *someone* gave a shit. But that didn't change matters at all.

"I can't tell you."

Wayne's voice was calm and cold when he replied. "No, I think it's more a case that you *won't* tell me."

"However you want to say it. I just can't."

Wayne sighed. "Right, then. I don't see that there's any other choice. I want you to go to your room and get ready for a punishment."

"For what?" Ellis shouted.

"Hm. Let's see. I'll allow you to choose. You've been lying to me for months. You left the house without letting me know where you were going, thus worrying me. You're refusing to answer me now. I think any of those qualifies, don't you?"

Ellis dipped his head, because he had no answer that would be satisfactory.

"Right. To your room, please. I'll be along shortly."

Ellis stood and trudged to his room, all manner of thoughts in his head, but with one in particular standing out.

This sucks.

CHAPTER TEN

WHEN WAYNE entered Ellis's room he found the man sitting in a chair, staring out the window. His breathing seemed erratic, his dark eyes surrounded by shadow. In the space of a few hours, somehow his sister had undone everything Ellis had accomplished.

Something about him touched Wayne deep inside, and he reined in his desire to be too firm.

Wayne spoke softly. "I'm going to give you one more chance. Tell me why you feel you're responsible for your sister's children."

Ellis didn't answer immediately. Wayne took the few steps to where Ellis sat and pointed at the floor. Ellis sneered, and Wayne gave an internal smile. *Does he actually think he's going to win on this?*

He kept his face straight. "Take your position, boy."

"Not a fucking boy," Ellis said in a low growl.

Wayne knew Ellis was lost. He needed focus. He had to be taken in a very firm hand.

And I'm just the man to do it.

Wayne reached out, grabbed a handful of Ellis's hair, and yanked him forward. "On your knees, Ellis."

Ellis let loose with a sharp cry but tumbled off the chair and onto his knees. He glared at Wayne with a look full of venom.

"I see. You want to do this the hard way by being stubborn," Wayne told him, ignoring the attitude. "Fine. There are many ways to deal with a brat. Until now I wasn't sure how I was going to punish you. But now that I'm looking at you, I'm thinking you might be in need of a spanking."

Ellis snapped his head back. "You are *not* spanking *me*."

"You agreed to follow my rules. In fact, I have it down in your writing. So unless you want to use the safeword you gave when you signed your contract—red—which stops this, but means we will be discussing it, you'll do what I tell you. I want you to strip off your clothes. Fold them and lay them neatly on the chair by the desk."

"What the fuck? You want me naked? What the hell for?"

Wayne ignored his outburst. "Then lean over the bed, your chest resting on the mattress, with your arms stretched out."

Ellis clenched his jaw. "Like fuck I will. I'm not a child."

Wayne did his best to stay calm, hearing the litany in his head. *Punishments should never be administered while angry.* "Your petulant behavior suggests otherwise. You've already earned fifteen swats: five for lying to me, five for withholding information, and five for your stubborn attitude. If you want to keep adding to the total, then by all means, continue. I'm going to make sure everything is secure, so I'll be back in a few moments. Be ready when I return."

Ellis glared daggers for a few moments before he stood up, grumbling as he did so. Wayne took his time, first ensuring the doors were locked, then turning off the lights. He put together a sandwich for Ellis, even though he didn't think it would be necessary, but he wanted to be prepared in case.

He wrapped the food in plastic before bringing both it and a bottle of water into the bedroom. Ellis was bent across the bed, his arse sticking up, presenting the most tantalizing picture. But tonight wasn't about the view—it was about helping take Ellis out of his head.

When he sat on the bed, Wayne noticed Ellis's sharp intake of breath. Ellis would deny it, he would fight it, but Wayne knew he needed this.

"I'm going to administer your punishment now, Ellis. I want you to count off as I do each stroke. If you lose count, we start again. Do you understand?"

"Yes," Ellis replied, his voice hoarse.

Wayne checked Ellis's reflection in the mirror on the wardrobe door before starting. Ellis stared ahead, his jaw set.

Wayne swatted him on the right cheek.

"One."

"No, that one was for not addressing me properly. Now I'll ask again. Do you understand?"

"I said yes," Ellis gritted out.

Another swat. "I can keep this up all night. And if my hand gets tired, I have a paddle I could use. Final time. Do you understand?"

"Yes… Sir," he spat, which led to yet another swat. Ellis glared at him in the mirror. "What the hell? I said it."

"Without a single bit of respect. You'll learn, though. Now let's begin. Remember, count each one off, or I start over."

Wayne knew it wouldn't take many before Ellis lost count. In fact, he was planning on it.

He brought his hand down with a loud crack for the first swat, and Ellis gave a start. "One," he ground out, loud and clear. Wayne continued, making sure the blows never landed in the same place twice. For the next four smacks, Ellis maintained his volume. By the eighth his voice began to trail off. By the tenth he was quieter still, and by the fifteenth, he stopped counting altogether. His eyes lost focus and he breathed more steadily.

Ellis had found his subspace.

After checking the rosy cheeks—and pushing down hard on the urge to sink his dick between them—Wayne manhandled Ellis onto the bed, then stripped down to his briefs. He grasped the bedspread from where it lay folded at the foot of the bed and tugged it, covering Ellis.

Wayne stared at his boy—*because that's what you are, even if you won't admit it yet*—and then lifted the cover and crawled in behind him before wrapping Ellis in an embrace.

"I've got you," he murmured, breathing Ellis in. "You're safe with me."

"Yes, Sir." His words were faint, tinged with fatigue.

The sound of deep, even breaths eventually lulled Wayne to sleep as well.

ELLIS WOKE first, rolling over and wincing as the pain in his arse flared again.

So it wasn't a dream. Wayne had actually spanked him.

No matter how much Ellis told himself he should be angry with Wayne for treating him that way, he couldn't. Not after Wayne delivered exactly what he'd promised. He had taken Ellis out of his own head for a while, allowing him to sleep, unplagued by the constant dreams of failure he had every time he dealt with Barb. That eternal knot in his stomach that pulled itself tight if he dared close his eyes hadn't materialized. As Wayne delivered each swat, it seemed like a layer of pain was peeled back, allowing Ellis a peek at the world as he hadn't seen it in such a long time. It had felt good, just as Jarod said. He'd let go, trusted Wayne as he always did, and the man had taken care of him.

Wait a minute, wait a minute. I don't want to want *this, damn it! Normal people don't do these kinds of things—do they?*

A snort behind him had Ellis twisting around to find Wayne stretched out, still sleeping. At first his presence startled Ellis, but he knew Wayne wouldn't try anything. Even if he didn't fully understand what was happening, Ellis knew that much to be true. He trusted Wayne more than he'd ever trusted anyone in his life. As long as they'd been partners, Ellis knew if Wayne got upset, it was always down to someone doing something stupid. He never stayed angry either. If he reprimanded someone on the squad, once it was done, that was that—case over. No residual anger, no harping back on it the next time someone made a mistake.

Ellis lay down again, surprised to find his naked body relishing the slight burn as his cheeks rubbed against the sheets. *Can I continue to do this? Let Wayne run my life? Make decisions for me? Take me in hand?* The thought sent a shiver through him. Already Wayne had shown respect and compassion for him. He'd given Ellis the best night of sleep he'd had in months. He demanded nothing, beyond what they'd agreed to.

Ellis scooted back a little more, until his body came in contact with Wayne's warmth. When his partner rolled over and wrapped an arm around Ellis's waist, his first thought was to jump up, but he didn't move. He hadn't been touched in so long, and it felt good, so why should he deny himself? Why shouldn't he be allowed to be at peace for a change?

No one needs to know, right?

WHEN WAYNE woke up, the first sound to reach his ears was the shower running. He wondered how long Ellis had been awake. A quick glance at the alarm clock told him he needed to be up and on his way. There wouldn't be time to make breakfast, so he'd have to ensure Ellis knew to eat something. Wayne got out of bed and realized he'd crawled in nearly naked last night. This morning. Whatever hell time they'd gone to bed. *I hope I didn't freak him out too badly.*

He searched for his clothes, surprised to see Ellis had folded and placed them next to his. After picking up the stack, he went to his room and got out a fresh set. He dressed quickly, went out to the kitchen, and halted in the doorway, gobsmacked by what he saw. Ellis had two bowls of muesli prepared and sliced some strawberries to go with it. He even had the carton of milk on the table.

"I hope you've got time for breakfast," Ellis said quietly.

"I really should go, but you went to all this trouble." Wayne's heart filled to bursting with pride. He knew the only reason Ellis had done this was his feelings of guilt, but the fact he'd done it at all meant a lot.

"Have a seat," he told Ellis. "Let's not have this go to waste."

Ellis sat and began to eat but wouldn't make eye contact with him. Maybe Wayne's near nudity in the bedroom had made him nervous.

"Just so you know, Ellis. When a punishment is administered, as long as it's resolved, the reason for it is forgotten. We didn't get anywhere last night, so today I want you to think about this. If you still won't tell me why you've taken responsibility for your sister, then I'm afraid we're at an impasse. I won't let it go, and if you continue to refuse to discuss it, then we've got a problem."

"Okay." Ellis jerked his head up. "I mean, okay, Sir."

Wayne grinned to himself. He rather liked seeing Ellis calm one minute, then flustered the next. Keeping him on his toes would be a good idea.

They finished their meal in silence. Ellis's mouth twitched.

"Something on your mind?" Wayne asked.

A deep sigh issued from Ellis's lips. "I want to answer your questions, but there is so much involved I'm not sure where I should start. It's not something I really want to talk about."

It was better than nothing.

"Mm-hmm. I can understand that. But you need to keep in mind that if you want me to help you, then you're going to have to open up and be honest with me. Without knowing what's going on in your head, I really have no idea how to proceed. I could do something that might make it so much worse for you, and that would do neither of us any favors."

Ellis turned his attention back to the tabletop, rubbing at an invisible spot on the surface. "I can't," he said quietly.

Wayne finished the rest of his breakfast, then rinsed his bowl out. "Right. Well, then, I'm not sure where we'll go from here. Maybe we both need to think on it. I'll be home at the same time. If you're not going to be here, at least do me the courtesy of calling."

Without waiting for an answer, Wayne grabbed his jacket and walked out the door. As he got in the car, he suffered a pang of regret. He knew he'd been hard on Ellis, but if he wanted to have any chance of breaking through the shell he had built up around him, Wayne had to keep chipping away at it. Only when it cracked could he bring Ellis out of it. Something was going on in his mind that had him knotted up inside. Someone had done this to him, broken him until he no longer had faith in himself.

He tapped the Bluetooth and told the phone to call Ellis.

"Hello?"

God, his boy sounded devastated. If Wayne was going to help, he had to do a little positive reinforcement.

"Hey. I forgot something before I left."

"What is it? Maybe I can bring it down."

"I forgot my hug," Wayne replied simply, smiling to himself when he heard Ellis exhale softly. "Do you think you can remember to remind me to get it when I come home?"

"I think I can do that," Ellis answered, his voice sounding lighter.

Before Wayne could hang up, he heard his name. "What's up?"

"Thank you" came the whispered reply.

Then he disconnected.

ELLIS FELT much lighter after Wayne called. He'd been angry with himself, his sister, hell, his whole damn family. If it weren't for them, he wouldn't be here right now. He'd be at work training beside Wayne and the team. Instead he was suspended and had nothing to do all day but think, which he'd be the first to admit was never his strong suit.

"What the hell do I owe them?" he grumbled as he wiped down the table. "I was happy. I'd finally gotten to the point where I thought I could be content with my life. I had mates, a job I love, and a best friend who'd do anything for me. Maybe I would have even found a woman to love. Goddammit!" he shouted as he pounded his fist onto the hardwood surface. "Wayne deserves to know the truth. He's taking a chance on me, giving me an opportunity that I'm royally fucking up. Who do I really owe here?"

The question was a valid one, but the answer wasn't so easy to come by. Ellis stewed about it while he cleaned, furiously scrubbing every surface. He had to tire himself out, if only to make that constant nagging voice in his head go back to sleep. Kitchen, bathroom, living room, both bedrooms—he cleaned them all from top to bottom. He dusted, swept, mopped the floors and walls, scrubbed the tub and sinks until his arms ached, his shirt was drenched with sweat, and still it wasn't enough.

Why are you bothering? You already know the outcome. You're going to mess up just like you always do, and Wayne will put you out. You're going to lose it all. Your best friend won't even want you.

At least in this, Ellis knew his bitch of an inner voice was lying. Wayne would always stand by him. He was the only person in Ellis's life who would.

Chapter Eleven

WAYNE WALKED into the flat and found Ellis asleep on the couch. He could smell the minty scent of the body wash from the shower and smiled at the thought of Ellis washing himself down. Not wanting to wake him, Wayne crept into the kitchen and could barely contain his shock. Even when he'd moved in, the kitchen had never been this clean or had smelled this fresh.

He went into the bathroom, and the scene repeated itself. It was immaculate. Everything put away on the shelves, the mirror wiped down, the tub and tiles shinier than when they were new. Ellis had put in a lot of work, and if Wayne was any kind of Dom, he needed to show his appreciation.

A quick call to Carlotti's and dinner was ordered, with an estimated arrival in thirty minutes' time. Ellis would be happy about that. Wayne went to his room and changed into a pair of tattered sweats, which he'd kept because they were comfortable, and an almost equally ratty T-shirt. He went back into the living room, lifted Ellis's feet so he could sit down, then pulled them onto his lap. He took the right foot in his hands and began to rub, gently at first, then more firmly as Ellis started to stir.

"Fuck, that feels so good," he said, his voice heavy with sleep.

"I'm glad you approve," Wayne replied happily.

Ellis's eyes popped open, his gaze focusing directly on Wayne. He tried to scramble off the sofa, but Wayne held him in place.

"Stay where you are."

Ellis blinked. "I'm sorry. I fell asleep. I meant to have dinner started because I appreciate everything you're doing. You don't know—"

Wayne chuckled. "Ellis? You're babbling. I don't mind that you fell asleep, okay? You obviously needed it after the thorough scrubbing you gave the place." He tilted his head to one side. "Care to tell me why? I didn't ask you to do it."

An expression flitted across Ellis's face. Sadness, anxiety, pain—all of them were clearly etched there for the world to see, if they bothered to look. Wayne's heart ached because he couldn't stand to see those emotions on his boy's face.

Ellis stared at him. "I needed…. I don't…."

The breath caught in Wayne's throat when Ellis sat up and threw himself into Wayne's arms.

"I said I wanted my hug. I didn't know you'd be just as eager," Wayne teased, squeezing for everything he was worth. Damn, it felt so good to hold him.

"I'm so sorry," Ellis whispered.

"For what?" Wayne asked, brushing his fingers over Ellis's short hair.

"Please don't give up on me, okay?"

Shit. What the hell happened? "You know I won't. Right?"

Ellis shook his head harshly. Wayne had never seen him like this. Whatever was going on inside him was tearing him apart. A flare of panic surged through Wayne, but he quashed it.

That won't help Ellis.

"I need you to look at me," Wayne said softly.

Ellis lifted his gaze and met Wayne's.

"I will *never* give up on you. I don't know what happened, and I don't care. There is nothing you can say that will shock me or make me regret having you in my life. If you're ever going to believe me about something, it should be this. I—"

Wayne stopped. He'd almost blurted out his true feelings, and that definitely wasn't needed right now. He took a calming breath.

"You're my friend, and I don't ever turn my back on friends."

Ellis whispered another apology, then tried to shift from Wayne's embrace. Wayne held him firm. "You're fine right where you are, I think. You need this closeness right now. In fact, I think we both do. Why don't you stretch out, close your eyes, and try to sleep a little longer?"

"Yeah. Okay." Ellis looked around for a moment before grabbing a cushion, placing it on Wayne's lap, and lying down, his head resting on it.

The urge to run his fingers through Ellis's hair was incredibly strong, but Wayne resisted, giving Ellis time to get comfortable. Ellis closed his eyes and his breathing became even. It took only a few minutes before Ellis drifted off again, but his sleep was clearly troubled; now and again he twitched, his brow furrowing.

Fuck it. Wayne stroked his boy's hair, keeping the movement light. *Can you feel that, boy? Can you feel how much I appreciate you? How much I love you?* As Ellis stilled, Wayne breathed more easily. *That's it.*

Twenty minutes later there was a soft knock on the door. Wayne lifted Ellis's head before easing himself out from under the cushion and up off the couch, then lowered Ellis down onto the cushion again. He paid for the delivery, gave a generous tip, and then came back into the living room, pizza box in hand. Wayne stood at one end of the couch, gazing at Ellis. He was exhausted and drained. Wayne wanted to let him sleep, but if Ellis had worked himself into this state, Wayne had to wonder if he'd eaten at all that day.

Hell, I need to eat too.

Wayne grabbed two plates from the kitchen, then put three slices of pizza on each. He went back over to the couch and looked down on a sleeping Ellis, unable to tear his eyes away.

We're going to get through this. I know we will.

Wayne placed the plates on the coffee table and then gently shook Ellis by the shoulder. "Ellis? Wake up. I've got something for you."

Eyes Wayne could easily lose himself in fluttered open. It took a few moments before they focused on the plate.

"You got me pizza?" Ellis croaked, sitting up and reaching for a plate.

"Well, I got it for both of us. Think of it as a thank-you for all your hard work today."

Ellis drew back his hand, staring at Wayne. "But why? I didn't answer your question."

Wayne sat next to Ellis and held out the plate, smiling when Ellis took it.

"No, you didn't. And we'll be talking about that soon. But today you went above and beyond any expectations I had of you, and I wanted you to know how proud and pleased I am of the initiative you took." He speared Ellis with a firm stare. "So shut up and eat your pizza."

Ellis gave a tired grin. "Yes, Sir. Thank you for the pizza."

"After that, if you want, we can watch a movie together."

"Would you mind if I called it a night? I'm so tired." Not that Wayne needed to hear Ellis's words—weariness was evident in the lines around his eyes and mouth, the way he held himself.

"Then I think you should turn in early. Before that, though, your phone, please."

Ellis slipped it out of his pocket and handed it to Wayne without argument, then dug into his pizza. "Damn, this is good," he moaned, reaching for his second slice.

"There's still some left in the box. I thought you might have it for lunch tomorrow."

Ellis swallowed his mouthful and stared at his plate. "I'm going to need to go home soon." His voice was hushed.

Wayne bit back his disappointment. "Oh? And why is that?"

"I can't keep paying for my place when I'm staying here. It doesn't make any sense."

Wayne knew Ellis had a point, but his desire to keep Ellis close overrode Wayne's common sense. "Then we'll go back to your place and you can give notice to your landlord. We'll pack your things up, and you can move in here." He awaited Ellis's reaction.

Ellis blinked. He blinked again. Then he shook his head. "I'm sorry. You want me to do… what?"

Wayne's heartbeat sped up. "Move in with me. Stay here and let me help you." He paused, frowning. "No, that's not right. Let me rephrase that. Stay here and share the place with me. Even if you decide you don't want us to continue what we've started, I'd like you to be here."

Ellis's gaze shifted down to his plate.

"I can't," he whispered. "I shouldn't even have allowed this to start. I'm sorry."

He started to stand, and Wayne put a hand on Ellis's arm. "Where are you going?"

"I need to go home. Trust me, you don't want to be involved in my mess."

Ellis stood and Wayne growled deep in his throat. Whoever had messed his boy up like this would most certainly pay for it.

"Sit down," he ordered. When Ellis didn't move, Wayne added, "Now."

Hesitantly Ellis took a seat.

Wayne tempered his rage at the unknown person or persons who'd messed with Ellis's head. "Okay, I don't know what's going on, but enough is enough. I get that whatever it is, you're afraid to tell me. While I wish you weren't, I promise to try and be a bit more patient. But *you've* got to try too. Think about why you're so hesitant to let me in. What is it that's eating at you?"

Ellis opened his mouth, but Wayne put up a hand. "No, don't answer. I want you to think on it. Spend the night. If you still feel like this isn't working out, then tomorrow we can talk about it. Okay?"

Ellis nodded. He turned to Wayne and said, "Can I be excused?"

"Of course. Warm bath, then get some sleep."

Without another word Ellis got up and trudged toward the bathroom. Wayne watched him go with a heavy heart.

This isn't over, Ellis. I'm not giving up on you, no matter how much you seem to think I should.

THE BUZZ of a phone woke Ellis, and he groaned and rolled over, reaching toward the bedside cabinet to grab his mobile. When he came up empty-handed, he sat up in bed, rubbing his eyes to clear the sleep from them.

Then he remembered. Wayne had his phone.

Aw, fuck.

He jumped from the bed and rushed to Wayne's door, hoping that the phone hadn't awoken him. *I shouldn't have stayed. I should have gone when I said I would.* He reached for the door handle, about to open it, when he heard Wayne's voice.

"Hello? ... No, I'm sorry. Ellis isn't available to babysit tonight, nor will he be in the foreseeable future."

Damn it! I'd really hoped Barb wouldn't call. Why the hell didn't Wayne turn off the bloody phone?

"My name is Wayne Dwyer, and I'm a friend of Ellis's. ... No, he's sleeping, and I won't wake him up for you. ... Right. If you persist in using that kind of language, then we clearly have nothing more to discuss."

Oh, this just gets better and better. She's probably drunk off her arse, and that *means she's swearing like a sailor.* He'd tried so hard to keep Wayne from finding out, and now with one phone call, she was about to ruin everything.

"For the record I *am* a police officer, but if you think calling will get you anywhere, please, go ahead, be my guest. Just make sure you give them my name correctly because I'm sure you wouldn't want to cause problems for anyone else. ... I'm sorry, what was that? Why won't I let you talk to your brother? Because he's run himself ragged, thanks to you."

Aw fuck. Wayne, please stop.

Ellis wanted to rush into the bedroom and take the phone away from Wayne. Right now he'd do just about *anything* to keep this from going further. *Then why the fuck won't my feet move?* He was rooted to the spot, listening as his life crumbled to bits before him.

Wayne's voice was hard, the same one Ellis heard him use when dealing with suspects. The voice that screamed *authority*.

"I've checked on you, Ms. Mann. I saw an arrest two years ago for possession of narcotics, and the note from the arresting officer said you were so high you didn't even know your name. See, you've already done enough damage to Ellis, and I simply won't allow you to infect him any further."

While part of Ellis was overjoyed Wayne was protecting him, another part knew everything he'd hidden was about to be pulled out into the light. Would any of his mates look at him the same again? Fuck, would *Wayne* be able to look him in the eye when he found out?

"Ms. Mann, can I be honest with you? I. Don't. Care what you want. Ellis will not be speaking to you this evening. Tomorrow I intend taking steps to ensure he has no more contact with you. … Fine. There's nothing more to be said. Your brother needs his rest now, so I'm going to say good night."

This can only end badly.

"Why, *you* are, Ms. Mann. Your children are *your* responsibility, and it's up to *you* to care for them or hire a babysitter whose job it is to watch them while you're… otherwise engaged. Please don't call this number again."

God, that hard edge to Wayne's voice sent a shiver through him.

He heard Wayne put the phone down. He wanted nothing more than to go back to his room and hide. Pretend none of this ever happened.

"Your sister is quite vocal, Ellis."

Ellis gave a start. The door opened, and Wayne stood there in a bathrobe, the room behind him bathed in a warm light.

"Why did you do that?" Ellis demanded. "What gives you the right?"

Wayne frowned and cocked his head. "You gave me the right when you signed the contract."

Ellis swallowed hard. *What. The. Fuck?* He crossed his arms in front of him and gripped his forearms to keep his hands from shaking. "Then we need to stop this right now. This is over, you hear me? This isn't for me. So *you're* going to tear up that contract and *I'm* going home, now. Tomorrow morning I'll see Lewis and tender my resignation."

His chest tightened and his stomach roiled. *Because there is no way I can face you after this.*

Wayne couldn't have looked worse if Ellis had struck him. His jaw went slack, and his face took on a pinched expression. "Ellis. Think about this. You don't have to—"

"Yes, I do," he interrupted. "Thank you for everything you've tried to do. I appreciate it, but…." *God, please help me get through this.* Ellis breathed in deeply and the words rushed out of him. "I don't want to see you again. You've messed with my mind, and… degraded me by making me do those things."

Fuck, don't cry, goddammit it.

Wayne held out a hand. "Ellis, I…." He took a step back, his expression bleak. "Okay, if this is what you want. I'm sorry I wasn't able to help you, and I hope you find the peace you're looking for." His voice sounded flat… dead.

Wayne turned and then staggered back into his bedroom, closing the door behind him.

Ellis gaped, a wash of cold flowing over his skin. He wasn't sure how he'd expected Wayne to react, but that swift agreement took his breath away.

This is what you wanted, right?

Now that he was standing outside Wayne's closed door, Ellis wasn't so sure.

He turned and rushed back to his—to the spare bedroom. He gathered up his clothes, stripped off Wayne's, and then put his own things back on. All the while that fucking voice in his head would not stop.

Go to Wayne. Explain it all to him. Beg his forgiveness.

Even if Ellis didn't want to admit it, he'd felt better after Wayne had taken him in hand. He was sleeping, eating right, his head finally clear. And now he'd fucked it up.

He stepped back into the living room. There was no light under Wayne's door, so hopefully he'd gone to sleep. *Maybe that's just as well.* He had a feeling if Wayne came out of his room, he wouldn't be able to keep from breaking down in front of him.

He stopped at the door and looked around. How weird was it that in the few days he'd been staying with Wayne, he felt more comfortable than he had in the last year in his own place? When Wayne asked him to move in, he had to force himself not to say yes on the spot because he knew if he accepted, ultimately Wayne would end up being hurt, and Ellis didn't want that at all.

He took a last look around the flat. A pain in his chest sucked away his breath. He'd finally found something he could call his own, something no one else could lay a claim on. Even though Wayne held the key, Ellis still had a feeling of rightness in his life that hadn't been there for a very, very long time. But to keep Wayne from being mired in the sinkhole his life had become, he was willing to walk away.

"Goodbye, Wayne."

THE SOFT click of the door still sounded thunderous to Wayne as he sat in his room. Letting Ellis walk out was the hardest thing he'd ever had to do, but his boy needed space, and Wayne needed to figure out how best to handle this situation.

He couldn't believe the woman on the phone was related to Ellis. She was loud and shrieking. When he refused to get into a shouting match with her, she went nuts, screaming about how Ellis would regret it. How he should know he had to take care of his family because that was the way he was raised.

The urge to hunt her down, drag her into a room, and force her to tell Wayne everything she knew about Ellis was tempting, but he needed to hear it from his boy's lips. Because if Wayne was certain about one thing, it was Ellis didn't want to go. His lips may have said he had to go, but the longing in his eyes told Wayne he wanted to stay more than anything.

He heard Ellis's car pull out of the parking space and rattle down the road. Wayne sloughed off his bathrobe and slipped back into his regular clothes. He fully intended to go after Ellis because no *way* was he about to let the man ruin his life. Sure, he told Wayne he didn't want to see him again, but that was deflection at best. He didn't want Wayne to see the pain, but they were way past that; Wayne had already seen it every day for more than a year.

He locked the door, went downstairs, and left the building. The night was reasonably quiet, even with the constant hum of traffic from the nearby main road. He got into his car and pulled out of his space. The drive to Ellis's house was only about twenty minutes, but Wayne deliberately drove slowly. *I know what I have to do, and tonight it gets done.*

Ellis was already home by the time Wayne pulled up in front of his building. He gazed up at the corner of the third floor, where he knew Ellis's flat was located. Wayne could see him at his window, his shadow pacing back and forth against the curtains. He got out of the car and walked up to the door. As Wayne approached, a man exited the building, holding the door open for him. Wayne gave him a smile, thanked him, and stepped inside. He used the stairs two at a time, and then there he was, outside Ellis's flat. He smiled to himself as he rang the bell. *You think this is over? Think again.*

"Just a minute," Ellis called out. The door opened, and Ellis gaped at him. "What are you doing here? I told you—"

"I know what you told me, but did you really think I'd accept that? Besides, you didn't give me your safeword, so I have to believe you didn't *really* intend for me to stay away."

"Wayne, I—"

"Sir."

"Please don't," Ellis whispered, his desperation obvious.

"Call me Sir," Wayne insisted.

"No, I can't…."

Wayne locked gazes with him. "Yet you want to. I can see it in your eyes. You long to submit to me, just like you have been since we started working together. You've always let me take the lead, to show you how things needed to be done. And you were grateful for it. You *needed* me, Ellis, and just like then, I'm here for you now. All you have to do is say the word."

Ellis's gaze was all over the place, not coming to rest on anything.

Wayne had to chuckle. "This is a very odd conversation to be having in the hallway, don't you think?" He paused. "Just say the word, Ellis."

"Please, Sir…," he whispered.

"Good boy," Wayne said, giving his boy a smile. "Can I come in?"

Ellis stepped back with only the slightest hesitation. "Yes, please."

CHAPTER TWELVE

WAYNE STEPPED into Ellis's hallway and Ellis closed the door behind them.

"Look, I know it's late, but I had to speak to you."

Ellis stood still, his hands by his sides. "Okay."

The words he'd turned over and over in his mind on the way over burst out of him. "You mustn't be hasty. You need to think things through. And as for quitting your job, please don't." Wayne met his gaze. "We can work it out."

Ellis's shy smile eased the clenched fist around Wayne's heart. "Why am I suddenly thinking of The Beatles?"

Wayne chuckled. "Oops. Now you know my guilty secret. I'm a closet Beatles fan."

Ellis's smile faltered. "Well, we all have our secrets."

Wayne reached into his pocket. "This is yours, I believe." He held out Ellis's phone. "I brought it in case you needed me." He couldn't suppress the thought right there at the forefront of his mind. *And you* do *need me.*

"Thank you." Ellis reached for it, and as he did so, it buzzed.

Wayne peered at the caller ID and frowned. "Do your parents always call you this late?"

Ellis went white as a sheet. His hands trembled and his eyes were wild, darting around the room as though he were searching for a means of escape.

What the hell? The hair rose on the back of Wayne's neck and along his forearms.

"What's wrong?"

"Don't make me talk to them," Ellis pleaded. "Please."

He'd never seen Ellis like this. He was actually afraid; Wayne could almost smell the fear rolling off him.

"Ellis?" Wayne reached out to try to calm him, but Ellis darted away. He rushed to his bedroom, closing the door with a bang. Wayne hurried after him. He pushed open the door to find Ellis pacing the length of the floor at the foot of his bed.

"What's going on? Talk to me. We've come so far. Don't step back now."

Ellis was trembling. "I can't talk to them. Please don't make me. They'll ruin everything."

Ruin everything? "What do you mean?"

Ellis turned away from him. "I can't tell you. You wouldn't understand."

Wayne glowered. "And why can't you? We've agreed to the truth, but now you're holding back." He walked over to Ellis, grabbed him by the arms, and then spun him round to face him.

Ellis tilted his head up, and the shine in his eyes spoke of tears unshed. "You shouldn't have come here. You should have just let me go. It's like I said. We can't continue it. I made a promise and I can't break it, no matter how much I wish I could."

Icy hands stroked down Wayne's spine. "A promise to whom?"

"My parents. They're…." Ellis pushed out a heavy sigh, his hands clenched into fists, his frustration evident in his pinched expression. "Let's just say that there will be repercussions and let it go at that." He swallowed hard. "You need to go now. It's fine. I'll deal with it."

Wayne gaped at him. "It is clearly *not* fine. And do you seriously think I'm going to leave and let you deal with whatever the hell it is on your own? You're *my* responsibility, Ellis, remember?"

Ellis stared at him. "I told you to tear up our contract."

"Well, I didn't. Did you really think I would? And here was I, thinking you knew me." Wayne couldn't help it. He reached out and cupped Ellis's cheek. "This is obviously tearing you up inside, so we're going to talk. You know I won't ever repeat any of it to another person, right? So you've *got* to tell me what's got you all snarled up inside."

Ellis dipped his chin. Wayne had never seen him so morose.

"Sit down," he said gently, withdrawing his hand. "And start at the beginning."

His boy sank onto the bed, his hands laced in front of him, and after a moment's hesitation, he began to speak, his voice almost a whisper. "I think it started when I was sixteen. No, it actually started much earlier than that. From as far back as I can remember, my father drilled it into my head that men took care of women. He said it was the natural order, and that we needed to follow it. I heard that every day of my life.

"When I turned twelve, he took me aside and told me that I was now a man, and as such, I had responsibilities of one. He told me that

Barb would be mine to care for. It was practice, he said, to prepare me for when I had a wife and family of my own. I tried to tell him I wasn't ready, but he was adamant. So of course everything Barb did reflected back onto me."

Ellis cupped his head in his hands. His voice shook as he tried to get the story out.

"When I turned thirteen, Barb got in trouble with a boy from school. He got her pregnant, and somehow it became my fault because I didn't protect her, even though she said she was in love with him."

"How could that have been your fault?" Wayne ached to put his arms around Ellis, but he restrained himself.

"They said I... wasn't there for my family." Wayne couldn't miss the tremor in Ellis's voice.

"But that's ridiculous. You were still a child. How could you be held responsible?" he demanded.

Ellis stared at him with wide eyes. "Because she was my responsibility." Another sigh. "I tried my hardest to keep her from getting in too deep, but she always found a way. Nothing I ever did was good enough. Another thing my father drilled into my head. When I didn't do as expected, if I failed Barb, there were... repercussions."

"What kind of *repercussions*?" Wayne demanded, though he wasn't sure he was ready to hear. His temper was already near fraying.

"The first time I argued with him, told him I didn't know why I had to be the one who helped her, he withheld my dinner. The next time, he locked me in the cupboard for an hour. After the third time, I finally got the message, and did my best not to argue."

"What message?"

Ellis sighed and pointed to a scar hidden beneath his brow. "I got a good thrashing. Then he left me in the cupboard while I was bleeding from a cut above my eye."

Wayne resisted the urge to growl. "And what about them? She was *their* daughter. Surely they had to take some responsibility." Ellis's face tightened even more, and Wayne wanted to kick himself. This was eating away at him. "So your sister got pregnant," he said, hoping to get Ellis back on track with his tale.

Ellis nodded. "No one wanted the baby, but there was no way they'd agree to an abortion. In the end it didn't matter, anyway. Somehow she miscarried and, believe it or not, that was my fault too." He sniffled.

There it was again, the urge to gather him up and hold him, but Wayne knew Ellis needed to get this out.

"She got into more and more trouble. Skipping school, joyriding. Stealing from the local shop. Smoking. Stuff like that. And *not once* did they call her on it. Instead they directed all their anger toward me. Why wasn't I looking out for her? She was *my* sister; I ought to have been there for her."

"Did you ever try to talk to your sister about some of her… choices?" Wayne asked, keeping his voice soft. "Because they were *her* choices, when it comes down to it."

Ellis snorted. "Of course, but she didn't listen to a *single bloody word* that I said. After that it got worse."

"Why? What happened next?" Inside Wayne was cold. Ellis's family sounded horrific.

"For some reason I was expected to keep the family together. Except when I went to train for the police, suddenly I was 'turning my back on my family' because I was taking on a dangerous career." He twisted his hands together. "They've never forgiven me for that. Most parents would be proud to have a son like me, but *no*, not them. Then when my sister had her first baby from another in a long string of boyfriends, everything changed."

Wayne didn't fight the urge this time. He took Ellis's hand in his, letting him know without words he was not alone.

Ellis glanced down and he briefly closed his eyes. When he opened them, he stared at the rug beneath their feet. "My parents wanted to know when I planned on getting married and having children." He grimaced. "They made it sound like only *my* kids would be legitimate or some such garbage. I don't like my sister much, but her kids are beautiful. They're bright and funny, and yes, they deserve better. As time went by, the questions became more frequent. 'Why don't you ever bring a girl home?' So I did. And then another. And another. Mum always found fault with them, which was fine because I had no real interest in any of them. But for my parents, I tried. So damned hard."

Wayne's chest was suddenly constricted. "What do you mean you had no real interest in any of those girls?" He tightened his grip on Ellis's hand. "What are you saying, Ellis?" When Ellis lowered his gaze, Wayne lifted his chin with gentle fingers. "Look at me," he demanded.

Ellis swallowed hard, but he didn't look away. "I… don't like women. Not like that, anyway. I tried for my parents' sake, and I almost convinced myself I could do it, but I just… can't. Those times at the bar, all those times you saw me picking up women? I'd leave with them, all right, but more often than not, I'd say I wasn't feeling well or something. There were a few I slept with because I figured I could learn to like it, or maybe meet someone I could fall in love with, but that never happened. But that night at the club, watching Alex and Leo on the stage? I got harder than I ever had with any woman."

Holy hell. Wayne stared at Ellis, his heart pounding. Slowly he lowered his hand.

Ellis pulled his hand free of Wayne's. "And now? Everything is about to fall apart. After the way you spoke to Barb, she probably got straight on to the phone to them, complaining that I wasn't doing what I should, that I was deserting her when she needed me. I'll bet anything you like that's why they're calling. They're probably mad that I won't help her. Not to mention the fact that I haven't been to see them for a few weeks, so that's probably pissed them off too. As soon as I do, though, it's going to be 'when are you getting married?' I just can't do this anymore."

The dam burst and Ellis bent over, sobbing into his hands. Wayne wrapped an arm around him, surprised when Ellis turned and buried his face in Wayne's chest.

"You don't know what it's been like," he wailed. "I've *tried* to be what they wanted. I've always done what I could to make them proud, but it's never enough. I do what I can for people, but everyone always wants more. Everyone wants *another fucking piece.* And the more I give, the more they want until there's just nothing left." He looked up at Wayne, his eyes wet and pleading. "They've used me up, Wayne. There isn't any more."

Wayne wrapped his arms around Ellis and held on. He'd known there was something there, but *this*? He hadn't expected this. *What kind of parents would do this to their son? Make him loathe himself, hide who he is, just to satisfy themselves? And to make him responsible for the poor decisions of another adult?* That went a long way toward explaining why Ellis was at the breaking point now.

"You listen to me, Ellis Mann. What they've done to you is neither right nor fair," Wayne murmured in Ellis's ear. "And you're wrong.

You're *not* used up. There is so much more to you, but you need to find it again. And I want to help you do that. Will you let me?"

He couldn't be sure Ellis heard him. All the pain that had impacted on his psyche seemed to be pouring out now. Instead of trying to talk to him, to get him to see himself the way Wayne saw him, he just held him, determined more than ever to protect him and help Ellis discover who he truly was.

Because there was no way he'd let him go now. Not when the truth of how much Ellis needed him had finally come out.

WHEN ELLIS woke he still felt as though he'd been hit by a bus. He was in bed, his entire body ached, his head pounded, and his eyes felt scratchy. The urge to go back to sleep hit him, but then he noticed something. He was being held. No, he was being cradled. Strong arms wrapped around him, holding him tight. He inclined his head to find Wayne asleep at his back, clutching Ellis to him. *Huh?*

Then the previous night came back to him in a flood of memories.

Telling Wayne everything. Breaking down. Wayne pulling him down onto the bed to hold him. Falling asleep in Wayne's arms and the quiet joy that spread through Ellis as he realized he felt safe. Protected. Cared for.

"Think quieter," Wayne murmured. "Some of us are still asleep."

Ellis tried to draw away, but Wayne tightened his grip.

"Stay where you are, lest you upset this delicate balance."

Ellis couldn't help the hysterical snort that burst from him. "Why are you here? You should have run out already."

Wayne opened his eyes slowly and focused on Ellis. "Why would I leave? I'm sure as hell not walking out when you finally need me."

Ellis broke his connection with Wayne. "Because now you know the truth. I'm not someone you can depend on. I let everyone down eventually."

Wayne gripped the back of Ellis's neck with a strong hand. "Stop that right now," Wayne snarled. "None of this—not one single iota—is your fault. How in the hell could any of it be? You were a child when all of this started, and that's the biggest problem here. The fact that they tried to make this all about you completely messed with your teenage mind. They forced you to accept responsibilities that weren't yours and set you up to fail because they couldn't, or more accurately, they *refused* to take care of their own problems."

"But I should have been watching Barb better. She wasn't a bad kid. She just fell in with the wrong people."

"And your parents tried to make it about you. Let me ask you something, and forgive me for being blunt here: do your parents care about your sister at all?"

Images from their childhood flashed through Ellis's mind. Christmas: she got a doll; he got a new bike. Her birthday: a cake from the local supermarket with a few candles on it. His birthday: a huge cake decorated with dragons and a castle and a party with mates from school.

"No, I don't think so."

"May I say I find it odd that you're supposed to look out for your sister, but then you say they didn't care for her."

Ellis shifted onto his back and stared at the ceiling. "It's all about what they think makes a man," he said slowly. "A man has responsibilities, cares for his family, steps up when he's needed, and most importantly, he never says no because family is *the* most important thing in life."

"Oh my God. Are you even listening to yourself?" Wayne's tone held an angry edge. "What happened to all of that when they were raising their daughter? I can understand now why she's angry. They treated her as if she didn't matter."

"In our father's eyes, she didn't," Ellis agreed. "Only boys can carry on the family name. To my father, girls are meant to support their men."

Wayne's eyes went wide and his expression showed his obvious disgust.

"You've got to understand how it is for him. My parents never argued because my mother understood her role in my father's eyes. He cared for her because she was his other half. That was his job. My sister was expected to find a man who would take care of her. But here's the important thing as far as my dad's concerned. When she does marry—if she ever does—Barb won't be a Mann anymore. She'll take on her husband's name, and that will be the end to that line of the family. As my father's only son, I'm expected to carry on his legacy. The future of the Mann family is right here." He cupped his balls through his boxers.

"Do you agree with his view on life?"

Ellis shook his head. "No. Never."

"But you still try to live up to it. You babysat for your sister whenever she called. You tried to hide who you were to make them happy."

Fuck. He'd told Wayne *nearly* everything. *Oh well, in for a penny....*

"My father has bone cancer. They found out last year."

Wayne shifted on the mattress. "I don't understand the correlation."

"He wants me to prove I can carry on for him after he dies. He wants me to have a wife and child—and it has to be a boy—to uphold our *proud* traditions." Ellis could hear the bitterness in his own voice. "I'm expected to take care of my family, so I need to find myself a wife."

"That's.... I'm sorry, Ellis, but that's insane."

In his heart he knew Wayne wasn't saying anything Ellis didn't already know. But they were his family. How could he deny them?

Wayne propped himself up on his elbow and gazed at Ellis. "May I ask you a question?"

The tone worried Ellis, but he agreed. Anything to distract himself from the sight before him—Wayne's bare chest with its dusting of dark hair, his nipples even darker.

"Have you ever been touched by a man?"

He'd dreamed it. Desired it. He'd lusted after enough of them. Malcolm from the rugby team. Daniel from science. Everett from the bar. But especially—

No, best to stop that line of thought right there.

"No. I can't do that."

"Can't or won't? There's a big difference here. If you can't do it, you're incapable. If you won't do it, you're trying to deny yourself. So which is it?"

"I can't. It would break my father's heart."

"No, that's a won't. You're doing what you said you've always done. Trying your best to make other people happy. But what about Ellis? What makes him happy?"

No one had ever asked Ellis what would make him happy. He knew his duty to his family, and what *he* wanted out of life wasn't important.

"I don't really know."

"You do," Wayne insisted. "Deep down in your heart of hearts, you know what means the most to you."

When he joined the police, it was the proudest day of his life. It meant something to him because in his eyes, it made sense. He would be taking care of a lot of people. He thought it would satisfy his father because it would show he had taken on even more responsibility. He thought it would make things better when Ellis told him the truth. But everything he planned had gone wrong. His father told him he was bitterly disappointed in Ellis's choices. He ranted about how police officers didn't make enough money to care for a family. How inconsiderate he'd been, thinking only of himself. His job would be fraught with danger, and if anything happened to him, God forbid, he could leave his wife and children without a means of support.

"I want to protect people," he answered. "It's why I wanted to become a police officer."

"It's a good job," Wayne agreed. "And you're incredible at it."

Warmth rushed to Ellis's cheeks.

"But you need to stop living for your father's expectations. Even if you were to marry a woman and raise a family, do you honestly think you'd be happy?"

"I like children," Ellis protested.

"I know. You talked about your sister's kids, and I could see in your face how much you love them. But think about what you just said. You like children. No mention of your wife. Would you be able to love her?"

Could he see himself married to a woman? He had some great friends who were women, but they could never be anything more. He'd gone home with a few women to try to show he could, but it was all physical. There was no emotion in it at all. And even the physical wasn't that great, because he worried the whole time about his performance. Was he pleasing her? Did she enjoy what they were doing?

"No," Ellis answered. "I don't know that I could love a woman like that."

"And would that be fair to her? Think about it. Five years down the line and you'd still be lying to her, to yourself. What then?"

Ellis's gut clenched. "Can we not do this?"

"Sure. We don't have to talk about it. But unless you face it, the problem won't ever go away, and I think you know that." Wayne sat up in bed and swung his legs out from beneath the duvet. "Pack your bags."

The abruptness of this change in direction made Ellis's head spin. "What? Why?"

"Because you're coming home where you belong. This isn't your place anymore, and I think you know it."

It wasn't. And he did. The times he'd been at Wayne's place, he'd been comfortable enough, but this time he felt like he belonged.

Wayne stood by the bed, hands by his sides, his gaze fixed on Ellis. "It's time to come home."

Chapter Thirteen

"How's the bath?" Wayne asked through the door.

"I don't know why I couldn't just take a shower at night," Ellis complained.

The door opened, and Wayne stepped into the steamy room. "So you're telling me you don't like taking baths? It doesn't feel good to let the warm water surround you and help to ease out the tensions?"

Ellis wanted to deny Wayne's words, but in truth, he loved the nightly bath Wayne insisted he take. He'd rarely taken a bath since he was a kid, and he'd forgotten how good it felt. It relaxed him, allowing calm to seep in and his stress to dissipate. He put his head back and rested it against the edge of the tub. Wayne's bath was big enough that he could relax, legs bent, and that was really saying something for someone of his build.

"Okay, maybe this *does* feel good," he admitted.

"Next time I go shopping, I'll buy some bath crystals for you."

Ellis jerked his head up, the sharp movement splashing water over Wayne and the floor. "What? Are you kidding?"

"No." Wayne appeared puzzled by Ellis's reaction. "Wouldn't you like something scented in the water?"

Ellis snorted. "Hell no. Bath stuff? Please. Next thing you know you'll be suggesting bubble bath. I sure as hell don't want *anything* in my water."

Wayne arched his eyebrows. "Ha. My *God*, you're a bad liar, do you know that? There's this little twitch you get in your lip every time you try to be less than honest with me."

A wet hand went up to cover his mouth. "I do not."

Wayne barked a laugh, his eyes twinkling. "You're simply adorable, you know that?"

When he heard the words, Ellis's heart thumped harder. He stared at Wayne with the backdrop of the light shining off his hair; even wrapped in sweats and a T-shirt, his body was stunning. *Fuck. How many times have I—*

Stop that!

"So what kind of crystals are we talking?" Ellis asked, wanting to move the conversation to a safer topic. "Because if you say lavender, I will not be held responsible for my actions."

Wayne's lips twitched. "Aw. What's wrong with lavender? I was always partial to magnolia or lily of the valley myself."

Ellis grimaced. "Ew. That's for little old ladies and those lacy things that your grandmother hung in the wardrobe or put in the drawer to make things smell… well, of lavender."

Wayne's face lit up when he smiled. "Relax. I get the message. Real Men Don't Like Lavender. If you must know, the one I was thinking of is called Therapeutic Bath. It's lemon and eucalyptus, and it says it'll help soothe aching muscles. Once you get back to work, you're going to need it. They've been killing us lately. I almost—and only almost—wish something would happen just so we wouldn't be crawling home every night."

"Do you really think I should go back?" Ellis asked. He still wasn't totally sold on the idea. His suspension and his own uncertainties about his future made him wary.

Wayne sat on the edge of the toilet. "Yes, I really do. You belong there with me, fighting the good fight. Someone has to keep London safe, and I really don't think there is anyone better for the job."

Ellis sagged into the warm water. "Thank you. I think sometimes I need to hear that. No one in my family gets that it's important to me, and sometimes it makes me doubt myself."

Wayne dipped his fingers into the water, then splashed Ellis in the face.

"Hey!" he sputtered. "What the hell?"

"I never want you to doubt yourself or your place. If you ever need someone who will listen, you only need to come see me. I'll always hear you out."

Ellis's chest warmed. "You mean that, don't you?"

Wayne started to reach out, then drew his hand back. He sucked in a deep breath and stretched out once more, cupping Ellis's cheek in his hand.

"I never say anything I don't mean, boy," he said softly.

Ellis almost pressed into Wayne's touch before he caught himself. His emotions felt so raw. He tried to ignore the fluttery feeling in his belly and the way the muscles in his stomach twitched. He pushed Wayne's hand away with a laugh. "Not a boy," Ellis reminded him.

Wayne sat back and his gaze narrowed. "Maybe one day you'll decide that you are. If that happens, keep in mind that you belong to me."

The lump in his throat made it hard for Ellis to speak.

"That won't happen," Ellis vowed.

Wayne stood up. He took a thick towel from the heated rack and laid it out for Ellis.

"I think it already has, but you're not ready to admit it," he replied, his voice smooth. He opened his mouth as if he were about to say more, but then snapped it shut. "But now's not the time to discuss this. It's almost bedtime. Dry yourself off and then get some sleep. I know *I* need some. I'll see you in the morning." He left the room quickly.

Ellis stared at the closed bathroom door. *Did I just say something to offend him?* He was starting to get a feel for Wayne's moods, and something was nagging at him, a sense that Wayne had left so swiftly just to get away from him. *Shit.*

Ellis pulled the plug and let the water drain out of the bath while he sat and watched it go. It made a sucking sound as it swirled down the hole.

"A bit like my life," Ellis mused aloud. "I thought I had everything under control, and then it all started being sucked away and I couldn't stop it."

But Wayne had changed that. He'd taken Ellis in and had begun to put things to right. His warmth filled Ellis with hope that, one day, he might actually be Ellis again and not the disappointing child of Charles and Emma Mann. Just thinking their names caused a spike of pain to lance through him. He didn't want to disappoint his parents, but Wayne had been right about that too.

"I'm my own man," he whispered. He hoped one day he'd actually believe it, though. Because Wayne was right about one other thing. Though Ellis tried to deny it or wished he could say it wasn't true, he was starting to think maybe the idea of actually belonging to Wayne—the one man who seemed to see the real him—might not be so bad.

He put on the robe Wayne had left out for him, opened the door, and walked down the hall to his room. He was surprised to see his phone plugged in to his charger by the bed. Usually Wayne took it when he got home from work. Ellis picked it up and brought the screen to life. Six missed calls from his parents.

Fuck. I knew this would happen.

He stared at the screen, his finger hovering over their names to return the call. *Don't. Just... don't.* Instead he turned the power off on the phone and tossed it into the drawer. He didn't want to think about them, and right then, he didn't have it in him to talk to them. Wayne must have left the phone in the bedroom to give Ellis the option.

Well, I've made my choice for tonight. Though I'm probably going to regret it later.

FRIDAY EVENING Wayne trudged to the door of his flat and leaned against the doorframe, almost too tired to reach into his pocket for the key. Everything from his feet to the follicles of his hair ached. The day had been all about training for coming up against a group of terrorists, and Lewis had made full use of the whole false town setup. Crawling over rooftops, up and down fire escapes and staircases—you name it, they'd done it. And of course when Lewis wasn't happy with their response times, they did it all over again. And again. Wayne's uniform stank to high heaven with sweat and dirt. When the day came to an end, all he wanted to do was get home to a long, long soak in the bath.

Opening the door proved to be a challenge for his protesting muscles. Who the hell put the handle so far up? He tried again with the same results. "Sodding thing," he grumbled.

The door opened, and he tumbled into Ellis's arms. Ellis had already taken his bath because Wayne could smell the crystals he'd sworn he wouldn't use. They scented his skin, the aroma filling Wayne's senses.

"What the hell? Are you okay?"

"Knackered," Wayne ground out.

Ellis practically carried him to the couch, set him down, and hovered over him.

"You look awful. How did you get dirt on your face?"

Wayne tilted his head slightly and glared at Ellis.

"Right. Sorry. Hang on." He started to walk toward the bathroom, stopped, turned around, and grinned. "Don't go away," he teased in a cheeky voice.

Wayne mumbled something. It was supposed to be "fuck you," but whatever came out didn't even sound like words. He lay on the couch, his head dropped back. Sleep had become a vital necessity, but the bedroom was too far away. Maybe he could stretch out on the couch?

A moment later strong arms lifted him off the sofa. "Just hold on, okay?"

"Hmm?" Wayne wanted to protest, but *damn*, Ellis's arms felt good. "Sometimes I forget how strong you are," he murmured.

Ellis carried him into the bathroom, where he sat him on the edge of the bath before proceeding to strip Wayne's clothes off. Wayne's nostrils were filled with the invigorating aroma that permeated the air. When he was naked, Ellis helped him into the bath, where he lay back.

"Okay, it's official. I'm in heaven." The water was just the right temperature. If he closed his eyes, he'd be asleep in seconds. *So close them. What's stopping you?*

Wayne closed his eyes, relaxed his body, and let the heat of the water and the wonderful aroma ease his aches. When a warm rag touched his face, Wayne's eyes popped open. Ellis knelt next to the tub, his eyes scrunched up. He wet the washcloth again, then rubbed it over Wayne's cheek.

"What—"

"Lie still," Ellis said softly. "Sleep if you want. I'll take care of you."

Wayne tried to stay awake as Ellis tenderly ran the cloth over his face, his shoulders, chest, stomach, legs. It was almost hypnotic. He closed his eyes again and lost himself in the water, the scents, and most of all, Ellis's gentle, hesitant touch as he cleaned him.

"That feels good," he admitted. Even that was a vast understatement. It felt *blissful*. The only way it could have been improved upon was if Ellis were in there with—

And you can stop right there, Wayne silently instructed his dick, which had thickened slightly.

Ellis's chuckle broke through to drag him back into the present. "I think you're done." He got Wayne to his feet and helped him out of the tub. Wayne was about to protest again when Ellis began to dry him off, but some part of his brain reacted incredulously. *Are you crazy? It feels amazing.*

Wayne kept his mouth shut. His body was half-asleep, but apparently his brain was working just fine. Ellis guided him toward the guest bedroom.

"I want you to sleep here tonight," Ellis murmured in his ear. "In case you need something. Don't try to get up without telling me, okay?"

A sleepy chuckle rolled out of him. "I'm okay, you know. I'm just shattered."

"And that's why you're going to sleep." Ellis laid Wayne on the bed, then stripped off his own clothes until he stood there in his underwear. He got Wayne under the covers, then crawled in himself before turning off the light.

"Good night, Sir," he whispered as the room was plunged into darkness.

Wayne wanted to stay awake now, to savor this, but the call of sleep was too great to ignore. The last thing he remembered before he went out like a light was a heavy arm across his waist and Ellis's head on his chest.

SATURDAY MORNING was heralded by peals of thunder and flashes of lightning. It felt as though the building were shaking, and on occasion, the lights flickered. Ellis pulled the covers up to his chin and snuggled down under them. He smiled at the fact that Wayne was still asleep. *How can he sleep through this?*

He let his mind drift back to the previous night. Wayne in the bath as Ellis had knelt next to him, scrubbing the dirt from his face, then moving to his chest. He'd hesitated at first, fearing the touch might seem too intimate, but his desire to take care of Wayne had overridden any other concerns. The sweet little noises Wayne made had thrilled him. They'd also made him… want more.

He'd lusted after men before, but Wayne was always different. He treated Ellis with respect, never talked down to him, and made him feel worthwhile. It was a lot more than any member of his family had done. He didn't want to admit it was this that had drawn him to Wayne in the first place, but after that realization, he'd begun to see more. Wayne's kindness to others, his strength and sincerity. He'd fallen in love with Wayne the day his father told Ellis the prognosis he wasn't going to live to see next year.

The memory was so vivid in his mind. They were in the pub, the guys joking around as they usually did when Derwent challenged Ellis to a round of darts. He'd tried to muster up the desire to play but couldn't. His father telling him he was dying was bad enough, but then to remind Ellis of his obligation to his family? It was all he could do to keep his lunch down.

"Leave him be, Derwent."

"Aw, is he too scared to play tonight? He's forever boasting about how good he is, and I'm feeling lucky."

Wayne's voice never faltered. "And I told you to leave him be. Can't you see he's not feeling well?"

Derwent mumbled under his breath and went off to play with Cassidy instead.

"You okay?" Wayne asked, leaning in close so as not to be heard.

"Yeah. No." Ellis sighed before he finally said, "I don't know."

"Right. Why don't you go home? Get some rest. If you need something, call me. I'll head home just in case."

"No, you don't have—"

"You're my mate, yeah? What kind of friend would I be if I didn't try to take care of you? Go home, take a nice, hot bath, and try to sleep."

The memory made Ellis snort. He'd forgotten how enamored Wayne was of the idea of Ellis taking a bath. But that night he'd taken one, and he had felt much better. As he lay in bed that evening, Wayne's kindness had comforted him, and while he slept, Ellis dreamed of his best mate.

Except we were more than just friends in those dreams, weren't we?

Wayne shifted, drawing Ellis back from his memories. He rolled onto his side and gazed at Wayne. Beyond the dark hair and intensely blue eyes, there was so much more. Wayne was gorgeous, but it was a beauty that started from the inside and worked its way out. *His* beauty was much more than skin-deep.

He thought back to Wayne's words from the night before. *"I think it already has, but you're not ready to admit it."* He'd thought about it since he signed the contract. *What must it be like to belong to a man?* It didn't seem to bother Alex at all. The look of rapture on his face when he had Leo's full attention was a sight to behold.

You know that's how Wayne looks at you.

A few seconds later, he had to accept his head was only telling him what he wanted to hear.

But he doesn't. After Ellis made his declaration that women didn't turn him on, he'd expected... something. Wayne had ignored it. He'd acted as if Ellis hadn't even said it. Maybe it made Wayne feel uncomfortable, knowing his friend had lied to him for years. Or perhaps the admission changed the way Wayne saw him.

He noticed a stray hair dangling over Wayne's eye and reached out to brush it away. Once he touched Wayne, though, he didn't want to stop.

It's not fair, is it? All those years you buried your desire for your friend because you knew it couldn't happen, and now that you've finally told him the truth, he doesn't seem to care. So not only have you gone against your family, you may very well have alienated your only real friend.

"What is it with you and thinking?" Wayne murmured. "You're forever doing it, and to be honest, I find it's quite distracting."

Ellis chuckled. "How is thinking distracting?"

Wayne opened his eyes and smiled. "Because you do it so hard. You throw yourself into it heart and soul. No one should have to think that hard. It's just not right."

"And what do you suggest?"

Wayne pulled his arm out from under the covers and placed his hand on Ellis's. "Life is going to happen no matter what we do. You've been fighting against it for so long and it's twisted you up inside. Maybe it's time to let someone else shoulder the burden for you."

Ellis humphed. "No one wants to be stuck with this, trust me on that."

Wayne squeezed his hand, and his expression grew serious. "I do. I've been telling you that, waiting for you to listen to me. But all that thinking you're doing? It's not letting you hear. Stop using your head and try using your heart for a change."

Use my heart?

Wayne sat up, the covers falling around his waist. "I'm going to get breakfast started. If you'd like, I'll even let you have a cup of coffee today."

"I can get breakfast started," Ellis said, sitting up in the bed.

"No, that's fine. You have a lie-in. It'll take a while, so just rest. And stop thinking. That's an order."

"Yes, Sir!"

Wayne gazed at him for a moment and then shook his head, smiling. He walked over to the chest of drawers, providing Ellis with a fantastic view of his firm arse. Wayne removed a pair of sweats from the bottom drawer and stepped into them, bending slightly, and Ellis had to fight the urge to sigh. *Fuck. Look at him.*

He left the room and Ellis lay back on the pillow. *Is Wayne right? Hell, has he ever been wrong?*

"Use my heart?" he muttered.

Ellis closed his eyes and let his mind drift. Wayne had once asked him what made him happy, and Ellis claimed he didn't know. But last night? He'd gotten his answer in an unexpected way. He'd held Wayne in his arms, caring for him, bathing him, and everything seemed to fall into place. For the first time in more than a year, Ellis had been content. Truly happy to his core. Because Wayne needed him.

"Fuck," Ellis whispered.

The truth his heart had been trying to tell him had finally reached his head. He wanted to belong to Wayne. To the only man he felt understood him, cared about him, protected him. And the one person in all the world Ellis could see himself being with. But he wasn't really sure what that meant in terms of Wayne's lifestyle. He needed to understand before he talked to Wayne about his revelation.

He quickly threw on his sweatpants and went into the kitchen, where Wayne stood scrambling some eggs.

"I thought you were going to get some more rest," he said, a frown on his face.

Ellis stood by a chair at the table. "I need to ask you something."

"And it couldn't have waited until it was time to eat?"

Ellis shook his head. "No, it's important. Well, to me, anyway."

"If it's important to you, it's equally important to me," Wayne replied, placing the bowl on the countertop.

"I was wondering what you thought about us going back to Secrets tonight. I want to see your world with a fresh set of eyes."

Wayne stilled and then blinked. "Maybe you should sit down," he said, waving a hand to the chair. He took one opposite Ellis. "We can go to the club if you'd like, but I have to warn you. What you're likely to see there will be very different compared to the other night. That was a party, one where friends gathered to celebrate. Tonight? The spanking you saw onstage will pale in comparison to what will probably be on display tonight. We're talking the potential to see whips, canes, or floggers being used. Group sex. Or any other number of things. I need you to be absolutely sure you want this."

Ellis's stomach clenched. *Maybe I should have thought this through some more.* He pushed the thought aside. Wayne had said to use his heart, and he was going to do that tonight.

Ellis sucked in a deep breath. "Yes, that's what I want. Can we go?"

Wayne got up and returned to the counter. "Yes, we can go."

He seemed a lot calmer about the prospect than Ellis did. *And that's just as well because I have no idea what I'm letting myself in for.*

CHAPTER FOURTEEN

AS THEY stepped into the club, Wayne put a hand around Ellis's waist, pleased when he moved closer. The crowd that night was boisterous, something he hadn't seen since the early days of Whispers, the club that was here before Secrets. The smell of leather, the sound of voices raised in pleas, groans, sighs, moans, and harsh cries, and the scent of release all mingled together to create a heady atmosphere. God, he missed this. Whispers was incredible years earlier, but time hadn't been kind to the club, nor the men who owned it. He was glad Jack and Michael had sold it rather than close down.

When a table became available near the bar, one of the guys tending rushed over to clear it. He had on an apron and not much else. Cute, but not nearly as sexy as Ellis. Speaking of his boy, Wayne smiled as Ellis moved a little closer still to him. The club in full swing had to be a bit of a culture shock for him. He guided Ellis to the table, then told him to take a seat.

Wayne couldn't take his eyes off Ellis. He'd put on some jeans so tight it almost seemed as though they'd been painted on. Wayne insisted Ellis go shirtless, though he allowed him a jacket. But the pelt of hair on his chest and stomach was too tempting to keep hidden away all night. The tight buds on his chest begged to be tweaked and nibbled, and Wayne ached to do just that. He wanted to make Ellis come apart as Wayne guided him into his new life.

Maybe this visit will allow that dream to become a reality.

"Remember what we talked about," Wayne reminded him. "The bracelet you're wearing says you're with me. It also signifies that you're not here to play. Don't talk to anyone unless I say it's okay. Keep your eyes lowered to the table at all times. If you're uncertain about anything, lean over and whisper to me. I promise you I will not leave your side tonight, and if you want us to go, let me know, and we're out the door."

"Okay." Ellis glanced down at his body. "Are you sure I'm dressed right?"

Right was a vast understatement, as far as Wayne was concerned. He was already fighting the urge to pull Ellis into his lap and kiss him until those brown eyes glazed over and Ellis was returning every kiss. "You look fine. Trust me. But I wish I had put a collar on you. I'm thinking something dark."

"A collar?" Ellis demanded and pressed his lips into a tight line. "What the hell for? I'm not a dog."

Wayne chuckled. "In my world a collar signifies ownership. Sometimes it's only for a night, but there are some that signify more. Those would be the equivalent of a wedding ring."

"That's… wow." Ellis glanced around the club. "I had no idea it could be like this." Wayne took the chair next to him, sitting close enough that their thighs were touching. He knew he didn't need to, but he thought his boy might feel better with his presence nearby.

"Is it always like this?" Ellis whispered, still taking in his surroundings. The way his breathing hitched as he watched a Dom caress his sub's chest with the soft tails of a flogger was adorable.

"No, I haven't seen a crowd like this in years." Wayne cast his gaze around the room. So much leather and man-flesh to be ogled. "It's great to see the place looking so full." He picked up the small menu from the table and perused it. The owners had certainly gone all out. Whispers never had a kitchen, but Secrets had all the amenities. He scanned the menu, looking for some finger food they could share.

When Wayne felt fingers sliding onto his leg, reaching for his hand, he caught them in a tight grip. Ellis visibly relaxed as Wayne held his hand, and a shiver ran through Wayne. *I am so proud of you.*

"Wayne? Hey, how's it going?"

Wayne looked up. "Vic! Great to see you. Missed you at the opening." He grinned. "Wow. Have you been living in the gym? I swear you've put on ten pounds of muscle since I last saw you." The large man flexed his arms, and Wayne laughed. "Now you're just showing off."

Vic chuckled. "Thanks for noticing. I've been working on my upper-body strength recently. Sorry I missed the opening. I was out of town. I tried to get back in time, but there was no way." He peered at Ellis. "And who's this pretty thing with you?"

Ellis tensed up slightly, and Wayne tightened his grip on Ellis's hand. "This is Ellis, my guest for this evening."

Vic inclined his head. "Pleasure to meet you, Ellis."

Ellis said nothing, staring at the table.

Wayne nudged him with his knee. "It's okay to say hello, boy."

"Hello," he said softly, a tremor running through him.

"Seems like a good one. Quiet and respectful," Vic said, then roared with laughter. "You need to take care of this one."

"Oh, I intend to," Wayne vowed. "What about you? Playing tonight?"

Vic grinned. "Just got done with a hot little number. The boy could suck the chrome from a hubcap with those lips."

Ellis gave a barely perceptible groan, and Wayne knew the topic might be uncomfortable. He decided it was best to change the tone of the conversation.

"No one special for you?"

"Nah. I like to play, but I'm not really one to settle down." He waggled his brows. "I'm only thirty-three; got plenty of years left before I get saddled with a ball and chain."

That comment brought a growl from Ellis's lips. He tightened his hand around Wayne's almost painfully. Wayne stared in amazement as Ellis lifted his gaze and glared at Vic.

"What the f—?" Ellis started to say, his tone dripping with anger.

"Eyes down, Ellis," Wayne snapped. Fortunately he complied immediately. Wayne gave Vic an apologetic glance. "Sorry, Vic. Ellis is new, so he's a little overwhelmed by everything."

"No problem at all." Vic leaned closer to Ellis. "Hey, Ellis?"

Ellis stared at the tabletop, his jaw set.

"You can answer, Ellis."

"Yes?" he replied, his tone clipped.

"Listen, I might tease, but I'm not serious. I'm sorry if I upset you."

Ellis simply dipped his chin.

"Have a good night, Wayne," Vic said as he turned and headed for the exit.

As soon as Vic was out of earshot, Wayne turned to Ellis. "That was rude," he growled.

Ellis snapped his gaze up. Wayne saw his flaring nostrils, his narrowed gaze, his anger clearly visible. "He was an asshole. He talked like guys were nothing more than a piece of meat."

This was the Ellis Wayne had fallen in love with. The confident, brash man who spoke his mind. While he liked his sweet, quiet boy, he wanted Ellis to be himself.

Now how can I chastise him when this is exactly what I was hoping to see?

Wayne kept his tone firm. "Regardless, he's a friend of mine, and you should have treated him as such."

Ellis grumbled and turned his head away.

"What did you say?" Wayne demanded. He hoped the glimmer of Ellis he'd seen peeking through wouldn't go away. His suspension had really shaken him, but Wayne wanted Ellis to emerge stronger than before. And he needed to turn to Wayne to help him accomplish that.

"I said I'm sorry."

Damn it. Not the breakthrough he'd hoped for. "Forgotten."

The server came over to the table and smiled wide at Wayne. "Can I get either of you something to drink or eat, sir?"

"An order of chicken quesadillas, please. And two mineral waters with lime."

"Of course, sir. I'll have those out to you right away."

The waiter turned and flounced away, exposing two pale white globes. Wayne smiled at the sight. *Now* there's *something Whispers never had before.*

"See something you like?" Ellis said, his voice full of attitude.

"Indeed," Wayne teased, giving the server's arse one last glance.

"Then why not go after him?"

The reply dripped with anger and hurt. Wayne turned toward Ellis, noting the pained expression.

"Because I don't want him," he replied. His heartbeat sped up. "In fact, I—"

"Good evening, gentlemen" came a soft voice behind them. Wayne twisted in his seat and smiled as Jarod approached the table.

"Nice to see you again, Ellis," Jarod said.

Wayne gave Ellis another nudge with his knee. "You're free to talk to him, Ellis."

Ellis lifted his gaze and smiled at Jarod, but there was sadness in his eyes. *Damn it.*

Jarod came to a halt by Ellis. "I was about to take a break. Eli said I looked tired, so he wanted me to go sit down for a while. I tried to tell him I was fine, but he gave me his 'don't argue with me, do what you're told' look, so I'm heading upstairs. Do you think you might want to come along?"

"Well, we've just ordered some food," Wayne said.

"I can have the kitchen hold the order for a bit," Jarod said hopefully. "Normally I wouldn't ask, but with Maxwell taking Mother out to see some of the London sights, it's...." Jarod sighed. "It's a little lonely. Eli said he'd come with me, but as you can see, we're very full tonight, and I don't want to take him away from the club."

Ellis looked at Wayne. "Would it be okay if I went? I'd like to talk with Jarod."

"Oh, I'm sorry, sir. I didn't realize—" Jarod started.

"No harm done," Wayne said with a wave of his hand. "Ellis, are you okay going with Jarod?"

"If that's okay with you."

It really wasn't. He liked having Ellis pressed against his side. The fact that Ellis seemed to feel safe with Wayne meant a lot. But if he expected Ellis to get comfortable in the club, he had to let him make friends. *And I get a good feeling about Jarod.*

"Where will you be taking him?" Wayne asked.

Jarod rubbed his chin. "I'd intended on going up to our apartment for a while, maybe have a cup of tea. If you'd prefer we can just as easily sit at the bar."

"What will your Master say if you have someone in your apartment?"

"I would definitely tell him before we went up. Again, if it's not right, we'll be happy to sit at the bar. I just thought Ellis might feel more comfortable talking where it's not so loud."

"You can take him with you," Wayne grudgingly allowed, "but if you could have him back in, say, thirty minutes?"

"Of course, sir."

Wayne stood and let Ellis step away from the table. "Thirty minutes," he stressed.

He sighed as Ellis walked away with the club owner. This was going to be a very long half hour.

WHEN THE elevator door closed, Ellis turned to Jarod. "Thank you."

"For what? You're doing me a favor, believe me. I haven't really spent much time alone since Eli and I got together, and I find it... uncomfortable to be by myself. I miss the sound of voices and doing things with others. Times like these I'd even prefer to go knit with my mother."

"Wow, that *is* desperate," Ellis teased.

"Sorry. I didn't mean it to sound like that. I love my mother. Knitting? Not so much. I'm better with crocheting."

Ellis looked at Jarod as the elevator reached the top floor. He could see a hint of something metallic under his shirt.

"What's that around your neck?"

Jarod's hand went up and he stroked the bit of steel that stood out against his light skin.

"My collar," he answered, his voice choked with emotion. "Eli collared me last year."

"Do you always wear it?"

Jarod led him down the hall. "Yes, it never comes off."

"What's it mean?" Ellis asked, even though he knew what Wayne had told him.

"Well, it's a symbol of our commitment to each other. The day of the ceremony, I got on my knees and vowed to him that I would always do my best to be worthy of him. In turn he promised to always take care of me."

Ellis couldn't deny how happy Jarod seemed. "Can I ask? Does it scare you?"

Jarod slid the key into the lock and pushed open the door. Ellis stepped inside and gaped. The place was amazing.

"Does what scare me? I'm not sure what you mean. The only thing that frightens me is the depth of my feelings for my Master. I never thought I would ever have the chance to feel this way again. Whether it was God or providence, I can't say, but no, I'm definitely not afraid."

"Oh. That sounds great," Ellis admitted. He couldn't think of what else to say.

Jarod busied himself in the kitchen putting together tea for them. He turned and smiled at Ellis. "Have a seat," he said, pointing to the stools at the breakfast bar. "You said you wanted to talk to me, so here I am. I'll listen and, if I can, try to offer advice."

Anxiety knotted in Ellis's stomach. He *did* have questions, but he really wasn't sure if he'd like the answers. He sat on a stool and took a deep breath. "What's it like being owned by another man? It sounds… wrong."

Jarod's eyes opened wide. "Oh God no. Imagine having someone who is there for you *all* the time. His very presence calms you, makes it so you can breathe. You asked me if it scared me. The idea of *not* having my Master is what scares me. After Phillip—my previous Master—died, I was terrified. I needed someone to care for because, without that, my life had no meaning. My mother reminded me that I wasn't meant to be alone. I'm not sure I would have done more than just exist."

That sounded familiar. Ellis was more certain than ever that he needed Wayne because the man infused Ellis with his strength, made it so he could carry on whether at work or, more recently, at home.

"So I see things have changed with your friend," Jarod said, sliding the mug toward Ellis. He gestured at the sugar caddy, then turned to the refrigerator and pulled out a carton of milk.

As Ellis added a splash to his tea, he said, "Maybe. I'm not sure."

Jarod slid gracefully onto one of the stools at the breakfast bar. "Did you want to talk about it?"

Ellis shook his head. "No, that's okay. I'm here to keep you entertained, remember?"

Jarod placed a hand atop Ellis's. "I'm always here to help a friend," he said, his tone solemn.

Finally Ellis couldn't hold it in anymore. "I told him something. I'd thought that once I did, I'd get a reaction from him, but he hasn't said a word about it."

"Okay. Maybe it's not what you're thinking."

A laugh bubbled out of Ellis. "That's the problem. I don't know *what* to think anymore."

"So tell me. Keep in mind, sometimes people can be clueless. Maybe what you're expecting requires something more from you. Or maybe he doesn't think it needs to be discussed."

Ellis dipped his head, not wanting to see censure in Jarod's gaze when he admitted the truth he hadn't told anyone but Wayne.

"I'm... gay."

"What a coincidence! Me too." Jarod laughed. "If you thought you'd shock me, you're wrong. At my age it takes a lot to do that. Besides, I thought maybe you were. I mean, you *are* in a gay BDSM club, right?"

"Hey! I was here to support my friend."

Jarod gave a single nod. "A noble intention. So what did you tell him that he didn't react to?"

Ellis snorted. "That I didn't like women… you know, like that."

"Ah, I see. How did you expect him to react?"

That was a good question. He'd wondered time and again how he'd wanted Wayne to react. "I don't know. Maybe a little bit surprised?"

"Can I ask you something? And you don't have to tell me. What's the relationship between you and… what did you say his name was? Wayne?"

"Yes, that's Wayne. He's my best mate. He's also my partner in the firearms division."

"Oh, that sounds interesting."

"He also…." Ellis's stomach tensed. "Oh God, it sounds so stupid to say it out loud."

There was the gentle yet reassuring touch of Jarod's hand on his. "Remember not much surprises me anymore."

"After we were here the last time, he told me he wanted to… to…." Ellis dropped his voice to a whisper. "Take me in hand. I've been staying with him for a while since I got suspended at work."

"Oh? Why were you suspended?"

Ellis could feel his cheeks heat. "I might have jumped on someone who called Wayne a queer."

"Ooh," Jarod said with a grin. "Now we're getting to the juicy stuff."

Jarod's jubilance was infectious, and Ellis couldn't help but laugh too. He went on to explain about Roberts, the resulting suspension, and his agreement to try things Wayne's way. He may also have mentioned the success he thought they'd had.

"Does that bother you?" Jarod wondered.

Ellis's cheeks warmed significantly. "Not as much as I thought it would," he admitted. "I… like him a lot."

"'*Like*'?" Jarod arched his eyebrows. "You hesitated for a second, so I have to wonder if that's what you were going to say."

Ellis gave him a mock glare. "Anyone ever tell you you're annoying?"

Jarod smirked. "Do you want that list alphabetically, or would you prefer it in chronological order? Now stop stalling."

"I think I… might…." His voice cracked a little. "I might be in love with him."

Jarod tilted his head to one side. "And the thought scares you?"

Ellis looked up, so many emotions at war within him, and no clue how to give them voice. "I don't know what it means to love a man. I'm not sure what it will mean to love a Dom either."

"I can answer that pretty simply because they're one and the same. A Dom, no matter what, is still a man. Unless we're talking a woman who is a Domme, but that's not the issue right now, and trying to sort it out would get us off track."

Jarod waggled his eyebrows, which had them both laughing. When they'd calmed down, Ellis dove back into the deep end of the conversation.

"I've never been in love before. I've got, shall we say, family issues." He held back a snort at how tame his proclamation was.

"Ah. I sometimes forget that not all parents were like mine. My mum and dad were always very supportive of me. I'm certain they knew I was gay long before I told them. The thing of it is, whether it's a man or a woman, love is love. It's sad that too many people don't seem to understand that."

"Like my parents," Ellis spat bitterly.

"So why do you think you want to belong to Wayne? You seemed uncertain the last time we talked."

Ellis tapped his fingers on the countertop. "It's a recent realization, I guess you could say. Wayne taking me in hand now, with my consent, shows me he's always been directing me, even if it was subtle before. I'm left wondering where I would be if not for him. And if I'm honest, I like how I feel when I'm with him."

"And how is that?"

Ellis thought for a moment. "Stronger. More in control. Calmer."

When Jarod grinned, Ellis wondered what he'd said.

"Sounds to me like you already know what you want."

That's the same thing Wayne said. Maybe it is *true.*

"The only way you're going to know is by talking to Wayne." Jarod glanced at his watch. "Speaking of which, we're going to be pushing the thirty minutes if we don't get down there now."

Okay, Ellis thought. *Time to decide if I want what Wayne is offering. And whether I can go through with it.*

CHAPTER FIFTEEN

WAYNE EXPELLED a sharp breath of relief when he saw Ellis and Jarod getting out of the lift. He had no idea why he'd been so nervous, but now that his boy was coming back toward him, he relaxed. Ellis joined him at the table and sat beside him again.

"Did you have a nice talk?" Wayne asked.

Instead of replying Ellis turned toward Jarod. "Did we?"

Jarod smile lit up his entire face. "I think we did. I'm going to go tell them in the kitchen that you're ready for your food. Gentlemen, thank you for being with us tonight. Should you require anything, don't hesitate to have one of the boys come find me."

He walked away, humming a familiar tune.

Wayne turned to Ellis. "I'm glad you're back. Felt weird not having you here."

"Aw, did you miss me?" Ellis asked, fluttering his eyes in typical teasing Ellis fashion.

"Yes, you cheeky brat. I missed you. Happy?" *This* was the Ellis he knew, the one who made him feel good inside.

Ellis laid his head on Wayne's shoulder. "Yeah, I'm happy."

Wayne caught his breath. He waited for the punchline to the joke, expecting Ellis to pop back up and tease him, but he didn't move an inch. He truly seemed content where he was.

How far can I take this?

Before he could say anything, the server brought a plate heaped with chicken quesadillas cut into small triangles, the centers oozing with salsa and Monterey Jack. He also placed two tall glasses on the table. "Jarod asked me to let you know these were compliments of the house. They're nonalcoholic cordials. Cherry mixed with sparkling water. They should go very nicely with your food."

Ellis sat up, and Wayne missed the connection instantly. The two of them sipped the drinks.

"Sweet but really good," Ellis said. "And the food looks tasty. I'm starving." He eyed the food intently. When he reached for a piece, Wayne made a split-second decision and smacked his hand.

"What the hell?" Ellis demanded, jerking his hand back. His lower lip jutted out slightly.

"Be still," Wayne ordered. He reached out and broke off a piece of one of the quesadillas with his fingers, then held it out for Ellis to take. "Open," he said quietly.

His heart thudded while he waited to see what Ellis would do. Ellis's gaze darted between the food and Wayne, who remained implacable. If Ellis refused, then he would let him feed himself, but right then, Wayne wanted nothing more than to show his boy how things were done.

Ellis leaned forward slowly and opened his mouth. Wayne could have died a happy man right there. He slipped the morsel between those waiting lips, then drew back his hand and leaned in closer.

"Sometimes a Dom likes to feed his boy," he whispered in Ellis's ear before straightening.

He waited for the usual comeback of "not a boy," but Ellis simply nodded. When Wayne picked up the next piece, Ellis leaned forward and accepted it without hesitation.

"Good," Wayne said, rubbing a hand over Ellis's leg. "You're making me so proud."

The comment seemed to jar Ellis, but after a moment, he smiled wide. "Thank you… Sir."

That did it. Wayne knew the time had come to claim what was his. He didn't want to frighten Ellis, but he had to have him in his life, in his home. Ellis was the missing half of him, and Wayne needed him to be whole.

He took Ellis's chin between his thumb and forefinger and turned so he could gaze into his boy's eyes. They widened a fraction, the pupils large. Wayne had wanted to do this at home, but he couldn't wait any longer. He leaned forward and placed his lips against Ellis's. The moment they touched, Ellis whimpered. Wayne kept the kiss light, needing to know how Ellis would respond. When he sat back, Ellis's lips were still puckered, as if he were begging for more. Wayne was addicted. Ellis's taste was strong; a trace of cherry mixed with taco seasoning, chicken, and Monterey Jack created a pleasant taste, and Wayne found it intoxicating.

"You can open your eyes now, Ellis."

"I don't want to," Ellis whispered.

"Why?"

"I dreamed about this more times than I can count. You're about to kiss me and… I wake up. I wondered what it would be like if I didn't. Would your lips be soft? Would your kiss be brutal? I could never find out, and it nearly killed me. I don't want this to be another dream."

"Open your eyes, Ellis."

Slowly he cracked them open. Wayne smiled at his hesitancy.

"See? Still here."

"Oh thank God," Ellis replied, so much emotion in his voice that it made Wayne's heart quake to hear it. "Can… can we talk about something? I've come to a decision and I need to share it."

Wayne's pulse raced as his mind went through the possibilities. "Is this conversation one we should have at home, or can we wait until we finish eating?"

Ellis glanced down at the plate. "Well," he said, dragging out the word. "I don't want the quesadillas to go to waste."

For the next thirty minutes, Wayne delighted in feeding Ellis small bits of food, and Ellis ate whatever Wayne gave him, a huge smile on his face. Wayne had never had anyone he could pamper like this, and didn't realize how much it would mean to him. Nor had he realized just how sensuous feeding someone could be. Now and again Ellis flicked Wayne's fingers with his tongue, and when he briefly sucked on one of them, Wayne had to bite back the groan that pushed at his lips, clamoring for release.

I could so get used to this.

"I'm stuffed," Ellis said, patting his stomach. He turned to Wayne with a look of concern. "You haven't eaten anything."

"I will now. I wanted you to have your fill first. Taking care of you is my primary responsibility."

Ellis nodded. "That's what I wanted to talk to you about. After I talked with Jarod, I realized how long you've been taking care of me. Even when it didn't get you anything, you still did it."

Wayne opened his mouth to protest, but Ellis held up a hand.

"I know you take care of all the guys on the squad, but with me, you went *way* above and beyond. I came to depend on you to be there for me. I needed you before I even understood what it meant. And you were always there."

When Ellis paused, Wayne waited. He wasn't going to break the moment, and he was content to let Ellis gather his thoughts.

"I guess what I'm saying is… I think you were right. I have always belonged to you. And if that's true…." Ellis looked him in the eye. "I'd like to belong to you… Sir."

Wayne could scarcely catch his breath. *Oh my God.* He'd wanted Ellis for years, but that didn't mean he'd ever believed it possible. It was rare enough to find a submissive who fit you perfectly, but to find one you'd known for so long?

Wayne forced himself to breathe evenly as he contemplated his next words. There was no way he wanted to screw this up. It still felt like a dream.

"We'd need to discuss a contract," he said at last.

Ellis frowned. "What? That doesn't make any sense. We've already got a contract."

"The contract we negotiated was for me to take you in hand, help you find yourself again. The new contract would go much deeper, sort of a grocery list of other things."

"Like what?" Ellis asked, head cocked.

"Do you recall watching Leo and Alex up on the stage? Public play is likely a part of their contract, as is spanking. There are negotiations for sex, roles, and so much more. What we have right *now* is a piece of paper. If we take this further, what we would be filling out would be a true Dom/sub contract." His heart pounded as he watched Ellis take this all in, the moment balanced precariously.

Ellis exhaled slowly. "Shit. I didn't realize it would be this involved."

For one horrible moment, Wayne was afraid to breathe. *Don't falter now. Don't let me down, Ellis.* Aloud he kept his voice even. "It is, and if you truly want to belong to me, a contract between us is a must so that there will be no misunderstandings."

Ellis sat quietly, and Wayne fought hard to keep himself from rushing in with both feet.

His heart pounding, he regarded Ellis with a calm he did not feel. "There is no shame in needing time to think about it. Nor would there be in changing your mind. This isn't something to be rushed into." In his head was a silent prayer. *Please don't change your mind.*

Ellis grinned. "I've been waiting six years. I don't think it could be called a rush, do you?"

The relief that flooded through Wayne meant he couldn't repress his smile. "Okay, then. We'll go home and sleep on it. Tomorrow morning we'll get up, I'll take you to breakfast, and then we can go back home and discuss it. Does that sound acceptable?"

Wayne had never seen Ellis smile so brightly. "Yes, Sir."

Without Ellis seeing, Wayne pinched himself so he, too, could be certain it wasn't a dream.

SLEEP WAS not on the agenda, apparently. Ellis rolled over in bed and stared at the blue LED numerals beside his bed. Midnight had come and gone, and he couldn't switch off his brain.

Not that this surprised him. He'd just made a huge decision, the ramifications of which were only now becoming clear to him. *I've just agreed to be owned by a man.* No, not just a man. He'd said yes to belonging to Wayne. His stomach quivered at the thought, equal parts excitement and nerves warring for dominance.

"Heh. Dominance." Ellis laughed nervously.

He knew they would be discussing things in depth the coming morning, and rapid-fire thoughts zipped through his head as to what that conversation might entail. When Wayne had said sex, Ellis had nearly leapt out of his seat. His sexual experience had been limited to a few fumbling attempts with women. Watching porn did nothing for him. He'd tried to watch gay porn a few times, but the guilt that always accompanied such activity meant he couldn't get hard. It was as if his subconscious refused to entertain the notion he could be gay.

"Goddammit," he muttered. "What happens if I can't function? If Wayne says my inability to get it up is a deal breaker?"

Something fluttered in the pit of Ellis's stomach at the thought he could lose Wayne before they even had a chance.

For God's sake. He couldn't lie there tormented by such thoughts. Like sleep was going to happen anyway. He got up and trudged into the living room. *Maybe I'll curl up on the couch and watch some television until I get sleepy.* It was certainly a better option than lying in bed, staring at the alarm clock.

To his surprise Wayne was already there, sitting on the couch in his sweatpants. He looked up as Ellis entered the room.

"Couldn't sleep either?" Wayne asked.

"No. I have a lot on my mind."

Wayne grinned. "Hmm. I couldn't imagine what you could possibly have to think about."

Ellis snorted. "Yeah, right."

Wayne patted the seat cushion next to him. "Come have a seat. I was going to heat up some milk to make cocoa. Would you like a mug?"

That warm feeling he got whenever Wayne did something to take care of him surged through his body. "Yes, please. If you don't mind."

Wayne levelled his gaze at Ellis. "I will never mind caring for you. I'm not sure what's going through your head, but get that firmly wedged in there now."

Ellis watched as Wayne got up and went into the small kitchen. When he returned with two steaming mugs, he went over to the cabinet next to the TV and opened it. He took out a bottle of Kahlúa and then added a bit of it to each mug.

"I don't normally do this," Wayne explained, stirring the liqueur into the cocoa. "I find it helps me to sleep, though. It doesn't take much, just a dash. Combined with the warm milk, it's delicious." He came back over to the couch, put the mug down beside Ellis, then took a seat next to him. "So did you want to talk about whatever is keeping you awake?"

"Not really," Ellis insisted.

Wayne cleared his throat. "Just so you know, once you've signed the contract? You won't be able to say no. I'll expect you to be open and honest with me at all times. Just as I'll need to be with you."

Ellis sighed and sipped his cocoa. "You were right. This is really good."

"And you're equivocating. Talk to me. Let me see if I can help."

Ellis stared into the depths of his mug. He didn't think making eye contact would be a good idea. "I'm afraid," he admitted.

"Of me?" Wayne wanted to know.

"No, definitely not of you." He took a deep breath. "You mentioned sex, and that got me thinking."

"Now you definitely have my attention. What were your thoughts?"

Ellis swallowed. "What… what happens if I can't maintain an erection?"

Wayne chuckled. "Trust me, you won't have any problems with it."

"But what if I do? When I had sex with women, I had to… think about other things. I would close my eyes and imagine I was with someone else. But then I'd start to feel guilty because I knew it wouldn't go anywhere. No matter what my dad said, there was no way I could envisage being married." He grimaced. "Just the thought was enough to make me flaccid."

"Honestly I don't think it will be a problem, but if you want, we could test it."

Ellis narrowed his gaze. "Test it how, exactly?"

Wayne grinned. "Do you trust me?"

"Right now? I'm not so sure." Wayne had an almost evil aura about him.

"I want you to put your cocoa down and lie back. Close your eyes if you want. Then I just want you to feel. That's your only job, okay?"

Ellis placed his mug on the table in front of him, then stretched his legs out. It felt silly, but he did trust Wayne. At the first featherlight touch of Wayne's fingers on his chest, Ellis jolted upright.

"What are you doing?"

Wayne regarded him calmly. "Trust me. Please."

Ellis settled back again and waited for Wayne to continue. He didn't have to wait long before Wayne was exploring his chest and stomach with deft fingers, brushing over the hair and rubbing his nipples. Ellis breathed easier, enjoying the sensations. Damn, it felt so good. When he felt Wayne's hands on his crotch, his first reaction was to pull away again. Fear surged through him, but he breathed through it. *Trust Wayne. He said to trust him.*

"That's my boy," Wayne whispered, slipping his fingers inside Ellis's underwear.

He wrapped a warm hand around his cock—his thick, hard, dripping cock. *Oh fuck.* How could he have doubted his ability to get it up around Wayne? He had been in his head every time Ellis attempted to have sex. Without Wayne in his mind, there was no way he would have ever been able to complete the act.

"Doing okay there?" Wayne asked quietly.

"Yes." *Oh hell yes.*

Wayne chuckled. "Not that I didn't already know. Your dick is like a rock."

He pulled him free of his briefs with those nimble fingers and began to run along the skin of Ellis's shaft, tickling the head. Then Wayne gripped him again, tight in his hot fist, and Ellis's skin tingled.

"I'm going to make you come, Ellis. I want you to do it for me, okay? You can do anything I ask of you because you're my boy. Right?" He moved his hand up and down Ellis's rigid shaft, the motion quickening.

Right? Hell, at this time if Wayne asked me to get up and flap my arms like a chicken, I would. Anything so long as he doesn't stop.

"Ellis?" Wayne asked again, amusement in his voice.

"God yes." Ellis couldn't think of anything beyond the hand that was bringing him closer to his climax.

"Yes, what?"

"Sir. Yes, Sir. Please."

"Please what? Tell me what it is you want, Ellis."

"I want you to make me come. Please." He took a deep breath. "Please, Sir, make me come."

"The problem we have here is that you're here to satisfy my needs. You're my boy to do with as I want. But your primary role in my life is to please me. And you *do* want to please me, right?" The voice was low, hypnotic.

Ellis's heartbeat sped up. "Yes, Sir. I want to please you." He wanted that with every part of him.

"Then come for me, Ellis."

Being given permission to let go of the fear, his previous failed attempts, of… *everything* surged through Ellis, becoming a hot point within him that travelled the whole length of his body, culminating in the most explosive orgasm of his life. He howled Wayne's name as shudders rocked him to his core.

All the while, Wayne never broke their connection. "I have you," he said quietly. "I'm not letting you go."

The words filled Ellis with joy.

As the jolts ebbed away, Wayne got up and went into the bathroom. He returned a few moments later with a warm cloth he used to wipe down Ellis's stomach and chest.

"You did so well," Wayne said softly.

Little by little Ellis came back to reality. He'd just had a mind-blowing, earth-shattering orgasm, and the man who'd caused it was now toweling him off and looking at him as though he were the most important thing in the world. When he was done, he carefully tucked Ellis's spent dick into his briefs.

"I should take care of you," Ellis murmured languidly as sleep began to catch up with him.

"No, you should go back to bed now. This was about you. *For* you. You did exactly what I asked you to, and I couldn't be prouder of you." Wayne leaned forward and pressed a kiss to Ellis's lips. "Go on now, back to bed."

Ellis got up, his limbs heavy. He turned toward Wayne, who watched him intently.

"Wayne?"

"Hm?"

"Thank you."

"Anytime… boy."

Ellis had always considered the word derogatory, used to demean people. Even when Wayne used it, Ellis figured he was at the very least trying to tease. But now he could hear the affection in Wayne's tone, and he realized the truth. It wasn't meant to bring him down at all. Instead it built him up. It let him know he could handle anything. And if he couldn't, there was someone who would always have his back.

He turned back to Wayne and closed the three strides that separated them. He leaned down and kissed Wayne on the lips. When Wayne cupped the back of his neck, Ellis opened his mouth, allowing Wayne inside. Wayne's soft murmur of approval only served to heighten the sensation, and Ellis exulted in the experience, lightheaded with the intensity of the brief but overwhelming kiss.

They parted, and Wayne smiled. "Good night, Ellis."

"Good night, Sir." He stood up and walked into his bedroom, his heart light for the first time since he'd arrived there.

CHAPTER SIXTEEN

BREAKFAST AT the local café was surprisingly intimate. Even without having Wayne seated next to him, Ellis was always aware of his presence. Whatever nerves he'd had dissipated under the weight of Wayne's gaze until he smiled, and then the soft wings of butterflies tickled his stomach. He'd never realized what it felt like to love someone and have that love returned.

Of course that didn't stop his nagging doubts from surfacing.

He never said he loved me. This is just like my parents. They were supposed to love me, but they only wanted me for what they could get. Who's to say Wayne's not the same? Maybe I just scratch an itch for him, and once that's done and gone, I will be too.

Ellis didn't want to believe his negative inner voice. *Wayne's not like that.* He had never once been anything less than what he appeared. Strong. Confident. And yes, a bit—*okay, more than a bit*—controlling. But that was what Ellis liked best about him. Wayne *exuded* control of his situation and his surroundings. Even before Ellis knew Wayne was a Dom, that fact was apparent to anyone if they only opened their eyes.

"What's that grin for?" Wayne asked around a mouthful of scrambled eggs.

"Oh, nothing, really. Just thinking."

"I'm fairly certain we've talked about you and that bad habit of yours," he said and took a sip of juice. "Eat your breakfast."

Ellis glanced down at his plate. Two scrambled eggs, a rasher of bacon, a sausage—*one sausage!*—and a bowl of fresh fruit. Before when they'd gone out to breakfast, this would have been more of a snack. Ellis would have had at least four eggs, six rashers of bacon, and a mound of hash browns, black pudding, and at least three sausages, not to mention mushrooms, baked beans, and toast. As soon as they sat down that morning, however, Wayne ordered for both of them. Ellis's initial indignant reaction soon passed. Although he really wanted to be annoyed, Ellis liked the fact Wayne made the decision.

Not that he'd tell him that, of course.

"When we've finished, I'll pay the bill. We're going to go back to the flat, and once we get there, you'll go to your room and strip off your clothes. Then you'll go into the living room and kneel by my chair with your head bowed while I get things together. You're not to speak unless I ask you a direct question."

A small shiver rippled through Ellis at Wayne's tone. Every time he heard it, the timbre buried itself in Ellis's mind, becoming more and more a part of him. *Perhaps that's why ultimately the decision to submit to Wayne was easy once I stopped fighting it.* Wayne was already deeply embedded within him.

"Yes, Sir," Ellis replied. What surprised him was even saying those two simple words helped him find peace within himself. When he began eating faster, his belly tightening with anticipation of what was to come, Wayne simply regarded him in silence, his eyebrows raised.

Ellis got the message, as clear as if Wayne had said the words out loud: *Slow down, boy.* He chewed his food slowly, savoring each mouthful, and Wayne's flash of a smile made him feel fantastic.

The moment they returned home, Ellis did as Wayne had instructed. At first he felt self-conscious about his nudity until he reminded himself it was what Wayne wanted, and somehow that made it okay. He got to the chair and knelt. Now *that* was a bitch. Men his size were simply not meant to be on their knees. Then he shivered at the thought of being on his knees for Wayne, and what Wayne might have him do while he was down there.

Will he want me to...? His shivers multiplied. *What will it be like to suck him? Will I like the taste? Will I get sick? Oh God. Don't let me get sick.*

"Ellis!" Wayne snapped.

Ellis opened his mouth but closed it again. *No speaking unless asked a question, remember?* A moment later Wayne was by his side. He put a hand on Ellis's head, running his fingers over Ellis's almost stubble.

"You were thinking again. I could hear it all the way in the other room."

"You can't hear thinking," Ellis grumbled, then covered his mouth. "You did that on purpose."

"Maybe I did," Wayne teased. "It still doesn't change the fact you've only been in here ten minutes, and already you've broken one of the rules I gave you for this morning."

"That's not fair," Ellis complained.

Wayne sat and continued to slide his fingers across Ellis's scalp. Ellis leaned in to the gentle touch. Damn, it felt so, *so* good.

"Do you realize you're purring?" Wayne whispered. "I admit I never thought you'd like being touched so much. Tell me what's on your mind. You have my permission to speak."

"If someone had told me a month ago that I would be on my knees in front of anyone, I would probably have punched them. But now? It's like… I don't know how to describe it."

"Like you've found your place?" Wayne suggested. "Maybe like something you'd always known was missing has now been slotted into place?"

"Yes," Ellis whispered. "That's it exactly."

His heart soared to know that Wayne understood, because Ellis wouldn't have been able to find the words and have them make sense. Each second he spent with Wayne, Ellis felt stronger, more in control.

"Okay, it's time to talk," Wayne announced.

Ellis sat back on his haunches, his knees beginning to ache a little. He raised his chin to gaze at Wayne, who smiled and nodded before producing a thick sheaf of paper. He set it on the small round table by the chair. Wayne leaned forward, his hands clasped together between his spread knees, and began to talk.

"BDSM means different things to different people. For some it's about pain; for others it's a lifestyle that they choose to follow twenty-four hours a day. For people like me, it's about guiding their submissive. Helping him become someone we can both be proud of. That's what I want with you, Ellis. Since we both have jobs, we obviously can't live the lifestyle all day, every day, but when we're within these walls, your goal is to meet all my needs, and mine is to fulfill all yours. Does that make sense so far?"

"Yes," Ellis said, his throat tight. *My life is about to change.* The thought made him dizzy.

"This contract covers a lot of information, not all of it relevant to our situation, but still something that needs to be gone over. We need to agree on our roles because knowing our places is very important."

"What about sex?" Ellis blurted. Ever since the thought of that blow job occurred to him, the prospect of having sex sent tremors coursing through him.

"Sex is covered too. Many, many different types of sex. Again, there will be some that we will probably not even contemplate after today, but still should be discussed. This will take us most of the afternoon, as I want to be sure you have all the information you need to make an informed decision when it comes time for us to sign." He locked eyes with Ellis. "I don't want you to feel pressured to do this. Signing this contract will not affect my commitment to you. Do you have any questions?"

"Yes. Can I get up? My knees are starting to ache."

Wayne laughed and rubbed the back of Ellis's neck. "Yes, you may get up. Learning to kneel takes time."

Ellis stood up, rubbed his knees, then sat on the couch next to Wayne's chair. Wayne handed him the stack of pages, and he couldn't help the ripple of excitement deep in his belly.

"Because I want to make sure of all your answers, we're going to go through these one at a time until both of us are certain that signing the contract is in both of our best interests. Understood?"

Ellis's breathing quickened. "Yes, Sir."

"Then let's begin."

WAYNE WATCHED as Ellis pored over the information, stopping on occasion to ask a question. He was amused by certain parts of the contract—role-play, feathers, and the like—and horrified by other parts—"People actually do that?"—but he continued to read and absorb what he'd read.

They both had several cups of tea while Ellis read. Wayne gnawed on his cheek because he still feared everything could go tits-up and Ellis could walk away. Not that he could even *entertain* such a thought. If that happened Wayne wasn't sure what he could do. Being a Dom was part of who he was, and no matter how badly he wanted Ellis, he couldn't simply turn that part off.

"I'm finished," Ellis announced.

"Let me see, please."

Ellis handed the papers to Wayne, who went through them page by page. Many of the items he refused came as no surprise. The look of utter distaste on his boy's face when they talked about bathroom play made it perfectly obvious that would definitely be a hard *no*. A few of the things he marked as soft limits, however, came as a complete surprise. Canes, whips, floggers—all of them were noted as *maybe*. And the parts that were definite *yes*es thrilled Wayne to no end. Ellis was agreeing to belong to him. To do as Wayne said while they were at home, to allow Wayne to help him wherever they were. He was willing to allow Wayne to make decisions for him.

Wayne had to force himself to breathe evenly. He always hoped— *God*, how he'd hoped—but he'd never really believed it could happen. It felt like his birthday, Christmas, and New Year all rolled into one.

"Are you absolutely certain about these?" Wayne asked once more. He wasn't really waiting for the bubble to burst, but he couldn't shake off that *this is too good to be true* feeling.

"Yes. Why? Aren't you?"

"Yes, I'm very happy with what you've marked down. I'm just surprised by the canes and things you noted as soft limits."

Ellis blushed. "After the spanking you gave me, I realized how good it felt. I figured I might be willing to try something a little more… intense."

Joy surged through him. "You don't know how happy I am to hear that. I'm actually quite adept with those instruments, and I look forward to pushing your limits."

"Do we sign now?"

Ellis's apparent eagerness made him want to laugh out loud. *He wants this. He* really *wants this.*

Wayne pulled a pen from his pocket and handed it to Ellis, who took a deep breath, then wrote his name. Everything Wayne had dreamed of was about to come true. Ellis handed the papers back to Wayne, who signed them as well.

Ellis now belonged to him, and it was time to celebrate.

And I know just how.

"Stand up," Wayne ordered.

Ellis complied right away, presenting himself before Wayne. His cock had thickened and now hung half-hard against his thigh.

"Undress me, please."

Ellis swallowed hard, then reached out with trembling hands to pull Wayne's shirt off. His hands fumbled with the belt, but as soon as he had it open, he slid Wayne's pants down to his shoes. He knelt down to try to get the shoes to come off, but wasn't having much luck with them.

"That's all right. Leave them for now. While you're down there, I want you to blow me. Do you understand?" His heart pounded as he said the words, his dick already past half-mast and still filling.

There was a second or two of hesitation before Ellis replied, his voice cracking slightly. "Yes, Sir." He shifted closer to Wayne until his face was directly in front of Wayne's bobbing cock. Ellis's breath warmed the head, and Wayne couldn't repress the shudder that slid down his spine. Ellis stared at the thick shaft, the skin stretched taut and shiny, the slit wet with precome.

"You don't have to do this," Wayne reminded him. He tried to imagine how he would feel in Ellis's position, up close and personal with his first cock. *What is going on in his head right now?*

Ellis said nothing but reached out a shaky hand and took Wayne's shaft in it. His fingers were cool.

"Answer me, Ellis. I need you to tell me this is what you want."

Ellis gaze flickered up, his eyes large, his pupils so big and black. His breathing was more rapid. "This… this is what I want," Ellis said, the slightest tremor in his voice.

He leaned forward and probed the tip of Wayne's throbbing erection with his tongue. He licked his lips as if trying to decide if he could do this, and Wayne's heart skipped a beat. Slowly Ellis opened his mouth wide and plunged it over Wayne's cock.

"Careful of your teeth," Wayne instructed, doing his best not to groan with the sheer pleasure of finally having his boy's mouth on him. "Curl your lips over them."

Ellis slowed down, doing as Wayne told him. It wasn't the best blow job Wayne had ever received, but Ellis showed a lot of enthusiasm for someone who'd never tasted a dick before.

"Good, that's so good," Wayne praised him.

The soft, happy little moan that followed sent Wayne's heart soaring.

Wayne cupped his hand over the back of Ellis's head, gently thrusting into the hot mouth. He kept his strokes measured, not wanting to choke him. Fuck. The feeling was incredible, and he knew that at this rate, it wouldn't be long before he would be shooting down Ellis's throat.

Then do it. Don't pull out. Feed him your load. Wayne's heartbeat raced and he tightened his grip on Ellis's head, stroking his fingers over the stubble.

"I'm going to come in your mouth and you're going to please me by swallowing it." There was no mistaking the shivers that coursed through Ellis's body. Wayne caressed his head, reaching lower to rest his hands on Ellis's shoulders. "Fuck, you're making me feel so damned good right now."

Ellis sucked harder, speeding up, and Wayne couldn't hold back any longer. He groaned and shot several jets straight down Ellis's throat, shuddering with the force of his orgasm. He was surprised when Ellis didn't flinch at all but kept suckling on the head as if he wanted every last drop. When the sensations became overwhelming, Wayne pulled back with a loud pop. Ellis stayed on his knees, a hesitant smile on his face.

"Did I do okay?" There was a note of anxiety in his voice.

Okay? That definitely wasn't the word Wayne would use. He'd been with many submissives before, all of them eager to please for the night. But Ellis? He'd shown an earnestness Wayne hadn't seen before, like he'd finally understood his place as Wayne's boy.

A boy who needed affirmation right then. Wayne stroked Ellis's cheek and cupped his chin, gazing into his eyes. "I can definitely say I can't wait to do that again."

Ellis's smile widened and his cheeks pinked. Wayne held out a hand to help him up, and when he stood, he pushed him back onto the couch. Ellis's cock stood rigid, thick and blunt like the man himself.

"You pleased me more than you know," Wayne said. His voice was husky, thick with desire for Ellis. He leaned over and licked at the drop of precome that beaded at the tip, grinning to himself when Ellis shivered. "You've never had a guy do this to you?"

Ellis's eyes were wide when he shook his head. "*No one* has ever done this to me."

"Good." The idea of being the first man to touch Ellis thrilled Wayne to no end. He wanted to introduce him to so many firsts. To be his guide on the journey they were taking. And now that they'd started, he hoped to hell they'd continue. The possibility Ellis might leave left Wayne feeling distraught. In the few weeks he'd been here, it already seemed he'd slotted himself perfectly into Wayne's life.

"Please," Ellis whispered.

"Please what?" Wayne teased. "Tell me what you want, boy."

Ellis narrowed his gaze, but he bit the corner of his lip. "Would you... suck me?" His belly quivered and his chest rose and fell rapidly.

Oh hell yes. Wayne had been dying to do just that. More than anything else right then, he craved his first taste of Ellis.

"Hold on to something," Wayne told him. "You're going to need it." And then in one swift motion, he took Ellis to the root, reaching out to stroke his furry balls.

"Oh my *God*," Ellis cried out, scrabbling his hands to clutch at the seat cushions, his belly becoming taut, his thighs trembling.

Wayne proceeded to reduce him to nonsensical babbling, going down on him again and again, deep-throating him each time. He saw Ellis digging his fingers into the upholstery, the muscles in his arms straining. He'd taken him to the very edge, and now it was time to force him over.

Wayne stroked Ellis's balls, tracing the fuzzy sac with his fingers until he slid them along Ellis's crack, rubbing over the hot, tightly puckered skin.

Ellis's shudders intensified.

Wayne didn't breach his hole. He didn't think Ellis was ready for that yet. *Soon, though.* He rubbed a single finger over the pucker again, giving it a light tap, and Ellis lurched up, arching his body, moaning as he spilled into Wayne's mouth.

Wayne closed his eyes and drank his boy down, every last drop of him, Ellis's dick still throbbing in his mouth. When his tremors subsided, Ellis flopped back onto the couch, panting heavily.

"I never knew," he muttered.

Wayne didn't have to ask what he meant. The blissed-out expression on his face told the whole story. "Come along, boy," Wayne said, holding out his hand.

Ellis didn't speak but merely took the offered hand. He rose to his feet and allowed Wayne to lead him to the bedroom—Wayne's bedroom. "This is where you'll be sleeping from now on. I want you with me, Ellis."

"You… do?" Ellis stared at him.

"Why should that be a surprise? I've been telling you how much I wanted you to belong to me, and now that you do, I've got no intention of letting you out of my sight."

Ellis smiled. "I like the sound of that."

"Now I think we may need to take a little nap. I think you sucked the energy right out of me."

Ellis was still laughing when Wayne pushed him down onto the bed.

Wayne doubted life could get any better.

As ELLIS lay sleeping, his arm draped over his chest, head back, mouth open, Wayne watched him. The constant furrow of his brow had smoothed out. The frown he'd seen on his boy's face so often had vanished, to be replaced by a slight smile. He snored softly, and to Wayne it sounded better than any Beatles song he'd ever heard because it came from the man who held his heart.

Ellis had let go today. He'd freed himself, finally, of the doubts and worries that he couldn't live as a gay man. He'd done what Wayne asked of him, not because it was demanded, but because he wanted to. And when he finished, he smiled sweetly. He'd been boneless, sated in a way he'd never experienced. No one had ever done for him what Wayne did. And if he had his say, no one ever would.

Tomorrow they'd have to return to the real world. One where people did bad things and it was their jobs to stop them. Where reality wasn't morning blow jobs, evening hot cocoa, and lazing in bed. Wayne hated the idea they'd have to face the world, because now that he had Ellis in his life, he realized exactly how much he had to lose.

And the thought frightened him to the depths of his being.

CHAPTER SEVENTEEN

THE ALARM beeped incessantly, heralding the arrival of Monday morning and the start of another work week. Wayne tried to reach over to switch it off, but realized he was pinned to the bed. Ellis was snuggled up against him, an arm across Wayne's chest.

Wayne let out a heavy sigh. "While I really want to say the hell with work, we need to get up. Wouldn't do to have you arriving late your first day after suspension."

"I don't want to get up. My butt hurts," Ellis complained.

Wayne chuckled. "I don't know what you're complaining about. It's not as if I gave you a load of strokes. And it *was* only your maintenance spanking."

Ellis huffed. "I distinctly remember someone looking a hell of a lot like you adding a few more and saying—and I quote—'Because I feel like it.'"

Wayne snickered. "Don't give me that. You loved every minute of it. If I had known spankings were such an incentive for you, I might have tried them when we were at work." What surprised him was how quickly Ellis had found his subspace, which was wonderful to see. Everything about him seemed to be wrapped in a bubble of tranquility. Ellis had smiled at him serenely and then seemed to let go of everything else.

Ellis quieted and turned over.

"What's wrong?" Wayne asked, putting a hand on Ellis's arm.

"We have to go back to work today. This changes things, doesn't it?"

"Every day changes something. What do you mean exactly?" Wayne asked, although he already knew the answer. He wasn't that happy to be going to work either. He wanted to be alone with Ellis. Work meant sharing him, being on view all the time, with no chance for them to be as close as Wayne wanted.

Our weekends are going to be so precious.

When he was a member of Whispers, he hadn't frequented the club during the week, but now? Wayne was seriously contemplating a couple of midweek visits.

Of course he'd never had anyone to share this part of his life before, and that was a heady realization. *We have all of that stretched out before us.*

He tried not to think about the job with its inherent dangers.

"What will you expect from me while we're at work? Do I have to call you Sir? What about the other guys? Do we tell them?" It was obvious from Ellis's questions that he'd been thinking a lot about this.

Wayne sat up and patted the edge of the bed. "Come here."

Ellis slid across and sat next to Wayne, who wrapped an arm around his shoulder. When Ellis put his head on Wayne's shoulder, he squeezed tighter.

"Did you ever tell any of the guys you're gay?"

"Oh hell no!" Ellis snapped. He drew back sharply, his face twisted in anger. "And don't you tell them either."

"Hey, I wasn't going to. That's *your* story to tell, not mine. Outing you is definitely not on the agenda."

Ellis turned back toward Wayne, his eyes downcast. "I'm sorry. I should have known you wouldn't do that. It's just… I don't want them to know."

Ellis's agitation worried him. "Okay, can you tell me why? They're your friends, and I'm certain they'd understand."

Ellis huffed. "Why would I tell them I'm gay when I'm not even used to the idea myself, if I'm honest? For so many years, I thought I couldn't have what I wanted, and now that I do, I don't really want to share it. Does that make sense?"

"It does. But when you're happy, don't you want others to know? Isn't your happiness multiplied by theirs?"

Ellis cocked his head. "You mean you don't care if they know about us?"

Wayne took Ellis's hand in his, massaging the back of it. "Not really, no. I can't be certain what Lewis would say about it, but that's a bridge to cross if we ever come to it." He lifted his hand to Ellis's neck and pulled him down until his head rested on Wayne's shoulder. "I've known that I'm gay since I was nine or ten. I've had years to get used to it, so I know how worried you are right now. Like I said, it's your story to tell. No one else has to know."

"But what about us?" Ellis murmured.

"There will always be us. I told you I'm not letting you go." He grinned. "Plus I have your signature on a very legal contract." Ellis laughed, and Wayne was glad to hear it. He rubbed his thumb over the back of Ellis's hand once more. "While we're at work, you can continue to call me Wayne. That's perfectly fine. I won't treat you any differently than I do the rest of the crew, and I expect the same from you."

"But we're living together," Ellis reminded him.

"Not officially. You still have your old apartment. I'd really prefer it if you gave that up and consider this your—*our*—home."

"You really want me to live here, don't you?"

"I do," Wayne answered honestly. "Having you here has made this a home. A place I look forward to coming back to every day because I know you're going to be here. But if you're dead set about staying in your place, fine. I can move there, if you want."

"Seriously?"

"Yes. Or if you'd rather, we could find a new place that will be all our own."

"You mean we could get a house?" Ellis asked, his voice tinged with excitement.

Wayne grinned. "With a white-picket fence and a dog named Muffy, if that's what you want."

"I'd like a house," he admitted. "No Muffy, though. But one with a small garden would be really nice. I've always liked the idea of inviting friends over for a barbecue or just sitting out in the evening and shooting the breeze. But I'm not sure we can have that."

Wayne was captivated by the idea. "Why couldn't we? It sounds like a great dream to me."

"Like I want them to see me kneeling by your chair," Ellis snarked.

Wayne sighed. "Look, I'm going to say this as plainly as I can. I don't want a slave. I want you. When we have guests over, I won't make you do anything you're uncomfortable with or that you'd be unwilling to do. I would like you to consider amending that if we have people from the club over, though. They would have their subs with them, and it would mean a lot to me to show you off."

Ellis bit his lip and tilted his head. "I'm not sure I'm at the point yet where I'm comfortable having others see me on my knees, but how about if I say I'm willing to work on it?"

Wayne stood and kissed Ellis on the temple. "That's all I can ever ask. Now do you want to shower first or start breakfast?"

"You go ahead and shower. I'll get breakfast started." Ellis got off the bed and strode toward the door, his naked arse still a bright red.

"Your cheeks are blushing," Wayne said with a laugh.

Ellis groaned and tried to cover himself.

"Stop," Wayne ordered.

Immediately Ellis stilled. Wayne walked over to him and ran a hand over the crimson flesh, delighting in Ellis's shivers.

"Don't hide from me, Ellis. You're mine, and I understand that you probably haven't realized the scope of that statement yet, but you will. Tonight when we come home, it'll be time to start your training."

"Training?" Ellis squeaked, an odd sound from a man of his stature.

Wayne nodded. "Being my submissive isn't just calling me Sir and kneeling by my feet." He waggled his brows. "And you're about to start a master class in it."

He chuckled when Ellis hustled out the door, a look of uncertainty on his face.

ELLIS COULDN'T believe he'd only been gone a week. It felt like months since he'd seen any of his team. They milled around him when he walked in, rubbing his head, patting his back, and telling him how much they'd missed his sorry ass. He winced when more than one person swatted him on top of Wayne's *maintenance* from the night before.

"All right, you lot, listen up. Today we're going to be heading back to the town," Lewis announced.

A chorus of groans went up.

"Shut it, all of you. We've got our Mr. Mann back with us, and he hasn't run a single simulation in the last week. We have to make up for lost time. So I want you in your gear in fifteen minutes, then ready to go. Move it!"

They bustled for the door, but Lewis shouted Ellis's name. "Not you, Ellis."

Ellis stifled a groan. *What now?* He waited for Lewis to a chorus of guys calling, "Ooooh, he's in trouble again!" It was good to be back.

Lewis handed him a stack of notes. "Your parents have been trying to reach you for days, apparently. They've been calling the Met switchboard, who passed these on. *Not* something they are particularly happy about, and the powers that be have been giving me grief over it. So call your parents and let them know that, in the future, they'll need to contact you through a different channel."

"Yes. Okay. I'm sorry." His heart sank.

"Nothing to be sorry for, Ellis. I just don't want it to become a habit." Lewis took a few steps, then turned back. "By the way, Ellis? It's good to have you back. I really wish I hadn't needed to do it. And I'm glad we got rid of Roberts, because no one on my squad will ever talk like that about another team member, not while I'm in charge."

Lewis left the room, shouting to the men that they had best hurry up. Ellis thumbed through the messages. All vaguely innocuous, but he could read the subtext. They were pissed they couldn't get in touch with him, that he hadn't returned their calls, and about how he'd treated Barb. His heart started hammering. He needed Wayne.

As if by some unspoken wish, Wayne was by his side, an arm around his shoulder.

"Are you okay?" he asked softly.

"They're angry. My father is insisting I call them." Ellis turned his gaze away from Wayne.

"Hey, look at me." Wayne cupped his cheek in his hand.

Ellis turned to face Wayne. "I don't know what to do," he said, his voice small.

"It's time to make a decision. You've been doing your best to be what they wanted since you were a young boy, but you're not him anymore. You've grown up, and now you need to figure out what you want."

What he wanted? That was easy. He wanted Wayne with an intensity he'd never experienced before. He *loved* Wayne. But to go against his parents—his family—was something he'd been brought up to believe was the ultimate crime. He turned to Wayne, his eyes burning.

Fuck it all, man. Stop crying.

Wayne brushed his thumb across Ellis's cheek. "You know there's nothing wrong with crying, right? Sometimes emotions just get to be too big to hold on to, and we need to let them out. There isn't anything wrong with that."

Before Ellis could answer, the door burst open and the team swarmed into the room, gear ready.

"Oy! Come on you—holy shit!" Phillips shouted.

Ellis twisted away from Wayne as though he'd been burned. "It... it's not what it looks like," he stammered.

"Hey, guys! Come in here."

The entire team of twelve men pushed into the room, gathering around Phillips, and Ellis started to inch toward the exit. This had all gone horribly wrong. He hadn't wanted anyone to know, and now that had all gone up in flames.

"Back off, Phillips," Wayne growled, stepping in front of Ellis.

Phillips ignored him. "So I came in here, and I found them together. Wayne was wiping away something from Ellis's face."

Fuck. Fuck. Just... fuck my life.

"What of it?" Wayne demanded. "I've helped each and every one of you to get something from your eye at some point."

"Wayne.... Don't." Ellis didn't want Wayne to take the heat for this. It wasn't fair to him. He faced Phillips, his face hot. "If you have something to say, it should be to me." He did his best to keep his voice steady.

"Oh, we have something to say all right," Phillips growled. "It's *about fucking time* you told us."

Ellis looked at Wayne, who shrugged. Ellis faced Phillips. "What the hell are you talking about?"

Phillips let out a patient sigh. "We've always known you two were together. All we had to do was look at you mooning over one another. It was downright sickening, you guys being all lovey-dovey. None of us ever get looked at like that."

"No," Ellis said. "We aren't...." He clammed up. *Man the fuck up for once. Do Wayne proud.* Ellis took hold of his courage. "Me and Wayne.... It's... new." His hands were trembling until Wayne reached over and took one in his.

"New? Hey, did someone have this year in the pool?"

What the fuck? Ellis couldn't believe he'd heard that right.

"Pool?" Wayne demanded.

"Yeah. Most of us figured the two of you were already together. Why do you think we refer to Ellis as 'the little woman'? Someone said you weren't, and they bet that this year would be the one. Who was it?"

"Me!" Lewis shouted gleefully. "Pay up!"

The guys grumbled as they reached into their pockets and began handing him five pounds each.

"Wait. So you guys don't care?" Ellis asked, completely floored by the exchange.

"Nah, mate. Why would we?" Lewis said, flipping through the bills. "You're both our friends. We couldn't care less what you two get up to as long as you're both happy."

Ellis breathed out a long sigh of relief.

Lewis tucked his winnings neatly into his wallet. "Let's go, people. We have to go take down a bunch of gun-happy terrorists so the people of London can sleep soundly in their beds at night."

"Yeah, and it's Marchant's team playing the bad guys," Phelps added.

Whoops and hollers echoed around the room. Cassidy grinned. "All right! Let's show them what we're made of."

As they marched out, several of the men congratulated Ellis and Wayne on their relationship, and for the first time in his life, Ellis breathed a little easier. He'd always been so terrified of people finding out about him. He wasn't under any illusion everyone would be as accepting as their mates—Roberts proved that—but he was satisfied the rest of the team wanted him and Wayne happy.

It went a long way to unclenching the knot that had formed in his heart years ago.

WAYNE WAS delighted to see Ellis back at work and even happier things hadn't gone as badly as he'd feared. He should have known their friends would have their backs. *After all these years, a family doesn't just turn away from you.*

He watched from his position as Ellis scampered up the side of one of the buildings. For such a big man, Ellis possessed an unexpected grace. It was partly what attracted Wayne in the first place. His boy did him proud in everything he attempted. Even when he didn't succeed on the first try—like when the simulation had them attempting to move the crowd out of an area under terrorist attack, and Ellis shepherded them down the wrong street—Ellis would come to Wayne, who would give him a pep talk, and the next time he would have no problems at all.

Today Ellis seemed to be on fire. He tore up the track on their run, beating his personal best time by six seconds. He climbed faster than the others, helping the ones who needed it. Wayne couldn't have been prouder of him. When they broke for a quick bite, he asked Ellis what was going on, and the answer he got shocked him.

"I'm going to talk to my parents," he whispered. "I can't keep avoiding them, because that will never get anything settled. But if you wouldn't mind, could you be there with me?"

Wayne glanced around and saw no one was looking, so he gave Ellis a quick peck on the lips. "I wouldn't be anywhere but by your side."

And that seemed to spur Ellis to work even harder.

Even if the team didn't care Ellis was gay, they still teased him a little more now. At first Ellis bristled. Wayne thought at one point he was going to come to blows when Phillips kept making kissing noises whenever the two of them were in close proximity. But when Ellis turned around, grabbed Phillips by the shoulders, and laid a big kiss on his cheek, Wayne laughed along with the rest of the team as Phillips turned scarlet.

Lewis didn't work them as hard as the previous week, and at the end of the day, he invited everyone out for a drink to spend his newly acquired fortune. Ellis asked if they could go along, and Wayne agreed to it.

After a quick shower and change of clothes at home, Ellis and Wayne drove into London to meet up with the others at their favorite pub, the Red Lion in Soho. The drinks were flowing—though Wayne insisted he and Ellis stick to mineral water—and spirits were high. As the night wore on and the men got more and more relaxed, Ellis challenged Wayne to a game of darts.

Derwent guffawed. "Are you crazy? We don't play darts in here at this time of night for a reason. This is the most dangerous dart pub in London."

Wayne nodded. "He has a point. When it's quieter, maybe." He knew what Derwent meant. The board was next to the downstairs back bar, far enough away from a table to be playable but near enough that anyone sitting there might end up skewered if a dart bounced off the board. Once the pub started filling up after five o'clock, the board was virtually useless.

Ellis flashed Wayne a wicked grin. "Does that mean you're... chicken?"

Wayne's eyes gleamed. "You're on."

Lewis snorted. "I'll go see if they have a box of Band-Aids behind the bar."

It was like old times. Ellis was a dart master and easily thrashed Wayne, then Phillips, and finally Derwent, who had stood on the side doing his best to distract Ellis. There was only one fatality—Derwent's leather jacket, which ended up with a dart to the shoulder. Wayne offered to stick a Band-Aid over it, and everyone laughed. At the end of the night, they got into Wayne's car and headed home.

Wayne closed the door to his flat behind them and locked it.

Ellis was still wearing that happy smile. "God, that was so much fun." He kicked off his shoes and left them standing neatly on the shoe rack in the hallway.

Wayne could see him almost glow. *This* Ellis was the one none of them had seen for over a year. The one who didn't care what the world thought of him.

"It was," Wayne agreed. "But you missed the start of your classes for tonight."

There was a moment's pause while his words sank in. Then Ellis sidled up next to him and kissed Wayne on the neck. "Maybe the teacher needs to punish me for being late," he teased.

The ease with which Ellis performed the intimate gesture made Wayne's heart soar.

"I think that is a great idea. It just so happens, I'd like to try and push one of your soft limits tonight."

Ellis gulped. "Already?"

"No time like the present, boy. Go into the bedroom and strip off your clothes. I'll be along shortly."

No argument. Ellis smiled and turned toward the bedroom, wiggling his bottom. Wayne chuckled, wondering how he was going to feel after their session ended.

"I can't wait," Wayne whispered to the empty room. Then he went to the toy chest and picked up his implement of choice, ready to get Ellis started on learning what it meant to belong to Wayne Dwyer.

CHAPTER EIGHTEEN

"WAYNE WON'T hurt you," Ellis told himself repeatedly, the words becoming a mantra in his head.

But you like a little pain. You loved it when he spanked your arse.

And Ellis had. Oh *God* yes. The feeling of Wayne's hand on him, smacking his cheeks in different places, the delicious sting as he brought the hand down over and over. How Ellis felt it all the way through his balls to his dick when Wayne aimed his blows upward. How quickly they both fell into a rhythm—Wayne's downward thrusts, Ellis lifting his hips off the bed, wanting more than anything for Wayne to land the next swat a little harder.

He had to admit he'd wondered what it would be like if Wayne used something instead of his hand. Something more… solid. He never thought he could enjoy being spanked, but *God*, it was amazing. No wonder Alex looked so blissed-out at the club's opening night. Ellis's first encounter with Wayne's hand wasn't an exercise in pain, but sensual pleasure.

He imagined himself in Alex's place with Wayne holding him down, swatting him over and over while the audience watched. There was no denying the thought made Ellis uncomfortable, but that didn't stop his cock from lengthening until he was rubbing his rigid shaft against the bed. Fuck, the friction was delicious. He could almost… almost….

"And what do you think you're doing?" Wayne's tone was laced with amusement.

Ellis twisted to look over his shoulder. "Oh. Wayne, I—" *Holy fuck.* His heartbeat raced.

Wayne glowered at him.

"I meant Sir, honest." His brain apparently had difficulty finding the words. Not that Ellis could blame it given the way Wayne looked. *Oh fuck.*

"Mm-hmm." Wayne folded his arms across that gorgeous chest. "So what were you up to when I walked in?"

Ellis tried to remember, but his brain was still in meltdown. Wayne had put on a pair of leather pants that were so tight Ellis could see the outline of his thick cock pointing down the right leg. He stood shirtless, his chest sprinkled with dark hair and barely covered by a crisscrossed leather harness.

He looked absolutely stunning.

Ellis licked his lips.

Wayne chuckled. "Do you like what you see?"

Finally Ellis found his voice. "Bloody hell, yes. I thought you looked good in a uniform, but *this*? Fuck."

"You've got a smart mouth on you, boy. I think after we have our lesson, I may have to put it to good use."

Ellis's mouth watered at the thought of Wayne's cock, the taste of his come. He groaned.

Wayne arched his eyebrows. "Problem?"

Ellis's snort escaped before he had a chance to stop it. "You're standing in front of me looking like a gift I desperately want to unwrap. Your dick is straining against those things you laughably call pants, and you ask if there's a problem?"

Wayne laughed and stepped closer to the bed. "Then why don't you come over here, get on your knees, and show me how much you want what I've got for you?" He slid his hands down his body until they framed his cock, pulling the leather even more tightly over it.

Like Ellis could refuse *that*. "Yes, Sir."

He slid off the bed, doing his best to keep his eagerness in check. He crawled over to where Wayne stood, glanced up at him, and then reached out a hand, sliding it over the soft, smooth leather. The hard cock jerked when Ellis rubbed it, and Wayne let out a sigh of lust.

"This wasn't what I had in mind."

Ellis stared up at him, still rubbing over Wayne's thick dick. "You make it sound like this is my fault."

"But it *is* your fault," Wayne growled. "I came in here knowing exactly what I wanted to do, and then you derail it all with those hungry eyes."

The laughter that had bubbled up through him died in his throat when he caught sight of what Wayne had laid on top of the ottoman at the foot of his bed. Slowly Ellis withdrew his hand and knelt up, his gaze locked on the two—*two?*—floggers, their long handles covered in leather, the thin, slender strips trailing over the edge of the ottoman.

"Oh."

Wayne's hand was on his shoulder, gently stroking him. "I did say we were going to push some limits, remember?"

Ellis gave a shaky laugh. "So one minute all I can think about is getting my lips around your thick cock, and the next?" He glanced at the floggers. "I want to know—no, I *need* to know—how they will feel."

"Nothing wrong with a little curiosity," Wayne murmured, his fingers light on Ellis's neck, sending shivers down his spine. "So what say we satisfy that curiosity?" He reached down and rubbed over his own erection. "This isn't going anywhere. In fact, by the time we're through, it might be even harder."

Before Ellis could come back with a witty retort, Wayne had helped him to his feet.

"Lean against the wall beside the bed, your hands flat on it, feet apart."

His breathing suddenly rapid, Ellis did as instructed. He bowed his head and stared at the floor, his heart pounding. His cock jutted out, heavy and full, a solid arrow of flesh pointing toward the wall. He let out a gasp when Wayne's body came into contact with his back, his chest hot, Wayne stroking him with his hands, caressing him. Ellis could feel that thick hardness pressing into his crack, and he swallowed.

"What is your safeword?" Wayne whispered into his ear, his warm breath tickling it.

"Red."

"Just so you know? This is not meant to hurt you, not this time. All I'm going to do is warm you up a little. Give you a taste of how sensual and erotic it can be."

Ellis's mouth dried up, his throat tight.

Wayne withdrew from him, and Ellis shuddered in anticipation. "Ready, boy?"

Ellis took a deep breath and found enough saliva to moisten his lips. "Ready, Sir."

The music took him by surprise. It was a quiet harmony of pipes and voices, soft and flowing. "What... what is that?" Whatever it was, it was an inspired choice. The music seemed to roll over his body, seep into him with its gentle cadences, bringing with it a peaceful air.

"It's by Peter Gabriel, and it's called *Passion*."

Yeah, a very inspired choice.

Ellis caught his breath when the tails of a flogger brushed down his back, no weight to them. He closed his eyes and inhaled, drawing the scent of the leather into him. Wayne trailed the flogger over his arse, pulling at one cheek before he drew the tails through Ellis's crease, the movement languid and sensual. Then it was gone.

The next thing Ellis knew, the flogger was on his shoulder, the soft leather tails draped over his chest. Wayne moved it gently so the tips tickled their way over his nipple.

It was nothing like he'd expected. It was like… the kiss of hummingbird's wings on his skin, the scent strong in his nostrils. And woven through it all was the music, its beautiful harmonies perfectly suited to the sensual touch of the leather all over his body. There was nowhere Wayne left untouched.

Ellis lost track of time, the combination of soft swooshes of the leather over his skin and the music lulling him into an almost hypnotic state.

Then the music changed, and with it, Wayne's strokes. From out of nowhere came the sound of drums, quiet but insistent, and the low chorus of voices rose with it. The tails now landed with more of a thud, not enough to cause pain, but definitely enough to make Ellis aware of them. Then he realized Wayne was working over his back with two floggers, alternating them to provide a constant barrage of sensation.

When Wayne stopped and rubbed over his skin with a gentle hand, Ellis arched into his touch.

"Are you all right?" Wayne asked, kissing between his shoulder blades.

"I'm fine," Ellis said, striving to keep his voice even. "Can… can we go on?"

"Of course." Another soft kiss and the strokes resumed, light strikes across his shoulders from both floggers, the air filled with the soft swish as they cut through it. After a minute or two, Wayne stopped to rub the skin where the tails had landed.

"Ready for something a little more vigorous? Remember, if you want me to stop, use your safeword."

"I'm ready." The next moment the leather tails connected with the fleshy part of his arse, landing with a thud. "Oh God." He felt it all the way through his body. Ellis breathed shallowly, feeling the perspiration pop out on his chest and back.

"It won't get any harder than that," Wayne promised him. Another hit, this time to his upper back. Heat spread over Ellis's skin, radiating out of him.

"Oh fuck," he gasped, arching his back as another strike landed, this time on the opposite arsecheek. He tensed for the next one and breathed more easily when Wayne resumed his sensual grazing over Ellis's skin, the tails swishing over his body, light and gentle. Wayne kept that up for several minutes, alternating between Ellis's back and his arse, thuds of leather connecting with his body and gentle, sensuous stroking.

Ellis gazed down at his own body, amazed to see the glistening string of precome suspended from his slit, swinging with each blow. There was no mistaking his body's reaction: Ellis liked it. He lost himself in the music, the pattern of strikes Wayne built up, the rhythmic strokes that sent him higher and higher....

Eventually he realized the music had stopped. Never mind that—*Wayne* had stopped. Instead of the touch of leather, he caressed him with gentle hands, then softly kissed his way down Ellis's back, and Ellis tilted his arse, wanting more, wanting to feel Wayne's mouth on his warm cheeks.

Then Wayne stood up, and Ellis wanted to groan in frustration.

"You're back," Wayne said quietly.

"I... I didn't want you to stop," Ellis whispered. It had felt... amazing.

Wayne chuckled. "Well, just because I'm done with the flogger doesn't mean we're finished for the night. How does your back and arse feel?"

"Okay. A bit warm, maybe. But it doesn't hurt."

"That's good."

Ellis giggled suddenly. "Much as I enjoyed the music, I did think of something more appropriate that you could have played."

Wayne stilled. "Oh really? And what would that be?"

Ellis snickered. "Michael Jackson's 'Beat It,' of course." There was a moment of quiet before Wayne swatted him on his arse. "Hey! Careful!"

"You deserve it for that crack." He chuckled. "Crack. Get it?" When Ellis groaned, Wayne kissed the back of Ellis's neck, and he shuddered. "Oh, you like it when I kiss you there." Wayne did it again. "Does it turn you on?"

"Y-yes," Ellis stammered. His dick was leaking copious amounts of precome, and he ached for Wayne to wrap his hand around it and bring him off.

"Turn around."

Slowly Ellis complied, his skin tight where the flogger had warmed it. Wayne had lowered his zipper to free his cock, which was still hard, thick at the base and pointing up. Wayne pumped it with a leisurely hand. With his other he reached down to where Ellis's dick was equally hard and wrapped his fingers around it. His gaze focused on Ellis, Wayne worked both their shafts, making Ellis moan quietly.

"Unless you desperately want to go to sleep right now," Wayne began, his eyes twinkling.

Ellis groaned. "You're kidding, right? No way are you leaving me to sleep in *this* state."

Wayne laughed. "Actually I have a much better idea." He squeezed Ellis's dick and worked it a little faster. "I'm willing to bet I can get you to beg me to fuck you."

Suddenly breathing seemed like a real chore.

Ellis shook his head harshly. "No. No way." He pushed aside the thrill that coursed through him at the thought of Wayne's cock pushing…. *No. No.*

"Oh, come on." Wayne slid his hand from root to tip, making Ellis want to moan even louder. "You're a betting man, right? I'll make a wager with you."

THE LOOK on Ellis's face said he was dubious at best. "What kind of wager?" Wayne could hear the note of suspicion in his voice.

Wayne released Ellis's dick and moved in closer until their bodies were touching and he could feel Ellis's cock, hard and wet, against his. Wayne leaned in, brushing his lips over Ellis's ear, making him shiver. "I'll bet you anything you want that I can get you to ask—no, *beg*—me to fuck you within fifteen minutes."

"Won't happen," Ellis said, shuddering once more when Wayne kissed his neck. "And stop that, you're fighting dirty."

Wayne chuckled. "So do we have a bet?"

Ellis pushed him away and looked him in the eye. "Okay, let me get this straight—so to speak. If you win you fuck me. If I win I get anything I want. Is that it in a nutshell?"

Wayne shrugged. "Well, anything within reason. I mean, I can't afford to buy you Buckingham Palace, but as long as it's reasonable, then yes, I'll go with that."

Ellis stilled, those brown eyes focused on Wayne. "What if I want to fuck *you*?"

Oh. Fuck. Wayne swallowed. *Talk about blindsided....*

Ellis smirked. "Oh, you're looking a little pale there, *Sir*. Maybe you're not as confident in your skills as you claim?"

He knew Ellis had him trapped by his own words. If he said no, he risked putting Ellis off. *But if I agree, I end up on the receiving end of Ellis's fat dick.* Nope. Not the way he wanted this to go. *Been there, done that, and I'll be happy not to do it again.* Then he paused. *I don't really have a choice in this, do I?*

Wayne sighed. "Okay, fine. If you win, you can claim your prize. You happy now?"

"Hell yes," Ellis said with a grin.

The words were on the tip of his tongue. *You won't be grinning when I'm through with you. Because you are going* down, *baby.*

"I want you to stand against the wall, just like you were before. Spread your arms. You can't move, so you're going to have to make sure you're balanced."

Ellis put his palms against the wall, and Wayne noticed a hitch in his breathing as he approached. "Remember, use your safeword if you need to. This is supposed to be good, but if it feels wrong, you can make it stop."

Wayne knelt down behind Ellis, swatted him twice on each cheek, then without warning, he put his hands on each firm globe and spread them.

"Oh God," Ellis groaned.

"The name's Wayne, and I haven't even started yet." He pressed his face to Ellis's crease and slowly licked over his hole, making sure to rub his scruff over there too. *Fuck, he smells good.*

"Fuck." Ellis shivered, his thighs trembling slightly.

Smiling to himself, Wayne repeated the action, only this time he pressed the tip of his tongue against Ellis's hole. He wanted to take his time, savor the moment, but hell, he *did* only have fifteen minutes. He pushed with his tongue, feeling the muscle resist him at first and then begin to loosen. Within a minute Ellis was pushing back, making it obvious he was loving it.

Wayne stroked over the hot pucker with his finger, pushing insistently until finally the tight ring gave way and he was inside.

"Oh my God," Ellis gasped. He spread his legs wider, his breathing loud and harsh.

Wayne flattened his tongue and laved the area with broad strokes before pushing in again. Ellis practically melted against the wall, which was exactly where Wayne wanted him.

He broke off from his delightful task. "Beg me to fuck you, Ellis."

"No, I won't," Ellis grunted out. Wayne would have believed him if it hadn't been for the way he thrust his arse back at the same time.

Wayne smiled and went back to work, this time using his tongue to spear his boy, pushing in as far as he could go. He could hear Ellis whimpering, and that helped him to redouble his efforts. He kept this up for a couple of minutes before taking a breather. "Are you ready to be fucked, boy?"

"Nope, I won't ask you to fuck me," Ellis replied breathlessly, shamelessly tilting his bottom for more of the same.

As the minutes ticked away, Wayne began to fear he'd overestimated his abilities. He tried every trick he'd ever learned: corkscrewing his tongue, quick jabs at the pucker, and blowing warm air over Ellis's hole.

There were plenty of groans, but although Ellis might have bent a little, he didn't break.

"Ha! Fifteen minutes," Ellis shouted triumphantly.

Well, fuck me. Then he realized that would be happening any second now.

Wayne got up, his knees aching. His hole clenched at the thought of Ellis claiming his prize. He hadn't bottomed since he was a horny teenager, and that was only the once.

"You win," he said sadly. "How do you want to do this?"

Ellis went over and lay on the bed on his back, drew his knees up to his chest, and growled out, "Fuck me."

Wayne's first thought was he was hearing things. He stared at Ellis, frowning. "But you won the bet. You don't have to do this."

Ellis gave him a patient look. "Yes, I won the bet, and now I want you to fuck me."

Something in Wayne's brain just wasn't firing. "I don't understand. You won, so you can claim your prize."

Ellis grinned. "Yes, and I want you to fuck me. I was on the brink of asking you when you first jammed your bloody magical tongue up my arse, but I wasn't about to give you the satisfaction of winning. You're already too cocky as it is." His grin faded and he gave Wayne a beseeching glance. "Wayne, please. Fuck me."

CHAPTER NINETEEN

WAYNE CRAWLED up Ellis's body, loving Ellis's soft gasp as Wayne dragged his heavy, full cock over Ellis's rigid shaft.

"That thing should be classed as a dangerous weapon," Ellis murmured.

Wayne waited until he was stretched out on top of him before responding with a gentle push of his dick. "Wait until it's inside you," he whispered. "It's going to feel good."

Ellis stared into his eyes. "Are you going to be taking it easy on me? Because I'm a big boy, Wayne." He grinned. "I can take whatever you dish out."

Wayne was so torn. He wanted to be gentle, to take care of Ellis, but the urge to let loose and fuck the come out of him was huge.

"How about we start off slowly and give you time to get used to having a cock inside you? When you're happy with that, *then* we can think about me taking you the way I want to."

Ellis's pupils grew larger. "And how is that?" His voice was husky.

Wayne leaned closer and kissed him on the lips, gently rocking his body on top of him. "I'm going to fuck you. I think the word speaks for itself, don't you?"

That catch in Ellis's breathing was delicious.

Wayne didn't give him time to respond. He closed in and kissed him, sliding his tongue deep as he swallowed Ellis's moan. Wayne stroked his neck and down over his chest, feeling Ellis's body quiver when he trailed his fingers lower to where Ellis's dick jerked into his touch. Wayne ignored it and rubbed the fur on Ellis's belly, enjoying the soft rasp of hair beneath his fingertips.

Ellis let out a low whine. "Bastard. You know damn well where I want that hand."

Wayne tut-tutted. "Is that any way to talk to your Dom? Especially one who was *thinking* about sucking your dick but is now reconsidering because of your attitude?"

Ellis laughed. "Oh, *I* get it. You're going to have fun with this, aren't you?"

Wayne was in no hurry. He wanted to savor every moment.

He kissed Ellis, loving how his boy threw himself into the kiss, his hands on Wayne's head, his shoulders, his back, always touching him. "Love how you kiss," he murmured against Ellis's lips.

"Love being kissed," Ellis fired back. He pulled back and gave Wayne a sexy grin that sent tendrils of heat spreading through him. "Of course it would feel even better if you were giving my cock the same attention."

Wayne grinned back. "Aw, am I neglecting your poor, unloved dick?" He edged down Ellis's body, moving at a leisurely pace until the head of Ellis's cock grazed his chin. Wayne met Ellis's gaze. "Have I ever mentioned that you have a beautiful dick?"

He gave Ellis no time to answer before lowering his head and taking his thick cock into his mouth.

"Oh fuck yeah," Ellis moaned, pushing up with his hips and thrusting into Wayne's mouth. Wayne concentrated on relaxing his throat, taking Ellis deep. Ellis's hands were on his head in an instant, gently but firmly keeping him there while he rocked up off the mattress, moving his hips faster, his breaths keeping time with his thrusts.

Wayne wanted to laugh for joy at Ellis's eagerness, but he had a mouth full of thick cock. When Ellis began to pant, his movements becoming less rhythmic, Wayne grabbed hold of his hips and pulled free of his dick, leaving it dripping. He traced the heavy shaft from head to root with his tongue until he reached Ellis's balls. Wayne buried his nose in the crease between Ellis's sac and his thigh, breathing in the rich male aroma.

"Why did you stop?" Ellis gasped out.

Wayne chuckled. "Because I wanted to do this." He closed his mouth around one of Ellis's fuzzy balls and sucked on it before pulling gently on the sac. Ellis's loud groan of pleasure was music to his ears. Wayne opened his mouth wide and drew both of them in, loving the way Ellis pushed out a long moan. Fuck, this was heady.

He sucked on the round orbs, reaching lower to rub over Ellis's hole once more. The saliva that had trickled down from his dick made it easy to sink a finger inside Ellis's hot channel, where his tongue had been just a few minutes ago.

"Oh God." Ellis stiffened, and Wayne reacted instantly, letting his finger lie still inside him.

"A little bigger than my tongue, right?" Wayne watched Ellis's face, waiting for a sign he could continue.

"Just a little." Ellis closed his eyes.

"Have you ever played with your hole before? You know, with a dildo or a vibrator? Even a finger?"

Ellis opened his eyes and stared at him. "No. That would have been too much like admitting that I was gay. Only gay guys do that."

"Oh, really? You think?" Wayne snickered. "Remind me to give you a guided tour of some porn sites. You'd be surprised how many straight guys love it." Gently he began to stroke his finger in and out of Ellis's tight channel. "How does that feel?"

Ellis's breathing sped up a little, but he nodded. "That... that feels good." When Wayne slowly withdrew his finger completely, he growled. "Not good. Put it back in there."

Wayne laughed and pulled open the drawer of the bedside cabinet to take out the lube. "Patience, Oh Impatient One. This will feel a whole lot better." He slicked up his finger and eased it back into Ellis's body, biting back his moan of pleasure when Ellis's hole tightened around it.

"Oh yeah, that's good." Ellis moved his hips, and Wayne responded by slowly fucking him with his finger, gradually building up speed and pushing in farther until he was knuckle deep. When Ellis was taking it easily and riding it hard, Wayne pulled free once more and went back to the drawer.

Ellis raised his head from the pillow. "Now what?"

Wayne held aloft the slim dildo he'd bought only two days before. "I thought we might begin with this."

Ellis gaped. "It's bright pink! Couldn't you have found one that was a nice *skin* color, at least? That thing is almost neon."

Wayne rolled his eyes. "Shut up, they only came in one color." He gave Ellis a sweet smile. "I think we might have a courgette in the fridge if you'd rather I start with that."

Ellis narrowed his gaze. "You are *not* fucking my arse with a vegetable." Then he gave a sigh. "Okay, bring on the bright pink thing."

Wayne squirted lube onto the jellylike dildo and then positioned himself on his knees between Ellis's spread legs. "It's not that long, and it's only an inch or so in width, so—"

"So it's nothing like your cock," Ellis finished for him, his gaze darting to where Wayne's dick still poked up toward his belly.

Wayne leaned forward, his weight on one hand, and bent low to kiss him on the mouth. "I was *going* to say so it will be good to get you ready for my dick. Because I want you to enjoy it." Another kiss, this time parting Ellis's lips with his tongue. "Can't wait to be inside you."

The mood changed just like that. Ellis's eyes darkened, his pupils growing larger. "Then get a move on and slide that into me."

Wayne pressed the head of the dildo against Ellis's tight pucker. "As you wish." Slowly he pushed, his gaze focused on the way Ellis's hole clung to the dildo, pulling it into him. "Fuck. This looks amazing."

Ellis lay still, his eyes closed. "Feels… strange. Not bad, just… weird." Then Wayne began to move it in and out of his channel, and Ellis moaned. "Oh God, that's… yeah, that's good."

Wayne got a rhythm going and then bent over to suck the head of Ellis's dick. He slid his lips down the thick shaft, and Ellis arched up off the bed, rolling his hips, his breathing shallow and harsh. He rocked between the dildo fucking him and Wayne's mouth sucking him.

Wayne loved the feel and taste of Ellis's cock, loved how Ellis pushed up with his hips to fill his mouth, how he rode the dildo, the low noises that burst from his lips every time Wayne thrust it into him.

Until it was no longer enough, and Wayne ached to be inside his boy.

Carefully he removed the dildo and placed it on the bed. "Ready for the real thing?"

"Thought you'd never ask," Ellis said, his voice rough with desire. He sat up, reached for Wayne's dick, and curled his fingers around it, squeezing it gently. "I want this inside me now."

Wayne nodded, his body buzzing with anticipation. He peered into the still-open drawer and pulled out a strip of three condoms.

Ellis stilled. "Do we need those?" He smiled. "I mean, it's not like you're going to knock me up, right?"

Internally Wayne groaned, trying not to think about the possibility of sliding bare into Ellis's hot, tight arse. That logical part of his brain, the part he always hated but had come to trust, shoved his mouth into gear.

"There are worse things than getting pregnant," he joked. "STIs, HIV…." He had never once fucked bare, having had the message burned early on into his brain: *Play safe.*

"But you're healthy, aren't you? Same as me?"

Wayne sighed. "Yes, but that's not the point…."

"Then I'd like to know what is." Ellis released Wayne's cock and leaned back on his hands. "We both have to undergo regular physicals, and they test for everything from HIV to housemaid's knee." He smiled. "But seriously you're safe, I'm safe, I'm a fucking virgin when it comes to anal sex—and it *is* going to be just us. Right?"

Wayne sighed. "Ellis, your safety is my primary concern. Yes, I have my paperwork from our last physical, but this is your first time, and—"

Ellis leaned forward until their mouths met in a fervent kiss, one that left Wayne wanting more. When they parted, Ellis sat back with a smile.

"If I'm honest? All I heard just then was blah, blah, blah. I know we're both safe. *You* know we're both safe." He gripped Wayne's dick and pumped it hard. "So shut up and get this dick in me *now*!"

It would be so easy to say yes, to yield to his desires....

Wayne's stomach churned. *But if I did that, I wouldn't be doing right by him. What kind of Dom would I be if I caved and ignored what I know to be right, just because the thought of going bareback is so all en-fucking-ticing?* His body already knew the answer to that one: his cock lost its rigidity.

Another thought: *How will he react if I refuse?* If?

When *I refuse, and there's only one way to find out.*

He took a deep breath. "I can't do that."

Ellis's eyes opened wide. "What?"

Wayne took hold of his hands. "Let me rephrase that. How about the two of us go together to get tested, and *then* we discuss this?" He lifted Ellis's hand and kissed it. "I won't do anything until I'm one hundred percent certain that I'm not putting you at risk. And before you ask, there will only ever be you, okay?"

Ellis gazed at him in silence for a moment. "I'm not going to win on this one, am I?"

Wayne chuckled. "I wasn't aware this was a contest. But no, you're not. You're my submissive, and I'm doing this to make sure you're safe. Because I intend spending a very long time with you, Ellis Mann. You got that?"

Ellis nodded slowly. "I've got it."

Wayne pushed out a sigh of relief. "Thank God." He took Ellis's hand and brought it to his dick. "And now you need to get me hard because all I want right now is to be inside you."

Ellis's eyes gleamed. "In that case…." He pushed Wayne onto his back and spread his legs with those large hands, then knelt between them and bent over Wayne's rapidly stiffening dick.

Wayne sucked in a huge breath as his cock was surrounded by wet heat. "Fuck, you're a quick learner."

Ellis said nothing but sucked him harder, flicking the head with his tongue. Wayne closed his eyes and enjoyed the cock worship, Ellis gentle as he cupped Wayne's balls with his fingers, pulling on his sac. When he pushed Wayne's legs toward his chest, Wayne's heart pounded.

What the hell?

The first hesitant touch of Ellis's tongue to his hole was electrifying.

"Fuck, Ellis," he moaned, shivering.

Ellis's only reaction was to lick over his hole again before kissing Wayne's spread cheeks.

Wayne couldn't remember the last time someone had rimmed him. He'd all but forgotten how fucking amazing it felt, as if all the nerve endings in his body suddenly fired up at the same time. His cock had never been this hard, and his balls ached. Ellis's tiny noises spoke of how much he too was enjoying the act. Wayne looked along Ellis's body to where his dick jutted out, weeping precome.

Now. I have to be in him now.

Wayne sat up and grabbed Ellis under his arms, tugging him until he was on top of him. "Kiss me," he said with a sigh, and Ellis's lips were on his in a heartbeat. With one hand Wayne cupped Ellis's nape while they kissed while he wrapped the other around both solid cocks, sliding it easily along their lengths. They gazed down to look at the sight of their dicks rubbing against each other, the heads glistening with precome.

"Oh shit," Ellis whispered. "And I thought *I* was big."

Wayne seized his mouth in a passionate kiss, sucking Ellis's plump lower lip between his teeth and pulling on it gently. "I promise it will fit. And I'll take it slow, all right?" He waited, watching Ellis's face.

Ellis smiled and kissed him, a faint tremor rippling through him. "Okay, fuck me," he said, his voice hoarse once more.

Wayne rolled Ellis off him and onto his back on the bed. "First things first," he said, grabbing a foil packet and tearing it open. He covered his dick and then slicked it up with lube. Wayne wrapped his hand around Ellis's cock and pumped it a couple of times before swiping between his arsecheeks with a slick hand.

"Okay, leg up, and you can hold it if you need to," he said, aiming his dick at Ellis's hole. "Stroke yourself too." He lay on his side, pressed up against Ellis's body, his shaft rigid.

Ellis kept his gaze focused on Wayne's face. "I'm ready," he said quietly.

Wayne pressed the head of his cock against Ellis's entrance and pushed, slowly, gently, just enough to let it ease into him. Then he stilled.

"Oh fuck." Ellis closed his eyes, moving his hand in a languid motion up and down his dick. His breathing sped up and he craned his neck to look down to where their bodies met. He dropped his head back onto the bed with a low moan, his eyes closed once more. "Fuck."

"I know," Wayne said, leaning over to kiss him and slipping his arm under Ellis's head. "Give it a moment."

Ellis's eyes popped open. "God, that's a thick dick."

Wayne chuckled and kissed him, taking his time. "And this is a tight hole," he said, inching his way a little farther inside him. Ellis groaned and Wayne stilled again, resisting the urge to groan aloud himself at the feel of Ellis's channel, so snug around his shaft. He leaned over to kiss him again, aware of the hunger building in his boy. Ellis turned his head to meet Wayne's kiss, feeding soft moans between his lips when Wayne began to move again, another inch into that tight heat.

Ellis stroked his length a little faster, starting to move his body, undulating his hips in a gentle roll Wayne recalled from when he'd tonguefucked him. Ellis moved with a grace that Wayne had seen so many times despite his size.

Ellis broke the kiss and met Wayne's gaze head on.

"Fuck me," he whispered.

Wayne nodded. "Going to fuck my boy." He rocked up with his body, moving slowly at first but gaining momentum. Ellis's hand kept pace with his cock, their rhythm taking a while to get going. Wayne brushed aside Ellis's hand and, wrapping his own around the wide dick, jerked it in time with his thrusts.

"Oh fuck yeah," Ellis groaned. "That's good. Yeah, like that."

Wayne shifted, his cock still deep inside Ellis. He grabbed Ellis's legs, lifting them into the air. He stared down to where his dick penetrated Ellis's body, filling him, and pushed out a moan. Wayne leaned over Ellis's body, pressing his knees to his chest, and slid faster, deeper, each thrust tearing a groan from Ellis's lips. Wayne's face was inches from

Ellis's, gazing at his boy's half-closed eyes, his parted lips, the flush spreading across his broad chest.

Ellis reached up and grabbed his head, pulling him down into a kiss, moaning into it, seeking Wayne's tongue with his own, the two of them breathing harshly.

"Look at you," Wayne marveled, staring at Ellis's face while he kept up a constant pistoning into that beautiful tight hole. "You look so fucking hot, taking my cock, pushing down on it." He gave a hard thrust and Ellis opened his eyes wide. "Yeah. *That* look. The look that tells me you're loving this, loving me fucking you."

Ellis had one hand on his dick, tugging it firmly, the other on the back of Wayne's head, drawing him lower into another brutal kiss, nothing soft about it, a clash of tongues and teeth. Wayne tried to slow down a little, not wanting this to be over, but he knew they were both too close. He pinned Ellis to the bed with his hands and rotated his hips, stirring his cock in the heat of Ellis's body before thrusting all the way into him until he was balls deep.

Ellis stared at him, mouth open, a low moan pouring from his lips. "Jesus!"

"A little too deep?" Wayne pulled out only to thrust in once more, filling Ellis to the hilt.

"Again," Ellis begged, pushing his body up off the bed to meet Wayne's thrusts.

Wayne pulled out and lay on his side once more, snugged up against Ellis's firm, warm body. He slid his dick back into him and then grabbed Ellis's thigh, lifting his leg again. With his other hand, he worked Ellis's cock while he fucked him, punching his dick into Ellis's channel until Ellis was crying out with every thrust, and Wayne knew he was about to come.

"That's it," he told Ellis breathlessly. "Come on, just let go and come for me."

Ellis reached for Wayne, cupping his cheek and moaning into his mouth as his cock creamed Wayne's hand, a thick stream of come that slid over his fingers. He trembled, his eyes locked on Wayne, and the sight was too much.

Wayne gave a hoarse shout as he shot his load into the latex, his dick as deep in Ellis as it could possibly be. He stayed there, his cock throbbing as he emptied his balls, his body shaking.

Oh my fucking God.

Never had an orgasm left him so weak, yet feeling as if he were invincible. There was nothing Wayne had ever experienced that came close.

ELLIS LAY in Wayne's arms, his body damp and his hole aching, but an ache he would gladly seek again and again. He stroked Wayne's face, unable to tear his gaze away. He could still feel the aftereffects of his climax, the tingling all over his body, and the tiny jolts of electricity that rocketed through him until at last he lay there, sated and warm.

He drew Wayne into a languid, lingering kiss, loving the feel of Wayne's hand on him as he stroked and caressed his way over his arms, chest, and belly. Wayne traced a line with his finger along Ellis's spent shaft, making him shudder.

"I'm guessing you're a little sensitive," Wayne said with a smile. His eyes gleamed. "So maybe now is not a good time to lick your dick clean."

Ellis groaned. "You're evil."

Wayne stared at him, his face glowing. "And you were wonderful."

He didn't know how to reply. He wanted to hold on to the feeling that flowed through him, spreading throughout his body in a slow, pulsing tide, a feeling of being... loved. He gazed at Wayne, wanting to give voice to the words that filled his heart.

I love you.

Ellis closed his eyes and drank it all in: the smell of sex, Wayne's heady scent that stirred his senses, the feel of their bodies pressed together, and the beautiful sense of peace that pervaded the room.

The words would have made it all perfect, but he held on to them, unable to shake off the fear that, once uttered, they would change everything.

CHAPTER TWENTY

"WHERE DO you want me to put these boxes?" Cassidy asked.

"In the kitchen, please." Wayne was standing in the middle of the living room, directing traffic. There weren't that many more to bring in from the cars, thank goodness.

Ellis still couldn't believe he was moving into Wayne's flat. He'd never thought it could happen. Once Wayne suggested it, everything got into gear quickly, and here he was, getting ready to meld his life with Wayne's.

After their first scene, Ellis had no choice but to admit how much he needed Wayne. He felt like he could fly when Wayne used the floggers, taking Ellis higher than he'd ever been. All the things he'd been worrying about—his parents, his future—all seemed to vanish into the ether as Wayne pushed him to his limits and beyond.

It was easy, really. I belong with my... oh fuck*... my Dom.*

The thought made him giddy.

Asking a few of the guys if they'd be okay helping Ellis move over the weekend resulted in quite a lot of good-natured catcalls and teasing, but every one of them agreed. And so the following Friday night after work, they got together to help make one of Ellis's dreams a reality.

"Hey, you need to feed the workforce!" Derwent yelled from the bedroom.

"Yeah, you promised pizza!" Cassidy shouted as he came through the front door with another box. "Make mine pepperoni with mushrooms, sausage, and salami."

Wayne caught Ellis's gaze and winked. "You sure do love your meat, Cassidy. Something you want to tell us?"

There was a brief pause as Cassidy stood in the doorway, gaping, and Derwent exploded into laughter.

Cassidy flushed. "I'll make you a deal. You don't say that again, and I won't tell the boys what I found when I peeked into the chest at the end of your bed." He shook his head and glanced at Ellis. "Are you certain you know what you're letting yourself in for? Because your man here is definitely a dark horse."

Derwent stared at Cassidy. "Aw, you can't say shit like that and not expect me to go take a look."

"No peeking!" Wayne said sternly, and Ellis did his best to repress a shiver.

There were some things that were *not* for sharing.

After a dinner of Carlotti's pizza and—for everyone but Ellis and Wayne—several beers, the guys left. Seconds after the last car had pulled out of the parking lot, Wayne's lips were on Ellis's neck, and this time he made no attempt to hide their effect.

"Alone at last," Wayne murmured into his ear. A minute later they were on the couch, naked, with Wayne kissing Ellis's neck, chest, and belly, obviously moving in a southerly direction.

Ellis was fine with that. More than fine.

At least until the phone rang.

Wayne froze, his mouth poised above Ellis's cock. Ellis wanted to groan in frustration as Wayne sat up and reached for the phone.

Wayne sighed. "It's your parents again." He held out the phone.

That was all it took to prick Ellis's precious bubble of happiness. They'd called every day for the last week, and he'd deftly ignored it. Wayne hadn't forced him to talk to them—for which Ellis was extremely grateful—but this was the last straw.

I'm about to make a new start in life, and there is no way I will allow anyone *to make me feel bad about it anymore.*

Except he knew this particular problem was not going to go away. There was only one thing to do. He waited until the phone fell silent and then took a deep breath.

"I'm going to call them," Ellis said, taking the mobile from Wayne's outstretched hand.

"Are you sure? We could just change your number."

It was a tempting thought. He huffed. "They'll just keep calling me on the phone or continue trying to contact me through work. No, it's best to have this out here and now, get it over with." He didn't need any problems on either front, and the time had come to deal with the situation. He gave Wayne a hopefully reassuring smile. "I have to do this. Just… don't leave, okay?"

Wayne took his hand. "I'm not going anywhere." He glanced down at his body. "Although I may put my clothes on again. You definitely don't need the distraction."

In spite of his trepidation, Ellis smirked. "That's a good idea." He peered down at Wayne's dick as it twitched. "Keep that warm for me."

Wayne laughed and leaned over to kiss him on the lips. "I'll be right here."

Ellis clicked to return the call, his gaze trained on Wayne's firm arse as he slipped into his sweats. When he heard the click, he dragged himself away. "Hello?"

"Where in the hell have you been?" his father snapped by way of greeting. "Your mother has worried herself sick, your sister's had to pay people to watch the kids, and you haven't even done us the courtesy of a call."

Ellis had to fight to keep a lid on his temper. He'd tried several times to contact Barb, but got no answer. He and his sister had problems, but he still loved her. And not being able to talk to Mark and Amanda left a hole in his heart. "Good to talk to you too, Dad."

"Don't backtalk me, Ellis. You've got a lot of explaining to do."

Ellis's stomach knotted. For an instant he felt like he was a kid again, being reprimanded for something over which he had no control. *Well, this time I do.*

"You know what? I really don't. Barb's an adult. It's up to her to make things work. I'm not her keeper. I can't be held responsible for another person's life."

There was silence, but Ellis could hear his father's harsh breathing.

"What's gotten into you? This isn't how you were raised. You know you have an obligation to your family."

"What about my family's obligation to me?" Ellis ground out. "Or does that not count? Has anyone ever asked what *I* want out of life? No, of course not. You were all so busy telling me what I was going to do, you never cared about my dreams."

His father made an exasperated noise. "Dreams? What have dreams got to do with anything? We're talking about family. You're going to be the head of your own family one day, and you need to know how to take care of them properly. When your son is old enough, you'll have to be the one to teach him the right path because I won't be around to help."

Ellis closed his eyes. He knew what his father was doing. He'd played on his children's guilt more than once in their lives. He would act as though he'd done so much for them, the poor father who'd sacrificed everything for his family. The truth was another matter entirely. The man had been selfish to the core. He'd forced Ellis into a role he didn't want and treated his daughter as though she were a commodity.

And yet knowing all that, I still feel guilty.

Ellis's voice dropped to a whisper. "Dad? I'm not you. I don't want to *be* you. I like my life just the way it is, and for that reason, I… I won't have a wife."

"That's nonsense. Of course you'll have a wife. You just haven't found the right woman yet. But one day it'll happen."

Another fallacy his father believed: all men were meant for women, and all women were meant to serve their husbands, an archaic notion Ellis never believed in. When he trained to be an officer, he worked side by side with some women who showed him the truth: they could handle anything a man could. But they were friends and couldn't ever be more than that.

Wayne sat beside him on the couch, watching him closely. Ellis looked at the man he loved. "No, Dad. I won't." He swallowed the lump that formed in his throat. "I tried so hard to be something I'm not. I did it for you and Mum. But that's not who I am. It's *never* been who I was meant to be."

Wayne gave him a wide smile, stroking Ellis's neck with his warm hand, giving him the strength to go on. Allowing him to get out the words he'd wanted to say to his parents since that day in high school when he got his first glimpse of a naked boy—and had had to hide his subsequent erection.

"I'm gay, Dad. I always have been, and I always will be. There will never be a wife for me. And… I've met someone who sees *me*. For the first time in my life, what *I* want is important to someone. He doesn't judge me or make me feel bad about being who I am. He's helping me to find out who I'm becoming."

Silence greeted his revelation, but not for long. "This is a joke, isn't it?"

"No joke, Dad."

"You're not gay. You have obligations. To us. To your sister. She's lost without you, Ellis. Don't let her—us—down."

Ellis couldn't believe his ears. "Oh my God, are you even listening to yourself? Barb is *thirty-five years old*, Dad. She's got two kids from two different men. You tried to make that my fault, but you know what? It wasn't. Neither was her having two kids. But that didn't stop you and Mum from making her feel guilty. You were never there for her when she was growing up—"

"She was your responsibility," his father snarled.

"She was *your* daughter!" Ellis shouted back. "It was up to you to raise her, not a thirteen-year-old boy who had no life experience. I had nothing to fall back on, Dad. Neither did Barb. You threw both of us in at the deep end and insisted we learn to swim, then walked away while we sank. Whenever Barb did something wrong, she was crying out for you to see her. To *help* her. But instead you tried to use her as an object lesson for me. *You* screwed up our family, Dad, not me. It was never about me at all."

His father sighed. "I told your mother you were weak. I always said our family line would die out because of you. And now it has."

Anger surged through Ellis, a white-hot, all-consuming fury. Wayne tightened his grip on Ellis's neck, the pain grounding him in the moment, but the fire in him would not be contained.

"Just stop for a second and listen to the crap that you're spouting, will you? Your family line has not died out! Are you even listening to me? Barb's kids are *your* grandchildren. They've got half of her DNA, so no matter who their fathers are, half of them is Mann."

"Those are not our family! Barb should have accepted her role in life. She was supposed to get married and become a quiet, nurturing wife. Not running around like some slut, opening her legs for any man who smiled at her."

Ellis wanted to throw up. His father's words were worse than any physical blow. *Oh my God—that is really how he sees us.* Yeah, things were hard for Barb, but Ellis knew she loved her children. She just had no sense of how things were done. How could she, the way their parents raised her? Some role models they'd been. She'd brought up her kids on her own with no help from them, which had only made things that much harder.

Ellis inhaled deeply, forcing himself to remain calm. Wayne's hand was still there on his neck, a reminder he wasn't alone.

"Wow. You know, Dad, I knew you had some messed-up ideas, but I guess I overlooked a lot of them because I loved you. But Barb and her kids have done nothing wrong. They certainly don't deserve to be treated this way. And right now? I'm ashamed of you."

His father let out a derisive snort. "You've got a nerve, especially after that little bomb you just dropped. Well, if that's how you feel, so be it. You're no son of mine."

Though he'd expected the words, the sharp pain that ran through him still caused Ellis to gasp.

"Dad—"

"You have no father or mother. We wash our hands of you. You were never anything more than a waste of space."

With that final insult, his father hung up.

That... that did not just happen.

Ellis sat there in stunned silence, barely noticing when Wayne pulled him close, rubbing his back, kissing his neck, and murmuring soothing words. He had no idea how many times Wayne had called his name before the words found their way through the fog that surrounded him.

"Ellis? What did he say?"

He sagged back against the seat cushions. "He told me I don't have a father anymore. But the joke's on him." It still felt like a dream. A horrible, surreal dream.

"Oh? How's that?" Wayne rubbed across Ellis's bare shoulders, the sensation comforting.

"He was never a father to me or Barb. He... he—"

It was no use. Ellis couldn't fight it any longer. He buried his face in Wayne's neck, tears streaming down his face. Wayne said nothing, just held him, letting his emotions run their course. After the tears had finally dried up, Wayne took him by the hand and guided Ellis to the bedroom, where he put him in their bed. He slid in beside Ellis and pulled him close.

Ellis laid his head on Wayne's chest. "I still can't believe he reacted like that." Maybe he'd always known, deep down, such a reaction was possible, but it was something else entirely to be confronted with the raw truth.

Wayne's arms were around him, warm and strong. "I know it hurts, boy. You may not believe me, but I'm proud of you. You stood up for yourself and for me. You became your own man today, and that's something no one can ever take away from you."

Ellis laughed, and the sound was sharp to his own ears. "My own man? That's funny. I'm your boy. You just said so."

Wayne chuckled. "Being one doesn't mean you're not the other. You're always going to be my boy, Ellis. When we're ninety and sitting in rocking chairs, I'll still be calling you boy."

The words comforted Ellis, at least a little bit. "Do you mean it?"

"I told you I never say anything I don't mean." Wayne tapped Ellis on the forehead. "You need to get it through your thick skull. This is it for both of us." He twisted his neck to gaze at Ellis. "I love you."

Oh God. He said it. He really said it. Finally.

"Really?"

Wayne reached down and swatted Ellis on the arse. "What did I just tell you? I never say anything I don't mean. So if I say I love you, what does that mean?"

"I love you too," Ellis whispered, tears starting all over again. "God, if you knew how long I've wanted to hear those words from your lips." He wiped at his eyes. "Fuck. When did I get to be such an emotional basket case? Look at me. I'm a mess."

"Never be ashamed of your feelings. Like your body, they all belong to me. If you're happy, sad, afraid, ashamed, all of those come to me. I will celebrate with you, comfort you, hold you, and encourage you."

"But isn't that your job?" Ellis said, trying to work up a smile and failing miserably.

Wayne kissed him on the forehead. "You're not just my job, boy. You're my life. Now lie still and let me hold you."

"Yes, Sir."

Ellis lay there, enjoying the way Wayne held him and loved him. It was going to take a while before he'd stop feeling bad about his confrontation with his father. *Why did it take me so long to stand up to him and make my voice heard?* His lack of action probably cost him his sister too because, whatever his father thought, Barb was desperate for their love and understanding. *Maybe she'll finally stand up for herself one day.* Yeah, somehow he doubted that.

"You're thinking again, aren't you?" Wayne asked.

"Sorry." Ellis slid his arm across Wayne's waist.

Wayne's sigh ruffled his hair. "You have nothing to be sorry for, but I can't let this go on right now."

Ellis craned his neck to look Wayne in the eye. "What do you mean?"

"I need to take you out of your head for a while. Get up and lie across the bed, face down, arms stretched out."

Ellis obeyed, moving slowly as if in a dream. He knew Wayne was probably right, but had no clue how he intended to go about it. His heartbeat raced as Wayne went to the chest at the foot of the bed. He knew what Wayne kept in there.

Wayne stood in front of him, clearly displaying the two floggers he'd used on Ellis during their first scene. Ellis breathed deeply. *He's right. I need this.*

"Do you remember your safeword?"

"Red, Sir."

"Good. I'm doing this because I love you, Ellis. If nothing else, always remember that."

Ellis believed him. With his whole heart, he believed Wayne loved him. He lowered his face to the bed.

"Are you ready, boy?"

"Yes, Sir."

"Good. Let's begin."

WAYNE LAUGHED when he walked into the bathroom and found Ellis trying to see over his shoulder while looking in the mirror.

"What are you doing?"

Ellis's shy smile was adorable. "I want to see your marks."

The stripes down Ellis's back were still a light shade of red, but very noticeable.

"They look beautiful," Wayne said, stepping closer and tracing a finger over them. "And you took them very well."

"But I can't *see* them," Ellis complained.

"Okay, fine. Just a moment."

Wayne went into the other room and arranged the mirror on the door with the one near the bathroom. It wouldn't be easy to see, but should allow Ellis to at least get a glimpse of them.

"Come out here," he called. When Ellis entered Wayne pointed to the spot in front of him. "Stand here." He positioned Ellis so he could see the bathroom mirror from the closet door.

"Oh my God," Ellis whispered, reaching a hand back and trying to touch them.

"Do you like them?" Wayne asked, stepping up behind Ellis and nuzzling his neck.

"I love them," Ellis answered. "Getting them, taking them, and being able to let go? All of that was absolutely amazing." He waggled his brows. "You really know your stuff."

"No, I just know you," Wayne said softly. "You did surprise me, you know."

"I did?"

Wayne nodded. "I'd increased the intensity of my strikes to make sure you really let go, but then you begged me to hit you harder."

Ellis stared at the marks on his back and buttocks. "It felt like you did, to a point."

Wayne kissed the back of his neck, loving the shiver that made its way down Ellis's spine. "You're right, I did, but I wasn't about to push you any more than that. You were already hurting."

"Don't you think I could have taken it?" Ellis asked quietly.

Wayne sighed. "That's not the point. It's my responsibility to ensure your emotional pains weren't related to your begging for more physical ones." He slid his hand down the curve of Ellis's back, down to his arsecheek. "But yes, you took it beautifully. I'm looking forward to learning what makes you soar. I want to be able to give that to you."

Ellis turned in his arms and kissed Wayne on the mouth. "Believe it or not, you already have."

"What do you mean?"

There was a distant look in Ellis's eyes. "For the last year, I wasn't sure what was going to happen to me. Every time I tried to live up to my father's expectations, I started hating myself a little more. I didn't want to be gay because I needed to provide for my family, the one I really didn't want. I'm not saying I don't like kids, mind you. I mean, I love Barb's, and when we're together, we always have a good time. But I just want to be Uncle Ellis, the one who will kiss a skinned knee, make a snack, pop some corn, and watch a scary movie with them because Mum is out for the night."

"How would you feel about us doing that?" Wayne asked. "The two of us, wrapped up under a blanket on the couch all weekend, a big bowl of popcorn between us while we have our own mini film festival? Hours upon hours of laughs, mindless violence, horror. Anything we want."

Ellis smiled. "I know you're doing this to take my mind off yesterday. Really, I'm okay."

The sadness in his boy's eyes said otherwise.

Wayne arched his eyebrows. "Ha. Not *everything* is about you, you know. I love watching films and eating loads of hot buttered popcorn. But having my boy beside me while we watch? That's going to make it extra special. So come on, don't be such a lump."

"A lump?" Ellis's eyebrows went up. "Okay, fine. You're on. How do we pick the films?"

"You pick the first one; I'll pick the next. We'll keep going until we're done, or until we can't move anymore because we've eaten way too much and we can't get off the couch."

"Fine. I know just the film, then." He gave Wayne a smirk.

Uh-oh. I get a bad feeling about this.

WAYNE GROANED as *The Hobbit* entered hour four. It wasn't a bad film, but when he suggested the marathon film-watching session, he thought there would be some variety. He glanced over as Ellis put another handful of popped corn into his mouth, his attention glued to the screen. Wayne slipped an arm over his shoulder and pulled him close.

Okay, maybe this isn't so bad after all.

By the time the film ended, Ellis had fallen asleep, his head on Wayne's lap. He sat there, stroking his boy's hair, and thought about how lucky he was to have this amazing man in his life after years of pining for him.

"Now who's thinking too hard?" Ellis mumbled. He shifted onto his back, opened his eyes, and smiled at Wayne.

"It's okay because I'm thinking about you," Wayne said, rubbing the side of Ellis's face.

"Oh, well, I guess that's fine, then." Ellis sat up. "Want to tell me what you were thinking about?"

"Six years ago I was sitting in a boring meeting. Then this guy walked in. He was a big bruiser of a man, but he had this… I don't know, vulnerability about him. It called to me on a level that no one else had ever done. When he introduced himself, he shook my hand, and I was amazed at how warm and alive he was. I told him my name, and he smiled. My stomach lurched, and I had to tear myself away because I knew I was staring at him.

"We became best mates, and over time, I realized I'd fallen in love with him, but since he didn't seem to see me as anything other than a friend, I hid my feelings because I'd rather have him in my life as a friend than not have him at all. Now I find out that he has feelings for me too, and I can't say how happy this makes me."

Ellis sat up and gave him a mock glare. "Who is this bastard? I'll kill him. You're mine, you got that?"

Wayne reached out and smacked Ellis lightly on the side of the head. His boy grinned and leaned in for a kiss.

"Thank you for not giving up on me," he whispered.

"That's something I'm never going to be able to do. To paraphrase a famous movie, I've got no intention of ever quitting you."

Ellis reached out and turned off the lamp, before stretching out on the couch and pulling Wayne down on top of him.

Wayne stared at his boy's face, illuminated by the glow of the TV screen. "I love you," he whispered.

"Why don't you show me just how much?" Ellis suggested softly.

"Why don't I?" Wayne replied, leaning in to take what now belonged solely to him.

CHAPTER TWENTY-ONE

ELLIS WAS having a conversation with his reflection.

"He's a fucking *slave driver*," Ellis complained to the mirror. "It's bad enough we're still doing all those drills at work, but then when we get home, it's all 'Ellis, take your clothes off so you can learn to kneel properly,' or 'Ellis, take your clothes off so you'll know the proper way to walk when we're in a club.' I think he just likes to see me with my clothes off."

"And do you blame me?" Wayne said from the door. He stood there, hands behind his back, grinning at Ellis.

Ellis jerked away from the mirror. "Sorry, Wayne. I mean Sir. I mean…." He sighed. "This is ridiculous. Why the hell do I need to know this stuff? You're not entering me into a talent contest or dog show that I'm aware of—are you?"

It had been almost two weeks since Ellis moved in with Wayne. Every day they carried out their training exercises or did physical training to keep fit, then came home for more of the same. Ellis was fed up. Even the weekends—like now—which he thought would be the two of them spending some quality time together, had become more in a series of Wayne cracking the whip.

And it's not even a real whip. The thought made his skin tingle. *Will he ever try that?*

"Didn't I tell you?" Wayne said, his eyes wide. "I've got you down for Crufts this year. Poodle category." When Ellis growled, he wagged his finger. "Bad dog. No treats for you."

"Watch where you're waving that finger, then," Ellis warned him. "This bad puppy might decide to bite it off."

Wayne smirked. "Okay, I was hoping you'd ask. If you'd like to know, I'll tell you, but please keep an open mind about this."

"Oh God," Ellis moaned. "I hate it when you say things like that."

Wayne chuckled. "I'd like us to go to the club," he said. "I want to be able to show you off."

Ellis shrugged. "Okay, that's fine. I wouldn't mind seeing Jarod again." That didn't seem so bad.

Wayne stepped into the bathroom and walked up behind Ellis. "No, you're misunderstanding me. I want you there as my submissive. I want you to be naked at my feet."

Ellis froze. "What the fuck? No. Absolutely not. I am not about to get starkers in a room full of strangers." He thought about the submissives he'd seen that opening night. Okay, so there were a *few* naked guys, but not everyone. "This is all you, isn't it? You just get off on seeing me naked."

"You won't be *completely* naked," Wayne said, bringing his hand to the front. He held a small wooden box. It was about eight inches long, plain, with no identifying marks. "This is for you."

Ellis took it, his heartbeat racing. Whatever was inside was obviously important, judging from Wayne's serious expression. Ellis opened it and stared, torn by two conflicting emotions. *If this is Wayne's idea of a joke, I should be laughing. If it's not, then I am not amused.*

"Handcuffs?"

Wayne smiled. "They're only part of it, and not the main part either."

Apart from the pair of interlocked handcuffs, the box contained a thin silver chain that shone in the light, and Ellis couldn't tear his gaze away from it.

"What's this for? And how will it make me not completely naked?"

Wayne's expression turned serious. "As long as you wear my collar, you're never naked or alone. A part of me is always with you. The fact that you're wearing this shows you that no matter what else, I'll always be by your side."

Ellis stared at the slender chain. *Oh wow. A collar?*

"I know that with our work and all, I can't give you a traditional collar, but I'd like you to wear this. It reflects our commitment to one another, and it's unobtrusive enough that no one would question why you were wearing it."

Wayne's words sank in, and it became clear what he held in his hands was something precious, not to be taken lightly.

Wayne shifted closer until his warm breath caressed Ellis's neck. "Will you wear my collar, Ellis?"

Oh God. He's serious. Ellis's heartbeat sped up. "Yes. Okay." He held out the box and Wayne lifted the chain from it. He slid it around Ellis's neck, made sure the clasp worked, and then let it go.

"This is a collar for now. At some point in the future, when we're both ready for it, I'd like it if you would consider wearing a permanent one. It will be something that only I have the key to, and you won't be able to remove it without my okay. But I don't want to rush things."

Ellis's thoughts drifted back to his conversation with Jarod. *"Those would be the equivalent of a wedding ring."*

Shit. Wayne is asking me to make what we have permanent. Wasn't he?

"Are you asking…?"

"For a permanent contract. Yes. I know it's fast because we just signed our initial one. But it's not like we haven't known each other for years. Like you said, you've always been mine. I just want everyone else to know it too. That's part of the going to the club thing. See, if we do this, we'd have a big celebration in the club, and we would have a lot of people there to witness it. I want you comfortable enough to do this, so I'd like to practice it. Plus I rather like the thought of your bare arse wiggling where I can see it as much as I want."

Ellis knew Wayne was using humor to deflect his nerves. He could see the tightness of his lips pressed into a thin, flat line. The wariness in his eyes. Any other day Ellis would have called him on it, but today?

"Okay, yes."

"Yes?" Wayne asked, sounding uncertain.

"I'm all for the no-rushing bit, but yes, I'd like that."

Wayne flashed his hand out and locked it behind Ellis's neck. He drew him in for a savage kiss, one that screamed passion and excitement, and Ellis went with that, melting into it. When he stepped back, Wayne's pupils were so big they almost blotted out his irises.

"Are you serious?"

Part of Ellis found Wayne's apparent reluctance to believe his own ears touching.

He smiled. "I have never been more serious in my life." He'd always wanted to be married—it was the one part of his father's dream Ellis actually wanted for himself—but he needed it to be with someone who completed him, made him feel like he was an equal partner, and loved him without hesitation.

Wayne gazed at him, still with the hint of hesitancy in his expression. "Do you think you might want to go to the club tomorrow night? I know you'll be uncomfortable, but I promise I'll be with you. There will be other subs there who are naked, so you won't be the only one. And if you're uncomfortable about the fact, then we can put you in something that will cover up your bits."

Ellis grinned. Wayne truly was the perfect man for him. He loved the way Wayne held him at night, the way he could be rough and passionate during sex but then tender when they made love. He truly didn't mind kneeling at Wayne's feet because when Wayne slid those fingers through his hair, Ellis felt… complete. For the first time in his life, he'd found his place.

"I'll try, but can we take something along with us, just in case?"

Wayne nodded instantly. "Of course. And remember you will always have your safeword. If you feel the least bit uncomfortable, you say it, and we'll get you out of there."

Once again Wayne showed that his concern was for Ellis, not for himself. And that made Ellis feel even more loved.

Wayne waggled his brows. "Meet me in the living room in five minutes so we can continue our training."

As soon as Wayne left, Ellis reached up and ran his fingers over the chain around his neck. This was a physical representation of Wayne's ownership, of his love. Warmth spread throughout Ellis's body at the realization.

"He loves me," he whispered, and even he could hear the awe and disbelief in his voice. It was so hard to believe Wayne hadn't simply given up on Ellis after he said that BDSM was sick and wrong, because he'd implied that Wayne was too.

WAYNE WATCHED as Ellis twitched. In the fifteen minutes since they'd arrived at the club and Wayne told him to kneel, Ellis couldn't seem to find a position that was comfortable. It took several moments before he finally settled, his head bowed. Wayne grinned to himself. *Time to have a little fun.*

"My drink is empty," he said, waiting to see how long it took for Ellis's irritation to surface.

"Yeah, well, at least you *have* a drink," Ellis growled, not looking up.

Wayne smiled to himself but kept his face straight, just in case Ellis glanced up. "No, boy. You're expected to get up and get me a refill." He held out his glass and waited.

Now Ellis popped his head up, and he settled his glare squarely on Wayne. "And you can kiss my furry behind. You did that on purpose."

Wayne grinned. "Maybe I did, but that doesn't excuse your bad manners. Now fetch me a drink," Wayne said, adding a little force to the order.

Ellis placed a hand on the table to steady himself as he stood, and Wayne couldn't take his eyes off him. Ellis was a large man, but he possessed a grace all his own, honed from their workouts. There wasn't a bit of padding to him. Ellis had worked hard to earn every one of the muscles he sported.

"You're a bastard, you know this, right?" Ellis said before grabbing the glass and heading over to the bar. Wayne enjoyed the view, Ellis's firm arse flexing as he moved. The urge to mark up those round cheeks was overwhelming.

Not today, he told himself. *Let's not run before we can walk.* Instead he raised his voice to call after Ellis.

"Yes, but I'm a bastard who's still waiting on his drink." He stifled a laugh when Ellis raised two fingers. Oh, his boy was cheeky. *But isn't that what I love about him?*

When he returned from the bar, Ellis placed the drink on the napkin Wayne had set out for a coaster. "Is there going to be anything else, *Sir*?" he demanded.

"Not at the moment, no." Wayne pointed at the floor. "You can assume the position again."

He heard the mutter and had to bite his cheek to keep from laughing. After Ellis had once again gotten comfortable, Wayne reached out and put his hand on his boy's head, rubbing Ellis's short hair.

"I'm very proud of you. I hope you know that," he whispered.

Though Ellis didn't respond, Wayne detected the shudder that went through him and the flush that crawled up his neck.

"Nothing to say, boy?"

Ellis shook his head. He inched closer, placing his head on Wayne's knee. "Nothing except please don't stop touching me."

Wayne had no intention of doing that.

They must have sat like that for half an hour, Wayne stroking Ellis's head, Ellis breathing evenly, apparently totally at peace. Wayne had never known such contentment.

"Can I ask you something?" Ellis murmured.

"Of course."

Ellis got up onto his knees, hands behind his back as Wayne had instructed him. "You know earlier, when you... took me for a walk around the club?" His gaze narrowed. "And there was I, thinking that Crufts comment was just a joke."

Wayne chuckled. "Aw, I was only showing you off." He scrubbed his hand over Ellis's head. "And you did it so well too."

Ellis gave him a look before lowering his gaze. "Yeah, well.... There was a guy tied to that giant cross thing."

"The St. Andrew's cross," Wayne corrected him. "What about him?" It had been a scene involving a flogger, a tawse, and ultimately, a whip.

Ellis paused, his face flushed. "Do you think... maybe, one day, we might...?"

Wayne's pulse raced. "Seriously?" It was something he'd dreamed of. He tilted Ellis's head up with his fingers and looked him in the eye.

Ellis swallowed. "Well, I... like it when you use the floggers when we're at home. It can't be that different doing it in the club."

Wayne chuckled again. "Okay, think for a moment. What usually happens when we're done with the floggers?" The act of marking his boy always had the same effect, and both of them enjoyed the aftermath.

Ellis stared at him. "You fuck me," he whispered at last.

Wayne nodded. "And what if we do as you suggest, and I fasten you to that cross... what about if, when we're finished, I want to take my boy right there and then in front of anyone who might be around?" Just thinking about it made his cock fill. The idea of fucking Ellis while he hung from the cross, sliding his dick between those newly warmed cheeks....

Fuck. Wayne wanted that.

Ellis had become very still. "I think I would be okay with that," he said quietly. He blinked. "Not right now, you understand. When I felt... ready."

What the fuck? Wayne was giddy with anticipation. He focused on Ellis's face, scanning it for any sign that he regretted his words. Ellis gazed back at him, his breathing a little faster but otherwise in control of himself.

Wayne leaned forward and kissed him on the lips, taking his time. "I like the idea too. Whenever you feel you're ready, just say the word," he whispered against Ellis's mouth, aware of the shudder that ran through him.

Looks like both of us want this.

Ellis chuckled. "You know, you didn't actually need to say that." He gestured with his head to Wayne's lap, where Wayne's erection pressed almost painfully against the zipper of his leather pants.

Wayne bit back the urge to growl. In his head he was already choosing his wardrobe for the event—a pair of tight leather chaps and a leather jock from which he could free his cock easily.

I'll probably be so turned on I'll come as soon as I'm inside him.

That did it. Wayne would ensure he jerked off before they got to the club.

He wanted it to last as long as possible.

CHAPTER TWENTY-TWO

WHEN THE phone rang, Ellis looked up from his place on the floor by Wayne's chair where he'd been kneeling for nearly an hour on a soft throw pillow Wayne had given him. If anyone asked him about it, he would deny finding any pleasure in the activity, but once he settled in, he found he quite liked being in this position. His mind calmed when Wayne reached out and absently stroked his head, and he had time to reflect on how he should be taking care of Wayne's needs. There was a lot of clarity to be found in leaving everything to his Dom.

Who would have thought it? Letting go got to be easier and easier as time went by.

Wayne looked over at the phone, then turned to Ellis. "It's your sister."

Ellis's heart began to thump in staccato bursts. He hadn't heard from anyone in his family for weeks. He'd actually adjusted to the fact he'd lost them all, though that took a while. He got there eventually. If they didn't want him around, that was fine.

He had Wayne, and that was all the family Ellis needed.

Some days he even believed it too.

So why is Barb calling now?

"What do I do?" he asked softly.

Wayne held out the phone. "Talk to her. Nothing will get settled if you don't."

His hands shaking, Ellis took the phone from Wayne. He sucked in a quick breath, then pushed speaker.

"Hello?"

"Uncle Ellis? It's Mark."

The boy's voice trembled, and Ellis was instantly on high alert. "What's wrong, Mark?"

"I don't know." He sniffled. "Mom's crying all the time, and Granddad won't let her come to see him. The last time she called, I heard her asking if she could please visit. When she hung up, she started crying on the couch, saying it was all too much."

Shit. That didn't sound good. "Where is she now?"

"In her room. She's been there all day."

Fuck. "Have you eaten?"

"There isn't any food in the house." He whimpered. "I'm scared. Amanda is crying all the time too. She wants Mum, but she won't open the door."

Ellis glanced up at Wayne, who nodded at him.

"I'll be right there, Mark. Don't tell your mum I'm coming. Get Amanda and go sit outside until I get there, okay?"

"Okay." The call disconnected.

"Wayne, I—"

Wayne's voice was like ice. "Get your jacket. We leave in five minutes." Then he rushed to the kitchen, reappearing a minute later with a box of muesli and some milk.

Ellis stared at him. "Muesli?"

Wayne paused long enough to frown. "Look, I don't know what they have, and this is the best thing I can lay my hands on at the moment. We can make arrangements for them when we get there. How old are your niece and nephew?"

"Mark is twelve. Amanda is eight."

Wayne growled. "Your father is…. Sorry. I'll shut up."

"No, you can say it. This just proves we're better off without him."

Wayne huffed. "*You* may be. But it sounds like your sister needs his help."

"Oh, I agree that she needs help, but she won't get it from him, not that he'd offer it in the first place." He sighed. "She always had me, you know. I was her anchor."

Wayne reached for his jacket and phone. "Yes, but at what cost? I mean, you weren't prepared for a family. You had no skills in that area either. I'm not happy with the fact you ran yourself into the ground, but at least now I'm starting to see the whole picture."

They left the flat and got into the truck, and Wayne peeled out of the parking area at breakneck speed. Ellis directed him to his sister's house, where they found Mark sitting on the lawn with Amanda. When they saw him, they rushed over and threw their arms around his waist.

"I missed you so much," he whispered into their hair.

"Mom said you didn't love us anymore."

Ellis knelt down and tucked a knuckle under Mark's chin. "I will *always* love you. Do you understand me?"

Mark gave a shaky nod. Amanda wouldn't let go of Ellis. She clung to him, her thin body wracked with sobs.

When Wayne cleared his throat, Ellis turned to him. "This is my friend Wayne. He's brought some cereal for you both for now. Later we'll see about making sure you've got food in the kitchen, okay?"

Both kids nodded. Ellis put his arms around their shoulders and all of them walked into the house. It was worse than usual. The kitchen was a disaster; the sink overflowed with dishes, the garbage stank, and the floors were sticky with something... purple. The living room was no better. Plates of old food sat on the couch, and there were soiled clothes strewn about. Ellis pushed down hard on his anger and turned to Wayne, who also seemed to be biting his tongue.

Wayne gazed at the kids and pasted on a bright smile. "Why don't I go do some dishes, then I'll get you both something to eat, okay?"

The kids looked to Ellis for confirmation, and he nodded. "Go on. I need to find your mum anyway." They turned and walked away with Wayne. He could hear him speaking to them in low tones, telling them what they could do to help.

Then it was Ellis's turn.

He stormed to his sister's room and rapped on the door. He could hear her sobs, and his heart ached a little bit at the broken sound.

"Barb, open the door."

Several loud, ugly sniffs followed. "You're not supposed to be here. Dad will be angry."

"Come on, open the door, honey." He kept his voice even like he did when he talked with people at the scene of a crime. "I'm here to help you."

"But...."

"Barb, you need my help. You know you do. Your kids haven't eaten and your place is a mess."

The door opened, and Ellis stifled a gasp. His sister, who had always been beautiful, looked as much a mess as her home. Her hair was greasy and her eyes were puffy, red, and streaked with mascara. Her skin was so pale that her smattering of freckles appeared to be blotches on her face. Before he even had his arms open, she threw herself at him, sobbing.

"I can't do this," she whispered. "It doesn't work without your help."

Ellis ran his fingers through her hair. "It does, but you need to learn how. And I'm going to help you."

"But Dad said—"

"What he said doesn't matter." Ellis knew his voice was hard, but it was time Barb faced facts. "He doesn't care about us. He never has."

"But he said—"

"That I'm not his son anymore? I never was. Think back. When was the last time he did anything for either of us beyond give us the basics in life? Even then we had to bow and scrape to get them. When you were in trouble, did he step in to help?"

"No, but...." She stepped back. "Just wait a minute, will you?" She took a deep breath. "Dad said you were... gay."

Ellis had to strain to hear her voice. "Yeah, so I'm gay. So what? I always have been, but I was too afraid to say so. It doesn't change anything. I'm still the same person who always helped with the kids and did my best for you. Right now my... Wayne is in the kitchen with Mark and Amanda."

Her expression was horrified. "You left them alone with a gay man?"

Ellis bit the inside of his cheek hard enough to note the coppery taste. "So did you. And Wayne would never hurt them. Neither would I. You *know* that."

She looked away. "I don't know what to believe anymore. Dad said that if you came here, I was to turn you away. He said you'd infect the kids."

A laugh, equal parts anger, frustration, and rage bubbled out of Ellis. "Infect them? It's not contagious, Barb. Believe me, it's taken me this long to finally admit to myself who I am. And if you listen closely, you'll hear Wayne in the kitchen doing dishes. He came to help. When has Dad ever done that?"

"Never, I guess."

"Don't guess. *Know.*"

She dipped her chin, and Ellis hoped she might actually be receptive to listening to him. He nodded for her to go back into her bedroom, then followed her inside and closed the door. He sat her on the edge of the bed, then sat down beside her, an arm draped over her shoulder.

"Think back, okay? When you were having trouble, who did Mum and Dad tell you to call?"

"You."

"When I was thirteen and you got pregnant, did they help you at all? Who made sure you went to your appointments? Who got on the bus with you and drove over half of London, all the while holding your hand?"

"You." Her voice was strained. Ellis hoped what he was saying would get through to her.

"Yeah, me, and I was only a year older than Mark is now. Would you expect him to do things like that?"

She shook her head, swallowing.

"When things got too overwhelming here, who did you turn to?"

Barb smiled. "It was always you." Then her smile faltered. "You were the only one who cared."

"I still care." He stroked her hair again. "We're going to figure this out, but it's going to be together. Mum and Dad can't be a part of this unless they can take responsibility for what they did to us, okay? Don't call them anymore. They're the reason we're both so messed up, you know."

"Ellis?"

When he heard Wayne's voice, Ellis let out a sigh of relief. He got off the bed, opened the door, and called out to him. "In here."

When Wayne entered the small room, Ellis turned to Barb. "Barb, this is Wayne. He's my… boyfriend."

Wayne smiled and winked at Ellis. He held out his hand, and very hesitantly, Barb took it. Wayne turned to Ellis. "I've got the kids eating, and we were able to clear away some of the dishes. I think a few of them might be better off tossed into the dustbin, though."

"Thank you," Barb said fervently.

"No thanks needed, I assure you." Wayne leaned against the door. "I have to ask, if things are this bad, why didn't you call Ellis yourself? Your children had to call Ellis because they were afraid."

Ellis stared at him. "Wayne, maybe now isn't the time to—"

Wayne glared at Ellis. "Let her answer the question."

Barb shuffled her feet. "I tried, you know. I thought I could do this, make them proud of me, show them that I could be a good mother. I did my best to keep up with everything, but then it all started to pile up again. So many clothes. So many dishes. No matter what I did, it wasn't enough. I tried to call Mum to ask her for help, but they refused and said I was on my own. So I tried again. And failed.

"Things got away from me. I used to be able to ask you for help, but I thought maybe, just this once, I could make someone proud of me because I could accomplish it on my own. As you can see from the state of the house, that didn't go so well."

"All of this is from a couple of days?" Ellis asked incredulously.

Barb pinned him with a glare. "You've babysat them. You know what it's like."

She wasn't wrong. Ellis could get them ready for bed, and if there was any way they could get dirty again, they'd find it.

"Okay, I understand. So what happened?"

"Mark wanted to make a jam sandwich for him and Amanda. He took the jam jar out of the fridge and dropped it. It shattered on the floor, and I just… lost it. I screamed at him, telling him he was supposed to take care of his sister, and his clumsiness wasn't helping her at all. That was when it hit me—I sounded like Dad."

Ellis's heart went out to her. "Aw, Barb."

"I tried to call them because I wasn't sure what to do. I mean, a woman my age who can't even take care of her own kids. What does that say about me?"

"It says you're a woman under tremendous stress." Wayne stepped closer. "And it says you need help. Despite what your father would have you believe, there is nothing wrong with being unmarried. Let me ask you something, and forgive me for being less than subtle. Do the fathers pay anything towards the kids' upkeep?"

Barb shook her head with a shuddering sigh.

"May I ask why?"

Her face went bright red. "I—I don't know who the fathers are. I used to go out… a lot when I was younger. I did some things I'm not really proud of. Hell, I've done things I'm not proud of most of my life." She peered closely at him. "You were the man I talked to when I called Ellis, right?"

Wayne nodded.

Barb sighed heavily. "I'm sorry I was so awful to you on the phone. When you said Ellis wouldn't help me, I got angry. Then when you told me that you knew about my past, I was mortified." She took a deep breath. "What you said was true. I did get arrested for narcotics, and I was high. It was a wake-up call for me. The officer who arrested me was also the one who brought me home. When I felt sick, he helped me into the bathroom, and stayed until he was sure I was okay."

"Sounds like a good cop," Wayne commented. He flashed Ellis a smile. "We work with a few guys like that."

"Then he sat me down and talked to me. He asked why I was making such a mess of my life. I told him what I did wasn't anyone else's concern. Then he asked about the kids. He reminded me that they could be taken away from me. Or that if I carried on the way I was, the chances were high that I'd OD, and then they'd be left alone with no one else. I couldn't have that."

Ellis wondered who her Good Samaritan was, and if he'd be able to find out. From the sound of it, he was in the right place at the right time. "I'm glad he didn't pull any punches," he said quietly.

Barb shook her head. "Oh, he did more than talk. He helped me get into treatment. It wasn't easy, and I hated every minute of it because there were plenty of times I thought it might be better to die. But I kept Mark and Amanda's picture in my wallet to remind me of why I was doing it. I looked at it every day and promised them I would get better. When it got to be too much, I'd call Ellis to watch the kids for a few hours so I could go see my counsellor. It got to the point where I was doing it every day." Her face fell. "And guess what? I failed. Again. Just like Dad said I would. Without a man to love me, I'm nothing."

She put her hands to her face and sobbed. Ellis pulled her in and held her. He looked at Wayne, needing his strength. Wayne moved to sit beside her, and together they both wrapped her in a hug.

Wayne put his lips close to her ear. "He's wrong, you know. Your father, I mean. The only person who can help you is you. And you're doing a good job. I know it's hard, and sometimes it gets overwhelming. What I don't understand is why you didn't simply tell Ellis?"

She sniffled and drew back, turning her attention toward Ellis. "Because El is the only one I ever wanted to be proud of me. He's a good brother—a good man. Dad always told me if I had a problem, it was Ellis's job to fix it. But El was always so afraid, and every time I messed up, he got this look on his face like my failure was his." She shrugged. "So basically I messed up two lives, and now I'm working on destroying two more. Maybe it would be better if the kids went somewhere else."

"Stop that!" Ellis's voice thundered out in the small room. "I've heard enough. We had a shit childhood; I won't deny it. But we're not those kids anymore, Barb. We had to grow up sometime. Wanna know something? I was afraid of failing you too. I wanted to be your rock, but I couldn't.

I wasn't even able to hold myself together. I—" Ellis swallowed hard. "I needed Wayne for that. He put me back together. He's the one I turned to when I needed help once I got my head out of my arse and admitted I needed him. So you see, there isn't anything wrong with needing help." He wiped her damp eyes with his hand. "And the kids wouldn't be better off with some stranger, or worse, separated. They're fine with their mum, but they need their Uncle Ellis too."

He glanced over to Wayne, who smiled and gave him a nod.

Ellis leaned in closer. "Let me help you, Barb."

"But… why?"

Ellis pulled her in tight again. "Because you're the only family I have now. And if you'll allow it, we'll be your family too."

"You have great kids." Wayne's voice was soft. "They helped with the dishes, knew where to put everything. They'll help you too if you give them a chance. But if you need help, you can call us. We'll do our best to figure it out. I will say, though… Ellis won't be available any time day or night. You've got to call me and we'll work out something. But we *will* help."

She leaned back and looked from Wayne to Ellis. "I love you, El."

"I love you too." He kissed her head, then wrinkled his nose. "But good grief, girl, you really need a shower."

Her reaction was something between a laugh and a sob.

"Why don't you go take a bath?" Wayne urged. "And we'll see about getting things back in order."

Barb stood and took a few steps toward the door before she whirled around and threw herself into Ellis's arms. "I'm sorry for everything I did, El. I should have been the one watching out for you, and I failed."

Ellis held her close. "No, you didn't. We were two children with parents who thought what they were doing was a form of love, but it wasn't. It was abuse. And with Wayne's help, I've broken that cycle and found my self-worth again. We need to do the same for you. And we will, I promise."

Barb left the room, and Wayne took Ellis in his arms.

He kissed him soundly. "So proud of you."

Ellis leaned in and took strength from his lover. "I just wish she'd told me. Maybe I could have helped."

"You did. You gave everything you had and then some. There are some lessons we need to figure out for ourselves, though. And I think maybe your sister is ready to learn them."

Ellis allowed Wayne to hold him for a few more moments. "It's too quiet out there. You know what they say; when you've got kids and it's quiet, something scary is going on."

Wayne chuckled. "And that's where you'd be wrong, smart arse. They're watching a cartoon. I told them after they finished their muesli they could have a little bit of television. And I *might* have said I didn't want any fuss or argument."

Ellis arched his eyebrows. "The big, bad Dom even has kids listening to him. I'm impressed."

"We'll see just how impressed you are when we get home. For now, though, we have a house to clean."

"Gladly, Sir."

Chapter Twenty-Three

"I'M MAKING some coffee," Ellis said as they came through the front door. "Do you want some?"

"Hmm?" Wayne was leafing through the mail he'd picked up from their box downstairs.

Ellis grinned. "Hello? Earth to Wayne. Come in, Wayne." He knew that would get a reaction.

Sure enough Wayne snapped his head up and stared at him. "Oh, we're feeling cheeky, are we? I'll have to do something about that."

Exactly the result Ellis had been hoping for. It was a week since they'd done anything remotely… kinky, which was what he called it in his own head. What surprised him was he'd missed it. They hadn't been to Secrets for a while either.

"And where is *your* head right now?"

Ellis blinked. "Sorry. I must have zoned out for a sec."

Wayne seemed amused. "What were you thinking about? And tell me the truth."

"If you must know, I was thinking that we hadn't been to the club for a while. Plus we haven't… done anything."

Wayne lifted his eyebrows. "'Done anything'? My, how coy we're sounding tonight. Could this be the same man I had tied to the bed last week, who begged me to f—"

"Yeah, okay, okay." Wayne had tried his hand at rope bondage, which Ellis found extremely arousing, especially when Wayne fashioned a cock ring from the rope. Staring at his dick, dark with blood and sticking up like a bloody flagpole, had turned Ellis on so much he'd begged to be fucked.

Who would have thought it? A side of him he never knew existed, and all it took to bring it to the fore was Wayne.

Ellis went to put the kettle on. He knew why he was in need of Wayne. The last few days there had been no training, and quiet days always made him restless. He knew it was part and parcel of the job, hence the rigorous training scenarios to keep them all ready for action.

Ellis loved it when the team was deployed. He liked the physicality of their operations, the need for mental agility, the adrenaline, every last damn bit of it.

As he was stirring the coffee, Wayne walked up to him and slipped his hands around Ellis's waist. Ellis leaned back, turning his head to find Wayne's lips awaiting him.

"I have news," Wayne murmured after kissing him slowly.

"Hmm?" Ellis wanted less talk, more kissing. Then Wayne's words broke through. "What news?" When Wayne didn't respond but kissed Ellis's neck, which was definitely not playing fair because the sod knew exactly what it did to him, Ellis moaned. "Unless you intend for us to strip off right this minute and get busy on the couch or the bed, stop that!"

Wayne ceased his sensual teasing and chuckled. He stepped back and held out an envelope, already opened. "This is for you."

Ellis gave him a questioning glance. "And this is why you read it? I don't recall you reading my mail as being part of our contract."

Wayne held up an identical envelope. "You're correct, but seeing as I knew what it contained…. And your physical well-being *is* my concern."

Just like that Ellis realized what he was holding.

He pulled out the folded sheet and scanned its contents. He grinned again, not because it informed him there were no nasty surprises lurking somewhere in his body, but because of its import.

"So," he said, stretching out the syllable.

Wayne's grin matched his own. "So I've been thinking about something I'd like to do at the club."

Ellis's heartbeat sped up a little. "Not here?"

Wayne shook his head. "For what I have in mind, we'd need… let's call them props."

"Oh?" He kept his tone nonchalant, but inside he was anything but. "That sounds complicated." *And exciting. And hot. Definitely hot.*

"Come and sit down for a moment," Wayne suggested, picking up his mug of coffee and heading for the living room. Ellis followed him, trying to keep a lid on his growing excitement. He was dying to know what Wayne had planned.

They sat on the couch. Ellis kicked off his shoes and put his feet on Wayne's lap, which drew an amused glance.

"Are we comfortable?" Wayne asked him in a dry tone.

"Extremely. Now talk. I want to hear about these props of yours."

Wayne chuckled. "Uh-uh. I want that part to be a surprise. But before I can put wheels in motion, I need to know something."

Ellis stilled, unable to escape the feeling something was coming at him. "Okay."

"If I wanted to do a scene with you at the club…," Wayne began, his gaze focused on Ellis.

The hairs stood up on Ellis's arms and the back of his neck. "You mean in front of people?"

Wayne nodded. "I figured you're more comfortable at the club now that we've been there a few times. So I guess I need to know if you're ready to do more."

Ellis's brain was whirring. "By 'more' are we talking a scene? Just a scene?"

Wayne gave a half smile. "And what follows."

His belly did a little flip-flop. "You mean sex." *Fuck.* Talk about pushing his boundaries.

Wayne rested his head against the back of the couch. "If you don't think you're ready for that, you just need to tell me. And that's perfectly okay, by the way."

Ellis's head was in a mess. The thought of being on show while Wayne did… whatever he had planned was tearing him in two opposing directions. Yes, it scared him to death, but there was also a small part of him that found the prospect exciting and arousing. He forced himself to view the situation calmly.

If I'm not happy, I can always use my safeword. I have nothing to worry about—right?

When he considered that, excitement won out over fear. *Do it.*

"Okay, let's go to the club." Ellis got out the words before he had chance to talk himself out of it.

Wayne beamed at him. "Good boy."

Ellis made a growl at the back of his throat. "And there you go with the dog stuff again. My name is *not* Fido, okay?"

Wayne stroked his hand over Ellis's stubbled head. "Whatever you say." He reached into the pocket of his jeans for his phone and lurched off the couch. "I just have to make a phone call first." He paused and gave Ellis a keen glance. "Tonight or tomorrow?"

Ellis's first reaction was to suggest Saturday night, but he knew that was only apprehension getting the better of him. "Can whatever it is you're arranging be ready for tonight?"

Oh God. The look on Wayne's face. He held his chin high, his eyes gleaming. "In case I forget to tell you later, I am so very proud of you."

The way Ellis was feeling right then, they wouldn't need Wayne's truck to get to the club. He was going to fucking *float* there.

THEY WALKED into the club, and Wayne sent Ellis to remove his clothing. The silver chain was already around his neck, and Ellis still reached up to touch it as if to check it was really there. Wayne had been tempted to put a leather collar on him, but he figured once Ellis caught sight of a leash, it might be a step too far.

"So where is he?" Eli strode across from the bar to greet him, hand extended.

Wayne shook it. "Getting changed. My request didn't cause you any challenges, I hope?"

Eli shook his head. "We had them in storage. I wasn't about to get rid of them: they come in very handy when there's a demonstration." He grinned. "Does Ellis know what you have planned?"

"Not exactly. You might want to stick around for when he sees it all."

Eli rubbed his hands together gleefully. "Like I'd miss this." He gestured toward the main floor with his arm. "And we're pretty packed tonight, so you're probably going to have quite a few onlookers."

Wayne's heartbeat raced. He knew Ellis wouldn't let him down, but then again, it had been quite a while since *Wayne* performed before an audience.

"You got butterflies?" Eli asked with another grin.

"Does it show?" Wayne inhaled deeply and took off his long coat, revealing his harness, tight leather chaps, and the leather jock that strained to contain his growing erection. His boots shone like glass.

"Not when you're wearing all that getup," Eli said, his tone warm with approval. "Here, give me your coat. I'll hang it up for you." He turned his head toward the changing rooms and nodded. "Always love it when a sub wears nothing but his boots."

Wayne followed his gaze to where Ellis was walking across to them, his back straight and his dick apparently leading the way, long, thick, and already past half-mast.

"Someone's eager," Eli said under his breath with a chuckle. "Let's see what happens to that gorgeous cock when he sees what's coming to him." He patted Wayne on the arm. "I think I'll leave you to it. I'll just go and stand over there and wait for the reaction."

Wayne laughed. "You're an evil man, aren't you?"

Eli cackled. "Nah, I'm just a Dom." He nodded toward Ellis as he approached. "Oh, and you'll be next to the stage. It's all ready for you," he said to Wayne as he walked off.

Ellis lowered his gaze as he came to stand in front of Wayne.

"Ready, Sir," he said in a low voice.

Wayne's heart filled with pride. "You look amazing. Lift up your chin so I can see those beautiful eyes."

Ellis complied, his gaze meeting Wayne's. "Permission to ask a question, Sir?"

"Certainly."

Ellis glanced around him. "*Now* can you tell me what we'll be doing tonight?"

Wayne laughed. "Of course. But first I have a question for you. Did you ever see the film *King Kong*?"

Ellis frowned. "Which version? I can think of three."

"Oh, any of them," Wayne said lightly. "So you have seen at least one?" Ellis nodded, and Wayne smiled. "Excellent. Then follow me."

ELLIS WALKED behind Wayne, his breathing a little faster than normal, his pulse racing in trepidation. He knew Wayne wouldn't do anything to hurt or embarrass him, but this mysterious scene was making him very nervous.

As they got closer to the stage, Ellis caught sight of the....

What the hell?

"Oh God. Now I know why you mentioned *King Kong*," he muttered.

He was looking at two huge wooden columns… except they weren't. Two tall posts rose up from triangular bases, a distance of maybe three feet between them. There were holes down each post, and rope wound around them spaced at equal distances. Ropes hung from the posts in three different locations, and a raised platform joined the bases together, maybe eighteen inches from the floor—a platform clearly intended for someone to stand on.

Ellis stared, his heart pounding. "Don't tell me. I'm Fay Wray and you're going to tie me to that, and then we're going to wait for this damn huge ape to arrive," he joked, although his mind had already begun turning the possibilities over and over. *What is he going to do to me?*

"I was always partial to Naomi Watts, myself," Wayne murmured, picking up the flogger that lay on the stage. He circled his arm, letting the tails swish through the air, and gave Ellis a grin. "And yes, it's time to monkey around!" He pointed toward the posts. "Up you get, *Fay*."

Ellis gave him a mock glare and climbed up onto the platform, his face turned to the wall behind it, away from the men who were standing by the stage, murmurs already rippling through them.

"Uh-uh, face this way," Wayne told him. "Let the dog see the rabbit."

His heart pounding, Ellis turned carefully until he was facing the main floor of the club and the members he'd tried to ignore. But as Wayne set to getting him ready, more and more eyes turned toward them. A shiver coursed through him as men moved closer to the stage. Fortunately for Ellis, Wayne was there. Wayne was *always* there.

Wayne walked over to him, nodding. "Hands held high, arms bent at the elbow. Legs spread." He put down the flogger, went behind Ellis, and got up onto the platform with him. "Slip your wrists through the loops of rope. There's enough length so you can pull down on them if you need to."

"Am I going to need to?" Ellis asked.

Wayne's grin only made his heart pound that much harder.

He stood still while Wayne made sure his wrists were comfortable. Then Wayne stepped off the platform and picked up the ropes that hung at hip height. He wound them around Ellis's muscular thighs, right at the top so Ellis could feel them against his balls. Wayne tested to make sure they weren't cutting off his circulation before bending down to fasten his legs in the same fashion, this time winding around the top of his boots.

"That's you all nicely trussed up," he said in a bright tone. He eased his fingers under the wide waistband of his chaps and pulled out something small, black, and folded. Ellis recognized the blindfold immediately: it usually lived in the drawer of their bedside cabinet. Wayne held it up. "Ready for this?"

Not being able to see what Wayne was up to added a whole new dimension to the proceedings. Ellis's pulse quickened and his mouth was suddenly dry. "Yes, Sir." The words came out as a croak.

Wayne got up onto the platform, his legs spread, his feet between Ellis's and the posts. Wayne grabbed one of the ropes and held on while he locked gazes with Ellis. "Are you sure? You know if you want this to stop at any—"

Ellis finally found some spit. "I'm sure, Sir. Go on, put it on me."

He was rewarded with Wayne's beautiful smile, his blue eyes shining. "Good boy."

This time Ellis had no desire to talk back as Wayne's lips met his in a passionate kiss, Wayne taking possession of Ellis's mouth with his tongue. Ellis responded eagerly, drinking in the heady aroma of Wayne, leather, sweat, and testosterone.

When they parted, Wayne murmured into his ear. "What is your safeword?"

"Red, Sir," Ellis whispered, his heart doing a dance.

Wayne nodded, still close to him. "It will also help to take your mind off the audience. Far easier to concentrate on me too. You can let go of what's around you and forget about being observed."

Ellis breathed a little easier. That made sense. He gave a single nod. "I'm ready, Sir." One last glance into Wayne's eyes before Wayne lowered the blindfold over his head and adjusted it, plunging Ellis into darkness.

He held himself still, focusing on the noises around him, trying to pick out Wayne from the cacophony of raised voices, the *thwack* of a paddle, the crack of a hand landing on bare flesh, or the *whoosh* of a whip as it sliced through the air. Ellis jumped when he felt Wayne stroke a warm, firm hand across his chest, pausing at his nipple to tweak it between fingertips. It felt good until both hands landed in a resounding slap on his pecs.

Ellis gave a jolt, relaxing a little when Wayne caressed his abs, moving lower until another set of slaps landed on his belly. He gasped, pulling his stomach in taut. Wayne tugged and tweaked his nipples with his fingers.

"This is going to be fun." Ellis could hear the glee in Wayne's voice. Then he moaned with pleasure when Wayne fastened his hot, wet mouth on one nipple and tugged its partner sharply.

"That feels… good," Ellis admitted before Wayne delivered a couple more hard slaps to his torso and chest.

He knew what Wayne was doing: he was preparing Ellis's body for where his strikes would land. Then he let out another low moan of pleasure when Wayne rubbed his beard over Ellis's belly. *Fuck.* It was such a sensual experience and not what he'd anticipated at all. Wayne was kissing his chest and abs, tracing a line from his sternum down to his pubes with his tongue. Ellis pushed out with his hips when Wayne gently cupped his balls in his warm hand, fondling them, rolling them through his fingers. All the breath left him, however, when Wayne gave a sharp downward tug on his sac.

"Have to keep you on your toes," Wayne said quietly. He slid those warm hands lower, avoiding his dick and moving on to his thighs, where he stroked and caressed the firm muscles before slapping him there too.

Ellis began to get the picture: that flogger was going to be everywhere. Wayne had started a pattern: he rubbed the muscles before slapping them. Ellis held on tight to the ropes, stiffening his body in anticipation of the next smack of hand against flesh. When the pause came, he knew what was coming.

Wayne was obviously reaching for his flogger.

Sure enough he felt the flogger move through the air before the tails landed on his skin, not fierce, just the lightest of touches. This continued for a moment before Ellis realized the tails were landing with a heavier thud on his pecs, his thighs, lighter on his belly, but there nevertheless. He felt *those* strikes right through him, felt the warmth that radiated out over his skin and through his body every time the leather struck. Then Wayne would pause, only to stroke over Ellis's skin once more, gently, lovingly, making Ellis yearn to be able to watch their progress.

Another pause and Ellis held his breath, straining to hear Wayne's steps, trying to gain any clue as to what was coming next. When the tails landed across his buttocks and back with a soft *whump*, he had his answer. Wayne varied his strikes, moving between Ellis's shoulders, back, arse, and thighs, although Ellis had the impression his target was primarily Ellis's backside.

"Let me hear you, boy."

Wayne's voice, loud and clear, sharpened Ellis's focus. "You like flogging my arse, don't you?" he gasped out. "Judging by how many times you keep aiming for it."

Wayne chuckled. "You should see it. What a beautiful shade of red. The way your cheeks jiggle when the flogger connects with them." He rubbed them with his hand, not gently but firmly, squeezing the heated flesh, and Ellis groaned. "That's it," Wayne praised him. "I want to hear you." More thuds from the flogger, landing indiscriminately and without warning, gave rise to a flurry of loud cries that burst from Ellis's lips. He sighed with relief when they ceased.

"He takes your flogger really well," someone said nearby.

"Yeah, and can't you tell he likes it?" another said with a chuckle. "Look at that cock. Practically begging to be sucked."

Before Ellis could even think of begging, Wayne encased his dick in the wet, hot heaven of his mouth. Wayne took him deeply before sliding his lips back toward the head, where he sucked hard. A long, slow lick on the underside of his shaft from his balls to his slit had Ellis thrusting his hips forward, wanting more. Then it was back to Wayne taking him so deeply that Wayne's nose was pressed into his pubes, rubbing his belly with one hand while he pulled on his sac with the other.

"Oh fuck, don't stop," Ellis begged.

"If my sub said that, I'd stop instantly," a deep voice rumbled out. "Just to make sure he appreciated my mouth."

Ellis sent up a silent but fervent prayer Wayne wasn't that evil.

Wayne licked and sucked, rolling his tongue over the head before licking down to the base, then repeating the journey in reverse. Ellis knew he could come just from Wayne's mouth on his cock, but he also knew there was more to come; he doubted Wayne was finished with the flogger. But until that moment, he was going to enjoy the experience. Wayne bobbed his head on his dick, gently moving his hand over Ellis's belly as he stroked him. From somewhere in front of him came more murmurs. They were obviously gathering an audience.

Ellis gave an involuntary shiver at the thought of all those men watching Wayne suck his cock, but such considerations were lost when Wayne took him deep into his throat and Ellis flung out a hoarse cry at how *fucking amazing* that felt. He moved his hips, pumping them as he tried to control his thrusts, but Wayne held him firm, those warm hands on his belly and arse.

When Wayne pulled away, Ellis wanted to beg him not to stop, but he knew better. He stood still, trying to focus once more on Wayne's movements, but his Dom was doing a good impression of a ninja. *Sneaky bastard.*

When the flogger landed with a heavy thud on his buttocks, Ellis let another harsh cry ring out.

"That's it. God, you sound good."

Ellis focused on Wayne's voice, his heart soaring to hear the love there. *Can they hear it too?* For Ellis it rang out as clear and steady as a beacon, cutting through the pain, the heat, and the exhilaration.

"Do you want to know just how good you look?" Wayne was closer, his voice lowered to a whisper Ellis had to strain to hear. Then suddenly Wayne was up on the platform again, his lips inches from Ellis's ear. "I've taken off my jock," Wayne whispered. "It wouldn't hold my cock any longer. Seeing you taking my strikes, watching your skin redden, hearing the sounds pouring out of you… it's such a fucking turn-on."

Ellis could feel Wayne's body heat, and then he felt something else—the hot slide of Wayne's bare dick against his.

"You feel that?" Wayne's voice was deep and husky.

"Yes, Sir," he whispered. *Feel it?* He wanted it with every fiber of him.

"You're going to take a little more for me, and then I'm going to fuck you right here while all these guys stand around watching you. They're going to watch my boy taking my dick." Ellis shuddered as Wayne kissed his neck and then sucked on it. "My bare dick," he added. "First time for both of us." Ellis jolted when Wayne tugged on his earlobe with his teeth. "You want that?"

Ellis had never been aware of how strong of an exhibitionist streak ran in him until that moment because *fuck yeah* he wanted that. His cock jerked up and his mouth flooded with saliva.

Then he couldn't hold back the whimper of frustration when Wayne climbed down off the platform.

The tails landed on his thighs in downward strokes, slowly at first but building until there was only a second's gap between them, alternating between legs. Now and again Wayne would ease off, and Ellis gasped to feel the leather caress his dick, softly and with none of its previous force. Then it was back to business, only now Wayne was focusing his strikes on Ellis's arse once again, the tails alternating between landing with a thud he felt through his body or with a sting as the tails were snapped onto his flesh.

Ellis took it all, already past the point where pain had begun to blur into pleasure, or at best, it was a heady amalgam of the two. It was the longest scene they'd done thus far, and he knew Wayne had been working up to this moment. Every time Wayne spoke of his pride in Ellis, it lit a fire inside Ellis's belly that licked and spread through him until his skin tingled everywhere.

When he realized the flogging had stopped, Ellis let out a long, drawn-out breath. *I did it. I took everything he had to give.*

"You were amazing." Wayne was right there, his breath tickling Ellis's face. Then he took Ellis's mouth in a lingering kiss, Wayne's hand gentle on his face and neck, caressing him, stroking him, the kiss spinning out until Ellis was dizzy from it.

Wayne removed the blindfold and Ellis blinked, his gaze instantly taking in the crowd of men who'd assembled in front of them. There had to be about fifteen to twenty of them, and most of them were grinning.

"You've got a good one there, Wayne. God, he's a big boy, isn't he?"

"In more ways than one," another added with a nod to Ellis's groin. "Tell me you share, please."

Wayne laughed and kissed Ellis on the lips. He locked eyes with him as he responded to the question. "Sorry, fellas. This one is all mine."

Ellis heaved a sigh of relief, not that he hadn't known that already.

Wayne got down and walked around to the rear of the posts. Ellis wanted badly to turn his head and watch, but he kept his gaze forward, jumping a little when Wayne smacked his arse. He held himself still the next time the slaps landed on his cheeks but couldn't help gasping when Wayne rubbed his beard over the heated flesh. Wayne kissed his buttocks, biting gently now and again before sliding a couple of fingers through his crease.

Ellis groaned and glanced down at his dick, a solid rod of flesh pointing upward. Precome suspended from the slit in a long, glistening string that waved through the air as he moved, like the thread from a spider's web.

"Okay, squat down, arms extended," Wayne instructed him. "Stick out that gorgeous arse."

Ellis complied, holding on to the ropes, his knees bent so he was in a sitting position, the ropes supporting him.

"Perfect." Wayne kissed the top of his crack. "I have a great view. Your cheeks are spread and your hole is just where I want it."

From behind him came the sound of tearing, followed by Wayne rubbing his slick fingers over Ellis's exposed hole. Wayne slid his other hand around Ellis's waist to wrap around his dick, and suddenly Ellis moaned from the double assault as Wayne tugged at his length while sinking two fingers into him, filling him.

"That's all you're getting." Wayne's voice was husky once more. "I have to be inside you." Ellis caught his breath at the words but groaned when Wayne pushed his hot, bare cock into him. "Oh God," Wayne said weakly. "That feels…."

Whatever else he'd meant to say was lost in a grunt as he thrust into Ellis's channel, filling him to the hilt. Ellis pushed back as best he could to meet him, unable to keep quiet. His loud cries of pleasure mingled with Wayne's groans and low growls as he fucked Ellis, Wayne gripping the ropes that wound around the posts. He punched his dick into Ellis's arse, burying it deep.

"Don't come until I say so," Wayne cried out between thrusts.

Ellis wanted to growl that he was already too fucking close, but he bit back the words and submitted to Wayne's sensual assault on his body.

Everything was conspiring to make this a short but epic fuck: the knowledge that they were being observed, the fact Wayne was fucking him bareback for the first time, the way Wayne's cock felt each time he slid it deep inside him, Wayne slipping his arm around Ellis to hold him and stroke him, Wayne's powerful thrusts that sped up, his groin slamming into Ellis's arse, and the way Wayne let the ropes take his weight, rocking his hips as he fucked Ellis with long, deep thrusts.

"Sir, I need to come," Ellis moaned, his balls tight, his body tingling. "Please let me come."

"Do it," Wayne grunted out, burying his dick deep. "I want to feel you come on my cock when I shoot my load inside you."

Heat surged through Ellis and he came with a shout, his come spattering onto the floor in front of him, dick jerking as it pulsed out the last drops.

"Fuck, you're so tight around my cock," Wayne ground out, and seconds later, Ellis felt the throb deep in his arse as Wayne came, his body curved around Ellis's, one arm around his waist.

"Love you, boy." The whispered words filled Ellis with a fierce joy.

"Love you too, Sir."

They hung there, Wayne's breathing harsh in his ear, Ellis's body shaking from his orgasm and flogging, Ellis aware of the round of applause that stuttered around the club.

Wayne gave a breathless chuckle. "I think they liked us."

Ellis gave an equally breathless snort. "Good, because we're not doing an encore."

Chapter Twenty-Four

ELLIS WALKED into the living room to the sound of his phone ringing. Wayne held it out to him. "Your sister."

Ellis glanced at the clock. They'd have to leave for work in an hour, but he had a few minutes to talk with Barb. He smiled to himself. The habitual terror he'd felt whenever she called failed to materialize. Their last few conversations had actually been almost pleasant. He and Wayne had watched the kids while Barb went out to look for a job, and they had a great time. They played board games—until the kids tired of them—and then Wayne and Mark played some ball outside while Ellis had a tea party with his niece. He hated to admit it, but sitting next to her as she set up the table with tiny china cups and her favorite stuffed animals was really sweet.

Of course he knew the teasing would follow. Like Wayne was going to let an opportunity like *that* get away from him. What Ellis hadn't anticipated was how long it would last. Wayne must have brought it up every day for a week, and not just at home either. When they were at work, Wayne would place a mug of tea on the table, then ask loudly if Ellis needed Mr. Flopsy to help him with the sugar. It made all the guys laugh, but instead of the surge of anger Ellis would have normally felt, he laughed right along with them.

Damn, it feels good to be myself again. He smiled over at the man seated beside him who was responsible. *I owe him my life. Literally.* When Wayne caught his gaze, Ellis mouthed *love you,* which made Wayne smile.

Enough smooching. Barb, remember?

"Hey, Barb."

"Hi, Ellis. Thank you both again for watching the kids," she started. "I wanted you to be the first to know I got the job."

"Really? Congratulations!"

"It's not much, but it's something. My counsellor helped me to get it. She's also got me involved in some parenting classes, and they're helping me get a handle on things. I still get stressed, but not like I used to. And I don't take it out on the kids." She was quiet for a moment. "Or you."

"I'm glad to hear it."

"Can I ask you a question?"

"Of course."

She made a humming sound. "Why did you let me treat you that way? Why didn't you just tell me to sod off?"

Ellis chuckled. "Do you want the truth, or do you want the story I told myself that helped to make it okay?"

"The truth. Please."

Ellis sat down on the sofa, smiling up at Wayne as he brought in a cup of decaf coffee. He mouthed *thank you*, then settled back. The lessons he'd learned thanks to Wayne were about to be imparted to his sister.

"Dad was right." He caught her startled intake of breath instantly. "I know how that sounds," he added quickly, "but in a manner of speaking, he was. I *am* responsible for helping my family. But one of the ways that I should have helped was by learning to say no. I ran myself ragged trying to be all things to all people, and that was tearing me apart. Like you, I needed someone to help me, and that turned out to be Wayne. He put me back on the path I needed to be on, and I'm grateful to him."

Wayne blew him a kiss, which caused Ellis's cheeks to heat.

"He seems like a good man," Barb said softly.

"He is. He's the best mate I've ever had, and I love him."

"I could see that when the two of you were here. Mark couldn't stop talking about how Uncle Wayne took him out and played with him. I'm… sorry I spoke so harshly about him. That wasn't fair to him, or to you."

"Neither of us were upset about it. Well, not really. The thing of it is, you and I were raised in a toxic environment. We did everything we could to make our parents love us. We tried to be the good kids, and when that didn't work…."

"I lashed out. I wanted them to just listen for once. Instead of telling me to go see you when I had a problem, I wanted their help."

"Exactly. And me? I was an idiot who thought the best way to do things was to show them I could take care of my sister. But I couldn't even care for myself. What they did to us amounted to child abuse." Ellis was still amazed he could look at the past so calmly. It was incredible what several weeks—and a healthy dose of Wayne—had done.

"And I was on that same path with Mark and Amanda. When she'd cry I would tell her to go talk to Mark because I couldn't handle it. And Mark? He's so much like you. He would do his best to take care of her, but…." She sobbed. "Ellis, I'm so, so sorry. I know I don't deserve your forgiveness, but I'm asking… *begging* for it. Even if you hate me, don't lose touch with the kids. They need their uncle in their lives."

Ellis sat up quickly, sloshing coffee over the rim of the cup. "Whoa. Wait. Where is this coming from?"

She sniffled. "My counsellor told me that I needed to think about the people I'd wronged. And it's a really, really long list. Your name is at the top of it."

"You never wronged me," Ellis said stridently. Wayne lifted his chin and stared, his forehead creased into a frown.

"Don't lie to me," Barb fired back. "Please. Not now. I did. I know it. I was a terrible person to you and my children. I can't even blame it on anyone else because I'm supposed to be the adult. I should have stepped up and taken responsibility instead of trying to foist it off on you because I couldn't handle it."

"And I should have talked to you and let you know how much of a toll it was taking on me. Do you really think that either of us is in the wrong here? We didn't communicate—which Wayne constantly reminds me is important—and that's on both of us. But Barb, you're my sister, and I love you."

"Really?"

Ellis smiled. "Cross my heart."

"I have an idea," Wayne said suddenly. "What if you, me, and your family take a trip this weekend? We'll go see the London Eye."

Ellis was almost giddy over the prospect. He'd seen the Eye—because who hadn't?—but he'd never ridden it. "Did you hear that?" he asked her.

"Yes. We'd love to go!"

"Then it's a date. We can do lunch too. We'll make a day of it."

"Thank you, Ellis. And thank Wayne for me. I'm glad I still have a family."

"Me too," Ellis replied.

They said their goodbyes and hung up. Ellis shifted closer to Wayne and kissed him. "Thank you."

"Nothing to thank me for," Wayne assured him. "I enjoyed spending time with the kids as much as you did. In fact, it made me call my own parents."

"Oh?"

"I hadn't talked with them in a while. While they may wish for another life for me, they still love me. Mum was floored that I called. She shouted to Dad, and the two of them kept me on the phone for hours talking my ear off. I told them about you, and Mum said she'd like to meet you. Dad wasn't nearly as enthusiastic, but he said you'd be welcome in their home."

Ellis frowned. "And where was I during this conversation?"

"That would be the day you were in the corner with a beautiful rosy red arse, hopefully reflecting on what a bad idea it is to sass me while we're at work."

Ellis snorted. "Hey, you started it."

Wayne's eyes gleamed. "And I finished it. But while I watched you kneeling in the living room with your nose pressed up against the wall, I got… I guess you could say homesick. My parents had been on my mind since that mess with yours. There were some hurt feelings there, mostly on my part, and I wanted to lay those to rest." Wayne put a hand on Ellis's neck and pulled him in for another kiss. "So you told your sister how much I helped you? You did the same for me."

Ellis's cheeks heated up. "So you're saying we're good for one another?"

"I'd say we're perfect for each other." He glanced at Ellis's phone. "And I'd also say that if you don't get your arse in gear, we're going to be late."

Ellis rushed from the room to get ready for work. He had a good feeling in the pit of his stomach. After more than a year, things were finally going his way.

THE DAY'S training exercises were almost at an end. Ellis was teamed up with Derwent, the two of them working to approach a pair of suspects as quietly as possible during a hostage scenario. Wayne was watching with the others on the sideline, his stopwatch in his hand. He always got a buzz from watching Ellis. *He can move bloody fast for a big guy.*

Wayne watched Ellis go up and over a wall, landing nimbly on the other side. He rushed toward the building where the "suspects" were located, then gave hand signals to Derwent, who covered the other exit. Then they both disappeared from view.

Wayne caught the klaxon from Phelps that signaled they'd finished the exercise, and he stopped his watch. The two of them had worked flawlessly, capturing Shaun and his partner in near record time. Ellis, Derwent, and the others exited the building, everyone smiling. He felt a flush of pride when Ellis and Derwent hugged one another. The smile on Ellis's face was the most genuine he'd seen at work in a very long time.

"Did you see that?" Derwent shouted to Wayne.

"I did," Wayne replied. "You two worked well together."

"Yeah, if he wasn't your—" Derwent lowered his voice. "—*whatever* the two of you have going," he whispered, "I'd consider stealing him for myself."

Ellis gave Wayne a startled look, which Derwent must have caught. He waved his hand toward Ellis.

"Don't get your undies in a twist, Mann. There's nothing wrong with a little spice in the bedroom. Hell, if I ever get a girlfriend, I may have to ask about borrowing some of your boyfriend's goodies. He's got some really interesting-looking items in that toy box there. Especially those little clips with the ring at the end. Not sure what they're for, but they looked wicked."

"Aha!" Wayne said triumphantly. "So you *did* peek after all." He leaned in close. "Those clips go on your nipples. That ring gets slipped over your cock. You stand up wrong or move too fast, and they deliver a nasty bite."

Derwent went pale. "You mean those are for use on a guy?"

"Well, duh," Wayne replied with a smirk. "What use would *I* have for something to use on a woman?"

"Oh shit. I didn't even think about that. Never mind. I don't want to borrow anything."

"Come on, Derwent," Ellis teased. "You'd probably love it."

"Nope, not for me, mate. You guys have fun with them."

"We do," Ellis assured him. Wayne had a good laugh about that.

It wasn't until they were driving home that Wayne realized Ellis had grown quiet.

"Is everything okay?"

"Hmm?" Ellis replied absently, his gaze fixed on the road ahead.

Wayne knew avoidance when he saw it. "All right, spit it out. You've obviously got something on your mind, and last time I looked, we don't keep secrets from each other."

Ellis studied his hands in his lap. "You know, I lied to Derwent earlier."

"Oh?" Wayne racked his brain to think what Ellis could be talking about.

"I told him we have fun with all your toys. But…."

"But?"

Ellis inclined his head to glance at Wayne. "I don't even know what you have in that chest apart from the floggers."

Wayne blinked. "You haven't opened it and taken a look?"

"You didn't say I could, so I didn't."

The simple statement floored him for a second. "I'm impressed. Seriously." He thought quickly. "Maybe we should take a tour of my— our—toys after dinner. I have some lovely things in there."

Ellis cleared his throat. "Why do I have the feeling 'lovely things' is a euphemism for 'implements of torture'?"

Wayne laughed. "Funny you should mention that word."

"Which one?"

"Torture." He fired Ellis a quick glance. "Do you know what CBT stands for?"

"No, but A, I think you're about to tell me, and B, I have another feeling that I'm going to be worse off for knowing."

Wayne kept his laugh internal. "CBT is cock and ball torture." He kept his eyes on the road and waited for the explosion.

Silence.

"Ellis?"

"You're kidding, right?"

Wayne had already decided what he was going to do that evening. "What if I told you that what I have in mind would end with you having probably one of the best orgasms of your life?"

"You'd have to go a long way to beat the one where you fucked me at the club."

Wayne smiled. Ellis had floated through the weekend after that scene.

"I'm not saying yes just like that, okay? I mean, there's the whole 'torture' aspect to think about, not just the end result."

Wayne chuckled. "I promise it sounds worse than it is." For what he had in mind, he'd need to do a little DIY when they got home, though. "Think about it. But if you decide to say yes, I'd need you to make the dinner while I... did something."

"What—turn the bedroom into a dungeon?"

"Just a few alterations, that's all. But it's a moot point if you say no."

Wayne pulled the truck into the parking lot in front of their building and switched off the engine. Ellis had gone quiet again, but Wayne let him. At least this time he knew what occupied his boy's mind. They got out of the truck and Wayne locked it. As they neared the main door, Ellis stopped him with a hand to his arm.

"Okay." His voice was low.

Wayne's heart almost skipped a beat. "Okay?"

"As in okay, let's do your fiendish torture of my delicate nether regions."

Wayne snorted as he pushed open the door. He leaned in close. "You forget I've seen your dick up close and personal, and trust me, honey, there is nothing delicate about it."

Ellis was still chuckling by the time they reached their front door.

WHAT THE hell did he need a pair of stepladders for?

Ellis tried not to dwell on it, but the question had plagued him constantly since Wayne went into the tall kitchen cupboard and removed the ladders before disappearing into the bedroom.

Stepladders? In the bedroom?

Ellis was dying of curiosity. Not that he'd peeped once into the room—Wayne had forbidden him to do that—but *God*, the temptation. Dinner was finished, the washing-up all dried and put away, and Wayne was in the bedroom again, humming away to himself. Ellis was sitting on the couch, trying to read the TV listings magazine, but it wasn't happening. His heartbeat wasn't anywhere near normal, for one thing.

Why did I say yes? I mean, cock and ball torture? Torture? What was I thinking?

He knew deep down his fears were groundless. Wayne would never do anything to hurt him.

Yeah, but he might like to watch me squirm. I wouldn't put that *past him.*

When the bedroom door opened and Wayne stood there, still in his jeans but his chest bare, the sight did nothing to help Ellis's nervous state. He sat on the couch, unable to move, his gaze focused on Wayne's face, the scruff of a beard and hint of a moustache, those long black lashes that framed gorgeous blue eyes....

"Well, if you're just going to sit there.... Changed your mind?"

Ellis pulled himself together and went with the truth. "I was just thinking what a beautiful man you are."

Wayne walked slowly over to him, bent down, and kissed him leisurely on the mouth. Ellis opened for him without hesitation, and in that moment, the kiss morphed into something with a lot more heat. Wayne straddled his lap, never once breaking contact, cupping Ellis's face in his hands. Ellis slipped his hands around Wayne's waist to stroke his back before gliding them over his warm skin to rub his chest and finally caress his neck, pulling him deeper. When Wayne began to rock against him, Ellis knew he had nothing to fear.

"I can feel you," Wayne whispered against his lips. "Feel how hard you are."

"Is that a bad thing?" Ellis asked with a smile.

"No, but it just means I'll have to be careful not to let you pop too quickly."

"'Pop'?"

Wayne shrugged. "Pop. Explode. Same thing." He grinned. "Ready to play?"

Ellis snorted. "But you don't mean 'play,' you sadistic ba—"

Wayne covered his mouth with a hand. "Be very, very careful what you say. You might regret it."

That shut him up fast.

Wayne got up off Ellis's lap and held out a hand. "Come on, see what I've been up to."

Ellis took it and Wayne hoisted him to his feet. He followed Wayne into the bedroom, darting his gaze around as he tried to see the results. The first things he saw were the steel rings that were now fixed to the wooden bed frame. They needed no explanation whatsoever. Then he looked higher.

"Er, Wayne? Why are there several hooks coming out of your ceiling?"

There was one above each corner of the bed, plus a central line of about four down the middle.

Wayne chuckled. "So you notice those but not what's on the bed itself?"

He diverted his gaze downward and saw lots of red rope laid out neatly in differing lengths and a—

Ellis jerked his head up and stared at Wayne. "What are you doing with one of those? Isn't that a vibrator for women?"

Wayne widened his eyes and laughed. "And how do you know about Magic Wands?"

Ellis glared at him. "I *have* dated women, remember? There *were* women in my life before you and that... lethal weapon of yours came into it." He stilled as he recalled a long-past conversation. Something about how powerful the vibrator was....

Oh fuck.

Wayne straightened, and it was as if he'd slipped on an invisible cloak that had DOM written all over it. His demeanor changed and his gaze grew more focused. "Strip, then lie on the bed on your back." He gave a flicker of a smile. "And I prefer to call it the Wand of Power, myself."

Yeah, that didn't help Ellis's nerves one little bit.

He stripped off quickly and got onto the bed, his gaze focused on Wayne, who was uncoiling the ropes. "Is this where I get trussed up like a Christmas turkey again?" he joked.

Wayne paused. "I need you to get into your head space," he said quietly. "I have a little preparation to do before we can start, and while I'm doing it, I want you focusing on being calm and relaxed. I know your nerves are getting the better of you—and don't deny it because you always retreat into humor when that happens."

Ellis stared at him, stilling instantly. "Wow. You really do know me."

Wayne leaned over the bed and kissed him, a brushing of lips, but it was enough. "Of course I do. I love you." He smiled once more. "Now hush and let me concentrate."

Ellis responded with a nod. "Yes, Sir."

"Arms above your head, hands towards the corners."

Ellis did as instructed, his heartbeat speeding up when Wayne fastened restraints around his wrists.

"Okay, now bend your legs, knees wide apart and ankles crossed." Wayne chuckled. "This is where you being flexible is a bonus."

Ellis spread his legs wide, his knees falling to the mattress. "This is also where all that yoga really pays off," he added. He ached to lift his head from the bed and watch as Wayne bound his ankles together with rope, but he knew better. He lay still, staring at the hooks in the ceiling. He figured he'd know soon enough where they fit in to the picture.

"This is the tricky part." Wayne picked up a long length and tied it to one of the rings in the bed frame. Then he slipped it through the ring on Ellis's wrist restraint. Ellis was fascinated by the journey this rope took as Wayne wound it around his thigh and calf, ending up at another ring at the foot of the bed. Wayne repeated this on the other side, mirroring the first rope's path until Ellis couldn't unfold his legs, the only movement left to him the ability to push up—a little—with his hips.

"Where did you learn to do all this?" he asked Wayne.

"One, I watched an expert at the club—that was what got me interested in the first place—and two, I had some training. I'm nowhere near as skilled as others, but I make it work for me without endangering the sub who ends up just where I want him." He grinned. "Which would be you right now."

Ellis was feeling surprisingly relaxed and comfortable despite his bonds. But when Wayne picked up another rope and stood on the bed, his heart began to pound.

Wayne tied the rope through the ceiling hook that was conveniently placed... right above Ellis's cock.

"Okay, this is getting... interesting."

Wayne laughed as he knelt on the bed. "Oh, I promise you it'll be a hell of a lot more than interesting when I'm done." He picked up the vibrator and tied the rope securely around it so it hung down, its bulbous head barely an inch from Ellis's achingly hard dick, low enough so it was an inch or two above his pubes.

What the fuck? Ellis couldn't resist the urge to lift his head as much as possible to watch the proceedings.

Wayne picked up another length of rope, tied it around Ellis's ankles, then through the knot that lay between his spread legs, clearly heading for his cock. Then he grabbed Ellis's sac and stretched it, pulling it away from his body before twisting the rope around and around it, separating it from his dick. Ellis caught his breath as Wayne slipped the rope around the thin neck of the vibrator between the head and the body until the flared ridge was pressed up against the body, the shaft against the oscillating head.

The head Ellis knew was going to vibrate. Powerfully.

Wayne leaned across the bed to pick up a mirror. "I want you to see what I can see," he said softly. He angled the mirror so Ellis saw *everything*: his balls, the skin stretched so tight that they were turning a purplish blue color, the delicate veins bulging out almost angrily as the blood vessels flared over the surface; his dick flushed dark red with blood and *fuck*, it was hard; and the precome that had already begun to bead at the head, glistening against the taut purple crown of his cock.

"Oh my God," Ellis said, swallowing. "That looks...."

"Amazing. You look amazing." Wayne slowly lowered the mirror and placed it on the bed, out of reach. "The ropes aren't tight enough so that you can't move, and the wand will move too. You'll be able to push up a little, and your cock will move through the rope. Although I recommend just lying back and enjoying it," he added with a grin.

"'Lying back'?" Ellis snorted. "Like I can do anything else in this state." He held his breath as Wayne stretched a hand toward the control.

"You have your safeword for if it gets too much," Wayne reassured him. "Ready?"

Ellis drew in a deep breath and forced himself to relax his muscles. "Ready, Sir."

Wayne smiled and pressed the button.

Fuck. It was intense right from the get-go every time the head of the vibrator buzzed against his shaft.

"Holy fuck," Ellis groaned. "That just sent my cock into warp speed."

"Give it a moment for your body to get used to the vibrations," Wayne told him. "Right now you're on the lowest setting."

"The lowest?" It was official; Ellis wasn't going to survive longer than five minutes. But after a minute, when he didn't come on the spot, he realized Wayne was correct: it started to feel really good, and he breathed a little easier. "It's like masturbating, but with someone else doing all the work." His cock was more rigid than ever, and he got the impression it wouldn't take much more to have him coming.

"Maybe it's time to turn up the volume."

Wayne's words pierced the sexual fog that surrounded his brain, and Ellis moaned. *Oh God.*

WAYNE COULDN'T take his eyes off Ellis. Every jerk of his cock moved the vibrator, and now and again Ellis would give a small thrust of his hips, clearly wanting more of the sensations. He watched Ellis's dick shudder when the oscillating head vibrated, noting the shivers that coursed through his body. Ellis appeared lost in a sexual haze, moaning constantly, his belly quivering, his chest rising and falling when the vibrations took their toll.

He gave Ellis a minute and then reduced the speed, unable to miss Ellis's harsh sigh. Wayne had tried it on his own cock and was astounded by the sensations. He knew if he left the vibrator where it was after Ellis ejaculated, it would simply extend his orgasm.

Wayne didn't think this first session would last all that long, however.

"Ready for some more?"

"I think... I'm really close," Ellis gasped out, his body shaking, the vibrator jerking more violently as it reacted to every movement of his dick.

"Can you feel your orgasm building?" he asked, gently stroking Ellis's bound thigh. *Fuck*, he looked so hot, the red ropes against his pale skin, the way he tried to push his cock against the vibrator, chasing the sensations. "Right now it's on a pulse mode, so you get a little respite." The head would oscillate for a few seconds and then cease.

"You're not going to leave me attached to this thing for hours, are you?" Ellis asked, his voice quavering.

Wayne laughed. "Er, no. It burns out its motor after about twenty-five minutes of continual use. But that's when it's on constant vibration, not like it is now. Not only that, if you use it for too long, it would cause some numbness."

"Thank God for small mercies," Ellis gasped.

Wayne grinned, reached out, and switched it from pulse to constant. Then he stepped back to watch his submissive lose it.

"Fuck! I can feel that all the way down into my nuts!" Ellis pushed his head back, his body straining against the ropes, his toes curling as come spattered from his cock. He attempted to arch up off the bed, but his bonds prevented it. More come pulsed out of him, and Ellis trembled, pushing out a stream of moans and low, hoarse cries. Wayne reached over and placed two fingers on his frenulum, holding it firmly against the wand.

Ellis's body jerked, but he still kept coming. "Oh fuck," he said weakly, his dick twitching as he emptied his balls, his spunk spluttering everywhere due to the vibrations. "Please… Sir, please…."

Wayne switched off the wand, and a huge sigh of relief poured from Ellis's lips, replaced by a loud cry when Wayne leaned over to lick the head of his cock.

"Ugh!" Ellis stiffened, his body rigid as Wayne slowly lapped the come from his shaft. "Fuck, that's so… s-sensitive."

Wayne chuckled and finished his cleanup. "I know."

"B-bastard," Ellis stuttered.

"No—*Sir*," Wayne corrected. "My, my, but you're a slower learner than I thought." Ellis's mutters under his breath were music to Wayne's ears. *This* was his boy, the man Wayne had fallen in love with. And when Ellis came down enough for Wayne to remove the ropes, he was going to put his boy under the sheets, strip off, climb in there with him, and hold him all night long.

CHAPTER TWENTY-FIVE

WAYNE PROPPED himself up on his arms and slowly, slowly filled Ellis's arse, pushing gently until his dick was buried to the hilt. Ellis's eyes were closed, his breathing shallow, his thick calves resting on Wayne's shoulders.

"God, this is addictive," Ellis murmured breathlessly.

"What is?" Wayne held still inside him and bent down to kiss him. "What's addictive?"

"The feeling of having your cock in my arse."

Wayne chuckled and slid out of him before thrusting a little harder. "What—this cock?"

Ellis groaned. "Bastard." But Wayne couldn't help noticing how he pushed down to meet Wayne's thrust. "Oh God, there."

Wayne rolled Ellis's body up off the mattress and speared his dick deep inside that tight channel. "There?"

Ellis opened his eyes wide. "Fuck yeah. Do it again."

Wayne slid his dick out and then pushed back inside all the way. "Tighten your arse around my cock."

Ellis bit his lip, concentration etched on his face. "Like that?" When Wayne let out a long moan of pleasure, he grinned. "Oh. Yeah. Like that." Once again there was that sensation of exquisite tightness.

Wayne caught his breath. "You're a fast learner." God, he wanted to let loose and just *take* Ellis, plow that tight arse until Ellis was begging to be allowed to come.

Then he thought about it. *Who's the Dom here?*

Wayne gazed into Ellis's eyes. "Hold on to me," he warned.

It took a second or two for the import of his words to sink in. Ellis swallowed hard and gripped Wayne's shoulders. "Okay."

Then Wayne was lost in a hot tide of intense fucking, sliding in and out of Ellis's body, not holding back as he drove his cock deep into him, each thrust punching the air from Ellis's lungs. Ellis dug his fingers deep into the shoulder muscle, his breathing becoming more rapid, his belly quivering. "You keep… this up… and I won't last…."

Wayne locked gazes with him. "Come when you're ready. But don't expect me to finish just because you do." Then he went right back to fucking his boy with a passion that slid from hot to white-hot as Ellis began to buck beneath him, his abs bunching up, the veins standing out on his arms as he held on to Wayne.

"That's it," Wayne encouraged him. "Just let go." He picked up speed, slamming into Ellis's meaty arse, feeling his flesh ripple from the impact.

"Oh fuck," Ellis moaned, and Wayne's groan matched his when his dick was gripped tightly. "God, I love you." Seconds later Ellis came, his come coating both of them, his body shaking.

Wayne shuddered and emptied his balls deep inside Ellis, his cock throbbing as he filled him, filled his boy. He lay on him, their bodies damp with sweat, both of them trembling from the force of their orgasms. "I love you," he whispered into Ellis's ear.

They lay like that for what seemed like hours, Wayne unwilling to pull out of him, loving the feeling of the two of them locked together. He was still holding his boy when they fell asleep.

IT HAD to be revoltingly early, but Ellis wasn't about to look at the clock. He was warm, with Wayne's arms wrapped around him. Sex just got better and better. He was starting to get used to going in to work with the most delicious aches in his body.

Except for those times when Derwent noticed and swatted him on the arse every chance he got. He stopped when Ellis leaned over and whispered, "Is that the best you got? Wayne does it a lot harder." Derwent had flushed and gone off to bother someone else.

Ellis's thoughts drifted from sex to what was fast becoming his favorite topic—Wayne. Because when he thought about how things were working out with Barb, he realized every good thing in his life right now came down to Wayne.

"Do you smell rubber burning?" Wayne asked, his voice filled with sleep.

Ellis gave a jolt. "What? No."

"Hm. Must be you thinking again."

Ellis grabbed his pillow and held it up to smack Wayne.

"You'd best think very carefully about what you're going to do with that."

Ellis stopped and put the pillow back down. "Just fluffing it, Sir," he said, trying to keep the grin out of his voice.

Wayne lay on his side and stroked his fingers across Ellis's chest. "What's going on in your head now?"

"Do you think we can go to the club tomorrow?"

Wayne furrowed his brow. "Tomorrow? Why would you want to go on a Wednesday?"

Ellis didn't think he had the words to explain the need within him. "I'd like to stop and talk with Jarod. You know, if that's okay. I've got something I want to ask him."

"And it's not anything I can help with?" Wayne asked.

Ellis would have to have been deaf to miss the note of hurt in his voice. He moved over and snuggled up against Wayne. "No, sorry. I have something on my mind, and I need to ask him about it. I guess you could say I need the view of a submissive."

The grin he got in return warmed Ellis through and through. This had been the biggest surprise of his life, finally admitting to himself and others he was gay and letting Wayne into his life despite Ellis's upbringing.

Wayne stroked his fingers over Ellis's hip. "I know I was a little rough earlier. Are you sore?"

Ellis's heartbeat sped up a little. "A little, but definitely not enough to make me say no." He smiled. "What do you have in mind?"

Wayne spent the next thirty minutes showing him.

ELLIS WAS buzzing with anticipation. Wayne was staying late to finish his reports on their training that day, but he told Ellis to go to the club. He'd meet him there when he was done. Then Wayne pushed him into the corner and told him to be ready when he got there, kissing him with such passion Ellis wanted to drop to his knees and blow his Dom in the bathroom.

Ellis strode into the club, went to the lockers, took off his shirt, and hung it up on the hook. His stomach fluttered as he anticipated what Jarod would say when they talked. Maybe Ellis was out of his mind for thinking about doing this, but everything in him was telling him this was right.

He stopped at the mirror to straighten the necklace Wayne had given him. He loved the way it gleamed in the light, a reminder that, even when he wasn't by Ellis's side, Wayne was there. Ellis stroked his neck, wondering what a real collar—like the one Jarod wore—would feel like. He reflected its weight might be a constant source of strength.

Ellis sighed. As much as he hated to admit it, he really did want that collar.

He exited the locker room and headed toward the bar. The club was already busy, and he had to admit it felt strange to be there without Wayne.

"Good evening. Can I get you something to drink?" the bartender asked.

"Not right now, but thank you. I was wondering if you could tell me whether Jarod was around."

"He is. Let me give him a call. Who shall I say wants to speak with him?"

For a moment Ellis's nerves got the better of him. "My name is Ellis, but please, let him know it's nothing important if he's busy."

The cute young man picked up the phone, spoke briefly, then hung up.

"Jarod said I should send you up. He's getting his mother ready to go to an art gallery with Maxwell and will be a few minutes. When you get in the lift, Jarod will know you're on your way."

The last thing Ellis wanted was to be an imposition, but he figured Jarod wouldn't have agreed to him going up to the apartment if he didn't have the time. He got into the lift, which took him up to the top floor. The door to Jarod's place was open, and as Ellis approached, he could hear a woman's voice.

"Can't we go to a strip club instead? I hear Thunder From Down Under is having a show tonight."

In spite of his nerves, Ellis had to smile. *This is his mother? She sounds like fun.*

He stepped into the apartment in time to see Jarod pinch the bridge of his nose. "Mother, you can't expect Maxwell to take you to a strip club. What will he be doing while you're ogling the dancers?"

"If I give him some five-pound notes, he can help me stuff their shorts." She laughed, and Ellis couldn't help but laugh too. Jarod glanced across and his face lit up in a smile. He rushed over to the door and dragged him to where his mother stood.

"Mother, this is Ellis. Ellis, this is Maggie, my mum."

Ellis held out a hand. "Pleased to meet you."

She stared openly at him before breaking into a wide smile. She turned to Jarod. "Okay, I'll make you a deal."

Jarod shook his head slightly. "Do I dare ask?"

"I'll stay if I can come downstairs and watch this one strip."

Jarod threw his hands in the air. "Oh, for heaven's sake, Mother!" He gave Ellis an apologetic glance. "Please forgive her. She has no filter on her mouth."

Ellis put his hand on Maggie's shoulder, leaned in, and gave her a peck on the cheek. "She's fine," he whispered.

He was surprised when she wrapped her thin arms around him and whispered into his ear, "You look like you could use a hug."

He'd known the woman less than five minutes, and she had him on the edge of tears. His own mother had never been the sort to dole out hugs, and to have Jarod's mum do it meant more than he was willing to say.

"I think you should let her go to the strip club," Ellis said, his voice choked with emotion.

Maggie stepped back and beamed another smile at him. "I like this one," she said brightly.

A knock on the door heralded the arrival of a tall, thin young man. He was cute and he definitely made an impression on Maggie, who rushed to him and took his arm.

"What do you say we ditch the gallery and hit the strip club?"

"Mother!" Jarod appeared aghast.

"What? I've got a purse bulging with pound coins and nowhere to put them."

"Maxwell, the gallery will be fine," Jarod huffed.

"Oh, but I don't mind taking her to the club," Maxwell insisted. "She's been talking about it all week, and she promised me she wouldn't ditch me to go home with one of the dancers again." He looked down at Maggie and winked. She giggled like a young girl and pressed herself against his side.

Ellis snorted. It was obvious Maxwell doted on Maggie.

"Wait—again? You *are* kidding, right? Oh my God." A loud sigh shuddered out of Jarod. "Fine. Take her wherever you want. Heaven forbid I should try to keep her out of trouble, especially now that she seems to have found herself an accomplice."

Maggie looked up at Maxwell. "See! I told you he'd cave. Let's go before he changes his mind."

"Mother," Jarod admonished. "If you get arrested, I'm not bailing you out this time."

She waved a hand at him. "That's fine. I learned some fun things in that police station. Remind me to talk to Eli about what Roberta told me regarding ice and blow jobs."

Jarod's eyes went wide. "Get her out of here. If *either* of you ends up in jail, there's going to be an opening for a new driver posted immediately after."

Maxwell stiffened. "Oh, maybe we shouldn't—"

"He won't fire you," Maggie promised. "He likes to pretend he's in charge, but I can get Eli to show him the error of his ways. Now let's go. All this money isn't going to get much use with us sitting here."

She hurried out the door with Maxwell in tow, and Jarod slumped into a chair. "That woman will be the death of me," he complained.

"Yeah, but you know you love it," Ellis replied. "You're lucky to have someone like that in your life." Based on only a few minutes' acquaintance, he thought Maggie was wonderful. Certainly nothing like his mother.

Jarod sat up straight and levelled his gaze at Eli. "I know. I've heard the horror stories from other people about their parents. I'm grateful for what I have, believe me. I just want to keep her out of trouble."

"You don't, really. She's a free spirit, and there are far too few of those people out there." As he knew only too well.

Jarod pushed up out of the chair. "You're right, of course. I've got to get downstairs. Can we talk in the club, or is this something you'd prefer to be private?"

"Can we talk here? It's nothing serious, to be honest, just a thought in my head, and I wanted to get some things straight."

Jarod pointed to the couch, sitting beside Ellis, an air of weariness about him.

"Is everything all right?" Ellis asked him.

"Hmm?" Jarod frowned briefly. "Oh, it's nothing. We're having a bit of difficulty, that's all." When Ellis gave him an inquisitive glance, he smiled, his brow clearing. "We've had an influx of new applications, and we can't seem to catch up with all the background checks. I shouldn't complain, of course. This is the price you pay for being popular." He leaned back against the cushions. "Now tell me what's on your mind."

Ellis drew in a deep breath. "How do you…? I mean…. Fuck."

Jarod patted Ellis's hand with his own. "Take a deep breath and relax. It's fine."

A cleansing breath definitely helped. Ellis peered at Jarod, and his reassuring smile helped quell Ellis's churning belly.

"How do you thank your Dominant?"

Jarod cocked his head. "I'm not sure what you mean."

"Well, see… I know you don't know me that well. Wayne and I both work for the police. This past year everything got really, *really* bad for me. I was lashing out in anger at my mates, doing my very best to fulfill what I'd thought of as my responsibility for my family, and failing at that. Everything in my life was chaos, and Wayne strode in, and even after I tried to push him away, he was still there for me. And I don't know the words to thank him."

With one quick move, Jarod leaned over and wrapped his arm around Ellis. "I guarantee you he knows. One thing about Doms is they watch. They listen. They have this annoying but reassuring habit of picking up on the stuff you're *not* telling them. If Wayne thought he wasn't doing right by you, he'd tell you so."

Ellis returned the hug. He'd never been hugged so much in one day, and it filled his heart to bursting. After they separated he continued. "I just feel like I need to let him hear the words."

"Then say them. No matter what else, he's going to understand. And he's going to be so happy that you told him you need him."

Jarod was right. All he had to do was say the words.

Now Wayne just needs to get here.

WAYNE HATED doing reports. He knew they were a necessary evil, but they always took so long. Tonight's were the worst. He had to explain in meticulous detail what occurred during their training session. Everything needed to be noted down to the smallest, most seemingly insignificant detail. The thing that bothered him the most, though, was it kept him away from Ellis, and he didn't like the idea of what belonged to him being in the club alone. It wasn't that he didn't trust others around his sub; he just wanted to be there if Ellis had questions.

He found Ellis splayed on the couch, his broad chest bare. *Shit, he looks amazing.* Wayne licked his lips. Ellis was talking with Jarod, who laughed at something his lover—his sub—said. When he saw Wayne approaching, Ellis looked up and smiled.

"Good evening, Sir."

The honorific on Ellis's tongue couldn't have sounded any sweeter, as far as Wayne was concerned. He approached the two men, assuming Ellis would take his position kneeling on the floor. Instead he reached out and grabbed Wayne's hand, tugging him until Wayne was sprawled in his lap.

"I'll leave the two of you alone," Jarod said as he stood. "Remember what I said, Ellis."

"I will. Thank you for the talk, Jarod. And if your mum gets arrested, let me know. I might be able to get her out."

Jarod laughed. "I'll keep that in mind." Then he was gone.

Wayne shifted, but Ellis held him tight. "Stay where you are," he insisted.

"This seems highly inappropriate," Wayne protested, half-joking.

"Maybe, but I need you close."

Wayne's heartbeat sped up a little. "Oh?"

"Yeah. I had a talk with Jarod, and he told me I needed to be honest with you about something."

Oh hell. "I'm listening." Wayne swallowed hard, his nerves fraying. He tried to project an aura of calm, but if even *he* could hear the tremors in his voice, then it was a safe bet Ellis could too.

Ellis wrapped his arms around Wayne and held him tight. "I need to thank you."

Okay, so definitely *not* what Wayne expected to hear. "For what?"

"You saw how things were going with me. It wouldn't have taken much to push me over the edge, and somehow you knew that. You held me together and refused to let go, even when I pushed."

Wayne's pulse eased down a notch. "I'm never going to let you go, so you should get used to that. You're where you belong, you know."

Ellis's cheeks pinked. "I need you, Wayne... Sir. I'm sorry for everything I put you through. I think giving you what you wanted—what I needed—helped."

"I'm going to be honest with you, Ellis. I'm glad to have my mate back, but I'm even happier to have my submissive by my side. You've given me the greatest gift anyone could, and I will cherish that for the rest of our lives."

He paused a moment, trying to decide if now was the time to bring up the thoughts he'd been having. *Hell yes. He's not going to get away.*

"Ellis?"

"Yes, Sir?

"I've been doing some thinking. About us and our future. I want to know if you're willing to extend our contract to a lifetime commitment."

Ellis was so still beneath him. "Really?" he asked, his voice cracking slightly.

"Really. I'd like you to wear my collar. I know you can't wear it at work—"

"Who says I can't?" Ellis asked sharply. "Derwent already knows, so it's not like it'll surprise him. Cassidy certainly knows after peeking in your toy box. And if I'm honest, I like the idea of people knowing I belong to you."

Wayne squirmed until Ellis let him go. He got up from his lap, sat on the couch, and pulled Ellis to him.

"You really have no idea what you mean to me," Wayne said, his voice hoarse. "Every dream I ever had involved you. Even when you were seeing other people, I...." The words died in his throat.

Ellis looked at him expectantly. "You what?"

"I... didn't sleep with anyone else. I did a few scenes at the club, but nothing sexual ever happened."

"What?" The shock in Ellis's voice was evident. "Why not?"

"Because deep in my heart, I felt like I would be cheating on you. You were always it for me, and no one could take your place."

"Fuck. Wayne, I'm sorry—"

"Stop. Don't be. I'm telling you this because I want you to know how serious I am about you. No one has ever measured up to you, Ellis Mann."

With one swift move, Ellis had Wayne pinned to the couch and was kissing him harshly. He ran his hands over Wayne's chest and stomach like a man possessed. When he drew back, Wayne could see his blown pupils and trembling lip.

"I love you," Ellis whispered. "So fucking much. I would love to wear your collar, Sir."

"I love you too, boy. I've always loved you, and I'm going to love you until the day I die."

"Take me home? Please. I need you."

Wayne didn't move.

Ellis let out a low growl. "Goddammit, if I have to, I'll throw you over my shoulder and carry you out. If you thought sitting in my lap was bad, wait until the other Doms see that!"

Wayne chuckled. God, he'd missed this cheeky bastard. And now he'd just agreed to be Wayne's. Could life be any more perfect?

CHAPTER TWENTY-SIX

"WHAT'S YOUR ETA, Temple?" The incident coordinator's voice was loud over the radio in the hushed ARV as they hurtled through the streets of East End London. Beside Wayne Ellis was quiet. Not that talking would make this one any more palatable.

Who the fuck fires a rifle at a playground full of kids? Wayne was still knocked for six. His stomach had been churning since the moment they received the call.

"Five minutes," Shaun replied confidently, turning sharply around a tight bend. Wayne admired the way he drove so expertly at high speeds.

In the front seat next to him, Derwent spoke up. "Do we have an update on the sit-rep?" They'd already seen the photos from the police helicopter, taken at a distance via a high-powered lens.

"The streets are cordoned off, and we have uniforms at every entrance to the area. Still no clearer on what set our guy off. He's been up on the roof for nearly an hour now. Armed officers are already on the scene, but they're awaiting your team. Unfortunately the block of flats where our suspect resides has the highest vantage point of the area."

"Yeah, we've already ruled out the likelihood of a clear shot based on the surveillance photos," Ellis said loudly. "Where are we being deployed, seeing as you already have officers on the scene?"

"A-Relief will take up position on the top floor of the newsagents on Bonner Road facing the main entrance to the school. They may get a clear shot at him, but it's unlikely. B-Relief will be on the top floor of the houses toward the rear entrance on Bishop's Way. They'll be closer, but again, it's not likely they'll get a clear shot. We're aiming to have five of your team on the roof. C-Relief will access the building by the main entrance on Approach Road, and Dwyer and Mann will take the door directly below the suspect. The police helicopter is ready to provide a distraction when you guys are in position, so he should be looking the other way when you make a move."

"Has the school got everyone inside, do we know?" Derwent asked.

"Not everyone, no. One of the teachers was in the playground with the kids when he started firing. She made them run to the far side of the building, out of his line of sight. They're pinned there, but they're safe. Officers are in touch with the teachers via the phone. They've told the staff to make sure everyone keeps away from the windows. And there's a little girl in the corner playground at the rear of the school. She tried to make a run for the building, apparently, but when he fired at her, she retreated. There's tree cover, so he can't get a clear shot, thankfully, but the police on the scene think she's going into shock."

"Poor kid." Ellis shook his head. "She must be terrified."

"So we'll have five men heading up to the roof, plus the teams on the ground."

Wayne already knew the primary school was a large, sprawling building located in a triangle of two quieter streets and a main road.

The irony of the situation was overwhelming. Their suspect, ex-military, had been under surveillance for a while once reports came in he had an illegal firearms collection. What no one anticipated was something pushing him over the edge into such a violent reaction. Wayne was pretty sure his thoughts echoed those of his colleagues.

What if we'd acted sooner? We could have prevented this. What the hell happened to shove him over the edge?

They couldn't have known, of course. The only reason Wayne and the others were involved was because of their detailed knowledge of the suspect. Otherwise the operation would have been handled entirely by Authorized Firearm officers.

"Here," Shaun barked as he pulled into the curb. No time was wasted as they put on their helmets and goggles over their balaclavas. Wayne checked they had radio connection and as they piled out of the ARV Shaun passed them their weapons. In the distance Wayne saw the yellow-and-black police tape that cordoned off the end of the street. The six-story block of flats was the tallest building on the horizon, and Wayne knew their suspect had a flat on the ground floor. Ahead of them were the uniformed police officers talking quietly into radio mics.

As Wayne and the others reached them, he caught the familiar drone of a helicopter.

Lewis's voice crackled in his ear. "Can you see the door from your position, Dwyer?"

"Affirmative." Wayne saw it directly ahead of them.

"You and Mann get ready to move into position when I give the signal. Derwent, you're on the ground. You should be able to see the child to the right of the entrance. Get ready to grab her as soon as the suspect is in custody or down."

Wayne knew shooting him would be the last option. No armed officer set out with the intention of killing a suspect. But he also knew when they did fire, the object was to stop the suspect, and that usually meant kill. Their record of fatalities was low—two since the decision was made to arm the police—but the public were often troubled by their strategy.

In films it all looks so simple. Shoot the gun out of the bad guy's hands or shoot him in the leg. Except Wayne knew all too well it wasn't possible to shoot that accurately, especially when dealing with a constantly moving target. The reality of armed policing was being prepared to make a life-or-death decision and to make it in the blink of an eye. "Shoot to kill" was the only definite way to stop a suspect.

The drone of the helicopter grew louder, and Wayne tensed, ready to move, his rifle held steady in his arms.

"Okay, move in!" Lewis barked, and the three made a run for the building, the police removing the tape to allow them access. They crossed the road and ran toward the door, the noise of the helicopter even louder. By the time they reached the door, the helicopter had begun to move away from their location.

"Oh shit," Ellis said quietly.

"What?" Wayne reacted instantly, following Ellis's gaze. Through the mesh of the fence that marked the boundary between the block of flats and the primary school, he saw the little girl. She was clinging to a tree trunk and crying, her long blonde hair half covering her face.

"Take Derwent with you. I'll stay with the kid."

Wayne didn't need long to work out the reason for the request: the little girl was about the same age, size, and coloring of Ellis's niece. "Fine. Just wait for my signal before you move in, okay?"

Ellis nodded.

"Let's go," Derwent said briskly.

Wayne gave Ellis a final nod before entering the building. They ran up the concrete stairs, Wayne listening to Lewis as he got the rest of the teams into position. He and Derwent paused at the top floor, waiting at the metal door that led to the roof.

"Wait for my signal," Lewis instructed them.

Time to put a stop to this bastard.

ELLIS STAYED close to the building, but his gaze never left the little girl. Her whimpers were clearly audible, and they went straight to his heart.

Poor kid. She was obviously terrified.

Then his heart missed a beat when she took a cautious step out from below the canopy of the trees, her face ashen.

"Stay there!" Ellis called out. "Honey, stay where you are."

She gave no sign of hearing him. Judging from her stance, Ellis reckoned she was about to head toward the school. *Shit.* He thought about asking for permission to go grab her but changed his mind just as quickly. There was no time. He made a split-second decision and lurched toward the fence, scaled it, and vaulted over the top to land in the playground.

The little girl was running for the school building, her cries growing louder. Ellis could see one of the teachers at a window, gesturing wildly for the child to go back, her mouth a wide O of panic.

Ellis was out of time. He ran at breakneck speed toward her, intercepting her before she had covered half the distance to the building. He scooped her up into his arms and turned to run back toward the trees, cradling her in his arms, holding her out of the gunman's line of sight.

The loud *crack* as a bullet missed him sent ice flooding through his veins, but it vanished in a bloom of intense heat that started in his thigh. Ellis tottered, holding on tight to the girl, but he knew he was going down. It was as if everything was happening in slow motion. He hit the ground, covering the girl with his body. He lay there frozen, his breathing labored. She screamed, but the sound grew fuzzier, drowned out by the waves of pain that spread through his body.

Wayne I love you oh fucking hell this hurts Wayne Wayne WAYNE!

He wanted it to be over, to be free of the crescendo of agony that bloomed in his body. Blackness welcomed him, and he closed his eyes and sank into its embrace.

WAYNE HEARD the shots as they burst through the door. *Oh fuck.* The first thing he saw was the suspect leaning over the parapet, aiming below, and fear shot through him like a bolt of electricity. *Ellis, you'd better be out of his line of fire.* His heart quaked at the thought of the little girl trapped down there.

"Put your weapon down now!" Phelps yelled, aiming his Glock at the middle-aged guy. The rest of the team had spread out in a line; he had nowhere to go.

The sniper straightened and swung his rifle around to take aim at them.

He never got the chance.

Wayne felt the familiar recoil as he discharged his weapon, hitting the guy cleanly through the chest and sending him flying backward onto the concrete roof, his head striking the ledge. There was no doubt he was dead.

Wayne rushed forward and peered over the ledge, an icy hand clutching his heart when he saw Ellis on the ground, blood slowly spreading beneath his leg. Judging from the way he was lying, the child was under him, pinned to the ground. Wayne could hear her screams.

"*Man down!*" He couldn't tear his gaze away.

"The ambulances are already on the scene." Lewis's voice was low. "They're on it, Wayne. And uniforms say he's alive." The wail of sirens below confirmed his words.

Phelps was at his side. "He'll make it. I'm sure he will."

"Let's get down there." Derwent was at his other side. "SOCO will be here to document the scene, and we'll need to make statements."

Wayne nodded, their words not really piercing the fog that enveloped his brain. *Ellis has been shot.*

Then it hit him. *I'm supposed to take care of him.*

Yeah. He sure made a good job of that.

By the time they exited the building, the street was alive with noise and flashing lights. The cordons were still in place, so the only people at the scene were emergency staff. Wayne glanced to the spot where Ellis had fallen, but there was no sign. His heartbeat raced, his hands clammy.

Lewis was striding toward them, his expression grave. "He's already on his way to hospital. Paramedics are taking care of the girl. She's in shock with a few scrapes from when she hit the ground, but nothing broken. Somehow Ellis made sure she was safe."

"How… how bad is he?" Wayne's stomach clenched as he awaited Lewis's response.

"Sniper got him through the thigh. The bullet exited just above his knee. Paramedics say he was bloody lucky."

Wayne wanted to scream. "Lucky?" He felt a hand on his arm as Derwent moved closer.

"Apparently the shot missed his femoral artery. If that had happened, he wo—"

"He'd have bled out," Wayne finished for him. He glanced across to where Ellis's blood still stained the concrete. *Shit.* A *lot* of blood. Then it struck him. A bullet from a high-powered rifle had to leave one hell of a mess. "His leg…."

Lewis winced. "Yes, it's not good."

Suddenly Wayne wanted to be anywhere but there. "Which hospital have they taken him to?"

"Royal London. It's closest and it's a major trauma center." Lewis lowered his voice. "You know you can't leave yet. Let them get to work on him. You can go when we're all done here. I'll get one of the uniformed officers to drive you there."

"And I'll go with you," Derwent added. "He's in the best hands, Wayne."

Fighting to contain his emotions was an uphill task. "Then let's get all the red tape done with so I can be with my—with Ellis." The words were there on his tongue. *With my boy.*

Wayne did his best to focus, pushing aside the creeping numbness that threatened to paralyze him. *Stay on top of it. Derwent's right; he's in the best hands.*

The thought did little to comfort him, but the sight of a black body bag emerging from the building, carried on a stretcher, was a stark reminder it could have been much, much worse.

WAYNE COULDN'T sit still. Not that he could have spent any length of time in those uncomfortable chairs anyway. He paced the waiting room, glancing up at the clock on the wall every couple of minutes. Ellis had already been in surgery for three hours. Wayne had given up asking for an update after meeting with the same reply each time: *"We'll let you know when there's any news."*

"Will you please sit down?" Derwent pleaded in a low voice. "Just watching you is wearing me out."

"What's taking them so long?" His body ached, and he knew it was due to tension.

"This isn't helping, mate. Just sit down, all right? When they have news, they'll find us. They said so, right?"

Wayne wanted to growl at him that he couldn't sit down, not when he had no idea how bad Ellis's injuries were. He bit back the words, however, and allowed Derwent to lead him by the arm to the plastic chairs.

"That's it." Derwent's tone held approval. "Lean back and close your eyes just for a minute." Wayne opened his mouth to tell Derwent how that was not going to happen, but Derwent held up his hand. "You're worn out. Do as you're told." He speared Wayne with a look. "Or are Doms no good at following orders?"

Wayne sagged into his chair, muttering under his breath about how a little knowledge was a dangerous thing. He closed his eyes and rested his head against the cool wall. All he could see was Ellis lying there on the hard ground, that dark blood slowly—

Can't go there. Thinking like that brought his emotions way too close to the surface. Wayne fought hard to push down on the fear that tightened his throat and his chest. *He's going to be all right. He's going to be all right.*

The next thing he knew, Derwent was shaking him gently. "Wayne? He's out of surgery."

He blinked and sat up straight. "What? When?" Wayne rubbed his eyes.

"The nurse just told me." Derwent paused and Wayne's heart sank. "What is it? Is he okay?"

Derwent nodded. "To be honest she said they're not supposed to share any information because we're not relatives, but she was being really nice because he's a copper. He's not awake yet. They have him sedated, and he'll be like that for a while. But she says his vital signs are good. They want to know who to contact."

Wayne sighed. He knew what he had to do. He just didn't want to do it. From his pocket he removed Ellis's phone and scrolled through his contacts.

A gruff voice answered. "Hello?"

"Mr. Mann? My name is Wayne Dwyer. Your son is in my unit at—"

"You have the wrong number."

Wayne pulled the phone away from his ear and checked the display. It was clearly listed as Ellis's father.

"Sir, I don't think you understand—"

"And I don't think you're listening to me. Like I said, you have the wrong number. We have no children," he barked into the phone.

Wayne's rage bubbled over. "You sanctimonious piece of crap. Ellis was just shot. He got hurt—maybe worse—protecting a little girl from being killed. He's a fucking hero, and you're going to—"

"Do you have a learning disability? Is that why you're not taking in a word I say? Okay, I'll make it easier for you. We. Do. Not. Have. Any. Children." A dull click announced their disconnection.

Wayne stared at the phone in disbelief. "That bastard!"

"Who? Ellis's father?" Derwent asked. "What did he say?"

"That son of a bitch has a son and daughter, and he just informed me he has no children. He rejected Ellis when he came out as gay."

"That's disgusting. God, who would do that to their child?"

Wayne dropped back into the chair. "Who indeed?" Now what? The only thing left to him was to call Barb. He hadn't wanted to upset her, but if Ellis's parents wouldn't even take Wayne's call....

Full of a weariness that was close to crushing him, Wayne made the call.

Chapter Twenty-Seven

ELLIS WAS swimming in an ocean of pain where the currents threatened to drag him down into fathomless depths, where countless skeletal fingers held on to him, their bony tips digging into his flesh. He struggled to break free, but his fight left him weak and helpless to do anything but sink faster, deeper, the water around him growing murkier, denser, with yet more horrors slinking toward him out of the inky blackness, reaching for him….

He wanted to cry with relief when his world began to grow lighter, the pain dissipating in a slow ebb until he was once more in the light, his eyes wet, and he unclenched his hands from their tight grasp of his sheets.

Thank God for pain meds.

"Ellis? Can you hear me?" A dim voice but increasing in volume.

He blinked and sought the speaker. A nurse leaned over him, her face kind. "Does that feel better?"

He opened his mouth to speak, to thank her for the blessed relief, but what came out was a croak. She brought a straw to his lips and he sucked greedily.

"Take sips," she instructed him.

Water had never tasted so good. When his throat was no longer parched, he pulled off the straw. "Thank you." His voice didn't sound like his own.

She smiled and put the plastic water bottle aside. Then she pressed a control into his hand. "Press this button when the pain gets too much. You're in control of the pain pump."

With the pain no longer muddying his head as much as before, it was easier to think more clearly. "Where… where am I?"

"You're in the high-level trauma center in the Royal London Hospital," she told him gently. "Do you remember what happened to you?"

Ellis managed a nod. "Got shot." A memory surfaced. "The little girl. Is… is she all right?"

"I don't know anything about a little girl." She inclined her head toward the door. "There are some people outside who want to see you. Do you feel up to a couple of visitors?"

In that instant Ellis knew exactly who was waiting beyond the white door, and his heart beat faster. "Please."

He watched as she opened the door and gestured to whoever waited there. Ellis wanted to weep when first Barb and then Wayne entered the room, their gazes locked on him.

"Hey," he managed before his throat tightened, and anything else he'd wanted to say died on his tongue as a fresh, raw pulse of pain surged through him. He jammed his thumb against the button and a sigh shuddered out of him to feel that slow release once more, banishing his pain.

Barb was at his side, leaning over him, her eyes damp. "Don't you ever do something like that again, do you hear me?"

A sound barely resembling a chuckle crept from his lips. "Nice to see you too, sis."

She stared at him, and then she pressed her warm lips against his cheek. "Love you." When she straightened, she smoothed a hand over his head.

"My turn."

Ellis's heart soared to hear that voice. He looked into Wayne's blue eyes, saw the lines etched around them, saw the deep shadows that circled them, and he knew they were his doing. But before he could say a word, soft lips descended on his and Wayne was kissing him, a slow, chaste, thorough kiss like he was learning Ellis's taste all over again.

"And I love you too," Wayne whispered.

Ellis knew Wayne wouldn't lie to him. "How… how bad is it?" He didn't dare lift his head to take a peek at his body for fear of what he'd find. The questions were right there on the tip of his tongue, however: *Do I still have my leg? Will I walk again?* He felt pain radiating through it, so he knew there was still some of it remaining.

It was Barb who answered. "Okay. I'll admit what the doctors told me was pretty complicated, so I'll give it to you in as easy a form as I can. The bullet went through your femur, shattering it above the knee. And you were bloody lucky not to lose your kneecap."

"Fuck." Ellis winced. That one word, "shatter," conjured up horrible images.

"The exit wound made a mess of the front of your thigh, and you lost a lot of blood. That bullet hit a lot of veins. The good news is that it missed your femoral artery," Wayne said softly. "Because otherwise we wouldn't be having this conversation."

Ellis knew what would be coming his way as soon as he was physically able. There would be A Conversation. He'd broken protocol. He put himself in the firing line.

Yeah, Wayne wouldn't let *that* go.

"And the bad news?" Because he knew, sure as anything, there *was* some coming right at him. When Wayne said nothing, Ellis stared at him. "Tell me. Now."

Wayne gazed at him unblinking. "We're talking immense tissue and nerve damage. We're also talking spending six months to a year in postoperative recovery and physical therapy, and that's just so you can walk again with a limp, possibly with a cane. And this is only down to the fact that you're young and in such good shape."

Those words stuck in Ellis's head. "A limp? A cane?"

Wayne nodded. "Sorry, babe, but this is serious shit."

Ellis swallowed. *Fuck.* He pushed down his dismay and locked gazes with his lover. "I'm assuming this is your way of breaking it to me gently, right?" He shook his head. "Well, if that's the worst over with, now tell me what they've done."

Wayne talked, Barb interjecting, and Ellis tried his best to take it all in. *Rods. Pins. Screws. Plates. Bone shards. More surgery.* It was a fucking nightmare, but hell, at least he was alive.

Then his earlier question came back to him. "What about the little girl?"

Barb's face glowed. "She's fine. You saved her life, Ellis."

"Her mother came to see you, but you were out of it," Wayne told him. "Doubtless she'll be back at some point."

She made it. The news was one bright point on an otherwise dark horizon.

"How long am I going to be in here?"

Wayne didn't break eye contact. "About one or two weeks."

And then what? The future loomed in front of him, uncertain and scary as fuck. *How will I cope when it's just me, and Wayne's at work?* That was another thing: would he still be able to work as an SFO? The prospect of using a cane made that possibility unlikely, but what were the alternatives? Ellis was not about to be tied to a desk in a police station for the rest of his life. He'd go nuts.

"Ellis." Wayne's voice was gentle, soothing. "Don't think about it now. Let's concentrate on getting you over this particular hurdle before you think about tackling what's coming."

He knew Wayne was right, but that still left one little niggling question.

"My parents…." He left it right there, afraid he already knew the answer.

Wayne said nothing, but he pressed his lips together in a thin, hard line. Barb's face tightened.

Ellis sighed. "Yeah. I figured as much. Don't bother replying." His breath caught as pain jabbed his leg with fresh spikes, and he hurriedly pressed the button.

Wayne was right. Thinking about anything could wait until the pain was manageable.

However long it might take to get to that point.

ELLIS AWOKE from an uneasy half sleep, covered in sweat, his leg throbbing violently. He searched on top of the sheets for the pain release button, scrabbling his fingers across the blanket.

"Hey." Wayne was there in an instant, his eyes heavy with sleep. He pressed the small device into Ellis's hand. "There you go. This what you're looking for?"

"Yeah, thanks." Ellis shuddered out a breath as the pain dissipated. When he could think a little more clearly, he blinked at Wayne. "What time is it? And why are you still here?"

Wayne leaned over him, stroking his face gently. "It's late. And the nurse let me stay. I think my arse is putting out roots in that chair, though."

Ellis stared at him. "Go home. Get some decent sleep. It's not like I'm going anywhere, right?" He knew he sounded bitter, but he couldn't hold it in.

Wayne locked gazes with him. "Okay, you need to stop that right now."

"Stop what?" Ellis feigned innocence.

Wayne arched his eyebrows. "I'm not stupid, all right? I know you're hurting, but—"

"Hurting?" Ellis gaped. "You have *no fucking idea* how much pain I'm in right now!" He wanted to scream. This was his own stupid, idiotic, moronic fucking fault, and that knowledge didn't make what he was going through any more palatable. He knew he was lashing out, but he couldn't stop all the anger from bursting out of him in a flood of hot rage.

Wayne didn't react as he'd anticipated. "Then tell me," he said quietly. "Don't try to shut me out."

Ellis inhaled deeply. "I feel like the bone is being pulled through my skin, only it doesn't want to come out, so it's being yanked, torn apart so they can get it out. Every little piece that's left? I can feel that too. Like shards being driven into muscle." He closed his eyes briefly before opening them to stare at Wayne. "If I'm honest with you, I wish they had just cut the damn thing off, because all they've done is set me up for a life of agony."

Wayne sighed. "Tell me something. If you could go back, would you let that little girl die instead of you being hurt?"

What the hell? "What? No, of course not. What kind of a question is that?"

Wayne's expression was patient. "The kind you need to remind yourself of. You saved her life, and yes, it cost you, but it's a choice you made then, and one you'd make again." He paused, moving closer until his face was inches from Ellis's, his eyes focused on him. "Let me ask you a different question. You're walking down the street now and you see someone in trouble. You know that if you stop and help them, it's going to hurt you." He tilted his head to one side. "Do you stand by and watch?"

"No," Ellis whispered, unable to tear his gaze away from Wayne's blue eyes.

"Right," Wayne said, nodding. "Because that's not the person you are. You can't stand to see anyone hurting. Given the chance you'd always choose to take the pain yourself." His hand was gentle on Ellis's face. "I'm sorry you got hurt, and I know there will be days when you might think maybe it would have made life a lot easier if you hadn't acted the way you did. But Ellis? Then you wouldn't be the man I've fallen in love with." He smiled. "Now try to sleep. I'll still be here when you wake up. I'm not going anywhere either. Not just yet."

Ellis wanted to fight the fatigue that rolled over and through him, but it wasn't happening. He could still feel Wayne's hand on his cheek as he drifted off into a dreamless sleep.

IT WAS morning. Maybe.

The days and nights were blurring into one another, and Ellis had lost all track of time. The pain was more manageable, but with more pain-free moments came longer bursts of clarity.

I'm going to be a burden on him, aren't I? He could see it all stretching out before him: Wayne coming home from a hard day at work, and there *he'd* be, dependent upon him, a drain on his time and energy. Ellis had already come to terms with the probability he wouldn't be able to continue as an SFO, but that didn't mean he liked the idea.

And then there was this whole new path they'd ventured down. BDSM. Yeah, that was going to be over before it really had a chance to get started. Because he had to face facts. His injuries were going to put physical limitations on what he could do. He couldn't see Wayne trussing him up like a Christmas turkey anymore, for one thing.

He doesn't need me messing up his life.

Well, at least there was one thing Ellis could do. He could make sure Wayne came to his senses before things went any further.

"You're awake." Wayne stood by the bed, a plastic cup of what was unmistakably tea in his hand.

Ellis scowled. "Have you just moved into the hospital or something? What about work? You still have a job, last time I looked."

Something flickered briefly in Wayne's eyes, but then it was gone. "I've taken a bit of time off. Right now you're more important than work."

For one moment Ellis's heart stuttered at the sentiment, but this wasn't helping.

"You can't think like that," he retorted. "Go back to work, Wayne. I'll get by."

Wayne stilled, his gaze focused on Ellis's face. "I know what you're trying to do, boy, and it's not going to work," he said softly.

Ellis closed his heart to that one word that threatened to reduce him to a quivering wreck. "And that's another thing. Let's be honest here. That part of our life is over."

Wayne widened his eyes. "Says who?"

Ellis groaned. "Don't you think *this*"—he gestured to his body—"is going to put a stop to things? I mean, can you see me being able to stand for long periods while you flog the shit out of me? Or contort myself into all kinds of kinky positions so you can tie me up?" He snorted. "It's not going to happen, so let's face that now."

Wayne straightened, his eyes flashing. "Okay, Ellis? Do me a favor and shut the fuck up for a minute."

That stopped him dead in his tracks. He stared at Wayne, his heartbeat racing.

"Don't think for a moment that I don't know what you're trying to do. I'm going to say this once, okay? You. Cannot. Push. Me. Away."

"I—"

Wayne ignored him. "I know you're hurting, but I am *not* going to let you lie there and feel sorry for yourself."

"I'll just mess up your life!" Ellis blurted out.

Wayne regarded him with that same patient expression. "When you needed someone to hold on to, who was always there fo—"

"This is different, and you know it!"

Wayne waited for a second or two before continuing. "I repeat, when you needed someone to hold on to, who was always there for you?" He glared. "Who, goddammit?"

"You," Ellis acknowledged in a quiet voice.

"Me." Wayne nodded. "Just like I'm here for you now. I'm not about to give up on you, even if you're prepared to give up on yourself."

"But what about the club?"

Wayne bent over him and stopped his words with a kiss. Ellis couldn't help himself. He closed his eyes and surrendered to the intimate connection. When Wayne drew back, he smiled at Ellis. "We'll figure it out, okay? Sure, things will be different, but nothing that we can't work through—together."

It sounded all well and good when Wayne put it like that, but Ellis couldn't shrug off the idea Wayne wasn't seeing things as clearly as he did.

We'll see.

CHAPTER TWENTY-EIGHT

WAYNE STEPPED into the room where their team normally assembled at the end of the day. Nothing had changed in the time since he and Ellis had been gone.

Has it only been a week? Wayne had lost all track of time, his world narrowing to the trek between his flat and Ellis's room in the hospital. Sleep had been an elusive commodity since the shooting, and Wayne had taken to dozing in the chair beside Ellis's bed when Ellis fell asleep.

Even though it was empty, the place still retained the smells of stale coffee, Derwent's aftershave, and other odors Wayne usually managed to ignore throughout the day. Now? It was like coming home in one sense, but in another, this place was now foreign to him because Ellis wasn't here.

No. He's in the hospital, balls-deep in a pity party.

Wayne was at a loss to know what to do for the best. He pushed aside the feeling that he was failing Ellis. Right then he had a job to do.

He stopped at Lewis's door and rapped on it lightly. Wayne's heart thudded in his chest. *This is going to change my—no, our—lives.*

"Enter," Lewis shouted.

When Wayne pushed the door open, Lewis looked up from the stack of papers in front of him. He gave a broad smile, stood, and stepped around the desk to where Wayne held out his hand. Ignoring it, Lewis wrapped Wayne in a hug.

"God, we've missed you," he murmured before he took a step back. "How's Ellis? When can we come see him?"

Wayne had been inundated with calls and texts asking after Ellis since the day he went into hospital. Everyone wanted to stop by to wish him well, but the nurses nipped that idea in the bud; they didn't want Ellis to get overly excited. Besides, visitors were limited to two at a time.

"It'll be a while yet, I'm afraid. The head nurse is pretty strict about how many people can get in to see him. She even gives me the evil eye when I approach the desk."

Okay, so he was exaggerating. The nurse was actually quite nice. She always gave him a smile because she said Ellis needed to see a friendly face. But she'd been pretty adamant about the number of visitors.

"Sit," Lewis insisted, cleaning off a stack of papers from a chair. "How's he doing?" He retook his seat behind the desk.

Wayne sagged into the chair. "Well, if I'm honest, he could be better. That's part of the reason I'm here to see you today."

Lewis averted his gaze, and Wayne knew what the outcome of this conversation was going to be. Nevertheless he had to ask.

"If Ellis is able to come back, will there be a spot for him? They say he won't be able to return to do field work, but what about something at a desk? A job that will still allow him to feel a part of the group?"

Lewis steepled his fingers. "Listen, you know how we all feel about Ellis. He's been the backbone of this team since he joined, but—"

"But what?" Wayne demanded, resisting the urge to jump to his feet. "You just told me how important he is. So what's with the 'but'?"

Lewis speared Wayne with an intense stare. "Okay, you want me to speak plainly? Fine. Ellis broke protocol. And I think we both know this isn't the first time."

Wayne gave a start and blinked.

Lewis nodded. "Yes, Wayne. I know about those other things Ellis did. And so you know, I am also aware that you covered for him in all those instances. I watched as Ellis sank deeper and deeper into whatever mire he found himself in. If it hadn't been for you trying to pull him out of it, I would probably have forced him to see someone. But he responds to you in ways he doesn't for anyone else."

Wayne snorted. "He's a good officer. He just needed someone to offer him a helping hand."

"And you did. I could see the difference every time he looked at you, especially lately. I knew the two of you were involved, and though I should have said something, I stayed silent because it wasn't hurting anybody. If anything it was helping Ellis. But then this happened, and I simply can't sweep this under the carpet. He put himself at risk, he endangered the life of a child, he—"

"He saved her bloody life!" Wayne barked. "She ran. He was the closest one to her. If he hadn't gone after her, she'd be dead."

Lewis slammed his hand on the desktop, causing a sheaf of papers to fall to the floor. He glared at Wayne. "That doesn't change the fact he broke every rule regarding situations like this. His leaving his post put his life in danger, as well as the lives of others in the unit. It wasn't his place to be on that playground. He should have been where you told him to stay. He should have tried talking to her, getting her to stay put. He put himself in jeopardy by not following the rules. Being shot? That was his own damn fault. And if you take the fact that he's important to you out of the equation, you'd know that too."

Wayne opened his mouth, then closed it. His training as a Dominant included not speaking in anger, to think before saying something that might cause regret. And although Lewis was definitely pushing those buttons right now, Wayne forced himself to calm down and try to see things objectively.

Lewis uttered a heavy sigh. "He messed up, Wayne, pure and simple. More than once. And as for finding him a desk job, you need to be honest with yourself. You know Ellis, probably better than most people. Do you think he'll be happy being confined to a desk, hearing about the action but not really being a part of it?"

Fuck no. Definitely not. Ellis always hated the downtime between ops, but he loved it when he was in the middle of the action. Wayne also knew Ellis had the capacity to learn new things, even though he denied it.

Lewis gazed at him earnestly. "I don't want you to think I'm being an arse, Wayne. I respect Ellis. I've seen firsthand the lengths he'll go to in order to get the job done. And I wish to God I could do more. But I have to be brutally honest here. If he comes back, it definitely won't be as an SFO. His injuries make that an impossibility, but you already knew that. As for remaining with us in some other capacity?" He sighed. "The bottom line is he didn't follow direct orders, and headquarters will take a dim view of that. Whether he saved the girl or not is immaterial."

Lewis was right. Wayne knew the rules, and so did Ellis. They'd discussed them before, and this time he deliberately disobeyed them. He might be a hero to the little girl, to her parents, and to a whole host of people in London, but in the eyes of the police, he broke a cardinal rule. With his service record, it wouldn't be enough to get him sacked, but it wouldn't reflect well on him either.

"I understand."

"No, I don't think you do," Lewis stated emphatically. "Ellis *is* a hero. In my mind anyone who wouldn't do what he did doesn't deserve the job. I have to enforce the rules, but it doesn't mean I necessarily agree with them. I saw the video, and that man risked everything to save that girl. I have no doubt that if he hadn't acted when he did, she would be dead."

Someone had videoed the scene on their phone from a window overlooking the playground, and it found its way onto the local news. Public opinion came down solidly in the "He is a hero" camp, and Wayne was so fucking proud to hear people talking about his boy like that.

Lewis continued. "My bosses agree that Ellis will be given a commendation. He's a fucking hero, Wayne, and you should be so very proud of him." His eyes were damp.

Wayne dipped his chin in acknowledgment.

"So tell me, what do the doctors have to say?"

The thought caused Wayne's stomach to lurch. "It's not good news. He's lucky, because it came close to the femoral artery. As it stands, if he's able to walk again, he'll need a cane for the rest of his life. I haven't talked with him about it yet, but I know for a fact he's going to be lost. I already plan on having him talk to a psychologist because finding out he can't return to work is going to crush him." Wayne hadn't found the right moment to broach the subject, but he knew it would have to be soon.

"Let's look at the positive, yeah? He's not dead, thank God. But now he needs to adapt to a different challenge, find a new path in life." Lewis cocked his head. "Will you stay with him?"

From anyone else the question would have made Wayne angry. But Lewis didn't know what Ellis meant to him.

"Yes. No question. He's always going to be my…." Wayne took a deep breath. He was tired of hiding behind terms like "boyfriend" and "lover" when what they meant to each other was so much more than that. "He's always going to be my boy," Wayne stated, chin jutted out.

Lewis arched his eyebrows. "So Derwent wasn't kidding about what he found in your chest, hey?" he said with a smile. "Good for you both. If that's what it was that brought Ellis back, then I'm proud of both of you." He held up his hands. "I'll admit I don't really understand it, but it's none of my business. If it makes the two of you happy, then good for you."

Derwent. Wayne was going to kick his arse.

"Just so you know," Lewis continued, "Derwent only told me because I'd marveled at the change in Ellis since the two of you got together. He grinned at me and said you were keeping him in line one way or another. When I asked what he meant, he hedged. Eventually he told me after making me swear not to tell anyone else. He considers the two of you his best mates, you know."

The words soothed the twisted knot in Wayne's stomach.

"We've got a clearer picture of what happened with our sniper," Lewis informed him.

"Yeah?" Wayne sat up. "Do we have any idea what set him off?"

Lewis nodded. "Uniform spoke with some of the kids. It seems they made a habit of throwing stones at his window, which was right by the school fence. He'd often yell at them to leave him alone, and he'd complained to the school on more than one occasion. Apparently the staff had told the kids to stay clear." Lewis shook his head. "You know kids."

Wayne scowled. "They threw stones at his window, and so he grabs a rifle, goes up to the roof, and starts firing at them?"

Lewis sighed. "Based on the reports coming in from his doctor and therapist, there's the theory that perhaps the sound of the stones triggered a memory. We know he suffered from PTSD and that he was discharged from the army on health grounds." He studied his hands on the desk. "We'll never know, will we? Maybe he had a psychotic episode and thought he was back in Afghanistan. We can just be thankful that no one else died."

Wayne closed his eyes. All he could see was Ellis in that hospital bed, the bandages that swathed his hip and upper leg, the look on his face that told Wayne when the pain was bad.

"Wayne?"

With a shiver he pushed aside his thoughts. "Hmm?"

Lewis regarded him thoughtfully. "If Ellis needs to see someone, the department will pay for it. We know how rough this is on both of you. And if you need more time off, that's okay. You're on a leave of absence for as long as you need, all right?"

Right then Wayne had no idea how long that would be. Maybe once Ellis was home and making progress, he'd know better, but in that moment, Wayne couldn't see more than a day ahead. There was a lot he needed to do before Ellis was discharged.

I have to make sure everything's ready for when I bring him home. Just the recollection of the notes the hospital had given him was enough to make him weary. He needed to spend some time in the flat, but each time he saw Ellis, he didn't want to leave his side.

Wayne fought the despondency that gripped him every time he sat by that bed. This wasn't like him, but he couldn't seem to shake it. Maybe because this was *Ellis*, his boy, his lover, the man who had rocked Wayne's universe and made his life complete.

He wanted Ellis whole again.

ELLIS LAY in bed, staring at the ceiling. The day had taken its toll physically and mentally, and yet each time he closed his eyes, he couldn't fall asleep. It was ironic Wayne hadn't been there; he'd spent so much time by Ellis's bedside, and the one day Ellis needed him, he did a disappearing act.

"Hey." Wayne's softly spoken greeting pierced the quiet of his room. "A little bird tells me I missed something important today." He walked over to the bed and bent to kiss Ellis on the cheek.

Ellis snorted. "Oh yeah, it was a real red-letter day. I can see the headlines now: 'Shot Cop Takes a Shower.'" He didn't miss how Wayne's face tightened, and inwardly he cursed.

"What else did you get up to?" Wayne sat on the bed, reaching for his hand.

"Let me see." Ellis pretended to consider the question. "This morning I went for a jog around the hospital grounds, then I flirted with the new nurse. He's a cute blond guy. Kind of small."

"Keep your eyes where they belong," Wayne growled. "And enough of the jokes. I know you're fed up of being stuck in here."

Ellis opened his eyes wide. "It's not like life will be much different when I get out of here, though, is it? I mean, what will I have to look forward to? They brought me my crutches today, and I had a go at walking." He could still feel the cold sweat that had popped out all over his body.

"How did that go?"

"Painfully, if you must know. I couldn't put any weight on my leg." Ellis had never felt so weak and helpless. He scowled. "And showering with your leg covered in plastic is a bloody pain in the arse."

"It's only while it's immobilized," Wayne reminded him, his voice gentle. "It won't be like that forever."

Ellis was in no mood to be placated. This had been bubbling below the surface all day, and he couldn't hold it in any longer. "You should see the list of notes they gave me. Signs to check for. What not to do. What to tell my dentist. My *dentist*, for fuck's sake!"

"I know, I read them too." Wayne's soft tone hadn't altered.

That gave him pause. "You have?"

Wayne nodded. "Of course. I needed to know how to... help you."

Ellis scowled again. "You mean look after me."

Wayne regarded him steadily. "Right now you need looking after, but that won't last." He smiled. "Not if I know you. You're a resilient, independent sod. You'll soon be up and around." His fingers curled around Ellis's. "My job is to support you, to push you when you need it, to be there to lean on when you need that too. And while we're on the subject, why do you think the hospital gave me those notes in the first place? They wanted to know that there'd be someone with you for the first two weeks after you leave here."

Ellis swallowed. "So I guess you're stuck with me, right?"

Wayne chuckled. "Not exactly how I'd put it, but yes." He bent over again and kissed Ellis, more slowly this time. "You've got me for as long as you need me."

"But... what about work?"

Wayne caressed his cheek. "I'm on an official leave of absence. The job will still be there when you're on your feet. Now we need to think about getting you home and used to using the crutches."

Ellis sighed. "It's going to be a while before we get to do the London Eye, isn't it?"

"Huh?"

He pulled his hand free from Wayne's grasp. "Barb visited me this afternoon."

Wayne studied him. "Oh? You *have* had a busy day, haven't you? Did Barb mention the trip?"

"No, I did. I told her I was sorry things had gotten in the way." He gestured to his leg.

"And what was her response?"

Ellis huffed. "She told me to shut up." Amongst other things.

"Good for her."

Ellis gaped. "Excuse me?" He glared at Wayne. "You're supposed to be on my side."

"I am. That doesn't mean I can't agree with your sister. She's worried about you, just like I am. So why don't you tell me what's at the root of this mood you're in?"

Ellis lost it. "Don't you think I'm entitled to be 'in a mood,' as you put it? I mean, look at me." He winced but didn't reach for the meds button.

Wayne became still, those blue eyes focused on Ellis's face. Ellis squirmed.

"You have control of your pain pump for a reason," Wayne said at last. "Use it if you need it."

"It's just another crutch—" Ellis started to say, but Wayne shook his head.

"Pain will set you back," he stated slowly. "Being *stubborn* will set you back. And as long as I'm around, I won't let you do something so stupid." Ellis opened his mouth to retort, but Wayne stopped his words with a couple of fingers to his lips. "I love you, remember? You're mine, Ellis Mann, and I look after what belongs to me."

Wayne's declaration warmed him, but his heart sank. *He doesn't see it, does he? How can we carry on as we were? Everything has changed.* Ellis knew there would come a day when Wayne would see things clearly, and when that day came….

All he could do until then was act like Wayne knew what he was talking about. "Yes, Sir."

Just saying the words broke his heart.

CHAPTER TWENTY-NINE

"YOU *HAVE* been busy, haven't you?" Ellis said as Wayne helped him down onto the couch and propped up his leg with cushions. The pain there had diminished from a roar to a dull ache that wouldn't go away, but he was trying his best to ignore it.

Except Wayne saw everything, especially the things Ellis tried to hide.

Wayne walked out of the kitchen with a glass of water and the full-to-bursting paper bag from the hospital that contained his pain meds. He passed Ellis the glass and opened the bag. "The nurse said to start with tramadol, so we'll do that." He pressed two capsules from a sheet of ten and handed them to Ellis. "Take these, and then I'll get started on lunch."

Ellis did as instructed. He still couldn't get over the changes in the flat. "When did you have the bath taken out?" he called to Wayne, listening to the noises from the kitchen. The bathroom had had a complete refit. Gone was the bath, replaced by a large walk-in shower with a glass door. And handles had appeared: there was one in the shower, another next to the toilet. A slip-proof mat was already in place in the shower.

Not that he wasn't grateful for the thought Wayne put into the refit. Not at all. But it was an expense, one Wayne didn't need if he wasn't working right then.

"Last week. Shaun recommended a good plumber." Wayne stood in the doorway and smiled. "You haven't seen the bedroom yet."

Ellis stared. "Why, what have you done in there?"

"New bed."

Ellis frowned. "What was wrong with the old one?"

"It was too high. This one, it's low enough that your feet will touch the floor when you sit on the edge."

More expense. Ellis's gut clenched. "What, you couldn't have just bought a stepladder for me?" he joked, aware of a sour taste in his mouth.

All he could think of was that he was going to be a financial and physical burden, a millstone around Wayne's neck.

Wayne arched his eyebrows. "Something on your mind?" He walked slowly over to where Ellis sat.

Ellis pushed out a heavy sigh. "I'm just concerned, that's all."

"About what?"

"You've obviously gone to a lot of trouble to make changes here to accommodate me. Changes cost money."

"I see. I hadn't realized that you had in-depth knowledge of my finances." Wayne seemed amused. Before Ellis could say another word, Wayne knelt in front of him, taking Ellis's hands in his. "Now you listen to me. If I couldn't afford it, I wouldn't have done it. Don't be worrying about my finances, okay? No one is about to come knocking on my door to throw us out into the street." He leaned forward and kissed Ellis on the mouth, a warm brushing of lips. "All you have to do is concentrate on getting stronger. The physical therapist took you through the exercises designed to help you build strength and flexibility while you're recovering, right?"

Ellis nodded.

"And you remember what she said about sitting down too—"

"I know, I know," Ellis interjected. "I mustn't stay in the same position for too long, and I have to change that at least once an hour."

"That's my boy." Wayne's eyes shone. "You're a fighter, always have been."

The only trouble was Ellis didn't feel like fighting. He felt like curling up into a ball, pulling the duvet over his head, and telling the world to go fuck itself. He had no idea what the future held for him, but he wasn't stupid. His days as an SFO were over. And when the pain fogged his head, it was difficult to see anything positive around him.

"Ellis."

With some effort Ellis pulled himself out of his thoughts and into the present. Wayne regarded him with eyes full of love.

"It's your first day out of the hospital. Let's take things nice and slow to begin with, okay?"

Wayne was right, of course. Ellis had been climbing the walls by the time they told him he could be discharged. He knew what lay ahead wasn't going to be easy. He had no way of knowing when he'd be able to put some, if any, weight on his leg again. The prospect of clunking around Wayne's flat on his crutches was a miserable one.

It's the first day. It's bound to get better, though.

Right?

WAYNE LAY in the darkness, unable to shut down his brain. Bringing Ellis home from the hospital was all he'd thought about that last week, but now that he was finally there? Wayne's mind was a mess. He knew the coming weeks wouldn't be easy, but they'd get through it. No, it was what came after that scared him. Wayne was used to planning ahead, making goals, keeping his focus—and right then his forward view was obscured by doubt and fear.

The prospect of going back to work in a couple of weeks filled him with dread. *I don't want to leave him.* Maybe it was Ellis's brush with death that clarified Wayne's thoughts. All he knew was he didn't want to waste a second.

He knew Ellis was still awake—his lover's breathing gave it away. For a moment Wayne was tempted to leave it, to let Ellis fall asleep when his body was ready, but he knew he couldn't do that.

Not if he could ease Ellis's mind.

"Want to talk about what's keeping you from sleeping?" he said quietly.

Ellis stiffened. "I could ask you the same thing." There was no trace of sleep in his voice.

"Close your eyes. I'm going to switch on the light." Wayne reached out and clicked on the lamp, flooding the bedroom with warmth. Ellis blinked a few times. Between them lay the wall of pillows Wayne had insisted on erecting, providing a buffer. The last thing he wanted to do was roll over in the night and hurt Ellis. He looked across to where Ellis's leg lay propped up on more pillows. "Are you in any pain?"

Ellis sighed. "Not much, but some, yeah." He stretched out a hand to where his painkillers lay beside a glass of water and popped two out of their foil. Ellis sat up, his weight on his elbows, and gulped down the capsules before sinking back onto the mattress with another sigh. "I suppose it will take time to get used to the new routine."

Wayne nodded. They'd gone through the ritual of cleansing the wound with soap and water and applying a fresh dressing over the incision. Wayne had insisted on helping. The nurse told him how important it was to check the incision at least once a day. Looking for increased redness, more fluid draining from it, or any indication the wound was opening up.

He had to bite back his dismay when he saw the wound for the first time. It brought home to him just how close he'd come to losing Ellis.

Ellis's breathing hitched, and Wayne glanced across at him. Ellis was staring at the ceiling, and when Wayne followed his gaze, he caught his breath too.

"Looks like you went to a lot of trouble for nothing," Ellis said, his tone somber, his eyes focused on the hooks Wayne had placed up there. "Because I don't think you're going to be tying me up any time soon."

"Wait a minute." Wayne leaned over him. "Do you really think I haven't already given this a lot of thought?"

Ellis blinked. "We don't even know if I'm going to be able to walk properly ever again. So I'm pretty sure hog-tying me is going to be a nonstarter."

Wayne sighed. "BDSM is all about negotiation, right? Before any scene we ask lots of questions. Are there any physical limitations I need to know about? Anything you can't do? So what's changed? Okay, I agree there will be certain positions that will be out-of-bounds, but we'll soon work out what can and can't be done." He grinned. "Besides, there isn't anything that can't be worked around with a bit of creativity and effort."

Ellis stared at him. "But what about… sex?" He swallowed.

"What about it?" Wayne didn't break eye contact.

"Well, for one thing, we're—we *were*—quite… rough when we fucked."

Wayne shrugged. "So? We do things a little differently." He peered intently at Ellis. "You're not telling me you're going to lose all interest in sex just because your leg got messed up, are you?"

"Well, no, but…."

Wayne reached under the duvet and removed a pillow from between them. He stroked Ellis's belly, keeping his movements leisurely and firm. He felt the muscles quiver beneath his fingertips. "Are you thinking about sex right this minute?"

Ellis shivered. "Yes."

Wayne nodded. "When was the last time you came?" Slowly he stroked lower, feeling the crisp curls of Ellis's pubes.

Another shiver. "The... the night before the op." Wayne detected the tremor in Ellis's voice.

"Mm-hmm." Wayne traced the length of Ellis's dick with a single finger, noting its increasing rigidity. "Well, I have an idea that might help you sleep." He curled his fingers around the thickening shaft.

"Oh?" Ellis's breathing sped up, his chest rising and falling.

Wayne nodded, his focus on Ellis's face. "See what you think." Swiftly he threw back the duvet that covered Ellis's erection and took him in his mouth, sucking on the wide head of his cock.

"Oh shit," Ellis hissed, a shudder rippling through him. He reached down and laid his hand on Wayne's head. "God, that feels good." A groan burst from his lips when Wayne began to bob on his cock, licking and sucking his shaft while he cupped Ellis's balls, gently manipulating his fuzzy sac.

Wayne hummed around the firm flesh, slowing down, determined that Ellis enjoy the act to the full. He traced the plump vein along the side of Ellis's dick with his tongue before taking him deep once again, noting how more tremors racked Ellis's body. He knew it wouldn't be long.

Sure enough more soft moans and sighs poured from Ellis's lips, and his breathing grew more rapid. "Close," he gasped out, holding Wayne in place with both hands.

Wayne held him immobile, making sure he did all the work, and was rewarded with a spurt of warm come that filled his mouth, pulsing again and again while Ellis shuddered through his orgasm. He drank it all down, savoring every drop until Ellis lay quiet, his breathing more even.

Wayne shifted up Ellis's body to look him in the eye. "Better?" he said with a smile.

Ellis returned it. "Much better." His gaze locked on Wayne. "And please get rid of those pillows. I want to feel your warmth against my body. I've waited two weeks for this, and I don't want a stupid buffer zone getting in the way."

Wayne nodded. "Okay, I'll just have to be extra careful not to jolt you." He threw the pillows to the floor and switched off the lamp. He couldn't miss Ellis's drawn-out sigh as Wayne moved closer, his body snugged against his lover's. "Does that feel better?"

Ellis's contented sigh said it all.

Wayne closed his eyes, his arm across Ellis's waist. "Go to sleep. Things will look brighter in the morning." He lay there in the blackness and listened as Ellis's breathing changed. Wayne let the rhythmic sounds pull him into a deep sleep.

ELLIS SAT on the couch, some reality show on the TV, but he wasn't paying the slightest bit of attention. It was simply a noise in the background, a distraction from the thoughts that collided inside his head.

As distractions went it was an epic fail.

Three weeks since his discharge from the hospital, and Ellis wasn't sure how much more he could take. He always considered himself a fairly patient man, but it took those last weeks to show him what a load of shit *that* assessment was. Patient? He heard what the doctors said: four to six months to recover, and that was dependent on the severity of his injury. Why he was expecting his progress to be faster than that, he wasn't entirely sure, but he assumed he'd be walking—or at least hobbling—around the flat by now.

And Wayne? Wayne was beginning to worry him.

When is he going back to work?

It wasn't that Ellis wanted to get rid of him from under his feet— make that *foot*—but the more time Wayne spent at home, the worse Ellis knew he was going to feel when Wayne finally stopped looking after him and went back to being a copper. Added to that were thoughts that hadn't occurred to him in the past, but they certainly were now: *what if he gets hurt too?* For all the dangers inherent in their careers, it was rare to actually consider the possibility of being caught in the line of fire.

Ellis had been given a sharp taste of reality.

"Do you want to tell me what's going on in that mind of yours?" Wayne stood in the doorway, two mugs of tea in his hands. "And don't fob me off again with 'Oh, it's nothing' because you've been like this for a few days now, and I'm not going to buy it." He sat next to Ellis and placed the mugs on the coffee table, far enough away from the cushions that supported Ellis's foot. Keeping his leg straight was infinitely better than trying to sit normally.

I suppose I owe him the truth, especially after everything he's done for me these past weeks.

Ellis leaned forward to reach for his mug, but Wayne got there first, picking it up and placing it in his hands. "Thanks," he said, settling back against the seat cushions. He took a sip before speaking. "I've been thinking about my future."

"Oh?" Wayne twisted to regard him. "What about it specifically?"

Ellis stared into the muddy brown liquid. "I'm not an idiot, Wayne. I know I'll never be an SFO again. So that means I'm going to need an alternative. I... I've been thinking about applying for a desk job." He couldn't look Wayne in the eye, too nervous he'd see his own assumptions mirrored there and know for certain he'd spoken the truth—that part of his life was truly over.

"Really? With the Met?"

Ellis nodded.

"But... not with the SFO."

That got his attention. Ellis snapped his head up. "Why not?"

Wayne shook his head. "Do you think for one second that you'd be happy watching your former colleagues go off on training days, ops, whatever, and see them at debriefings, all talking about what they'd been doing? You always loved the locker-room banter, the post-mortems...."

Ellis let out a growl. "Fine. Rub it in, why don't you? What's the difference whether I hear all the chatter there, or from you when you come home from work?" Wayne coughed, spluttering his tea, and Ellis gave him a keen glance. "All right. What aren't you telling me?"

Wayne cleared his throat. "I guess I have a couple of confessions to make."

Ellis opened his eyes wide. "Should I be nervous here?"

"It's not much, and I haven't done anything concrete about it yet, but...." He took a slurp of tea. "I've been considering the possibility of not going back to work."

The quiet in the living room was so thick Ellis could almost taste it.

"Why?" he said after a moment, his head in a whirl. Wayne loved his job. He *lived* for it.

Wayne studied his own mug. "Seeing you lying there, your blood on the ground.... It changed something in me. I never minded the danger before. That was part of the job, the thrill, the buzz. But nearly losing you like that brought home to me how close I came to losing the most important thing in my life."

"Oh fuck, Wayne." Ellis's heartbeat raced. "I'm here, aren't I? A little bit the worse for wear, sure, but I'm still here." God, all he wanted to do in that moment was kiss Wayne, let him feel Ellis's lips against his. But he knew there was more to come, and he needed to keep a cool head.

Wayne slid a hand across the cushion and wrapped his fingers around Ellis's. "Yes, you're here, but for the first time, I had to face the possibility that one day I could walk out that door and... not come back. And I couldn't do that to you." His face tightened, and Ellis's chest constricted.

"You said a couple of confessions."

Wayne nodded. "I've been doing some job hunting."

That stopped Ellis dead. "What? Since when?"

Wayne gave a shrug. "I started a couple of weeks ago, not really giving it one hundred percent. But what I've found so far doesn't fill me with hope."

"What kind of jobs have you been looking for?" Ellis still couldn't believe Wayne was seriously considering leaving the service.

"At first I was only looking at jobs that wouldn't be monotonous, but you know what? That describes about 90 percent of the jobs out there. So right now I'm open to suggestions." He squeezed Ellis's hand. "I haven't handed in my resignation yet. I was going to wait until I definitely had a job to go to."

A cold hand crept around Ellis's heart. "Should I be worried about our finances? I know I have some money put away—originally it was to help Barb out if she needed it—but it's not a fortune. We could last—"

Wayne stopped his words with a quick kiss. When he drew back, he smiled. "I've been able to put money aside too. For a long while, my only expenditure outside of the basics was my fees for the club. We're not in a dire financial state, I promise. No one is about to turn up on our doorstep and toss us out on our ear."

Ellis cocked his head to one side. "'Our' ear? This is *your* place, Wayne." Not that hearing Wayne refer to them in that manner didn't send a rush of warmth through him.

Wayne shook his head. "*Our* place. You're not my roommate, nor my tenant. This is your home too. We're a couple, right?"

If Ellis had been warm before....

Ellis leaned against Wayne's shoulder. "What a pair we are. I can't carry on as an SFO, and you want out. You know what would be great? If we could find jobs where we can still work together."

Wayne kissed his temple. "Yeah, I'd already thought about that, but all I could come up with was working as security guards."

Ellis craned his neck to stare at Wayne. "Really? Sitting behind a desk, staring at a monitor all day? Maybe working nights?" He sighed. "I was thinking of something a little more... active."

Wayne cackled. "There's always porn."

Jesus Christ. "Er, no. No. And…. No. And before you ask, I am *not* becoming a stripper, go-go boy, or kissagram." He snorted. "I mean, can you *see* me in those tiny little gold lamé shorts, dancing on a bar top?" Ellis gave an exaggerated shudder.

Wayne growled. "Now I'll have that image in my head all night." Ellis laughed, loving how Wayne slipped his arm around him and held him. "I see a flaw with your plan," Wayne said quietly. "You wouldn't cope with an active job."

Ellis said nothing, but his heart sank. *I'd be the one holding us back.*

Wayne pulled him closer. "Now listen. *We* have savings. *We* are in this together. So don't worry because we're not in dire straits yet. Okay?"

Ellis managed a nod. "Okay." Inside he was less optimistic.

The future was once again looking like a scary place. He knew in his heart Wayne would be there for him, would look out for him because, hey, wasn't that what Doms did? All the same, it was difficult to brush aside his fears.

Maybe I just need to trust him.

CHAPTER THIRTY

"YOU'RE SURE you don't want me to stay?" Ellis stared at him, and Wayne sighed. "I know, that's the fourth time I've asked you that, isn't it?"

Ellis smiled. "The fifth, actually, but who's counting? Look, it's just going to be me being put through my paces again by the physical therapist. You've been there, seen it, sat there for a couple of hours while they do their checks and then make me sweat like a bastard. Just think how happy I'll look when you turn up to take me home."

Wayne chuckled. "In that case how about I organize something nice for dinner? A special treat?"

A more genuine smile greeted his words, but Wayne couldn't miss the lines around Ellis's eyes, the air of fatigue and anxiety that clung to him. "That sounds great." Ellis leaned forward and kissed him on the cheek. "I'll buzz you when I'm nearly done. Don't switch your phone onto silent again." Another weary smile. "At least if it's on vibrate, you can enjoy the sensation of it going off in your pocket."

Wayne laughed. "See you later." He left Ellis on his chair outside the doctor's consulting room and walked off along the hallway. With a final wave, he lost sight of Ellis as he disappeared through the door that led to the lifts.

Now that he was alone, Wayne could afford to let down the mask. Keeping up a cheerful appearance was draining, but he couldn't let Ellis see how he really felt. It was the first time he'd been away from Ellis since they brought him home from hospital, and Wayne had a good case of cabin fever going. Even their groceries were delivered. Wayne was grateful for the brief respite, but what he really wanted was to talk to some friends.

What he needed was a visit to Secrets.

Only when he got there, one glance told him there was no one around he knew, at least well enough to talk to about this. It was only three in the afternoon, and most of his friends wouldn't be there until the evening. He took out his phone and scrolled through his contacts. He thought about calling Vic or maybe Aaron and Sam, but he realized he'd probably end up becoming maudlin, and he had no desire to subject his friends to that particular version of Wayne.

Maybe this isn't such a good idea after all. Maybe I should just go shopping for that special dinner I promised him and then wait for his text.

"Hello, sir" came a voice from beside him.

Wayne turned and smiled to find one of the club owners. "Oh, hi, Jarod. How are you this afternoon?"

"Doing well, thank you for asking. I... I was hoping to find out how Ellis is keeping?"

Wayne detected the note of anxiety in Jarod's voice. He liked that Jarod had become Ellis's friend and confidante. And Wayne knew he had Jarod to thank for helping Ellis to understand his need to belong with Wayne.

"If you have a moment, I can bring you up to speed."

"Yes, I'd like that very much. Would you mind if Eli joined us? He's been asking if I'd heard anything."

It warmed Wayne the new owners were turning out to be such a caring couple. "Aren't you busy?"

Jarod gestured around him. "As you can see, things are quiet. So yes, we can both afford some time." He cocked his head. "Besides, it looks like you need a shoulder or two right now."

Damn. Jarod didn't miss much. "Yes, please. I'd like that."

Jarod rushed to the bar. A few moments later, he returned with Eli and three mugs of tea.

"I know you didn't ask for it, sir, but you look like you could use a cup. If you prefer, I'd be happy to get you something else."

Wayne took the cup gratefully and sat on the leather couch in the reception area. "This is perfect. Thank you so much." The tea's aroma relaxed him.

"So how is Ellis? We've been worried, but I didn't want to intrude." Eli sipped his tea. "It's a relief to see you here, to be honest. I think Jarod was this close to paying you guys a visit."

Wayne took a deep, calming breath. "I take it you saw the video on the news?"

"We both did," Eli informed him. "Jarod was so overwrought I had to take him out of his head for a while." Wayne noticed when Jarod shifted closer to Eli, and smiled when his Dom snaked an arm around his shoulders.

A thought passed fleetingly through his head. *That's what Ellis needs. Only I don't know how to give that to him.* He'd never felt this helpless.

"Seeing him go down was horrifying. I can't imagine how you felt." Wayne could hear the pain in Jarod's hushed tone.

The images had burned themselves into Wayne's memory forever. He could see it play out frame by frame. Every step Ellis took closer to safety for him and the precious package he protected. The sound of the gun, Ellis stumbling, then falling, but covering the child with his body. Wayne shivered, and warm tears ran down his cheeks. *Fuck. So close to losing it all.* He gave himself a shake and wiped savagely at his damp eyes. *Get a grip, Dwyer.*

Eli touched his arm. "Hey, why don't you come upstairs with us? It'll be quieter, and you can have some privacy."

Wayne nodded as he tried to rein in his emotions. He allowed Eli to escort him to the lift, but once inside, he sobbed. Wayne was surprised when the two men wrapped their arms around him.

"It's okay to let it out," Eli assured him.

Wayne took him at his word, and for the first time since that horrific day, he let it all come tumbling out of him: the pain, the fear, the anguish. Even after they got him into their apartment, he couldn't seem to stop crying. *Ellis could have died. He came so damn close because he valued another life over his own.*

Eli pushed Wayne into a seating position on the couch, then turned to Jarod. "Pet, why don't you get him something a little stronger?"

"Yes, Sir," Jarod replied and scurried off. A few moments later, he returned with a glassful of amber liquid, which he placed in front of Wayne on the low table.

"I shouldn't—" Wayne protested.

"Yeah, I think you should," Eli countered. "It's only a small glass, after all. So drink." He took a seat next to Wayne while Jarod sat in the armchair, watching them.

Though he knew he should bristle at the order, Wayne picked up the glass and downed the contents in one gulp. It burned all the way down to his stomach, then smoothed out into a warmth that flooded his system.

"Thank you," Wayne said softly.

Eli smiled and patted his arm. "You're very welcome. Do you want to tell us what's going on? We're good listeners, and I promise we won't repeat any of it."

Wayne leaned back and took a breath. "The shot shattered his femur. They had to use rods, screws, and plates to put everything back together again. He says the pain is manageable, but that's not what is bothering me. It's obvious he's depressed. He doesn't say as much, but it's like he's ready to give up."

"Then you can't let him," Eli stated firmly. "When Jarod had his heart attack, he tried to push me away. I wouldn't let him because I knew he needed me just like I needed him. Ellis already knows how much he needs you. Maybe he just needs a refresher."

"It won't be easy," Jarod added. "Ellis seems like he can be pretty stubborn, but he also looks to you for strength. You give him what he needs to make it through the day. Keep that in mind." He regarded Wayne steadily. "There's something else, isn't there?"

"Pet?" Eli said, his brows knitted.

"The expression on his face. He's upset about Ellis, but there's something else too."

"You're too perceptive," Wayne said. He studied his hands laced in his lap. "I've been giving serious consideration to quitting my job."

"Really?" Eli arched his eyebrows. "Wow. Why?"

"Ellis needs me to take care of him. His parents disowned him, and his sister is already trying to get a handle on her own life. He can't go back to his job, and after everything that's happened…."

"It changes things, doesn't it?" Eli's voice was soft. When Wayne regarded him with an inquiring gaze, he gave a sad smile. "You got a taste of what life would be like if you'd lost him, and now you're hyperaware of your own mortality. I know none of us know how long we have on this earth, but if you're in a dangerous job like yours…." He shrugged. "I don't blame you, mate, really."

Jarod returned his gaze to Wayne. "Do you have any idea what you want to do?"

Wayne shrugged. He wasn't sure exactly what they could do until the full extent of Ellis's limitations was known.

"Ellis could come back, but he would be stuck sitting at a desk, and that would only serve to depress him further. I want to find something where he can do easy work now, and then if possible, we can move on to something a little more intensive. I've broached the idea of finding security jobs somewhere, but he didn't seem all that keen. Not that I can blame him after the career we've had."

"Do you honestly think that would make either of you happy?" Eli asked. "I know we haven't talked much, but from what Jarod tells me, neither of you strike me as the type that would settle for that kind of life."

It was true. Wayne hated the thought of Ellis wasting away in a job he hated.

"No, neither of us would enjoy it," Wayne admitted.

"I thought as much. Then do me a favor." Eli's expression grew serious. "Don't go rushing into this. Look around until you find something that feels right. There has to be a job out there that will suit both of you."

"And about this part of your life," Jarod added. "Don't let him think that it's over." He glanced at Eli. "I have a good idea how Ellis is feeling because that was me until Sir showed me the error of my ways." He smiled. "In a way I'll never forget."

Eli grinned. "Me neither." He gave Wayne his full attention. "Let's be practical for a moment. With an injury like his, we're talking scenes that won't require a lot of standing or kneeling in one position for great lengths of time, right?"

Wayne nodded. "Kneeling is going to be out of the question." That thought gave him a pang. The memory was right there: Ellis at his side, on his knees, head bowed.

"Right, then we start there. Whatever you plan has to take that into consideration." Eli waggled his eyebrows. "Time to get your thinking cap on."

"I like the idea of you and Ellis working together," Jarod said suddenly. "You already make a great team, so it makes sense." He put down his cup and gazed at Wayne, nodding. "Yes. You need to pursue this."

There was something in Jarod's expression that piqued Wayne's interest. Maybe it was the way his eyes lit up.

Eli obviously caught it too. "Pet." There was a warning note in his voice.

Jarod blinked and regarded his Dom. "What? I was just… thinking."

Eli shook his head. "You forget. I know you."

Wayne's phone buzzed in his pocket and he pulled it out to glance at the screen. "Oops. It's Ellis giving me a time check. I'd better go." He got up from the couch. "Thanks for the tea, guys. I'll stay in touch and let you know how the job hunting is progressing."

"You'll both be in my thoughts," Jarod said warmly. Wayne caught his breath when he stepped closer and gave Wayne a brief but firm hug. When he released Wayne, Jarod smiled. "And be sure to give Ellis a hug from me."

"I will." Not for the first time, Wayne reflected on whatever had brought Eli and Jarod to the club because Secrets was all the better for it.

"THAT WAS delicious." Ellis smacked his lips. "Crispy duck and pancakes has always been my favorite Chinese dish." He was pleasantly full, and the nap after he arrived home from hospital did wonders for his mood.

Wayne cleared away the plates and headed for the kitchen. "There's more to come."

Ellis grinned. "You got dessert too? What have I done to deserve this?"

A moment later Wayne was back, moving behind him and wrapping his arms around Ellis, his lips at Ellis's neck. Ellis couldn't suppress the shiver that made its way down his back. Wayne kissing him there was guaranteed to arouse him. The mere fact that Ellis's dick was stiffening a little was a welcome event. Apart from that impromptu blow job, there had been little desire on his part to indulge in more sensual pleasures; the pain messed up his wiring.

Maybe things are looking up. Then he snickered internally. His cock certainly was.

"You've done nothing but simply be you," Wayne whispered before kissing his neck again. "The man I fell in love with."

Ellis shuddered as Wayne kissed down his neck. "You… you mean the man who lets you tie him up and flog the shit out of him before fucking him raw in front of a bunch of guys."

Wayne chuckled, tickling Ellis's ear. "Well, there *is* that too."

When Ellis's phone began to vibrate its way across the coffee table, he wanted to growl. *Not now.* Not when his body was tingling with anticipation. God, he hoped Wayne was on the same page. He loved how Wayne was careful with him, always making sure Ellis was comfortable, but there had been little evidence Wayne wanted to do more than hold him.

Ellis didn't want to be held. He wanted Wayne to make love to him.

Wayne pulled his arms from around Ellis and walked over to pick up Ellis's phone. "Jarod's calling you," he said, passing him the phone.

"Really?" Ellis connected the call. "Hey, Jarod, this is a surprise."

"Hi. Well, after Wayne told us how you were doing, I felt it was okay to call."

Ellis regarded Wayne. "Oh? Wayne didn't say he'd been in touch with you."

"He dropped by this afternoon."

"Did he?" Ellis didn't break eye contact with Wayne, who was keeping a straight face.

"The reason I'm calling is to find out if you two will be home for the next hour, and if so, are you up to receiving a couple of visitors? Eli and I have something we'd like to discuss with you."

"Hang on, I'll ask." Ellis put the phone to his chest. "Eli and Jarod want to pay us a visit. Like now."

Wayne frowned. "How odd. I'm okay with it if you are." He darted his gaze around the flat, and Ellis chuckled.

"Relax. Everywhere is spick-and-span as usual. And that's fine."

Wayne nodded. "Then tell them it's okay. I'll put some coffee on." He grinned. "I might even allow you to have some."

Ellis gave him a mock glare and returned to his call. "That's okay, Jarod. We'll be expecting you." They disconnected and he stared at Wayne. "You went to the club? While I was in therapy?" Something in his stomach rolled over at the idea of Wayne going to the club for something Ellis couldn't give him right then.

"I popped in to make sure they knew what was happening. They gave me a cup of tea."

That sounded so like Jarod that Ellis's fears were assuaged. Then a thought occurred to him. "You've hardly left my side since I came out of the hospital. You know, if you want to go out for a drink with the boys or see friends, I'm all right with that. I don't expect you to be stuck at home with me all the time."

Wayne arched his eyebrows. "Sure, because why on earth would I want to spend time with you?" Before Ellis could react, he said, "I mean, I must be such a masochist, looking for jobs where we can work together." He peered intently at Ellis, who squirmed. "I don't see it as being 'stuck' here with you, you got that?"

"Okay." Ellis tried to change the subject. "Speaking of jobs, has anything remotely interesting come your way yet?" He pushed back his chair, grabbed his crutches, and hoisted himself to his feet to hobble over to the couch. To his relief Wayne didn't try to help him, but stood to one side, his gaze trained on Ellis.

When Ellis sank into the couch, however, Wayne was there with cushions. He sat beside Ellis, perched on the seat edge. "I did see a couple of jobs advertised today…."

Ellis stared. "And?"

"A dance club in Soho wants a bouncer, and there's a department store in the West End that is hiring security guards."

Ellis liked neither of the options. "So in one job you get to deal with drunks, and in the other, get bored to death."

Wayne shrugged. "I didn't say I was going to take either of them, did I? It's only that there isn't much out there right now." Then he sighed. "To be honest there are probably lots of jobs out there. It's just that right now my heart isn't in it. I'm more concerned about seeing you restored to health."

When the door intercom buzzed, Ellis gave a start. "I didn't expect them so soon."

Wayne got up and walked into the small entrance hall. "Hello?" Ellis barely caught the voice at the other end. "We're on the third floor. You can take the stairs or the lift." When he came back into the living room, he smiled. "They're eager to see you."

Ellis laughed. "I think they were already on their way when Jarod called." A minute or two later, the doorbell rang. He peered at the doorway, smiling when Jarod hurried into the room. "Hey, good to see you. Excuse me if I don't get up," he joked.

Jarod came over and bent down to hug him. "Good to see you too." He glanced at Ellis's leg and his face fell.

Ellis patted his arm. "I am assured I will be walking on this leg within three to five months. Okay, so I won't be dancing the tango again—"

"You mean you could dance the tango before?" Wayne asked with a smirk, guiding Eli into the room.

Ellis glared at him and mouthed *fuck off*, to which Wayne just guffawed. Ellis ignored him and regarded Jarod and Eli with a smile. "It's going to take a lot of effort, but I'll be walking, albeit with a cane. Until then I have my crutches."

"Yeah, and don't get in his way—he's pretty lethal with those things," Wayne joked.

Jarod ignored both of their attempts at humor. He sat down next to Ellis and then turned his head to regard Wayne.

"We'd like you to come and work for us," he said decisively. "Both of you."

CHAPTER THIRTY-ONE

WAYNE STARED at Jarod. "Work… for you? As what, exactly?"

Jarod turned to Eli, who gave him a nod. Jarod smiled at Wayne. "After you left this afternoon, I got to thinking. We've been swamped with applications for the club, and we're having real difficulty finding time to go through all the necessary background checks. We vet all applicants."

"You mentioned this when I came to see you at the club," Ellis interjected.

Jarod nodded eagerly. "Well, it's got to the point where we've admitted defeat. There aren't enough hours in the day, not when we're into running the club hands-on. So when you mentioned working as security guards, it got me thinking." Jarod tilted his head to one side. "What about private security? You could do your own work like we did with the club. You could start small, you know, doing background checks for companies and the like. You have the contacts and know how to find out information about people. And if you think it would work, we could be your first clients."

"We're not taking a handout," Wayne snapped.

Jarod shook his head vehemently. "Oh no. Not a handout. We need someone we can trust. You could start working for us straightaway, and Ellis can join you when he's more mobile. The two of you could decide then how you want to grow. You could either hire staff and direct them or do jobs on your own. Either way the two of you would be in charge together."

"I have to admit, when Jarod first shared his idea, I loved it right away," Eli said. He turned to Wayne. "If you think this is something that might interest you, we have space available on the third floor of the building. It's empty now, but we were looking at things we could do with it. What if we set you up with an office there, so you can have an actual business front? It has a separate entrance, so clients wouldn't be traipsing through a BDSM club. There's a lift that can be accessed so Ellis could make it upstairs with no problems. And as Jarod said, we're already in dire need of someone to help us sort through the applications."

Wayne's head was in a whirl. He glanced across at Ellis, who sat there with an equally stunned expression.

"Well," Wayne began slowly, "you've certainly given us something to think about."

"Which is exactly what I was about to say," Jarod added. "Don't feel you have to give us your answer right this minute. I expect you'd like to discuss it between you. After all, this will affect both of you." He sniffed the air. "Do I smell coffee?"

Eli laughed. "Subtle as usual."

Wayne laughed too. "I've just made some. Why don't I pour us all some coffee, and then we can have a chat?"

"If you're sure we're not intruding," Jarod stressed.

Wayne really liked him. "Not at all. And besides, if this comes off, the four of us are going to be working together, so getting to know one another sounds like a good idea, don't you think?"

"A very good idea," Eli said with a grin. He peered toward the kitchen. "Any biscuits to go with the coffee?" he asked in a hopeful tone. Jarod made a rumbling noise in his throat, and Eli gave him a plaintive glance. "I know, I know, you're watching my diet, but come on, pet. Just this once?"

Ellis cleared his throat. "This assumes we have any biscuits in the flat." He peered at Wayne. "Do we?"

Wayne sighed. "Damn. There was me hoping to keep the peanut butter chocolate cookies a secret too."

Ellis gaped. "We have cookies? Get them out here!"

Wayne chuckled and went into the kitchen. Eli and Jarod's visit seemed to have lifted Ellis's mood, for which Wayne was profoundly grateful.

Let's see if his good mood prevails once they've gone. Wayne hadn't missed Ellis's earlier reactions before Jarod's call. The last month had been tough. Ellis hadn't shown any signs of wanting to make love, and Wayne hadn't pushed him. He had no idea, after all, of what Ellis was going through physically. But this evening was different. Wayne's kisses seemed to have had an effect, and he was eager to see if Ellis wanted more.

"So, WHAT do you think about Jarod's idea?" Wayne asked as they undressed for bed. He came around to Ellis's side of the bed to help him out of his sweatpants, pausing as he eased the fabric over Ellis's thigh. The wound was looking much better. There would always be scars, and sometimes it was difficult to believe the amount of metal now inside Ellis's body.

"It's worth considering," Ellis replied with a casual shrug. He stretched up, pulling his T-shirt up and over his head. Wayne took the opportunity to gaze at his lover's body. Ellis had lost weight, and the slightly leaner look made him all the sexier.

Wayne continued pulling the sweatpants off gently and then sat back on his haunches, staring at Ellis, noting his long cock, his balls hanging low. Wayne resisted the urge to lick his lips, but *damn*, the thought was right there…

Ellis put his T-shirt to one side and gave Wayne a quizzical glance. "What are you looking at?"

Wayne smiled. "A beautiful man." He grinned. "What, you expect me not to look when you go commando?" He drew back the sheets and helped Ellis into the bed before walking around to his side and removing his briefs. He climbed under the sheets and lay on his side, gazing at Ellis. "You don't seem that enthused about the job offer."

Ellis folded his arms under his head and stared at the ceiling. "I'm still taking it all in, I suppose. I mean, it's a big decision."

Wayne studied him for a moment. "Yes. Exactly. This would be both of us starting a new life. We'd be business partners as well as life partners."

Ellis didn't respond.

"But this has to be something we both agree on because otherwise it won't work."

Still no word from Ellis. Wayne felt an uneasy pressure in his belly.

"I know how much you loved that job," Wayne said quietly. "You haven't officially resigned yet. Do you want to stay with the team, albeit in a desk job? Because I do know how you—"

Ellis reached out swiftly and covered Wayne's mouth with his hand. "Just… shut up for a minute, okay?"

Wayne stared at him, nodding. Slowly Ellis withdrew his hand and looked him in the eye.

"It was never about the job," Ellis said earnestly. "It was always you. The one constant in my life has always been you. I loved our work, but you're the person who made it something I cared about. I can't imagine going back without you, and I don't see how my life would work if I tried to go forward alone. I guess what I'm saying is I love you, Wayne."

Warmth pulsed through Wayne in a slow tide. He shifted closer and leaned over Ellis. "I love you too," he whispered before moving to take his mouth in a leisurely kiss. Ellis responded in a heartbeat, locking his arms around Wayne's neck, pulling him in to deepen the kiss. Wayne couldn't help stroking over his warm chest and fuzzy belly.

Ellis broke the kiss and stared at him. "It's… been a while, hasn't it?" His breathing had quickened.

Wayne nodded. "That doesn't mean we have to do anything."

Ellis smiled, and the light in his eyes made Wayne's insides flutter. "And what if I want us to do… something?"

Oh God. Falling asleep was suddenly the last thing on Wayne's mind.

"What did you have in mind?" His throat was dry.

Ellis gave a lazy smile and reached down to where his dick had started to fill. "Surprise me."

Wayne chuckled. "I believe you were the recipient of the last blow job. My turn."

Ellis widened his eyes. "We're taking turns now?"

"No, it's usually going to be your job, but I'm feeling generous tonight."

Ellis grinned. "How does sticking your cock in my mouth make *you* generous?"

"Because you love the taste, the way it pushes into your throat, the way you can look into my eyes while I fuck that beautiful mouth."

Ellis sounded hoarse. "When you put it that way…."

Wayne got to his knees and knelt beside Ellis, pumping his thickening dick with a languid hand. "Swing yourself around so your head hangs over the edge of the bed."

Ellis licked his lips, then turned his body. His movements were slow but methodical. Wayne was so proud of him. He could still see pain in the expression but also evidence of Ellis's iron will. He let Ellis move at his own pace, determined not to rush or help him unless he asked. This had to be his decision. When Ellis finally lay flat on the bed, his neck bent over the edge, Wayne got off the mattress and placed himself at Ellis's head.

"Thank you," Ellis whispered.

"For what?" Wayne asked, bending his legs to rub his cock along Ellis's cheek.

"I wasn't sure whether I was… a man anymore. You're always there, helping, taking care of me. I needed to do this on my own to prove I still can."

Wayne smiled. "You're a man, trust me. And you're my boy, a fact that I'm going to prove to you now. I want you to open wide for me. You can just lie there. I'll do all the, um… *hard* work."

Ellis snorted, then opened his mouth. Wayne stepped closer, put his hands on the bed on either side of Ellis, then guided his cock into the waiting warmth. He groaned as it slid in deeper than ever before down Ellis's throat. "Fuck," he growled as he looked down at his boy. "If you need me to stop, tap on my leg."

When Ellis shook his head slightly, Wayne began to pump in slowly. Ellis groaned and put his hands on Wayne's arse like he needed him deeper still. *God, this is heaven.* He'd never done this before, but it quickly vaulted to the top of his favorite positions. Ellis's eyes were wide as Wayne pushed in again.

"Fuck, that feels amazing," he said. "Use your tongue too. When I pull out, trail it along the shaft, swirl it around the head."

He pulled out slowly, loving the suction. Ellis's tongue was talented; there wasn't any doubt about that. Wayne could easily spill into that incredible mouth, but that wasn't what he wanted, and it sure as hell wasn't what Ellis needed. He pumped a few more times, slowly sliding in, then pulling out. He wasn't in a hurry, and he intended on satisfying both of them before they were done. When he pulled fully out of Ellis's mouth, his boy blinked a few times.

"What's wrong? Ellis asked, wiping a hand over his lips.

"Nothing. But this isn't enough. I want your arse."

Ellis stilled. "I don't know—"

"What are you thinking about?" Wayne crouched at Ellis's head. "Tell me."

"It's just that… we've been so careful, avoiding doing anything that might cause me pain."

Wayne stroked his cheek. "Well, I do know. Trust me. I won't hurt you."

His gaze met Ellis's, and he could see the uncertainty there. This was important. If Ellis couldn't trust Wayne would take care of him, he was afraid their relationship would suffer. A D/s lifestyle required trust, and Wayne needed to be sure he still had Ellis's. When Ellis finally gave a slow nod, Wayne breathed a sigh of relief.

"Thank you," he said.

Ellis narrowed his eyes. "I'm always going to trust you. You're the one thing in my life that I've always been able to put my complete faith in. I'm scared, but I won't—I can't—let that stop me."

Wayne kissed him slowly and thoroughly. "Lie on your side. Put your sore leg on top."

As Ellis moved to obey, Wayne could feel the surge of electricity that flowed between them. Ellis was his, would always be his. And he'd prove it however many times Ellis needed.

Wayne slipped pillows under Ellis's leg, supporting it. "Comfortable?"

Ellis nodded, his breaths more rapid. "Come on, Wayne. I need to feel you inside me. Been too long without that."

"Oh, you *are* feeling horny tonight, aren't you?" Wayne loved how Ellis pushed aside his fears and just went with it.

"Too much talking," Ellis flung back.

Wayne spooned up behind him, his rigid cock sliding between Ellis's arsecheeks, already slick with precome. Wayne rocked, rolling his hips as he slid faster, loving the friction, the sounds pouring from Ellis's lips. He leaned forward to whisper in Ellis's ear. "You ready for my cock?"

"Fuck yes, I'm ready. Now get it in there and stop asking stupid questions."

Wayne chuckled and reached behind him for the lube. He swiped his slick hand through Ellis's crease and then positioned his dick at Ellis's hole.

"Hey, wait—what?"

Wayne froze. "What's wrong?"

Ellis twisted to stare over his shoulder at Wayne. "What are you doing?" He pushed Wayne back.

Wayne blinked. "I'd have thought that was obvious. That *was* you just now telling me to 'get it in there'?"

Ellis shook his head. "Yeah, but not without a condom."

Okay, Wayne was officially baffled. "But why?"

Ellis half twisted his body to regard Wayne with a pained expression. "Surgery, remember? Blood transfusions? We need condoms. They tested me at my last appointment, so in three months' time if—*when*—I test negative, then we can ditch them, but until then, safety first."

The thought had never even entered Wayne's mind. All he thought about was being buried in Ellis's body again, that tight arse encasing his cock. Ellis coming apart as Wayne took him. The two of them reconnecting, giving Wayne the opportunity to prove to Ellis his place in Wayne's life.

Thank God one of us is on the ball.

"I'm sorry," he apologized. "I should have—"

"It's fine," Ellis interrupted. "But like you look out for me, I'm going to make sure to look out for you too." He rolled back onto his side.

Wayne kissed his shoulder. "I love you, Ellis. So much that it hurts sometimes." He grabbed the lube and a condom and placed them on the bed.

"Yeah, yeah. Well, I'm going to hurt *you* if you don't do something soon with that dick. Enough sweet talk. My arse isn't going to fuck itself."

"Do I need to remind you who the Dom is around here?" Wayne growled. "Now shut up. No talking unless it's to cry out 'Oh God' or something."

"A bit sure of yourself?" Ellis teased.

Wayne smacked him lightly on the arsecheek, careful not to jostle his leg. "No talking starts now." He stroked a finger over Ellis's slick hole. When he took in a sharp breath, Wayne stopped. "Does that hurt?" he asked.

Ellis shook his head.

"Talk to me," Wayne insisted.

"Don't talk, talk. Make up your damn mind! And put that finger in me. Now. Please?"

Wayne chuckled. God, he loved this cheeky sod. He pushed his finger in up to the knuckle, then made short jabs, spreading the lube around.

"God, I wasn't sure I'd ever be able to do this again," Ellis moaned, trying to push back onto the finger.

"Where there's a will and all that," Wayne replied, keeping up his movements. He pulled the finger free, put another daub of lube on it, then slowly pushed in two fingers.

"Oh fuck yes," Ellis groaned. "God, I missed this."

Wayne grinned to himself. "Trust me, my cock missed it more. It can't wait to get back inside of you."

"Then do it," Ellis insisted.

"I thought you liked my fingers inside your arse?"

"Wayne, please. I need a lot of normal right now. Forget about spending forever loosening me up. I can take it, I promise. Just… I need you, Sir."

As always the word made Wayne's heart soar. He wiped his fingers over his dick, and after dropping the bottle of lube to the floor, he tore open the packet and unfurled the condom down his stony length. Ellis wanted him. Was begging him. Who was he to deny his boy?

He scooted down on the bed, grabbed his shaft, and rubbed it along Ellis's crack to spread more lube.

"Are you ready for me?" Wayne asked, his voice husky.

"Yes, Sir."

Wayne put the head of his cock against Ellis's opening and pushed as slow as he could, breaching Ellis.

"Oh fuck yes," Ellis moaned.

"Does it hurt?" Wayne stilled, waiting for the go-ahead, although he ached to thrust deep into Ellis's tight channel.

"A little burn, but it's so damned good."

Wayne continued to push in an inch at a time. It was exquisite feeling Ellis around his cock once more.

"I'm probably going to blow in an embarrassingly short time," Wayne admitted once he was fully seated.

"Don't care. We can do it again later."

"How's your leg?"

"Wayne? Shut the fuck up. Don't remind me about my leg; don't ask me about how I'm feeling. Just fuck me. Remind me that you still want me."

Want him? Hell yes, Wayne wanted him. He pulled out slowly, then shoved his cock back inside, which caused Ellis to grunt. It wasn't easy, but Wayne found a rhythm. He put a gentle hand on Ellis's hip to keep him still as he hammered his arse.

"You mean like this?" Wayne demanded. "You want me to fuck you hard? Fine, but don't say I didn't warn you."

He drilled deeper inside Ellis, who moaned, twisting his head from side to side. "Yes, please. Please. Please."

Wayne kept pace with the litany of Ellis's pleas, pushing harder, deeper, moving faster. He stayed mindful of Ellis in case he noticed any discomfort, but Ellis only moaned. As he neared his completion,

Wayne reached a hand around and gripped Ellis's iron-hard shaft, smiling to himself when Ellis cried out. It took a few strokes for him to get a steady motion going, but once he did, he pounded Ellis's arse while jacking his cock.

"You're going to come for me, boy. Do it now."

"Sir!" Ellis cried out, his orgasm racing through him. He shot hard, his come arcing over the bed to fall onto the floor. Ellis clenched his cheeks, tightening even more around Wayne's cock.

"Fuck," he groaned as Ellis's amazing arse milked his orgasm from him, his muscles tightening around Wayne's dick. Wayne was locked inside him, imprisoned in heat while his cock pulsed out the last of his come into the latex.

As his orgasm subsided, he kissed the back of Ellis's neck. "Love you so much," he murmured.

When Ellis didn't reply, Wayne slid free and pulled Ellis onto his back. He lay there with a blissed-out expression.

"Are you okay?" Wayne asked.

Ellis blinked several times, then focused his gaze on Wayne. "That…. Fuck. I don't even know how to describe it."

"I take it that it was good for you?"

"Don't fish for compliments," Ellis teased. "You know you're a stud. And I'm glad to be your boy."

Wayne leaned down and took a kiss. Ellis finally said the words Wayne had been longing to hear. Ellis was glad to be his boy. Wayne had just been given a great gift, and he would always cherish it.

"Now do you think maybe you could help me into the bathroom so we can get cleaned up?" Ellis asked.

"Why? I'm just going to get you dirty again in a few minutes."

Ellis reached up and put his hands on Wayne's shoulders to pull him close. "Confident?"

"With you? I always will be."

CHAPTER THIRTY-TWO

Four months later

WAYNE HELD the door open for Ellis, who walked stiffly into the club, his cane in his hand. They hadn't gone a few feet when guys approached them, patting Ellis on the back and greeting him warmly. Wayne loved the expression of astonishment on his boy's face. "I think they're glad to see you," he said quietly as yet another guy walked up to Ellis and gave him a tight hug.

"But… it's not like I've been here all that often," Ellis remonstrated. "How come they remember me?"

"I can answer that one." Eli strode toward them, grinning. "For one thing, you two did a bloody hot scene. Remember that one? And for another…." He shook his head. "You're a bloody hero, you ninny." He clasped Ellis to him in a warm hug. "Glad to have you back, mate."

Ellis smiled. "It's good to be here." He gave Wayne a glance. "He's been doing a great job, Jarod tells me. I figured it was time to join the team."

Wayne put his arm around Ellis's waist. "I for one am delighted to have you on board. It will be wonderful to work with you again." He'd gotten used to going home to Ellis, but he couldn't deny he wanted this. The two of them in business together. Ellis had been working from home the last month or so, but as the summer drew to a close, he'd announced he was ready to join Wayne in their office.

"Ellis!" Jarod walked over, his arms wide. "You made it!"

Ellis chuckled as he accepted Jarod's hug. "It's good to be mobile again." He waved his cane in the air. "And this is much better than the crutches."

"Hmm. He still manages to give me a poke with it," Wayne commented. "And his aim is deadly." Ellis did an eye roll, and Wayne laughed. "Yeah, you know I'm right."

"Are you two here so Wayne can put you to work? Because if that's the case, I think I'll veto it right now. It's Saturday night, for God's sake." Eli waggled his eyebrows. "Or are you here to play?"

Wayne didn't miss the way Ellis stiffened. When Wayne had suggested going to the club, Ellis was slow to agree. He reasoned he wasn't ready. A few days later, however, he'd apparently changed his mind, talking animatedly about spending time with Eli and Jarod.

The last few months had been a wasteland, as far as scenes went. Their sex life was improving in leaps and bounds, and Wayne felt confident enough to push Ellis's boundaries in bed. But any mention of doing something more than that, and Ellis clammed up. Wayne had on more than one occasion opened his toy chest and gazed in frustration at its contents. It was as if the scenes they'd shared had never taken place.

Enough is enough. Wayne wanted his boy back, the same boy who loved the touch of his flogger. And if what he planned came off, by the end of the night, Ellis would once again be his submissive, heart, body, and soul. Everything was ready—he hoped.

As if Eli read his thoughts, the club owner cleared his throat. "Those documents you were waiting for have arrived, by the way." He gave Wayne a meaningful stare. "They're ready for you to look at whenever you want."

Wayne nodded, his heartbeat racing. "Thanks. I might need to see them before we leave tonight." Eli returned his nod, his eyes bright.

"Hey," Ellis piped up. "No work talk, remember what Eli said?"

Wayne gave him a friendly swat to the butt.

Jarod's phone buzzed, and he withdrew it from the pocket of his leather pants. "Excuse me," he said to Wayne and Ellis before peering at the screen. His gaze met Eli's. "It's Ben." Both men seemed excited by the call. Jarod answered the phone. Wayne noted his furrowed brow and his terse responses. A moment later he was practically vibrating. When he disconnected, he was shaking so hard Eli went behind him and wrapped his arms around Jarod's waist.

"Pet? What's wrong?"

"Annie had some problems, so they had to deliver the baby by C-section."

Eli paled and released him. "Fuck. Is she okay?"

Jarod nodded hurriedly. "She's doing fine now, but they were really worried for a while." His face relaxed into a smile. "We're uncles."

Eli beamed. "Seriously? Boy or girl? Names? Give me some details, damn it."

"Sounds like it was ultimately good news," Wayne said.

Jarod turned to him, nodding, his face alight. "Our friends were supposed to have their baby a few weeks ago. They had to induce her."

"Jarod," Eli growled. "Details."

Jarod put his arms around Eli. "I'm proud to announce the arrival of Beth-Ann Winters, at five pounds even and Zachary Alexander Winters at five pounds three ounces."

Eli hugged Jarod to him, kissing him fervently on the mouth. "That's wonderful! We'd better organize a visit to Manchester soon." When they parted, Eli gave Wayne a grin. "By the way, we have something for you two."

"Oh?" For one heart-stopping moment, Wayne thought he was about to reveal their secret, but then he pushed aside his fear. *Eli wouldn't do that.* Then he recalled what other secrets he and Eli shared. *Oh. It's here. Perfect.*

If all went according to plan, it was to be a night of surprises for his boy.

Jarod smiled at Ellis. "To be honest it's more for you."

Ellis frowned. "Me?"

Jarod nodded. "Come with me." He led them across the main floor of the club, which was already packed. Vibrant noise filled the air, and Wayne's pulse quickened to hear it. God, he'd missed this. Ellis walked slowly at his side, leaning heavily on his cane, darting his gaze around the floor, his expression impassive.

It was not the reaction Wayne had hoped for.

Jarod and Eli stopped at the side of the stage, but before Wayne and Ellis reached them, Ellis halted and turned to regard Wayne with a solemn expression, his hand laid on Wayne's arm.

"This... this isn't going to work."

Wayne cocked his head to one side. "What isn't?"

"This." Ellis gestured to the men around them. "Maybe... maybe we need to dissolve our contract." He swallowed. "I'm sorry. I've wanted to say something for weeks now, but every time the occasion arose, I wimped out. But being here, seeing all this...." He bowed his head. "I'm sorry, Wayne."

Wayne was struggling to get his head around it all. "Are you saying you want to leave me?" His heart stuttered at the mere thought. *Please, God, no. I can't lose him. Not now. Not after everything we've been through.*

Ellis jerked his head up, his eyes widened. "Fuck no. I love you, and that's not going to change. But...."

"But?" Wayne peered intently at Ellis. "What are you trying to say?" Around them scenes took place, men engaged in the blissful exchanges of power Wayne had loved for so many years, but in that moment, all he could see was Ellis's strained, pale face.

Ellis squirmed and lowered his gaze again. "If you... need someone else to give you what you're looking for, I'd understand. I wouldn't stand in your way. Let's face it: I'm not exactly going to be able to bend over backward for you anymore."

"Since when have you ever been able to bend over backward?" Wayne said with a laugh. "You've always been flexible, I grant you, but—"

"You know what I mean," Ellis snapped.

Fuck, the pain in his eyes.

Yeah, enough was definitely enough.

Wayne straightened. "You know what? To be honest with you, I've had it with your pity party."

Ellis's eyes bulged and he reared back as though Wayne had just slapped him.

Good. That got his attention.

"Come with me," Wayne ordered before striding toward the stage where Eli and Jarod still stood, watching the proceedings. He turned when he realized Ellis hadn't budged. "Now, boy."

Ellis flinched but walked slowly over to him. When he reached the stage, Wayne pointed to an empty spot. "Stand there."

"What, no kneeling?" Ellis's tone was bitter.

Wayne couldn't hold back his sigh. "I know you can't kneel. I *am* aware of your limitations, but you know what? One of the things we discussed when we got together was for me to push your limits. And I'm going to do that now."

"In spite of everything I just said?" Ellis's face flushed.

Wayne moved closer until he could feel the heat radiating from Ellis's body. "I heard everything you said, but right this minute, I'm not listening to your words. I'm listening to what my senses tell me. And you *want* this, Ellis, though you may try to deny it."

Ellis was quiet, his chest rising and falling. The flush on his cheeks was still in evidence.

"Tell me you didn't love how it felt when I flogged you here. Tell me you didn't like knowing all those guys were watching us, envying me because all this—" He gestured to Ellis's body, his dark blue T-shirt stretched tight over his chest and arms, his jeans barely containing his thighs, thick with muscle. "—all this is mine. My boy." Wayne edged closer still until his lips were almost touching Ellis's ear. "Tell me you didn't love being my boy, and we can leave right now." He pulled back, his gaze focused on Ellis's face.

Ellis's Adam's apple bobbed. "You know I can't tell you any of those things." His voice cracked.

Wayne nodded. "Then here is where you trust me again." When Ellis nodded, he forged ahead. "If you feel the slightest discomfort, you tell me. Do I make myself understood?"

Ellis took a deep breath. Another nod.

"Words, Ellis. I need you to tell me you understand."

"Yes, I understand."

Wayne arched his eyebrows. He was going to make sure Ellis got the message. *I'm in control here.* "You understand… what?"

Ellis swallowed. "I understand… Sir."

Wayne fell silent. He took a step back and indicated Eli and Jarod. "Let's see what surprises lie in store for you, shall we?"

Ellis nodded and walked stiffly to where Eli and Jarod stood beside their latest piece of equipment.

"We all enjoyed watching you in your scene," Eli began, and Jarod grinned.

"Members are still talking about it."

Eli flashed him a hard stare and then brought his attention back to Ellis. "But we know from talking to Wayne that such apparatus would bring you great discomfort, so we bought this with you in mind."

ELLIS STARED at the bench between Eli and Jarod. It was padded and covered with black vinyl. What was unusual about it was its design. There were slimmer arms to it that clearly moved out from the main part of the bench so it resembled a headless body with arms and legs. Along every edge were V-shaped clips.

"It's a flogging bench," Eli told him. "You lie on this, face up or down, it doesn't matter, and then you are tied to it using the clips. What's important for you is that your leg would be supported."

"We wanted to make sure that if you did a flogging scene, you wouldn't be on your feet or putting pressure on your knee," Jarod added.

Ellis blinked. "You got this… just for me?"

Jarod smiled. "We look after our members. So when Wayne contacted us suggesting that we might—"

"This was your idea," Ellis blurted, turning to regard Wayne.

"Yes, and he did it for you," Eli butted in. "So now we're going to leave the two of you to play." Another grin. "Have fun. That *is* what Secrets is here for, right?" He put an arm around Jarod's waist and the two men walked off toward the reception area.

Wayne focused on Ellis. "Alone at last," he said with a wicked smile.

For some reason Ellis's pulse quickened. "Hardly, in a club full of men." He could hear the tremor in his own voice.

Wayne shook his head. "Tune them out. Right now I want all your attention." He reached out, pulled Ellis's T-shirt up to his neck, and leaned in to lick a stripe from Ellis's navel to his sternum, laving the area with his tongue.

Ellis couldn't repress his shiver. "Oh God," he said weakly.

Wayne chuckled against his skin. "There's my boy." He moved to take Ellis's nipple between his teeth, tugging slightly at it while he got busy tweaking the other with his fingers. Ellis wanted to whimper, to tell him how fucking amazing that felt.

Then he remembered where he was. It was sort of expected.

"Yes, Sir," he whispered. "Don't stop, please."

"Begging already?" Wayne's soft laughter reverberated through Ellis's body. "Damn, I'm good." When he pulled free, Ellis wanted to growl with frustration.

Wayne straightened, his eyes gleaming. "Strip for me. Now."

Like he could refuse Wayne anything.

His heart pounding, Ellis pulled off his T-shirt, dropping it to the floor before popping the button on his jeans.

"Let me," Wayne said, his voice husky. He pulled down the zipper, taking his time. And then Ellis caught his breath as Wayne eased his agile fingers under the waistband to slowly lower his jeans over his hips, his burgeoning shaft obvious in his boxers. He loved Wayne's careful manner, how mindful he was of Ellis's leg. Ellis stared down at him as Wayne laid a trail of gentle kisses over his scars.

"Oh wow." It was such an intimate act. In that moment Ellis forgot about the club, the men standing around them watching them, Eli, and Jarod. All he could see was Wayne.

Wayne paused, gripping the elasticated waist of Ellis's boxers. "And what do we have here?" he said with a grin, sliding them to the floor. Ellis's cock bobbed up, already past half-mast. "Someone is eager."

Ellis's breathing hitched. "That... that would be me." Finally he was naked, the temperature of the club just perfect.

Wayne pointed to the bench. "Facedown, arms outstretched. When you're comfortable, especially your leg, we'll proceed."

Ellis sat down on the bench and carefully rolled onto his belly, placing his limbs on the arms, the vinyl cool against his skin. His thigh ached a little, but that was due to the walk from the car, and besides, he could dial that out. He turned his head to one side. "Ready, Sir."

For a moment nothing happened, and Ellis's heartbeat raced. Then Wayne stroked a gentle hand down his back and squeezed his arse. "It's been a while since this beautiful body bore my marks."

Ellis forced out a chuckle. "I thought I said we weren't doing an encore?"

Wayne's breath warmed his ear. "Yeah, but I'm the Dom, so suck it up. Besides, you know you have your safeword."

Ellis knew all right, but he also knew Wayne would have to really freak him out for Ellis to consider using it.

"Okay, being serious for a minute." Wayne crouched down by Ellis's head. "Do you want to call a halt to this? You did say no encores, after all." His brow was furrowed.

Ellis had to laugh. "Yeah, but when I said that? I meant not right that second. You'd just fucked the come right out of me and all over the floor, remember? I was knackered."

He saw the wave of relief that crossed Wayne's face. "Then we're okay?"

Ellis smiled. "More than okay." He meant it. The idea excited him. His dick was wedged against the bench, so hard it ached.

When he felt that first touch of the rope as it snaked across his back, it brought a question to mind.

"Permission to speak, Sir?"

"Go ahead."

"You really did plan this, didn't you? Right down to having ropes ready?"

Wayne laughed. "Didn't I tell you? I used to be a Boy Scout. I like being prepared." Quickly he bound Ellis's wrists to the bench arms, then did the same with his ankles. "That feel okay? No discomfort?"

Ellis sighed. "Stop mollycoddling me. I'm fine, honest. If I wasn't, I'd tell you." He took a deep breath. "Come on, Sir. Let me feel it. I've missed this."

The soft tails of a flogger trailed across his shoulders. "Me too," Wayne said quietly.

That first thud of leather against his flesh was like coming home.

Ellis lost himself in the moment: the swish of the flogger as it cut through the air; the light sting of its tails as they connected with his arsecheeks; the smell of leather; the low cries that filled his ears, a man lost in bliss, until he realized they were his cries. Wayne paused now and then to rub his back and arse, his hand firm but gentle, his voice low as he told Ellis how "fucking beautiful" he looked, how his noises made Wayne's heart soar.

I'm soaring too. It was true. Ellis let himself go and gave himself up to the sensations that coursed through him, nonsensical words pouring from his lips as he submitted to Wayne with every fiber of his being. As the strikes petered out, he breathed deeply, overwhelmed by the feeling of peace that filled him. *I needed this.* But all too soon, another need began to burn within him, growing white-hot as the idea took root. He reared up his head and twisted to look at Wayne, his breath catching in his throat at the sight of him, shirt unbuttoned to reveal a chest glistening with perspiration, his sleeves rolled up, his face bright with joy.

Wayne's erection was all too obvious.

"Take me," Ellis begged. "Now. Please."

Wayne dropped the flogger to the floor and leaned forward to kiss Ellis's upturned face. "You want that?"

Ellis barked a harsh laugh. "Damn it all, do you have to do that every time I demand that you fuck me?"

"Do what?"

"Try to talk me out of it instead of rolling over and saying, 'Yes, Ellis.'" He grinned. "I thought it was the submissive who had all the power?" He knew he was pushing it, but fuck it, all he wanted that second was Wayne reaming his arse. Ellis craved that connection, that wonderful moment when they were not two, but one.

Wayne returned his grin as he slowly unzipped his jeans and fished out his long, hard cock, pointing straight at Ellis. He grabbed hold of Ellis's good leg and spread him wide before coming to stand between Ellis's parted thighs.

"Here you go, Wayne," someone called out.

Wayne raised his hand and caught a packet of lube. "Thanks, Vic."

"My pleasure," the deep voice boomed. "Now fuck that gorgeous arse."

"You sure you don't share?" another voice shouted.

Wayne's gaze locked on Ellis, with a look so hot Ellis's hole clenched. "Positive. This is my boy." He smiled. "Face forward."

Ellis did as instructed, his heart hammering. Wayne spread his cheeks and Ellis gave a tiny start as the cool lube trickled down his crack. Then he gasped when the blunt head of Wayne's dick pressed against his hole.

"This is going to be quick," Wayne warned him. Before Ellis could reply, hot flesh inched its way into his channel, stretching him, filling him to the hilt.

"Fuck, that feels good. So full," Ellis moaned, trying to move, but his bindings made that impossible.

"You're going to lie there while I mount you," Wayne said breathlessly. "You won't be able to come, not until I say so."

Ellis shuddered, the words inflaming his urgent need even more. "Come on, then," he pleaded. He cried out as Wayne slid all the way out of him, only to thrust back in, filling him again. "Oh fuck yeah." The friction where his cock lay trapped against the bench was exquisite torture, and Ellis knew he was seconds away from orgasm.

Wayne thrust into him two, three, four times until Ellis felt the telltale throb inside him and heard Wayne's wordless cry of ecstasy.

"Yours," Ellis whispered as Wayne kissed across his shoulders and back, his dick still buried inside Ellis's body. Everything became a blur as Wayne untied him and helped him sit before reaching down to grasp Ellis's cock, tugging hard.

"Come."

Ellis groaned and covered Wayne's hand with his warm spunk. Then Wayne was on his knees in front of Ellis, kissing him over and over while feeding him one word between Ellis's lips.

"Mine."

CHAPTER THIRTY-THREE

"HOW'S THE back?" Jarod asked, a twinkle in his eye. The four of them sat at a table in the farthest corner of the bar, the remains of a shared plate of snacks between them.

Wayne loved the quiet, peaceful sigh that rolled out of Ellis. "Fine." Ellis glanced at Wayne. "Thank you again."

"What for?"

"For not listening to me before."

Wayne feigned innocence. "I have no idea what you're talking about."

Ellis leaned across the table and caught hold of Wayne's hand. "You know exactly what I'm talking about. Me being stupid and asking you to tear up our contract."

"Oh, that." Wayne grinned. "What makes you think I ever listen to you?" He laughed at Ellis's expression and squeezed his hand. "Only joking. I'm just glad I was able to show you how much you love this. That you're still my boy."

Ellis's face glowed. "Yes, Sir. That I am."

Beside Wayne, Eli gave a cough. "I think now you might want those documents, right?"

Wayne's heartbeat raced. "Yes. Perfect." Eli gave a nod and got up from the table.

Ellis heaved an exaggerated sigh. "What am I going to do with you? We just got finished doing an amazing scene, and you want to do some work? This doesn't bode well for our life together, you know."

Wayne smiled. "On the contrary. I think this is the perfect way to start." He gazed toward the club office to see Eli approaching, a deep square box in his hand.

Ellis narrowed his eyes. "You're up to something. I know the signs."

He laughed. "Damn. You know me too well." Eli handed him the box with a wink. Wayne thanked him and placed it on the table. Ellis focused on it, but he said nothing, merely giving Wayne an inquiring glance, his hand still curled around Wayne's.

"So much has happened in the last five months," Wayne began, "that one important issue got lost somewhere along the line. To be fair, this is mostly my fault. I was more concerned with helping you to heal."

Ellis regarded him with a puzzled stare. "What issue?"

"We didn't have a chance to formalize our agreement, so I intend on correcting that today." Wayne smiled. "This was why it was so important to me that you acknowledged how much you needed this part of our life together." He let go of Ellis's hand and lifted the lid of the plain black box.

Ellis's eyes widened at the sight of the metal collar, fashioned from steel. Wayne caught the hiss of escaping breath.

"There are many different types of collars in our lifestyle. Some are intricate and delicate, others are cold and harsh." He gazed at Ellis, his heart full of love. "This one is like you. Unyielding. Strong. And permanent. Once I put this on, I will be the only one who can remove it. I know you're fairly new to all this, but I'm sure you realize that a collar is akin to a vow for us. It means that you will be mine, and only mine, for the rest of our lives." He paused, eyes locked on Ellis. "That is if you decide you still want to wear it."

"I…." Ellis paused.

Wayne held up a hand. "Don't answer yet because I haven't finished talking. If you accept this collar, we're both going to be starting a new life. You're agreeing to walk, cane and all, down the path with me, by my side always. Business partners as well as life partners. We're going to be moving forward with the family we're building—your sister, niece, and nephew will belong to both of us. But like I said months ago, this has to be something we both agree on because otherwise it won't work." He fell silent.

Ellis sat quietly for a few moments. "Oh, *now* you're done? Do I get the chance to talk?" He met Wayne's direct gaze. "I can't make any promises about the future. I think we both know that nothing is ever set in stone. But for as long as I have on this earth, I want to be with you, however that will be." He grinned. "I can't say I won't be hard to live with, and I know my road to recovery may not be over, and I'll probably be a right bastard pretty often. But there is no one I would rather have with me than you—Sir." Ellis bowed his head. "I'm ready for my collar."

With slightly trembling fingers, Wayne removed the thick band of burnished stainless steel from its box and held it out. *This is really happening.* After years of watching Ellis, never once daring to think anything could ever come of his feelings, to see him now, Wayne's collar about to adorn his neck, was….

He had no words.

ELLIS HELD his breath as Wayne opened the collar at the front and slipped it around his neck, snapping it shut. He released it as Wayne locked the collar with a key and then closed the cover over it. Ellis reached up to finger the cool metal that felt remarkably comfortable around his neck, as though it had been made to fit him. He tugged at the ring. It was really there, a solid circle of metal, unmissable.

He drew in a long breath. "Wow."

Wayne seemed as overcome by the act as he was. "Yeah, but a good wow."

Ellis nodded, aware of the metal against his skin. "This is real, right? I mean, I'm not dreaming this." He let out a cry when Wayne suddenly reached out and pinched both nipples between his fingers. "Ouch!"

Wayne shrugged. "Just wanted to show you that yes, you *are* awake." He smiled, and the light in his eyes made Ellis's stomach flutter. "My boy," he said softly.

"Yours," Ellis agreed wholeheartedly. He leaned closer and kissed Wayne on the mouth, drinking in his scent, his presence. "I love you," he murmured against Wayne's lips.

Wayne's fingers were on the back of his head, pulling him in, deepening the kiss with a passion that made Ellis's heart pound. Nothing else existed in that moment, just him and Wayne locked in a kiss, their arms around each other.

Then someone coughed and the spell was broken.

"Congratulations, guys."

Ellis surfaced to see a dark-haired man, his chest covered in a mat of hair, a harness snug across it, wearing leather pants and boots. He nodded toward Ellis, smiling.

Wayne beamed. "Aw, thanks, Aaron." He shook Aaron's extended hand.

Aaron held up a tube container. "I wanted to grab you earlier this week when I saw you coming into the club, but somehow I didn't get the chance."

"Yeah, it's been a busy week," Wayne admitted. "Eli and Jarod are keeping me busy." He gave them a quick smile. "Business is brisk."

Ellis loved that their venture was off to a good start, especially since word was getting around and they'd received calls to work for other companies.

Aaron placed the tube on the table. "I don't know if now is a good time, but I wanted you to have this." He grinned. "Sorry it's a bit late."

Wayne's face lit up. "Hey, thanks. And your timing is perfect. Let's see what you've done." He shifted his chair closer to Ellis's and made room.

Aaron opened the tube and pulled out a roll of papers he unfurled on the table. Ellis peered at them with interest. He could see they were architectural drawings, clearly house plans.

"I've got the preliminary work done," Aaron told Wayne. "So just like we discussed, two floors, a master bedroom, as well as three guest rooms. A fireplace, a large kitchen with a breakfast bar. And of course a room off the master that will double as an office space if you want to work from home. If not, it would make a great dungeon."

Ellis's muscles tightened. *Dungeon?* He thought about what Wayne would put in such a room, and he grinned internally. *A room for all his toys.* Then it struck him. *Wait a minute. A house?*

"What is this?"

"Huh?" Wayne said absently, tracing the lines on the paper with his fingers. Then he jerked up his head. "Oh. Sorry. This is a rough sketch of our new home. If you're still interested, of course."

New home? "I don't understand."

Wayne smiled. "Remember a while ago when we talked about a house? White-picket fence? A dog called Muffy? Oh, wait, you vetoed the dog."

A rush of warmth flooded through Ellis. *A house?*

"Well, Aaron is an architect. I asked if he'd be willing to draw up some plans, and he said yes. Now don't get me wrong. Nothing is written in stone. You can feel free to give your opinions if you want to change things. Having said that, I really liked what he's come up with."

Ellis was still reeling. A house?

Wayne took his hand. "If we want it, this will be our home. I want to start a new life with you, Ellis. New jobs, a new collar, and a new home. And see this here?" He tapped the papers. "This will be our balcony leading off the master bedroom. That's where our rocking chairs are going to go, so when we're ninety, we can sit and watch the world go by while we sip our tea and hold hands."

God, how does he do this? Draw out so many emotions in me? Ellis wasn't sure if he should laugh or cry or give a whoop of joy. Then he thought about Aaron's description. "Do we really need four bedrooms?"

Wayne smiled. "If our family ever needs a place to stay, they'd be welcome."

Now Ellis knew which emotions were in control. Warm tears slid down his cheeks and he tightened his grip on Wayne's hand. Wayne said nothing but reached up to wipe away his tears with gentle fingers. Ellis pulled himself together. "I love you so much. But we have to be practical. How can we afford this?"

Aaron cleared his throat. "Sam, my partner, works for a bank. The paperwork is already approved for a loan. The house is yours, guys. You just need to say yes."

Holy fucking hell. From someplace deep inside him, a slow release of joy began.

"Well?" Wayne squeezed his hand. "Are you interested?"

Ellis laughed. "Are you serious? Of course I'm interested. Yes, yes, yes!"

Wayne stared at him for a second, and then Ellis was seized in a fierce hug that took his breath away.

"Excellent!" Jarod's voice pierced Ellis's bubble of happiness. "Eli has just said we're going to gather at the bar for a small celebration. All welcome."

Around them were noises of approval, and everyone moved away from the table. Aaron patted Wayne on the back. "You two coming?"

Wayne smiled. "Just give us a minute, okay?" Aaron nodded and left them. Wayne slowly released Ellis and sat back. "So am I forgiven for going ahead and getting the ball rolling with Aaron without saying a word to you?"

Ellis chuckled. "What can I say? It was a lovely surprise. In fact, it's been a night for surprises." He gazed at Wayne, hoping his eyes betrayed what he was feeling right then. "Thank you," he whispered.

Wayne cupped his cheek. "Don't thank me. This is for both of us. Now what do you say to investigating whatever goodies Eli has set up on the bar? I don't know about you, but I'm hungry again." He grinned. "This starting-a-new-life business is obviously giving me an appetite." He got up and handed Ellis his cane. Ellis took it and followed Wayne toward the bar, his brain finally catching up on the proceedings.

Everything changed in the space of a few hours.

As they neared the bar, the crowd of men gathered there applauded them, offering their congratulations on the collaring. At the opposite end of the bar, however, one young man stood alone in the corner, his back to them.

Ellis knew a punishment when he saw one.

Wayne's friend Vic followed Ellis's gaze. "Don't even think about leaving that spot," he growled at the young man.

Ellis tried not to grin when his words elicited a plaintive whine. "But I'm hungry."

"You should have thought about that earlier. No more talking, Rob, or you'll be going to bed without any dinner."

Yeah, Ellis was really trying hard not to laugh. He'd seen Vic with Rob once or twice, and he knew the man cared for the cheeky boy in the corner. He brought his attention back to Wayne, who was waiting for him at the bar, two glasses in front of him.

Ellis stood at his side. "You'll forgive me if I don't kneel."

Wayne grinned. "Maybe just this once." He grabbed Ellis's hand and squeezed it, his face alight with happiness.

Ellis was no fool. He knew there would be trials ahead for them—more surgeries and doubtless more missteps as they started working together—but he realized that through whatever lay hidden from them in the future, Wayne would always be there for him. He leaned over and put his head on Wayne's shoulder.

He would spend the rest of his life with this man. His lover.

His Dom.

K.C. WELLS started writing in 2012, although the idea of writing a novel had been in her head since she was a child. But after reading that first gay romance in 2009, she was hooked.

She now writes full-time, and the line of men in her head clamoring to tell their story is getting longer and longer. If the frequent visits by plot bunnies are anything to go by, that's not about to change anytime soon.

K.C. loves to hear from readers.

E-mail: k.c.wells@btinternet.com
Facebook: www.facebook.com/KCWellsWorld
Blog: kcwellsworld.blogspot.co.uk
Twitter: @K_C_Wells
Website: www.kcwellsworld.com

PARKER WILLIAMS began to write as a teen, but never showed his work to anyone. As he grew older, he drifted away from writing, but his love of the written word moved him to reading. A chance encounter with an author changed the course of his life as she encouraged him to never give up on a dream. With the help of some amazing friends, he rediscovered the joy of writing, thanks to a community of writers who have become his family.

Parker firmly believes in love, but is also of the opinion that anything worth having requires work and sacrifice (plus a little hurt and angst, too). The course of love is never a smooth one, and happily-ever-after always has a price tag.

Website: www.parkerwilliamsauthor.com
Twitter: @ParkerWAuthor
Facebook: www.facebook.com/parker.williams.75641
E-mail: parker@parkerwilliamsauthor.com

COLLARS & CUFFS

AN
UNLOCKED
HEART

K.C. WELLS

Collars and Cuffs: Book One

Since the death of his submissive lover two years ago, Leo hasn't been living—merely existing. He focuses on making Collars & Cuffs, a BDSM club in Manchester's gay village, successful. That changes the night he and his business partner have their weekly meeting at Severinos. Leo can't keep his eyes off the new server. The shy man seems determined to avoid Leo's gaze, but that's like a red rag to a bull. Leo loves a challenge.

Alex Daniels works at Severinos to scrape together the money to move out on his own. He struggles with coming out, but he's drawn to Leo, the gorgeous guy with the icy-blue eyes who's been eating in his area nearly every night.

Leo won't let Alex's hesitance get in the way. He even keeps him away from the club so as not to scare him. And as for telling Alex that Leo is a Dom? Not a good idea. One date becomes two, but date two leads to Leo's bedroom… and Alex discovers things about himself he never realized—and never wanted anyone to see.

www.dreamspinnerpress.com

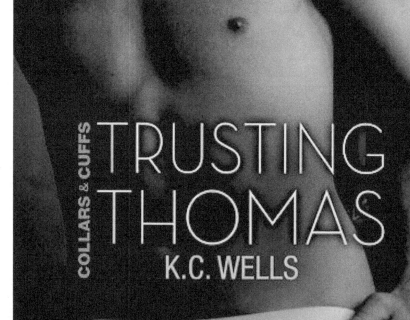

COLLARS & CUFFS

TRUSTING
THOMAS

K.C. WELLS

Collars and Cuffs: Book Two

Christmas is a time for goodwill to all, but Collars and Cuffs co-owner Thomas Williams receives an unexpected gift that chills him to the bone. A Dom from another Manchester club asks Thomas for his help rescuing an abused submissive, Peter Nicholson. Thomas takes in the young man as a favor to a friend, offering space and time to heal, but he makes it clear he's never had a sub and doesn't want one.

Peter finds Thomas's home calm and peaceful, but his past has left him unwilling to trust another Dom. When Thomas doesn't behave as Peter expects, Peter's nightmares begin to fade, and he decides he'd like to learn more about D/s life. A well-known trainer of submissives, Thomas begins to teach Peter, but as the new submissive opens up to him, Thomas finds he cares more for Peter than he should. Just as he decides it's time to find a permanent Dom for Peter, they discover Peter's tormentor is still very much a threat. With their lives in danger, Thomas can't deny his feelings for Peter any longer. The question now becomes, can Peter make it out of the lions' den alive, so that Thomas can tell his boy that he loves him?

www.dreamspinnerpress.com

COLLARS & CUFFS NOVEL

SOMEONE TO
KEEP ME

K.C. WELLS & PARKER WILLIAMS

Collars and Cuffs: Book Three

Eighteen-year-old Scott Keating knows a whole world exists beyond his parents' strict control, but until he gains access to the World Wide Web, he really has no idea what's out there. In a chat room, Scott meets "JeffUK." Jeff loves and understands him, and when he offers to bring Scott to the UK, Scott seizes his chance to escape his humdrum life and see the world. But when his plane touches down and Jeff isn't there, panic sets in.

Collars & Cuffs favorite barman and Dom-in-training, Ben Winters, drops his sister off at the airport and finds a lost, anxious Scott. Hearing Scott's story sets off alarm bells, along with his protective instincts. Taking pity on the naïve boy, Ben offers him a place to crash and invites him to Collars & Cuffs, hoping his bosses will know how to help. Scott dreams of belonging to someone, heart and soul. Ben longs for a sub of his own. And neither man sees what's right under his nose.

www.dreamspinnerpress.com

A

DANCE WITH
DOMINATION

K.C. WELLS

Collars and Cuffs: Book Four

Recently returned to the UK after living in the States since he was eleven, Andrew Barrett is determined to keep busy and make a new life for himself. He works full time as a copywriter and strips at a club on Canal Street on weekends. But it still leaves him too much time to think. Then he finds the BDSM club, Collars & Cuffs, where at twenty-nine, he is their youngest Dom. Young doesn't mean inexperienced, however. All this activity keeps him focused with no time to dwell on the past. But the past has a way of intruding on the present.

It's been four long years since Gareth Michaels last set foot inside Collars & Cuffs. But when he finally summons his courage and steps back into his former world, he finds the man who drove him away is still a member, and what's more, he wants Gareth back. Two men in pain need the freedom they find in each other, but it takes another man's horrific plans to make them see it.

www.dreamspinnerpress.com

COLLARS & CUFFS

DAMIAN'S DISCIPLINE

K.C. WELLS & PARKER WILLIAMS

Collars and Cuffs: Book Five

The man who pimped Jeff may be in prison, but Jeff is still living the nightmare, selling himself to men and relying on pills to manage. Then he meets Scott, a young American man who could easily have been where Jeff is now. Scott's friends extend a helping hand to Jeff, and he grabs it.

Leo and Thomas bring Jeff to stay with Dom Damian Barnett until they can find him someplace more long-term. Still grieving from losing his sub to cancer two years before, Damian agrees to help. But when he glimpses the extent of the damage, Damian wants to do more than offer his guestroom. Jeff is not a submissive, but Damian can see he desperately needs structure in his life. It's up to Damian to find an answer.

He never expects that what he discovers will change both their lives.

www.dreamspinnerpress.com

COLLARS & CUFFS

MAKE ME
SOAR

K.C. WELLS

Collars and Cuffs: Book Six

Anyone who frequents Collars & Cuffs knows Dorian Forrester is built for pain, including Dorian himself. But everyone has it wrong. For six years, Dorian's chased a feeling that remains tantalizingly out of his reach. Unteachable, Dorian can take anything and everything a Dom can throw at him. Still, it's not enough. Dorian needs… something more. Something he won't find at Collars & Cuffs.

Dorian's search takes him out of the safe environment he's known for years, out of his depth, and into a realm of deep, dark trouble.

Alan Marchant has been watching Dorian with interest for a while and knows there's more to Dorian than his label of "pain slut" suggests. When Dorian disappears, Alan and his friend Leo set out to find him. But the disoriented young man discovered cowering in a hotel room is not the Dorian they know and love. That Dorian is shattered. It's up to Alan to pick up the pieces and show Dorian there are better ways to fly.

They may be off on a new journey together, but their destination will rock them both to the core.

www.dreamspinnerpress.com

COLLARS & CUFFS

DOM OF AGES

K.C. WELLS & PARKER WILLIAMS

Collars and Cuffs: Book Seven

Eli may only be thirty, but he has had enough of pretend submissives. When he spies Jarod in a BDSM club, everything about the man screams submission. So what if Jarod is probably twenty years older than Eli. What does age matter, anyway? All he can see is what he's always wanted—a sub who wants to serve.

Jarod spent twenty-four years with his Master before Fate took him. Four years on, Jarod is still lost, so when a young Dom takes charge, Jarod rolls with it and finds himself serving again. But he keeps waiting for the other shoe to drop. Because there's going to come a point when Eli realizes he's a laughingstock in the club. Who would want to be seen with a fifty-year-old sub?

After several missteps, Eli realizes that in order to find happiness, they will need friends who will understand. At a friend's insistence, he visits Collars & Cuffs, where they are met with open arms. As they settle in to their new life, Eli begins to see things differently and he dares to think he can have it all. Until a phone call threatens to take it all away….

www.dreamspinnerpress.com

Made in the USA
Las Vegas, NV
26 May 2022

49406015R00187